THIEF OF HEARTS

NEW YORK TIMES BESTSELLING AUTHOR
TESS GERRITSEN

H HARLEQUIN® SELECTS™

Recycling programs
for this product may
not exist in your area.

ISBN-13: 978-1-335-40662-0

Thief of Hearts
First published in 1995. This edition published in 2022.
Copyright © 1995 by Terry Gerritsen

Beneath the Badge
First published in 2008. This edition published in 2022.
Copyright © 2008 by Rita B. Herron

All rights reserved. No part of this book may be used or reproduced in any manner whatsoever without written permission except in the case of brief quotations embodied in critical articles and reviews.

This is a work of fiction. Names, characters, places and incidents are either the product of the author's imagination or are used fictitiously. Any resemblance to actual persons, living or dead, businesses, companies, events or locales is entirely coincidental.

For questions and comments about the quality of this book, please contact us at CustomerService@Harlequin.com.

Harlequin Enterprises ULC
22 Adelaide St. West, 41st Floor
Toronto, Ontario M5H 4E3, Canada
www.Harlequin.com

Printed in U.S.A.

CONTENTS

Internationally bestselling author **Tess Gerritsen** is a graduate of Stanford University and went on to medical school at the University of California, San Francisco, where she was awarded her MD. Since 1987, her books have been translated into thirty-seven languages, and more than twenty-five million copies have been sold around the world. She has received the Nero Award and the RITA® Award, and she was a finalist for the Edgar Award. Now retired from medicine, she writes full-time. She lives in Maine.

Books by Tess Gerritsen

Call After Midnight
Under the Knife
Never Say Die
Whistleblower
Presumed Guilty
In Their Footsteps
Thief of Hearts
Keeper of the Bride

Visit the Author Profile page at Harlequin.com for more titles.

THIEF OF HEARTS

Tess Gerritsen

In memory of Jim Heacock

"In thy face I see / The map of honor, truth, and loyalty."

—William Shakespeare, *Henry VI, Part II*

In memory of Jim Heacock
"In thy face I see the map
of honor, truth, and loyalty."
—William Shakespeare *Henry VI, Part III*

Prologue

Simon Trott stood on the rolling deck of the *Cosima,* and through the velvety blackness of night he saw the flames. They burned just offshore, not a steady fire, but a series of violent bursts of light that cast the distant swells in a hellish glow.

"That's her," the *Cosima*'s captain said to Trott as both men peered across the bow. "The *Max Havelaar.* Judging by those fireworks, she'll be going down fast." He turned and yelled to the helmsman, "Full ahead!"

"Not much chance of survivors," said Trott.

"They're sending off a distress call. So someone's alive."

"Or was alive."

As they neared the sinking vessel, the flames suddenly shot up like a fountain, sending out sparks that seemed to ignite the ocean in puddles of liquid fire.

The captain shouted over the roar of the *Cosima*'s engines, "Slow up! There's fuel in the water!"

"Throttling down," said the helmsman.

"Ahead slowly. Watch for survivors."

Trott moved to the forward rail and stared across the watery inferno. Already the *Max Havelaar* was sliding backward, her stern nearly submerged, her bow tipping toward the moonless sky. A few minutes more and she'd sink forever into the swells. The water was deep, and salvage impractical. Here, two miles off the Spanish coast, was where the *Havelaar* would sink to her eternal rest.

Another explosion spewed out a shower of embers, leafing the ripples with gold. In those few seconds before the sunlike brilliance faded, Trott spotted a hint of movement off in the darkness. A good two hundred yards away from the *Havelaar,* safely beyond the ring of fire, Trott saw a long, low silhouette bobbing in the water. Then he heard the sound of men's voices, calling.

"Here! We are here!"

"It's the lifeboat," said the captain, aiming the searchlight toward the voices. "There, at two o'clock!"

"I see it," said the helmsman, at once adjusting course. He throttled up, guiding the bow through drifts of burning fuel. As they drew closer, Trott could hear the joyous shouts of the survivors, a confusing babble of Italian. How many in the boat? he wondered, straining to see through the murk. Five. Perhaps six. He could almost count them now, their arms waving in the searchlight's beam, their heads bobbing in every direction. They were thrilled to be alive. To be in sight of rescue.

"Looks like most of the *Havelaar*'s crew," said the captain.

"We'll need all hands up here."

The captain turned and barked out the order. Seconds later the *Cosima*'s crew had assembled on deck. As the bow knifed across the remaining expanse of water, the men stood in silence near the bow rail, all eyes focused on the lifeboat just ahead.

By the searchlight's glare Trott could now make out the number of survivors: six. He knew the *Max Havelaar* had sailed from Naples with a crew of eight. Were there two still in the water?

He turned and glanced toward the distant silhouette of shore. With luck and endurance, a man could swim that distance.

The lifeboat was adrift off their starboard side.

Trott shouted, "This is the *Cosima!* Identify yourselves!"

"Max Havelaar!" shouted one of the men in the lifeboat.

"Is this your entire crew?"

"Two are dead!"

"You're certain?"

"The engine, she explodes! One man, he is trapped below."

"And your eighth man?"

"He falls in. Cannot swim!"

Which made the eighth man as good as dead, thought Trott. He glanced at *Cosima*'s crew. They stood watching, waiting for the order.

The lifeboat was gliding almost alongside now.

"A little closer," Trott called down, "and we'll throw you a line."

One of the men in the lifeboat reached up to catch the rope.

Trott turned and gave his men the signal.

The first hail of bullets caught its victim in midreach, arms extended toward his would-be saviors. He had no chance to scream. As the bullets rained down from the *Cosima,* the men fell, helpless before the onslaught. Their cries, the splash of a falling body, were drowned out by the relentless spatter of automatic gunfire.

When it was finished, when the bullets finally ceased, the bodies lay in a coiled embrace in the lifeboat. A silence fell, broken only by the slap of water against the *Cosima*'s hull.

One last explosion spewed a finale of sparks into the air. The bow of the *Max Havelaar*—what remained of her—tilted crazily toward the sky. Then, gently, she slid backward into the deep.

The lifeboat, its hull riddled with bullet holes, was already half submerged. A *Cosima* crewman heaved a loose anchor over the side. It landed with a thud among the bodies. The lifeboat tipped, emptying its cargo of corpses into the sea.

"Our work is done here, Captain," said Trott. Matter-of-factly he turned toward the helm. "I suggest we return to—"

He suddenly halted, his gaze focused on a patch of water a dozen yards away. What was that splash? He could still see the ripples of reflected firelight worrying the water's surface. There it was again. Something silvery gliding out of the swells, then slipping back under the water.

"Over there!" shouted Trott. "Fire!"

His men looked at him, puzzled.

"What did you see?" asked the captain.

"Four o'clock. Something broke the surface."

"I don't see anything."

"Fire at it, anyway."

One of the gunmen obligingly squeezed off a clip. The bullets sprayed into the water, their deadly rain splashing a line across the surface.

They watched for a moment. Nothing appeared. The water smoothed once again into undulating glass.

"I know I saw something," said Trott.

The captain shrugged. "Well, it's not there now." He called to the helmsman, "Return to port!"

Cosima came about, leaving in her wake a spreading circle of ripples.

Trott moved to the stern, his gaze still focused on the suspicious patch of water. As they roared away he thought he spotted another flash of silver bob to the surface. It was there only for an instant. Then, in a twinkling, it was gone.

A fish, he thought. And, satisfied, he turned away.

Yes, that must be what it was. A fish.

Chapter 1

"A small burglary. That's all I'm asking for." Veronica Cairncross gazed up at him, tears shimmering in her sapphire eyes. She was dressed in a fetching off-the-shoulder silk gown, the skirt arranged in lustrous ripples across the Queen Anne love seat. Her hair, a rich russet brown, had been braided with strands of seed pearls and was coiled artfully atop her aristocratic head. At thirty-three she was far more stunning, far more chic than she'd been at the age of twenty-five, when he'd first met her. Through the years she'd acquired, along with her title, an unerring sense of style, poise and a reputation for witty repartee that made her a sought-after guest at the most glittering parties in London. But one thing about her had not changed, would never change.

Veronica Cairncross was still an idiot.

How else could one explain the predicament into which she'd dug herself?

And once again, he thought wearily, it's faithful old chum Jordan Tavistock to the rescue. Not that Veronica didn't need rescuing. Not that he didn't want to help her. It was simply that this request of hers was so bizarre, so fraught with dire possibilities, that his first instinct was to turn her down flat.

He did. "It's out of the question, Veronica," said Jordan. "I won't do it."

"For me, Jordie!" she pleaded. "Think what will happen if you don't. If he shows those letters to Oliver—"

"Poor old Ollie will have a fit. You two will row for a few days, and then he'll forgive you. That's what will happen."

"What if Ollie doesn't forgive me? What if he—what if he wants a…" She swallowed and looked down. "A divorce," she whispered.

"Really, Veronica." Jordan sighed. "You should have thought about this before you had the affair."

She stared down in misery at the folds of her silk gown. "I didn't think. That's the whole problem."

"No, it's obvious you didn't."

"I had no idea Guy would be so difficult. You'd think I broke his heart! It's not as if we were in love or anything. And now he's being such a bastard about it. Threatening to tell all! What gentleman would sink so low?"

"No gentleman would."

"If it weren't for those letters I wrote, I could deny the whole thing. It would be my word against Guy's then. I'm sure Ollie would give me the benefit of the doubt."

"What, exactly, did you write in those letters?"

Veronica's head drooped unhappily. "Things I shouldn't have."

"Confessions of love? Sweet nothings?"

She groaned. "Much worse."

"More explicit, you mean?"

"Far more explicit."

Jordan gazed at her bent head, at the seed pearls and russet hair glimmering in the lamplight. And he thought, *It's hard to believe I was once attracted to this woman.* But that was years ago, and he'd been only twenty-two and a bit gullible—a condition he sincerely hoped he'd outgrown.

Veronica Dooley had entered his social circle on the arm of an old chum from Cambridge. After the chum bowed out, Jordan had inherited the girl's attentions, and for a few dizzy weeks he'd thought he might be in love. Better sense prevailed. Their parting was amicable, and they'd remained friends over the years. She'd gone on to marry Oliver Cairncross, and although *Sir* Oliver was a good twenty years older than his bride, theirs had been a classic match between money on his side and beauty on hers. Jordan had thought them a contented pair.

How wrong he'd been.

"My advice to you," he said, "is to come clean. Tell Ollie about the affair. He'll most likely forgive you."

"Even if he does, there's still the letters. Guy's just upset enough to send them to all the wrong people. If Fleet Street ever got hold of them, Ollie would be publicly humiliated."

"You think Guy would really stoop so low?"

"I don't doubt it for a minute. I'd offer to pay him

off if I thought it would work. But after all that money I lost in Monte Carlo, Ollie's keeping a tight rein on my spending. And I couldn't borrow any money from you. I mean, there are some things one simply *can't* ask of one's friends."

"Burglary, I'd say, lies in that category," noted Jordan dryly.

"But it's not burglary! I wrote those letters. Which makes them *mine*. I'm only retrieving what belongs to me." She leaned forward, her eyes suddenly glittering like blue diamonds. "It wouldn't be difficult, Jordie. I know exactly which drawer he keeps them in. Your sister's engagement party is Saturday night. If you could invite him here—"

"Beryl detests Guy Delancey."

"Invite him anyway! While he's here at Chetwynd, guzzling champagne—"

"I'm burgling his house?" Jordan shook his head. "What if I'm caught?"

"Guy's staff takes Saturday nights off. His house will be empty. Even if you *are* caught, just tell them it's a prank. Bring a—a blow-up doll or something, for insurance. Tell them you're planting it in his bed. They'll believe you. Who'd doubt the word of a Tavistock?"

He frowned. "Is that why you're asking *me* to do this? Because I'm a Tavistock?"

"No. I'm asking you because you're the cleverest man I know. Because you've never, ever betrayed any of my secrets." She raised her chin and met his gaze. It was a look of utter trust. "And because you're the only one in the world I can count on."

Drat. She would have to say that.

"Will you do it for me, Jordie?" she asked softly. Pitifully. "Tell me you will."

Wearily he rubbed his head. "I'll think about it," he said. Then he sank back in the armchair and gazed resignedly at the far wall, at the paintings of his Tavistock ancestors. Distinguished gentlemen, every one of them, he thought. Not a cat burglar in the lot.

Until now.

At 11:05, the lights went out in the servants' quarters. Good old Whitmore was right on schedule as usual. At 9:00 he'd made his rounds of the house, checking to see that the windows and doors were locked. At 9:30 he'd tidied up downstairs, fussed a bit in the kitchen, perhaps brewed himself a pot of tea. At 10:00 he'd retired upstairs, to the blue glow of his private telly. At 11:05 he turned off his light.

This had been Whitmore's routine for the past week, and Clea Rice, who'd been watching Guy Delancey's house since the previous Saturday, assumed that this would be his routine until the day he died. Menservants, after all, strived to maintain order in their employers' lives. It wasn't surprising they'd maintain order in their own lives, as well.

Now the question was, how long before he'd fall asleep?

Safely concealed behind the yew hedge, Clea rose to her feet and began to rock from foot to foot, trying to keep the blood moving through her limbs. The grass had been wet, and her stirrup pants were clinging to her thighs. Though the night was warm, she was feeling chilled. It wasn't just the dampness in her clothes; it was the excitement, the anticipation. And, yes, the fear.

Not a great deal of fear—she had enough confidence in her own ability to feel certain she wouldn't be caught. Still, there was always that chance.

She danced from foot to foot to keep the adrenaline pumping. She'd give the manservant twenty minutes to fall asleep, no longer. With every minute that passed, her window of opportunity was shrinking. Guy Delancey could return home early from the party tonight, and she wanted to be well away from here when he walked in that front door.

Surely the butler was asleep now.

Clea slipped around the yew hedge and took off at a sprint. She didn't stop running until she'd reached the cover of shrubbery. There she paused to catch her breath, to reevaluate her situation. There was no hue and cry from the house, no signs of movement anywhere in the darkness. Lucky for her, Guy Delancey abhorred dogs; the last thing she needed tonight was some blasted hound baying at her heels.

She slipped around the house and crossed the flagstone terrace to the French doors. As expected, they were locked. Also as expected, it would be an elementary job. A quick glance under her penlight told her this was an antique warded lock, a bit rusty, probably as old as the house itself. When it came to home security, the English had light years of catching up to do. She fished the set of five skeleton keys out of her fanny pack and began trying them, one by one. The first three keys didn't fit. She inserted the fourth, turned it slowly and felt the tooth slide into the bolt notch.

A piece of cake.

She let herself in the door and stepped into the library. By the glow of moonlight through the windows she could see books gleaming in shelves. Now came the hard part—where was the Eye of Kashmir? Surely not in this room, she thought as the beam of her penlight skimmed the walls. It was too accessible to visitors, pathetically unsecured against thieves. Nevertheless, she gave the room a quick search.

No Eye of Kashmir.

She slipped out of the library and into the hallway. Her light traced across burnished wood and antique vases. She prowled through the first-floor parlor and solarium. No Eye of Kashmir. She didn't bother with the kitchen or dining areas—Delancey would never choose a hiding place so accessible to his servants.

That left the upstairs rooms.

Clea ascended the curving stairway, her footsteps silent as a cat's. At the landing she paused, listening for any sounds of discovery. Nothing. To the left she knew was the servants' wing. To the right would be Delancey's bedroom. She turned right and went straight to the room at the end of the hall.

The door was unlocked. She slipped through and closed it softly behind her.

Through the balcony windows moonlight spilled in, illuminating a room of grand proportions. The twelve-foot-high walls were covered with paintings. The bed was a massive four-poster, its mattress broad enough to sleep an entire harem. There was an equally massive chest of drawers, a double wardrobe, nightstands and a gentleman's writing desk. Near the balcony doors was a sitting area—two chairs and a tea table arranged around a Persian carpet, probably antique.

Clea let out an audible groan. It would take hours to search this room.

Fully aware of the minutes ticking by, she started with the writing desk. She searched the drawers, checked for hidden niches. No Eye of Kashmir. She moved to the dresser, where she probed through layers of underwear and hankies. No Eye of Kashmir. She turned next to the wardrobe, which loomed like a monstrous monolith against the wall. She was just about to swing open the wardrobe door when she heard a noise and she froze.

It was a faint rustling, coming from somewhere outside the house. There it was again, louder.

She swiveled around to face the balcony windows. Something bizarre was going on. Outside, on the railing, the wisteria vines quaked violently. A silhouette suddenly popped up above the tangle of leaves. Clea caught one glimpse of the man's head, of his blond hair gleaming in the moonlight, and she ducked back behind the wardrobe.

This was just wonderful. They'd have to take numbers to see whose turn it was to break in next. This was one hazard she hadn't anticipated—an encounter with a rival thief. An incompetent one, too, she thought in disgust as she heard the sharp clatter of outdoor pottery, quickly stilled. There was an intervening silence. The burglar was listening for sounds of discovery. Old Whitmore must be deaf, thought Clea, if he didn't hear *that* racket.

The balcony door squealed open.

Clea retreated farther behind the wardrobe. What if he discovered her? Would he attack? She'd brought nothing with which to defend herself.

She winced as she heard a thump, followed by an irritated mutter of *"Damn* it all!"

Oh, Lord. This guy was more dangerous to himself than to her.

Footsteps creaked closer.

Clea shrank back, pressing hard against the wall. The wardrobe door swung open, coming to a stop just inches from her face. She heard the clink of hangers as clothes were shoved aside, then the hiss of a drawer sliding out. A flashlight flicked on, its glow spilling through the crack of the wardrobe door. The man muttered to himself as he rifled through the drawer, irritated grumblings in the queen's best English.

"Must be mad. That's what I am, stark raving. Don't know how she talked me into this…"

Clea couldn't help it; curiosity got the better of her. She eased forward and peered through the crack between the hinges of the door. The man was frowning down at an open drawer. His profile was sharply cut, cleanly aristocratic. His hair was wheat blond and still a bit ruffled from all that wrestling with the wisteria vine. He wasn't dressed at all like a burglar. In his tuxedo jacket and black bow tie, he looked more like some cocktail-party refugee.

He dug deeper into the drawer and suddenly gave a murmur of satisfaction. She couldn't see what he was removing from the drawer. *Please,* she thought. *Let it not be the Eye of Kashmir.* To have come so close and then to lose it…

She leaned even closer to the crack and strained to see over his shoulder, to find out what he was now sliding into his jacket pocket. So intently was she staring, she scarcely had time to react when he unexpectedly grasped the wardrobe door and swung it shut. She jerked back into the shadows and her shoulder thudded against the wall.

There was a silence. A very long silence.

Slowly the beam of the flashlight slid around the edge of the wardrobe, followed cautiously by the silhouette of the man's head.

Clea blinked as the light focused fully on her face. Against the glare she couldn't see him, but he could see *her*. For an eternity neither of them moved, neither of them made a sound.

Then he said, "Who the hell are *you*?"

The figure coiled up against the wardrobe didn't answer. Slowly Jordan played his torchlight down the length of the intruder, noting the stocking cap pulled low to the eyebrows, the face obscured by camouflage paint, the black turtleneck shirt and pants.

"I'm going to ask you one last time," Jordan said. "Who are you?"

He was answered with a mysterious smile. The sight of it surprised him. That's when the figure in black sprang like a cat. The impact sent Jordan staggering backward against the bedpost. At once the figure scrambled toward the balcony. Jordan lunged and managed to grab a handful of pant leg. They both tumbled to the floor and collided with the writing desk, letting loose a cascade of pens and pencils. His opponent squirmed beneath him and rammed a knee into Jordan's groin. In the onrush of pain and nausea, Jordan almost let go. His opponent got one hand free and was scrabbling about on the floor. Almost too late Jordan saw the pointed tip of a letter opener stabbing toward him.

He grabbed his opponent's wrist and savagely wrestled away the letter opener. The other man struck back just as savagely, arms flailing, body twisting like an eel. As Jordan fought to control those pummeling fists, he snagged his opponent's stocking cap.

A luxurious fountain of blond hair suddenly tumbled out across the floor, to ripple in a shimmering pool under the moonlight. Jordan stared in astonishment.

A woman.

For an endless moment they stared at each other, their breaths coming hard and fast, their hearts thudding against each other's chests.

A woman.

Without warning his body responded in a way that was both automatic and unsuppressibly male. She was too warm, too close. And very, very female. Even through their clothes, those soft curves were all too apparent. Just as the state of his arousal must be firmly apparent to her.

"Get off me," she whispered.

"First tell me who you are."

"Or *what?*"

"Or I'll—I'll—"

She smiled up at him, her mouth so close, so tempting he completely lost his train of thought.

It was the creak of approaching footsteps that made his brain snap back into function. Light suddenly spilled under the doorway and a man's voice called, "What's this, now? Who's in there?"

In a flash both Jordan and the woman were on their feet and dashing to the balcony. The woman was first over the railing. She scrambled like a monkey down the wisteria vine. By the time Jordan hit the ground, she was already sprinting across the lawn.

At the yew hedge he finally caught up with her and pulled her to a halt. "What were you doing in there?" he demanded.

"What were *you* doing in there?" she countered.

Back at the house the bedroom lights came on, and a voice yelled from the balcony, "Thieves! Don't you come back! I've called the police!"

"I'm not hanging around *here,*" said the woman, and made a beeline for the woods.

Jordan sighed. "She does have a point." And he took off after her.

For a mile they slogged it out together, dodging brambles, ducking beneath branches. It was rough terrain, but she seemed tireless, moving at the steady pace of someone in superb condition. Only when they'd reached the far edge of the woods did he notice that her breathing had turned ragged.

He was ready to collapse.

They stopped to rest at the edge of a field. The sky was cloudless, the moonlight thick as milk. Wind blew, warm and fragrant with the smell of fallen leaves.

"So tell me," he managed to say between gulps of air, "do you do this sort of thing for a living?"

"I'm not a thief. If that's what you're asking."

"You act like a thief. You dress like a thief."

"I'm not a thief." She sagged back wearily against a tree trunk. "Are you?"

"Of course not!" he snapped.

"What do you mean, *of course not?* Is it beneath your precious dignity or something?"

"Not at all. That is— I mean—" He stopped and shook his head in confusion. "What *do* I mean?"

"I haven't the faintest," she said innocently.

"I'm *not* a thief," he said, more sure of himself now. "I was…playing a bit of a practical joke. That's all."

"I see." She tilted her head up to look at him, and her expression was plainly skeptical in the moonlight. Now that they weren't grappling like savages, he realized she was quite petite. And, without a doubt, female. He remembered how snugly her sweet curves had fit beneath him, and suddenly desire flooded through his body, a desire so intense it left him aching. All he had to do was step close to this woman and those blasted hormones kicked in.

He stepped back and forced himself to focus on her face. He couldn't quite make it out under all that camouflage paint, but it would be easy to remember her voice. It was low and throaty, almost like a cat's growl. Definitely not English, he thought. American?

She was still eyeing him with a skeptical look. "What did you take out of the wardrobe?" she asked. "Was that part of the practical joke?"

"You…saw that?"

"I did." Her chin came up squarely in challenge. "*Now* convince me it was all a prank."

Sighing, he reached under his jacket. At once she jerked back and pivoted around to flee. "No, it's all right!" he assured her. "It's not a gun or anything. It's just this pouch I'm wearing. Sort of a hidden backpack." He unzipped the pouch. She stood a few feet away, watching him warily, ready to sprint off at the first whiff of danger. "It's a bit sophomoric, really," he said, tugging at the pouch. "But it's good for a laugh." The contents suddenly flopped out and the woman gave a little squeak of fright. "See? It's not a weapon." He held it out to her. "It's an inflatable doll. When you blow it up, it turns into a naked woman."

She moved forward, eyeing the limp rubber doll. "Anatomically correct?" she inquired dryly.

"I'm not sure, really. I mean, er…" He glanced at her, and his mind suddenly veered toward *her* anatomy. He cleared his throat. "I haven't checked."

She regarded him the way one might look at an object of pity.

"But it *does* prove I was there on a prank," he said, struggling to stuff the deflated doll back in the pouch.

"All it proves," she said, "is that you had the foresight to bring an excuse should you be caught. Which, in your case, was a distinct possibility."

"And what excuse did *you* bring? Should you be caught?"

"I wasn't planning on getting caught," she said, and started across the field. "Everything was going quite well, as a matter of fact. Until you bumbled in."

"What was going quite well? The burglary?"

"I told you, I'm not a thief."

He followed her through the grass. "So why did *you* break in?"

"To prove a point."

"And that point was?"

"That it could be done. I've just proven to Mr. Delancey that he needs a security system. And my company's the one to install it."

"You work for a *security* company?" He laughed. "Which one?"

"Why do you ask?"

"My future brother-in-law's in that line of work. He might know your firm."

She smiled back at him, her lips immensely kissable, her teeth a bright arc in the night. "I work for Nimrod Associates," she said. Then, turning, she walked away.

"Wait. Miss—"

She waved a gloved hand in farewell, but didn't look back.

"I didn't catch your name!" he said.

"And I didn't catch yours," she said over her shoulder. "Let's keep it that way."

He saw her blond hair gleam faintly in the darkness. And then, in a twinkling, she was gone. Her absence seemed to leave the night colder, the darkness deeper. The only hint that she'd even been there was his residual ache of desire.

I shouldn't have let her go, he thought. *I know bloody well she's a thief.* But what could he have done? Hauled her to the police? Explained that he'd caught her in Guy Delancey's bedroom, where neither one of them belonged?

With a weary shake of his head, he turned and began the long tramp to his car, parked a half mile away. He'd have to hurry back to Chetwynd. It was getting late and he'd be missed at the party.

At least his mission was accomplished; he'd stolen Veronica's letters back. He'd hand them over to her, let her lavish him with thanks for saving her precious hide. After all, he *had* saved her hide, and he was bloody well going to tell her so.

And then he was going to strangle her.

Chapter 2

The party at Chetwynd was still in full swing. Through the ballroom windows came the sounds of laughter and violin music and the cheery clink of champagne glasses. Jordan stood in the driveway and considered his best mode of entry. The back stairs? No, he'd have to walk through the kitchen, and the staff would certainly find that suspicious. Up the trellis to Uncle Hugh's bedroom? Definitely not; he'd done enough tangling with vines for the night. He'd simply waltz in the front door and hope the guests were too deep in their cups to notice his disheveled state.

He straightened his bow tie and brushed the twigs off his jacket. Then he let himself in the front door.

To his relief, no one was in the entrance hall. He tiptoed past the ballroom doorway and started up the curving staircase. He was almost to the second-floor landing when a voice called from below.

"Jordie, where on earth have you been?"

Suppressing a groan, Jordan turned and saw his sister, Beryl, standing at the bottom of the stairs. She was looking flushed and lovelier than ever, her black hair swirled elegantly atop her head, her bared shoulders lustrous above the green velvet gown. Being in love certainly agreed with her. Since her engagement to Richard Wolf a month ago, Jordan had seldom seen her without a smile on her face.

At the moment she was not smiling.

She stared at his wrinkled jacket, his soiled trouser legs and muddy shoes. She shook her head. "I'm afraid to ask."

"Then don't."

"I'll ask anyway. What happened to you?"

He turned and continued up the stairs. "I went out for a walk."

"That's all?" She bounded up the steps after him in a rustle of skirts and stockings. "First you make me invite that horrid Guy Delancey—who, by the way, is drinking like a fish and going 'round pinching ladies' bottoms. Then you simply vanish from the party. And you reappear looking like that."

He went into his bedroom.

She followed him.

"It was a long walk," he said.

"It's been a long party."

"Beryl." He sighed, turning to face her. "I really *am* sorry about Guy Delancey. But I can't talk about it right now. I'd be betraying a confidence."

"I see." She went to the door, then glanced back. "I *can* keep a secret, you know."

"So can I." Jordan smiled. "That's why I'm not saying a thing."

"Well, you'd best change your clothes, then. Or someone's going to ask why you've been climbing wisteria vines." She left, shutting the door behind her.

Jordan looked down at his jacket. Only then did he notice the leaf, poking like a green flag from his buttonhole.

He changed into a fresh tuxedo, combed the twigs from his hair and went downstairs to rejoin the party.

Though it was past midnight, the champagne was still flowing and the scene in the ballroom was as jolly as when he'd left it an hour and a half earlier. He swept up a glass from a passing tray and eased back into circulation. No one mentioned his absence; perhaps no one had noticed it. He worked his way across the room to the buffet table, where a magnificent array of hors d'oeuvres had been laid out, and he helped himself to the Scottish salmon. Breaking and entering was hard work, and he was famished.

A whiff of perfume, a hand brushing his arm, made him turn. It was Veronica Cairncross. "Well?" she whispered anxiously. "How did it go?"

"Not exactly clockwork. You were wrong about the butler's night off. There was a manservant in the house. I could have been caught."

"Oh, no," she moaned softly. "Then you didn't get them…"

"I got them. They're upstairs."

"You *did?*" A smile of utter happiness burst across her face. "Oh, Jordie!" She leaned forward and threw her arms around him, smearing salmon on his tuxedo. "You saved my life."

"I know, I know." He suddenly spotted Veronica's husband, Oliver, moving toward them. At once Jordan extricated himself from her embrace. "Ollie's coming this way," he whispered.

"Is he?" Veronica turned and automatically beamed her thousand-watt smile at Sir Oliver. "Darling, there you are! I lost track of you."

"You don't seem to be missing me much," grunted Sir Oliver. He frowned at Jordan, as though trying to divine his real intentions.

Poor fellow, thought Jordan. Any man married to Veronica was deserving of pity. Sir Oliver was a decent enough fellow, a descendant of the excellent Cairncross family, manufacturers of tea biscuits. Though twenty years older than his wife, and bald as a cue ball, he'd managed to win Veronica's hand—and to keep that hand well studded with diamonds.

"It's getting late," said Oliver. "Really, Veronica, shouldn't we be going home?"

"So soon? It's just past midnight."

"I have that meeting in the morning. And I'm quite tired."

"Well, I suppose we'll have to be going, then," Veronica said with a sigh. She smiled slyly at Jordan. "I think I'll sleep well tonight."

Just see that it's with your husband, thought Jordan with a shake of his head.

After the Cairncrosses had departed, Jordan glanced down and saw the greasy sliver of salmon clinging to his lapel. Drat, another tuxedo bites the dust. He wiped away the mess as best he could, picked up his glass of champagne and waded back into the crowd.

He cornered his future brother-in-law, Richard Wolf, near the musicians. Wolf was looking happy and dazed—just the way one expected a prospective bridegroom to look.

"So how's our guest of honor holding up?" asked Jordan.

Richard grinned. "Giving the old handshake a rest."

"Good idea to pace oneself." Jordan's gaze shifted toward the source of particularly raucous laughter. It was Guy Delancey, clearly well soused and leaning close to a buxom young thing. "Unfortunately," Jordan observed, "not everyone here believes in pacing himself."

"No kidding," said Wolf, also looking at Delancey. "You know, that fellow tried to put the make on Beryl tonight. Right under my nose."

"And did you defend her honor?"

"Didn't have to," said Richard with a laugh. "She does a pretty good job of defending herself."

Delancey's hand was now on Miss Buxom's lower back. Slowly that hand began to slide down toward dangerous terrain.

"What do women see in a guy like that, anyway?" asked Richard.

"Sex appeal?" said Jordan. Delancey did, after all, have rather dashing Spanish looks. "Who knows what attracts women to certain men?" Lord only knew what had attracted Veronica Cairncross to Guy. But she was rid of him now. If she was sensible, she'd damn well stay on the straight and narrow.

Jordan looked at Richard. "Tell me, have you ever heard of a security firm called Nimrod Associates?"

"Is that based here or abroad?"

"I don't know. Here, I imagine."

"I haven't heard of it. But I could check for you."

"Would you? I'd appreciate it."

"Why are you interested in this firm?"

"Oh…" Jordan shrugged. "The name came up in the course of the evening."

Richard was looking at him thoughtfully. Damn, it was that intelligence background of his, an aspect of Richard Wolf that could be either a help or a nuisance. Richard's antennae were out now, the questions forming in his head. Jordan would have to be careful.

Luckily, Beryl sauntered up at that moment to bestow a kiss on her intended. Any questions Richard may have entertained were quickly forgotten as he bent to press his lips to his fiancée's upturned mouth. Another kiss, a hungry twining of arms, and poor old Richard was oblivious to the rest of the world.

Ah, young lovers, sizzling in hormones, thought Jordan and polished off his drink. His own hormones were simmering tonight as well, helped along by the pleasant buzz of champagne.

And by thoughts of that woman.

He couldn't seem to get her out of his thick head. Not her voice, nor her laugh, nor the catlike litheness of her body twisting beneath his…

Quickly he set his glass down. No more champagne tonight. The memories were intoxicating enough. He glanced around for the tray of soda water and spotted his uncle Hugh entering the ballroom.

All evening Hugh had played genial host and proud uncle to the future bride. He'd happily guzzled champagne and flirted with ladies young enough to be his granddaughters. But at this particular moment Uncle Hugh was looking vexed.

He crossed the room, straight toward Guy Delancey. The two men exchanged a few words and Delancey's chin shot up. An instant later an obviously upset Delancey strode out of the ballroom, calling loudly for his car.

"Now what's going on?" said Jordan.

Beryl, her cheeks flushed and pretty from Richard's kissing, turned to look as Uncle Hugh wandered in their direction. "He's obviously not happy."

"Dreadful way to finish off the evening," Hugh was muttering.

"What happened?" asked Beryl.

"Guy Delancey's man called to report a burglary at the house. Seems someone climbed up the balcony and walked straight into the master bedroom. Imagine the cheek! And with the butler at home, too."

"Was anything stolen?" asked Richard.

"Don't know yet." Hugh shook his head. "Almost makes one feel a bit guilty, doesn't it?"

"Guilty?" Jordan forced a laugh from his throat. "Why?"

"If we hadn't invited Delancey here tonight, the burglar wouldn't have had his chance."

"That's ridiculous," said Jordan. "The burglar—I mean, if it *was* a burglar—"

"Why wouldn't it be a burglar?" asked Beryl.

"It's just—one shouldn't draw conclusions."

"Of course it's a burglar," said Hugh. "Why else would one break into Guy's house?"

"There could be other…explanations. Couldn't there?"

No one answered.

Smiling, Jordan took a sip of soda water. But the whole time he felt his sister's gaze, watching him closely.

Suspiciously.

The phone was ringing when Clea returned to her hotel room. Before she could answer it, the ringing stopped, but she knew it would start up again. Tony must be anxious. She wasn't ready to talk to him yet. Eventually she would have to, of course, but first she needed a chance to recover from the night's near catastrophe, a chance to figure out what she should do next. What Tony should do next.

She rooted around in her suitcase and found the miniature bottle of brandy she'd picked up on the airplane. She went into the bathroom, poured out a splash into a water glass and stood sipping the drink, staring dejectedly at her reflection in the mirror. In the car she'd managed to wipe away most of the camouflage paint, but there were still smudges of it on her temples and down one side of her nose. She turned on the faucet, wet a facecloth and scrubbed away the rest of the paint.

The phone was ringing again.

Carrying her glass, she went into the bedroom and picked up the receiver. "Hello?"

"Clea?" said Tony. "What happened?"

She sank onto the bed. "I didn't get it."

"Did you get in the house?"

"Of course I got in!" Then, more softly, she said, "I was close. So close. I searched the downstairs, but it wasn't there. I'd just gotten upstairs when I was rudely interrupted."

"By Delancey?"

"No. By another burglar. Believe it or not." She managed a tired laugh. "Delancey's house seems to be quite the popular place to rob."

There was a long silence on the other end of the line. Then Tony asked a question that instantly chilled her. "Are you sure it was just a burglar? Are you sure it wasn't one of Van Weldon's men?"

At the mention of that name, Clea's fingers froze around the glass of brandy. "No," she murmured.

"It's possible, isn't it? They may have figured out what you're up to. Now *they'll* be after the Eye of Kashmir."

"They couldn't have followed me! I was so careful."

"Clea, you don't know these people—"

"The hell I don't!" she retorted. "I know *exactly* who I'm dealing with!"

After a pause Tony said softly, "I'm sorry. Of course you know. You know better than anyone. But I've had my ear to the ground. I've been hearing things."

"What things?"

"Van Weldon's got friends in London. Friends in high places."

"He has friends everywhere."

"I've also heard…" Tony's voice dropped. "They've upped the ante. You're worth a million dollars to them, Clea. Dead."

Her hands were shaking. She took a desperate gulp of brandy. At once her eyes watered, tears of rage and despair. She blinked them away.

"I think you should try the police again," Tony said.

"I'm not repeating that mistake."

"What's the alternative? Running for the rest of your life?"

"The evidence is *there.* All I have to do is get my hands on it. Then they'll *have* to believe me."

"You can't do it on your own, Clea!"

"I can do it. I'm sure I can."

"Delancey will know someone's broken in. Within twenty-four hours he'll have his house burglarproof."

"Then I'll get in some other way."

"How?"

"By walking in his front door. He has a weakness, you know. For women."

Tony groaned. "Clea, no."

"I can handle him."

"You *think* you can—"

"I'm a big girl, Tony. I can deal with a man like Delancey."

"This makes me sick. To think of you and…" He made a sound of disgust. "I'm going to the police."

Firmly Clea set down her glass. "Tony," she said. "There's no other way. I have some breathing space now. A week, maybe more before Van Weldon figures out where I am. I have to make the most of it."

"Delancey may not be so easy."

"To him I'll just be another dimwitted bimbo. A rich one, I think. That should get his attention."

"And if he gives you too much attention?"

Clea paused. The thought of actually making love to that oily Guy Delancey was enough to nauseate her. With any luck, it would never get that far.

She'd see to it it never got that far.

"I'll handle it," she said. "You just keep your ear to

the ground. Find out if anything else has come up for sale. And stay out of sight."

After she'd hung up, Clea sat on the bed, thinking about the last time she'd seen Tony. It had been in Brussels. They'd both been happy, so very happy! Tony had had a brand-new wheelchair, a sporty edition, he called it, for upper-body athletes. He had just received a fabulous commission for the sale of four medieval tapestries to an Italian industrialist. Clea had been about to leave for Naples, to finalize the purchase. Together they had celebrated not just their good fortune but the fact they'd finally found their way out of the darkness of their youth. The darkness of their shared past. They'd laughed and drunk wine and talked about the men in her life, the women in his, and about the peculiar hazards of courting from a wheelchair. Then they'd parted.

What a difference a month made.

She reached for her glass and drained the last of the brandy. Then she went to her suitcase and dug around in her clothes until she found what she was looking for: the box of Miss Clairol. She stared at the model's hair on the box, wondering if perhaps she should have chosen something more subtle. No, Guy Delancey wasn't the type to go for subtle. Brazen was more his style.

And "cinnamon red" should do the trick.

"I've checked the name Nimrod Associates," said Richard. "There's no such security firm. At least, not in England."

The three of them were sitting on the terrace, enjoying a late breakfast. As usual, Beryl and Richard were snuggling cheek to cheek, laughing and darting amorous glances at each other. In short, behaving pre-

cisely as one would expect a newly engaged couple to
behave. Some of that snuggling might be due to the unexpected chill in the air. Summer was definitely over,
Jordan thought with regret. But the sun was shining,
the gardens still clung stubbornly to their blossoms and
a bracing breakfast on the terrace was just the thing to
clear the fog of last night's champagne from his head.

Now, after two cups of coffee, Jordan's brain was finally starting to function. It wasn't just the champagne
that had left him feeling muddled this morning; it was
the lack of sleep. Several times in the night he'd awakened, sweating, from the same dream.

About the woman. Though her face had been obscured by darkness, her hair was a vivid halo of silvery
ripples. She had reached up to him, her fingers caress-
ing his face, her flesh hot and welcoming. As their lips
had met, as his hands had slid into those silvery coils
of hair, he'd felt her body move against his in that sweet
and ancient dance. He'd gazed into her eyes. The eyes
of a panther.

Now, by the light of morning, the symbolism of
that nightmare was all too clear. Panthers. Dangerous
women.

He shook off the image and poured himself another
cup of coffee.

Beryl took a nibble of toast and marmalade, the
whole time watching him. "Tell me, Jordie," she said.
"Where did you hear about Nimrod Associates?"

"What?" Jordan glanced guiltily at his sister. "Oh, I
don't know. A while ago."

"I thought it came up last night," said Richard.

Jordan reached automatically for a slice of toast.

"Yes, I suppose that's when I heard it. Veronica must have mentioned the name."

Beryl was still watching him. This was the downside of being so close to one's sister; she could tell when he was being evasive.

"I notice you're rather chummy with Veronica Cairncross these days," she observed.

"Oh, well." He laughed. "We try to keep up the friendship."

"At one time, I recall, it was more than friendship."

"That was ages ago."

"Yes. Before she was married."

Jordan looked at her with feigned astonishment. "You're not thinking...good Lord, you can't possibly imagine..."

"You've been acting so *odd* lately. I'm just trying to figure out what's wrong with you."

"Nothing. There's nothing wrong with me." *Save for the fact I've recently taken up a life of crime,* he thought.

He took a sip of tepid coffee and almost choked on it when Richard said, "Look. It's the police."

An official car had turned onto Chetwynd's private road. It pulled into the gravel driveway and out stepped Constable Glenn, looking trim and snappy in uniform. He waved to the trio on the terrace.

As the policeman came up the steps, Jordan thought, *This is it, then. I'll be ignominiously hauled off to prison. My face in the papers, my name disgraced...*

"Good morning to you all," said Constable Glenn cheerily. "May I inquire if Lord Lovat's about?"

"You've just missed him," said Beryl. "Uncle Hugh's gone off to London for the week."

"Oh. Well, perhaps I should speak with you, then."

"Do sit down." Beryl smiled and indicated a chair. "Join us for some breakfast."

Oh, lovely, thought Jordan. What would she offer him next? *Tea? Coffee? My brother, the thief?*

Constable Glenn sat down and smiled primly at the cup of coffee set before him. He took a sip, careful not to let his mustache get wet. "I suppose," he said, setting his cup down, "that you know about the robbery at Mr. Delancey's residence."

"We heard about it last night," said Beryl. "Have you any leads?"

"Yes, as a matter of fact. We have a pretty good idea what we're dealing with here." Constable Glenn looked at Jordan and smiled.

Weakly, Jordan smiled back.

"A matter of excellent police work, I'm sure," said Beryl.

"Well, not exactly," admitted the constable. "More a case of carelessness on the burglar's part. You see, she dropped her stocking cap. We found it in Mr. Delancey's bedroom."

"She?" said Richard. "You mean the burglar's a woman?"

"We're going on that assumption, though we could be wrong. There was a very long strand of hair in the cap. Blond. It would've reached well below her—or his—shoulders. Does that sound like anyone you might know?" Again he looked at Jordan.

"No one I can think of," Jordan said quickly. "That is—there *are* some blondes in our circle of acquaintances. But not a burglar among them."

"It could be anyone. Anyone at all. It's not the first break-in we've had in this neighborhood. Three just this year. And the culprit might even be someone you know. You'd be surprised, Mr. Tavistock, what sort of misbehavior occurs, even in your social circle."

Jordan cleared his throat. "I can't imagine."

"This woman, whoever she is, is quite bold. She entered through a downstairs locked door. Got upstairs without alarming the butler. Only then did she get careless—caused a bit of a racket. That's when she was chased out."

"Was anything taken?" asked Beryl.

"Not so far as Mr. Delancey knows."

So Guy Delancey didn't report the stolen letters, thought Jordan. Or perhaps he never even noticed they were missing.

"This time she slipped up," said Constable Glenn. "But there's always the chance she'll strike again. That's what I came to warn you about. These things come in waves, you see. A certain neighborhood will be chosen. Delancey's house isn't that far from here, so Chetwynd could be in her target zone." He said it with the authority of one who had expert knowledge of the criminal mind. "A residence as grand as yours would be quite a temptation." Again he looked directly at Jordan.

Again Jordan had that sinking feeling that the good Constable Glenn knew more than he was letting on. *Or is it just my guilty conscience?*

Constable Glenn rose and addressed Beryl. "You'll let Lord Lovat know of my concerns?"

"Of course," said Beryl. "I'm sure we'll be perfectly all right. After all, we do have a security expert on the premises." She beamed at Richard. "And he's *quite* trustworthy."

"I'll look over the household arrangements," said Richard. "We'll beef up security as necessary."

Constable Glenn nodded in satisfaction. "Good day, then. I'll let you know how things develop."

They watched the constable march smartly back to his car. As it drove away, up the tree-lined road, Richard said, "I wonder why he felt the need to warn us personally."

"As a special favor to Uncle Hugh, I'm sure," said Beryl. "Constable Glenn was employed by MI6 years ago as a 'watcher'—domestic surveillance. I think he still feels like part of the team."

"Still, I get the feeling there's something else going on."

"A woman burglar," said Beryl thoughtfully. "My, we *have* come a long way." Suddenly she burst out laughing. "Lord, what a relief to hear it's a *she!*"

"Why?" asked Richard.

"Oh, it's just too ridiculous to mention."

"Tell me, anyway."

"You see, after last night, I thought—I mean, it occurred to me that—" She laughed harder. She sat back, flush with merriment, and pressed her hand to her mouth. Between giggles she managed to choke out the words. "I thought *Jordie* might be the cat burglar!"

Richard burst out laughing, as well. Like two giddy school kids, he and Beryl collapsed against each other in a fit of the sillies.

Jordan's response was to calmly bite off a corner of his toast. Though his throat had gone dry as chalk, he managed to swallow down a mouthful of crumbs. "I fail to see the humor in all this," he said.

They only laughed harder as he bore the abuse with a look of injured dignity.

* * *

Clea spotted Guy Delancey walking toward the re-freshment tent. It was the three-minute time-out be-tween the third and fourth chukkers, and a general exodus was under way from the polo viewing stands. Briefly she lost sight of him in the press of people, and she felt a momentary panic that all her detective work would be for nothing. She'd made a few discreet inqui-ries in the village that morning, had learned that most of the local gentry would almost certainly be headed for the polo field that afternoon. Armed with that tip, she'd called Delancey's house, introduced herself as Lady So-and-So, and asked the butler if Mr. Delancey was still meeting her at the polo game as he'd promised.

The butler assured her that Mr. Delancey would be at the field.

It had taken her the past hour to track him down in the crowd. She wasn't about to lose him now.

She pressed ahead, plunging determinedly into the Savile-Row-and-silk-scarf set. The smell of the polo field, of wet grass and horseflesh, was quickly over-powered by the scent of expensive perfumes. With an air of regal assuredness—pure acting on her part—Clea swept into the green-and-white-striped tent and glanced around at the well-heeled crowd. There were dozens of tables draped in linen, silver buckets overflowing with ice and champagne, fresh-faced girls in starched aprons whisking about with trays and glasses. And the ladies—what hats they wore! What elegant vowels tripped from their tongues! Clea paused, her confidence suddenly wavering. Lord, she'd never pull this off...

She glimpsed Delancey by the bar. He was stand-ing alone, nursing a drink. *Now or never,* she thought.

She swayed over to the counter and edged in close to Delancey. She didn't look at him, but kept her attention strictly focused on the young fellow manning the bar.

"A glass of champagne," she said.

"Champagne, coming up," said the bartender.

As she waited for the drink, she sensed Delancey's gaze. Casually she shifted around so that she was almost, but not quite, looking at him. He was indeed facing her.

The bartender slid across her drink. She took a sip and gave a weary sigh. Then she drew her fingers slowly, sensuously, through her mane of red hair.

"Been a long day, has it?"

Clea glanced sideways at Delancey. He was fashionably tanned and impeccably dressed in autumn-weight cashmere. Though tall and broad shouldered, his once striking good looks had gone soft and a bit jowly, and the hand clutching the whiskey glass had a faint tremor. *What a waste,* she thought, and smiled at him prettily.

"It has been rather a long day." She sighed, and took another sip. "Afraid I'm not very good in airplanes. And now my friends haven't shown up as promised."

"You've just flown in? From where?"

"Paris. Went on holiday for a few weeks, but decided to cut it short. Dreadfully unfriendly there."

"I was there just last month. Didn't feel welcome at all. I recommend you try Provence. Much friendlier."

"Provence? I'll keep that in mind."

He sidled closer. "You're not English, are you?"

She smiled at him coyly. "You can tell?"

"The accent—what, American?"

"My, you're quick," she said, and noted how he puffed up with the compliment. "You're right, I'm

American. But I've been living in London for some time. Ever since my husband died."

"Oh." He shook his head sympathetically. "I'm so sorry."

"He was eighty-two." She sipped again, gazing at him over the rim of her glass. "It was his time."

She could read the thoughts going through his transparent little head. *Filthy rich old man, no doubt. Why else would a lovely young thing marry him? Which makes her a rich widow....*

He moved closer. "Did you say your friends were supposed to meet you here?"

"They never showed." Sighing, she gave him a helpless look. "I took the train up from London. We were supposed to drive back together. Now I suppose I'll just have to take the train home."

"There's no need to do that!" Smiling, he edged closer to her. "I know this may sound a bit forward. But if you're at loose ends, I'd be delighted to show you 'round. It's a lovely village we have here."

"I couldn't impose—"

"No imposition at all. I'm at loose ends myself today. Thought I'd watch a little polo, and then go off to the club. But this is a far pleasanter prospect."

She looked him up and down, as though trying to decide if he could be trusted. "I don't even know your name," she protested weakly.

He thrust out his hand in greeting. "Guy Delancey. Delighted to make your acquaintance. And you are…"

"Diana," she said. Smiling warmly, she shook his hand. "Diana Lamb."

Chapter 3

It was three minutes into the fourth chukker. Oliver Cairncross, mounted on his white-footed roan, swung his mallet on a dead run. The thwock sent the ball flying between the goalposts. Another score for the Bucking'shire Boys! Enthusiastic applause broke out in the viewing stands, and Sir Oliver responded by sweeping off his helmet and dipping his bald head in a dramatic bow.

"Just look at him," murmured Veronica. "They're like children out there, swinging their sticks at balls. Will they never grow up?"

Out on the field Sir Oliver strapped his helmet back in place and turned to wave to his wife in the stands. He frowned when he saw that she was leaning toward Jordan.

"Oh, no." Veronica sighed. "He's seen you." At once she rose to her feet, waving and beaming a smile of wifely pride. Sitting back down, she muttered, "He's so bloody suspicious."

Jordan looked at her in astonishment. "Surely he doesn't think that you and I—"

"You *are* my old chum. Naturally he wonders."

Yes, of course he does, thought Jordan. Any man married to Veronica would probably spend his lifetime in a perpetual state of doubt.

The ball was tossed. The thunder of hoofbeats, the whack of a mallet announced the resumption of play.

Veronica leaned close to Jordan. "Did you bring them?" she whispered.

"As requested." He reached into his jacket and withdrew the bundle of letters.

At once she snatched them out of his hand. "You didn't read them, did you?"

"Of course not."

"Such a gentleman!" Playfully she reached up and pinched his cheek. "You promise you won't tell anyone?"

"Not a soul. But this is absolutely the last time, Veronica. From now on, be discreet. Or better yet, honor those marriage vows."

"Oh, I will, I will!" she declared fervently. She stood and moved toward the aisle.

"Where are you going?" he called.

"To flush these down the loo, of course!" She gave him a gay wave of farewell. "I'll call you, Jordie!" As she turned to make her way up the aisle, she brushed past a broad-shouldered man. At once she halted, her gaze slanting up with interest at this new specimen of masculinity.

Jordan shook his head in disgust and turned his attention back to the polo game. Men and horses thundered past, chasing that ridiculous rubber ball across the field. Back and forth they flew, mallets swinging, a tangle of sweating men and horseflesh. Jordan had never been much of a polo fan. The few times he'd played the game he'd come away with more than his share of bruises. He didn't trust horses and horses didn't trust him and in the inevitable struggle for authority, the beasts had a seven-hundred-pound advantage.

There were still four chukkers left to go, but Jordan had had his fill. He left the viewing stands and headed for the refreshment tent.

In the shade of green-and-white-striped awning, he strolled over to the wine bar and ordered a glass of soda water. With so much celebrating this past week, he'd been waking up every morning feeling a bit pickled.

Sipping his glass of soda, Jordan wandered about looking for an unoccupied table. He spotted one off in a corner. As he approached it, he recognized the occupant of the neighboring table. It was Guy Delancey. Seated across from Delancey, her back to Jordan, was a woman with a magnificent mane of red hair. The couple seemed to be intently engaged in intimate conversation. Jordan thought it best not to disturb them. He walked straight past them and was just sitting down at the neighboring table when he caught a snatch of their dialogue.

"Just the spot to forget one's troubles," Guy was saying. "Sun. Sugary beaches. Waiters catering to your every whim. Do consider joining me there."

The woman laughed. The sound had a throaty, hauntingly familiar ring to it. "It's rather a leap, don't you think, Guy?" she said. "I mean, we've only just met. To run off with you to the Caribbean…"

Slowly Jordan turned in his chair and stared at the woman. Lustrous cinnamon red hair framed her face, softening its angles. She had fair, almost translucent skin with a hint of rouge. Though she was not precisely beautiful, there was a hypnotic quality to those dark eyes, which slanted like a cat's above finely carved cheekbones. *Cat's eyes,* he thought. *Panther's eyes.*

It was her. It had to be her.

As though aware that someone was watching her, she raised her head and looked at Jordan. The instant their gazes met she froze. Even the rouge couldn't conceal the sudden blanching of her skin. He sat staring at her, and she at him, both of them caught in the same shock of mutual recognition.

What now? wondered Jordan. Should he warn Guy Delancey? Confront the woman on the spot? And what would he say? *Guy, old chap, this is the woman I bumped into while burgling your bedroom....*

Guy Delancey swiveled around and said cheerily, "Why, hello, Jordan! Didn't know you were right behind me."

"I...didn't want to intrude." Jordan glanced in the woman's direction. Still white-faced, she reached for her drink and took a desperate swallow.

Guy noted the direction of Jordan's gaze. "Have you two met?" he asked.

Their answer came out in a simultaneous rush.

"Yes," said Jordan.

"No," said the woman.

Guy frowned. "Aren't you two sure?"

"What he means," the woman cut in before Jordan could say a word, "is that we've *seen* each other before. Last week's auction at Sotheby's, wasn't it? But we've never actually been introduced." She looked Jordan straight in the eye, silently daring him to contradict her.

What a brazen hussy, he thought.

"Let me properly introduce you two," said Guy. "This is Lord Lovat's nephew, Jordan Tavistock. And this—" Guy swept his hand proudly toward the woman "—is Diana Lamb."

The woman extended a slender hand across the table as Jordan turned his chair to join them. "Delighted to make your acquaintance, Mr. Tavistock."

"So you two met at Sotheby's," said Guy.

"Yes. Terribly disappointing collection," she said. "The St. Augustine estate. One would think there'd be *something* worth bidding on, but no. I didn't make a single offer." Again she looked straight at Jordan. "Did you?"

He saw the challenge in her gaze. He saw something else as well: a warning. *You spill the beans,* said those cheerful brown eyes, *and so will I.*

"Well, did you, Jordie?" asked Guy.

"No," muttered Jordan, staring fiercely at the woman. "Not a one."

At his capitulation, the woman's smile broadened to dazzling. He had to concede she'd beaten him this round; next round she'd not be so lucky. He'd have the right words ready, his strategy figured out…

"…dreadful shambles. Pitiful, really. Don't you agree?" said Guy.

Suddenly aware that he was being addressed, Jordan looked at Guy. "Pardon?"

"All the estates that have fallen on hard times. Did you know the Middletons have decided to open Greystones to public tours?"

"I hadn't heard," said Jordan.

"Lord, can you imagine how humiliating that must be? To have all those strangers tramping through one's house, snapping photos of your loo. I'd never sink so low."

"Sometimes one has no choice," said Jordan.

"Certainly one has the choice! You're not saying you'd ever let the tourists into Chetwynd, would you?"

"No, of course not."

"Neither would I let them into Underhill. Plus, there's the problem of security, something I'm acutely tuned in to after that robbery attempt last night. People may *claim* they're tourists. But what if they're really thieves, come to check the layout of the place?"

"I agree with you on that point," said Jordan, looking straight at the woman. "One can't be too careful."

The little thief didn't bat an eyelash. She merely smiled back, those brown eyes wide and innocent.

"One certainly can't," said Guy. "And that goes triply for you. When I think of the fortune in art hanging on your walls…"

"Fortune?" said the woman, her gaze narrowing.

"I wouldn't call it a fortune," Jordan said quickly.

"He's being modest," said Guy. "Chetwynd has a collection any museum would kill for."

"All of it under tight security," said Jordan. "And I mean, *extremely* tight."

The hussy laughed. "I believe you, Mr. Tavistock."

"I certainly hope you do."

"I'd like to see Chetwynd some day."

"Hang around with me, darling," said Guy, "and we might wangle an invitation."

With a last squeeze of the woman's hand, Guy rose to his feet. "I'll have the car sent 'round, how about it? If we leave now, we'll avoid the jam in the parking lot."

"I'll come with you," she offered.

"No, no. Do stay and finish your drink. I'll be back as soon as the car's ready." He turned and disappeared into the crowd.

The woman sat back down. No shrinking violet, this one; brazenly she faced Jordan. And she smiled.

From across the refreshment tent Charles Ogilvie spotted the woman. He knew it had to be her; there was no mistaking the hair color. "Cinnamon red" was precisely how one would describe that glorious mane of hers. A superb job, courtesy of Clairol. Ogilvie had found the discarded hair-color box in the bathroom rubbish can when he'd searched her hotel room this morning, had confirmed its effect when he'd pulled a few silky strands from her hairbrush. Miss Clea Rice, it appeared, had done another quick-change job. She was getting better at this. Twice she'd metamorphosed into a different woman. Twice he'd almost lost her.

But she wasn't good enough to shake him entirely. He still had the advantage of experience. And she had the disadvantage of not knowing what *he* looked like.

Casually he strolled a few feet along the tent perimeter, to get a better look at her profile, to confirm it was indeed Clea Rice. She'd gone heavy with the lipstick and rouge, but he still recognized those superb cheekbones, that ivory skin. He also had no trouble recognizing Guy Delancey, who had just risen to his feet and was now moving away through the crowd, leaving Clea at the table.

It was the other man he didn't recognize.

He was a blond chap, long and lean as a whippet, impeccably attired. The man slid into the chair where

Delancey had been sitting and faced the Rice woman across the table. It was apparent, just by the intensity of their gazes, that they were not strangers to each other. This was troubling. Where did this blond man fit in? No mention of him had appeared in the woman's dossier, yet there they were, deep in conversation.

Ogilvie took the lens cap off his telephoto. Moving behind the wine bar, he found a convenient vantage point from which to shoot his photos, unobserved. He focused on the blond man's profile and clicked off a few shots, then took a few shots of Clea Rice, as well. A new partner? he wondered. My, she was resourceful. Three weeks of tailing the woman had left him with a grudging sense of admiration for her cleverness.

But was she clever enough to stay alive?

He reloaded his camera and began to shoot a second roll.

"I like the hair," said Jordan.

"Thank you," the woman answered.

"A bit flashy, though, don't you think? Attracts an awful lot of attention."

"That was the whole idea."

"Ah, I see. Guy Delancey."

She inclined her head. "Some men are *so* predictable."

"It's almost unfair, isn't it? The advantage you have over the poor dumb beasts."

"Why shouldn't I capitalize on my God-given talents?"

"I don't think you're putting those talents quite to the use He intended." Jordan sat back in his chair and returned her steady gaze. "There's no such company as Nimrod Associates. I've checked. Who are you? Is Diana Lamb your real name?"

"Is Jordan Tavistock yours?"

"Yes, and you didn't answer my question."

"Because I find you so much more interesting." She leaned forward, and he couldn't help but glance down at the deeply cut neckline of her flowered dress.

"So you own Chetwynd," she said.

He forced himself to focus on her face. "My uncle Hugh does."

"And that fabulous art collection? Also your uncle's?"

"The family's. Collected over the years."

"Collected?" She smiled. "Obviously I've underestimated you, Mr. Tavistock. Not the rank amateur I thought you were."

"What?"

"Quite the professional. A thief *and* a gentleman."

"I'm nothing of the kind!" He shot forward in his chair and inhaled such an intoxicating whiff of her perfume he felt dizzy. "The art has been in my family for generations!"

"Ah. One in a long line of professionals?"

"This is absurd—"

"Or are you the first in the family?"

Gripping the table in frustration, he counted slowly to five and let out a breath. "I am not, and have never been, a thief."

"But I saw you, remember? Rooting around in the wardrobe. You took something out—papers, I believe. So you *are* a thief."

"Not in the same sense *you* are."

"If your conscience is so clear, why didn't you go to the police?"

"Perhaps I will."

"I don't think so." She flashed him that maddening grin of triumph. "I think when it comes to thievery, *you're* the more despicable one. Because you make victims of your friends."

"Whereas you make friends of your victims?"

"Guy Delancey's not a friend."

"Astonishing how I misinterpreted that scene between you two! So what's the plan, little Miss Lamb? Seduction followed by a bit of larceny?"

"Trade secrets," she answered calmly.

"And why on earth are you so fixated on Delancey? Isn't it a bit risky to stick with the same victim?"

"Who said *he's* the victim?" She lifted the glass to her lips and took a delicate sip. He found her every movement oddly fascinating. The way her lips parted, the way the liquid slid into that moist, red mouth. He found himself swallowing as well, felt his own throat suddenly go parched.

"What is it Delancey has that you want so very badly?" he asked.

"What were those papers you took?" she countered.

"It won't work, you know."

"What won't work?"

"Trying to lump me in your category. *You're* the thief."

"And you're not?"

"What I lifted from that wardrobe has no intrinsic value. It was a personal matter."

"So is this for me," she answered tightly. "A personal matter."

Jordan frowned as a thought suddenly struck him. Guy Delancey had romanced Veronica Cairncross, and then had threatened to use her letters against her. Had he done the same to other women? Was Diana Lamb, or someone close to her, also a victim of Guy's?

Or am I trying to talk myself out of the obvious? he thought. The obvious being, this woman was a garden-variety burglar, out for loot. She'd already proven herself adept at housebreaking. What else could she be?

Such a pity, he thought, eyeing that face with its alabaster cheeks and nut brown eyes. Sooner or later those intelligent eyes would be gazing out of a jail cell.

"Is there any way I can talk you out of this?" he asked.

"Why would you?"

"I just think it's a waste of your apparent…talents. Plus there's the matter of it being morally wrong, to boot."

"Right, wrong." She gave an unconcerned wave of her hand. "Sometimes it isn't clear which is which."

This woman was beyond reform! And the fact he knew she was a thief, knew what she had planned, made him almost as guilty if she succeeded.

Which, he decided, she would not.

He said, "I won't let you, you know. While I'm not particularly fond of Guy Delancey, I won't let him be robbed blind."

"I suppose you're going to tell him how we met?" she asked. Not a flicker of anxiety was in her eyes.

"No. But I'm going to warn him."

"Based on what evidence?"

"Suspicions."

"I'd be careful if I were you." She took another sip of her drink and placidly set the glass down. "Suspicions can go in more than one direction."

She had him there, and they both knew it. He couldn't warn Delancey without implicating himself as a thief.

If Delancey chose to raise a fuss about it to the police, not only would Jordan's reputation be irreparably tarnished, Veronica's, too, would suffer.

No, he'd prefer not to take that risk.

He met Diana's calm gaze with one just as steady. "An ounce of prevention is worth a pound of cure," he said, and smiled.

"Meaning what, pray tell?"

"Meaning I plan to make it bloody difficult for you to so much as lift a teaspoon from the man and get away with it."

For the first time he saw a ripple of anxiety in her eyes. Her brightly painted red lips drew tight. "You don't understand. This is not your concern—"

"Of course it is. I plan to watch you like a hawk. I'm going to follow you and Delancey everywhere. Pop up when you least expect it. Make a royal nuisance of myself. In short, Miss Lamb, I've adopted you as my crusade. And if you make one false move, I'm going to cry wolf." He sat back, smiling. "Think about it."

She *was* thinking about it, and none too happily, judging by her expression.

"You can't do this," she whispered.

"I can. I have to."

"There's too much at stake! I won't let you ruin it—"

"Ruin *what*?"

She was about to answer when a hand closed over her shoulder. She glanced up sharply at Guy Delancey, who'd just returned and now stood behind her.

"Sorry if I startled you," he said cheerily. "Is everything all right?"

"Yes. Yes, everything's fine." Though the color had

drained from her face, she still managed to smile, to flash
Delancey a look of coquettish promise. "Is the car ready?"

"Waiting at the gate, my lady." Guy helped her from
her chair. Then he gave Jordan a careless nod of farewell. "See you around, Jordan."

Jordan caught a last glimpse of the woman's face,
looking back at him in smothered anger. Then, with
shoulders squared, she followed Delancey into the crowd.

You've been warned, Diana Lamb, thought Jordan.
Now he'd see if she heeded that warning. And just in
case she didn't...

Jordan pulled a handkerchief out of his jacket pocket.
Gingerly he picked up the woman's champagne glass
by the lower stem and peered at the smudge of ruby red
lipstick. He smiled. There, crystal clear on the surface
of the glass, was what he'd been looking for.

Fingerprints.

Ogilvie finished shooting his third roll of film and
clipped the lens cap back on his telephoto. He had more
than enough shots of the blond man. By tonight he'd have
the images transmitted to London and, with any luck,
an ID would be forthcoming. The fact Clea Rice had
apparently picked up an unknown associate disturbed
him, if only because he'd had no inkling of it. As far
as he knew, the woman traveled alone, and always had.

He'd have to find out more about the blond chap.

The woman rose from her chair and departed with
Guy Delancey. Ogilvie tucked his camera in his bag
and left the tent to follow them. He kept a discreet distance, far enough back so that he would blend in with
the crowd. She was an easy subject to tail, with all that
red hair shimmering in the sunlight. The worst possible

choice for anyone trying to avoid detection. But that was Clea Rice, always doing the unexpected.

The couple headed for the gate.

Ogilvie picked up his pace. He slipped through the gates just in time to see that head of red hair duck into a waiting Bentley.

Frantically Ogilvie glanced around the parking lot and spotted his black MG socked in three rows deep. By the time he could extricate it from that sea of Jaguars and Mercedes, Delancey and the woman could be miles away.

In frustration he watched Delancey's Bentley drive off. So much for following them; he'd have to catch up with her later. No problem. He knew which hotel she was staying at, knew that she'd paid for the next three nights in advance.

He decided to shift his efforts to the blond man.

Fifteen minutes later he spotted the man leaving through the gates. By that time Ogilvie had his car ready and waiting near the parking-lot exit. He saw the man step into a champagne gold Jaguar, and he took note of the license number. The Jaguar pulled out of the parking lot.

So did Ogilvie's MG.

His quarry led him on a long and winding route through rolling fields and trees, leaves already tinted with the fiery glow of autumn. Blueblood country, thought Ogilvie, noting the sleek horses in the pasture. Whoever *was* this fellow, anyway?

The gold Jaguar finally turned off the main road, onto a private roadway flanked by towering elms. From the main road Ogilvie could just glimpse the house that lay beyond those elms. It was magnificent, a stone-and-turret manor surrounded by acres of gardens.

He glanced at the manor name. It was mounted in bronze on the stone pillars marking the roadway entrance.

Chetwynd.

"You've come up in the world, Clea Rice," murmured Ogilvie.

Then he turned the car around. It was four o'clock. He'd have just enough time to call in his report to London.

Victor Van Weldon had had a bad day. The congestion in his lungs was worse, his doctors said, and it was time for the oxygen again. He thought he'd weaned himself from that green tank. But now the tank was back, hooked onto his wheelchair, and the tubes were back in his nostrils. And once again he was feeling his mortality.

What a time for Simon Trott to insist on a meeting.

Van Weldon hated to be seen in such a weak and vulnerable condition. Through the years he had prided himself on his strength. His ruthlessness. Now, to be revealed for what he was—an old and dying man—would grant Simon Trott too much of an advantage. Although Van Weldon had already named Trott his successor, he was not yet ready to hand over the company reins. *Until I draw my last breath,* he thought, *the company is mine to control.*

There was a knock on the door. Van Weldon turned his wheelchair around to face his younger associate as he walked into the room. It was apparent, by the look on Trott's face, that the news he brought was not good.

Trott, as usual, was dressed in a handsomely tailored suit that showed his athletic frame to excellent advantage. He had it all—youth, blond good looks, all the women he could possibly hope to bed. *But he does not yet have the company,* thought Van Weldon. *He is still afraid of me. Afraid of telling me this latest news.*

"What have you learned?" asked Van Weldon.

"I think I know why Clea Rice headed for England," said Trott. "There have been rumors...on the black market..." He paused and cleared his throat.

"What rumors?"

"They say an Englishman has been boasting about a secret purchase he made. He claims he recently acquired..." Trott looked down. Reluctantly he finished. "The Eye of Kashmir."

"*Our* Eye of Kashmir? That is impossible."

"That is the rumor."

"The Eye has not been placed on the market! There is no way anyone could acquire it."

"We have not inventoried the collection since it was moved. There is a possibility..."

The two men exchanged looks. And Van Weldon understood. They both understood. *We have a thief among our ranks. A traitor who has dared to go against us.*

"If Clea Rice has also heard rumors of this sale, it could be disastrous for us," said Van Weldon.

"I'm quite aware of that."

"Who is this Englishman?"

"His name is Guy Delancey. We're trying to locate his residence now."

Van Weldon nodded. He sank back in his wheelchair and for a moment let the oxygen wash through his lungs. "Find Delancey," he said softly. "I have a feeling that when you do, you will also find Clea Rice."

Chapter 4

"To new friends," said Guy as he handed Clea a glass brimming with champagne.

"To new friends," she murmured and took a sip. The champagne was excellent. It would go to her head if she wasn't careful, and now, more than ever, she needed to keep her head. Such a sticky situation! How on earth was she to case the joint while this slobbery Casanova was all over her? She'd planned to let him make only a few preliminary moves, but it was clear Delancey had far more than just a harmless flirtation in mind.

He sat down beside her on the flowered settee, close enough for her to get a good look at his face. For a man in his late forties, he was still reasonably attractive, his skin relatively unlined, his hair still jet black. But the watery eyes and the sagging jowls were testimony to a dissipated life.

He leaned closer, and she had to force herself not to pull back in repulsion as those eyes swam toward her. To her relief, he didn't kiss her—yet. The trick was to hold him off while she dragged as much information as she could out of him.

She smiled coyly. "I love your house."

"Thank you."

"And the art! Quite a collection. All originals, I take it?"

"Naturally." Guy waved proudly at the paintings on the walls. "I haunt the auction houses. At Sotheby's, if they see me coming, they rub their hands together in glee. Of course, this isn't the best of my collection."

"It isn't?"

"No, I keep the finer pieces in my London town house. That's where I do most of my entertaining. Plus, it has far better security."

Clea felt her heart sink. Darn, was that where he kept it, then? His London town house? Then she'd wasted the week here in Buckinghamshire.

"It's a major concern of mine these days," he murmured, leaning even closer toward her. "Security."

"Against theft, you mean?" she inquired innocently.

"I mean security in general. The wolf at the door. The chill of a lonely bed." He bent toward her and pressed his sodden lips to hers. She shuddered. "I've been searching so long for the right woman," he whispered. "A soul mate…"

Do women actually fall for this line? she wondered.

"And when I looked in your eyes today—in that tent   I thought perhaps I'd found her."

Clea fought the urge to burst out laughing and managed—barely—to return his gaze with one just as steady. Just as smoldering. "But one must be careful," she murmured.

"I agree."

"Hearts are so very fragile. Especially mine."

"Yes, yes! I know." He kissed her again, more deeply. This was more than she could bear.

She pulled back, rage making her breath come hard and fast. Guy didn't seem at all disturbed by it; if anything, he took her heavy breathing as a sign of passion.

"It's too soon, too fast," she panted.

"It's the way it was meant to be."

"I'm not ready—"

"I'll *make* you ready." Without warning he grasped her breast and began to knead it vigorously like a lump of bread dough.

Clea sprang to her feet and moved away. It was either that or slug him in the mouth. At the moment she was all in favor of the latter. In a shaky voice she said, "Please, Guy. Maybe later. When we know each other better. When I feel I know *you*. As a person, I mean."

"A person?" He shook his head in frustration. "What, exactly, do you need to know?"

"Just the small things that tell me about you. For instance…" She turned and gestured to the paintings. "I know you collect art. But all I know is what I see on these walls. I have no idea what moves you, what appeals to you. Whether you collect other things. Besides paintings, I mean." She gave him a questioning look.

He shrugged. "I collect antique weapons."

"There now, you see?" Smiling, she came toward him. "I find that fascinating! It tells me you have a masculine streak of adventure."

"It does?" He looked pleased. "Yes, I suppose it does."

"What sort of weapons?"

"Antique swords. Pistols. A few daggers."

Her heart gave an extra thump at that last word. *Daggers.* She moved closer to him. "Ancient weaponry," she murmured, "is wonderfully erotic, I think."

"You do?"

"Yes, it—it conjures up knights in armor, ladies in castle towers." She clasped her hands and gave a visible shiver of excitement. "It gives me goose bumps just to think of it."

"I had no idea it had that effect on women," he said in wonder. With sudden enthusiasm he rose from the couch. "Come with me, my lady," he said, taking her hand. "And I'll show you a collection that'll send shivers down your spine. I've just picked up a new treasure—something I purchased on the sly from a very private source."

"You mean the black market?"

"Even more private than that."

She let him guide her into the hallway and up the stairs. *So he keeps it on the second floor,* she thought. Probably the bedroom. To think she had gotten so close to it that night.

Somewhere, a phone was ringing. Guy ignored it.

They reached the top of the stairs. He turned right, toward the east wing—the bedroom—and suddenly halted.

"Master Delancey?" called a voice. "You've a telephone call."

Guy glanced back down the stairs at the gray-haired

butler who stood on the lower landing. "Take a message," he snapped.

"But it—it's—"

"Yes?"

The butler cleared his throat. "It's Lady Cairncross."

Guy winced. "What does she want?"

"She wishes to see you immediately."

"You mean *now?*"

Guy hurried down the stairs to take the receiver. From the upper landing Clea listened to the conversation below.

"Not a good time, Veronica," Guy said. "Couldn't you…look, I have other things to do right now. You're being unreasonable. No. Veronica, you mustn't! We'll talk about this some other— Hello? Hello?" He frowned at the receiver in dismay, then dropped it back in the cradle.

"Sir?" inquired the butler. "Might I be of service?"

Guy glanced up, suddenly aware of his predicament. "Yes! Yes, you'll have to see that Miss Lamb's brought home."

"Home?"

"Take her to a hotel! In the village."

"You mean—now?"

"Yes, bring the car 'round. Go!"

Guy scampered up the steps, snatched Clea by the arm and began to hustle her down to the front door. "Dreadfully sorry, darling, but something's come up. Business, you understand."

Clea planted her heels stubbornly into the carpet. "Business?"

"Yes, an emergency—client of mine—"

"Client? But I don't even know what you *do* for a living!"

"My chauffeur will find you a hotel room. I'll pick you up at five tomorrow, how about it? We'll make it an evening."

He gave her a quick kiss, then Clea was practically pushed out the front door. The car was already waiting, the chauffeur standing beside the open door. Clea had no choice but to climb in.

"I'll call you tomorrow!" yelled Guy, and waved.

As the chauffeur drove her out through the gates, Clea clutched the leather armrest in frustration. *I was so damn close, too,* she thought. He'd been about to show her the dagger. She could have had her hands on it, were it not for the phone call from that woman.

Just who the hell *was* Veronica?

Veronica Cairncross turned from the telephone and looked inquiringly at Jordan. "Well? Do you think that call did the trick?"

"If it didn't," he said, "then your visit will."

"Oh, must I really go see him? I told you, I want nothing to do with the man."

"It's one sure way to flush that woman out of the house before she does any damage."

"There must be some other way to stop her! We could call the police—"

"And have it all come out? My late-night foray into Guy's house? Those stolen letters?" He paused. "Your affair with Delancey?"

Veronica gave a vigorous shake of her head. "We certainly can't tell them *that.*"

"That's what I thought you'd say."

Resignedly, Veronica picked up her purse and started for the door. "Oh, all right. I got you into this. I suppose I owe you the favor."

"Plus, it's your civic duty," observed Jordan. "The woman's a thief. No matter what bitter feelings you have for Guy, you can't let him be robbed blind."

"Guy?" Veronica laughed. "I don't give a damn what happens to *him.* It's your lady burglar I'm thinking of. If she gets caught and talks to the police…"

"Then my reputation is mud," admitted Jordan.

Veronica nodded. "And so, I'm afraid, is mine."

Clea kicked off her high heels, tossed her purse in a chair and flung herself with a groan across the hotel bed. What a ghastly day. She hated polo, she despised Guy Delancey and she detested this red hair. All she wanted to do was go to sleep, to forget the Eye of Kashmir, to forget everything. But whenever she closed her eyes, whenever she tried to sleep, the old nightmares would return, the sights and sounds of terror so vivid she thought she was reliving it.

She fought the memories, tried to push them aside with more pleasant images. She thought of the summer of '72, when she was eight and Tony was ten, and they'd posed together for that photo that later graced Uncle Walter's mantelpiece. They'd been dressed in identical tans and bib overalls, and Tony had draped his skinny arm over her scrawny shoulder. They'd grinned at the camera like a pair of shysters in training, which they were. They had the world's best teacher, too: Uncle Walter, con man *extraordinaire,* damn his larcenous heart of gold. How was the old fellow faring in prison these days? she wondered. Uncle Walter would be up for parole soon. Maybe—just maybe—prison had changed him, the way it had changed Tony.

The way it had changed her.

Maybe Uncle Walter would walk out of those prison gates and into a straight life, sans con games and grifters.

Maybe pigs could fly.

She jerked as the phone rang. At once she reached for the receiver. "Hello?"

"Diana, darling! It's me!"

She rolled her eyes. "Hello, Guy."

"Dreadfully sorry about what happened this afternoon. Forgive me?"

"I'm thinking about it."

"My chauffeur said you're planning to stay in the village for a few days. Perhaps you'll give me a chance to make it up to you? Tomorrow night, say? Supper and a musicale at an old friend's house. And the rest of the evening at mine."

"I don't know."

"I'll show you my collection of antique weapons." His voice dropped to an intimate murmur. "Think of all those knights in shining armor. Damsels in distress…"

She sighed. "Oh, all right."

"I'll be by at five. Pick you up at the Village Inn."

"Right. See you at five." She hung up and realized she had a splitting headache. Ha! It was her just punishment for playing Mata Hari.

No, her *real* punishment would come if she actually had to bed that dissolute wretch.

Moaning, she rose to her feet and headed toward the bathroom to wash off the smell of polo ponies and the greasy touch of Guy Delancey.

* * *

Delancey was scarcely sober when he came to fetch her the next evening. She debated the wisdom of climbing into the car with him behind the wheel, but decided she had no choice—not if she wanted to see this through. All things considered, the dangers of riding with a tipsy driver seemed almost insignificant. Risk was a relative thing and this was the night for taking risks.

"Should be a jolly bunch tonight," said Guy, dodging traffic along the winding road. High hedgerows obscured the view of the road ahead; Clea could only hope that some car wasn't zooming toward them from the opposite direction. "I don't go for the music, really. It's more for the conversation afterward. The laughs."

And the drinks, she thought, clutching the armrest as they whizzed past a tree with inches to spare.

"Thought it'd be my chance to introduce you," said Guy. "Show you off to my friends."

"Will Veronica be there?"

He shot her a startled glance. "What?"

"Veronica. The one who called yesterday. You know, your client."

"Oh. Oh, *her.*" His laugh was patently forced. "No, she's not a music fan. I mean, she's fond of rock and roll, that sort of rubbish, but not classical music. No, she won't be there." He paused, then added under his breath, "Lord, I hope not, anyway."

Twenty minutes later his hopes were dashed when they walked into the Forresters' music room. Clea heard Guy suck in a startled breath and mutter, "I don't believe it" as a russet-haired woman approached them from across the room. She was dressed in a stunning gown of cream lawn, and around her neck hung a magnificent strand of pearls. But it wasn't the woman whom Clea focused on.

It was the woman's companion, a man who was now regarding Clea with a look of calm amusement. Or was it triumph she saw in Jordan Tavistock's sherry brown eyes?

Guy cleared his throat. "Hello, Veronica," he managed to say.

"I'd heard there was a new lady in your life."

"Yes, well…" Guy managed a weak smile.

Veronica turned her gaze to Clea, and offered an outstretched hand. "I'm Veronica Cairncross."

Clea returned the handshake. "Diana Lamb."

"We're old friends, Guy and I," Veronica explained. "*Very* old friends. And yet he does manage to surprise me sometimes."

"I surprise *you?*" Guy snorted. "Since when did you become a fan of musicales?"

"Since Jordan invited me."

"Oliver is so trusting."

"Who's Oliver?" Clea ventured to ask.

Guy laughed. "Oh, no one. Just her husband. A minor inconvenience."

"You are an *ass,*" hissed Veronica, and she turned and stalked away.

"Takes one to know one!" Guy retorted and followed her out of the room.

Jordan and Clea, equally cast adrift, looked at each other.

Jordan sighed. "Isn't love grand?"

"*Are* they in love?"

"I think it's obvious they still are."

"Is that why you brought her here? To sabotage my evening?"

Jordan picked up two glasses of white wine from a passing butler and handed a glass to Clea. "As I once said to you, Miss Lamb—or is it Miss Lamb?—I've taken on your reformation as my personal crusade. I'm going to save you from a life of crime. At least, while you're in my neighborhood."

"Territorial, aren't you?"

"Very."

"What if I gave you my solemn oath not to cut into your territory? I'll let you keep your hunting grounds."

"And you'll quietly leave the area?"

"Provided you carry out your side of the bargain."

He eyed her suspiciously. "What are you proposing?"

Clea paused, studying him, wondering what made him tick. She'd thought Jordan Tavistock attractive from the very beginning. Now she realized he was far more than just a pretty face and a pair of broad shoulders. It was what she saw in his eyes that held her interest. Intelligence. Humor. And more than a touch of determination. He might be an incompetent burglar, but he had class, he had contacts and he had an insider's familiarity with this neighborhood. By the looks of him, he was an independent, not a man who'd work for someone else. But she might be able to work *with* him.

She might even enjoy it.

She glanced around at the crowded room and motioned Jordan into a quiet corner. "Here's my proposition," she said. "I help you, you help me."

"Help you do what?"

"One itty-bitty job. Nothing, really."

"Just a small burglary?" He rolled his eyes. "Where have I heard that line before?"

"What?"

"Never mind." He sighed and took a sip of wine. "What, may I ask, would I get in return?"

"What would you like?"

His gaze focused with instant clarity on hers. And she knew by the sudden ruddiness of his cheeks that the same lascivious thought had flickered in both their brains.

"I'm not going to answer that," he said.

"Actually, I was thinking of offering up my expert advice in exchange," she said. "I think you could use it."

"Private tutelage in the art of burglary? That *is* a difficult offer to turn down."

"I won't actually help you do it, of course. But I'll give you tips."

"From personal experience?"

She smiled at him blandly over the wineglass. *Time to inflate the old résumé,* she thought. While burgling had never actually been her occupation, she did have a knack for it, and she'd rubbed shoulders with the best in the business, Uncle Walter among them. "I'm good enough to make a decent living," she said simply.

"A tempting proposition. But I'll have to decline."

"I can do wonders for your career."

"I'm not in your line of work."

"Well, what line of work *are* you in?" she blurted in frustration.

There was a long silence. "I'm a gentleman," he said.

"And what else?"

"Just a gentleman."

"That's an occupation?"

"Yes." He smiled sheepishly. "Full time, as a matter of fact. Still, it leaves me enough leisure for other pursuits. Such as local crime prevention."

"All right." She sighed. "What *can* I offer you just to stay out of my way? And not pop up at inconvenient times?"

"So that you can finish the job on poor old Guy Delancey?"

"Then I'll be out of here for good. Promise."

"What does he own that's so tempting to you, anyway?"

She stared down at her wineglass, refusing to meet his gaze. No, she wouldn't tell him. She couldn't tell him. For one thing, she didn't trust him. If he heard about the Eye of Kashmir, he might want it for himself, and then where would that leave her? No evidence, no proof. She'd be left twisting in the wind.

And Victor Van Weldon would go unpunished.

"It must be quite a valuable item," he said.

"No, its value is rather more…" She hesitated, searching for a believable note. "Sentimental."

He frowned. "I don't understand."

"Guy has something that belongs to my family. Something that's been ours for generations. It was stolen from us a month ago. We want it back."

"If it's stolen property, why not go to the police?"

"Delancey knew it was hot when he purchased it. You think he'd admit to its ownership?"

"So you're going to steal it back?"

"I haven't any choice." Meekly she met his gaze, and she saw a flicker of uncertainty in his eyes. Just a flicker. Was he actually buying this story? She was surprised how rotten that made her feel. She'd been telling a lot of lies lately, had justified each and every one of them by reminding herself this was what she had to do to stay alive. But lying to Jordan Tavistock felt somehow, well...*criminal.* Which made no sense at all, because that's exactly what *he* was. A thief and a gentleman, she thought, gazing up at him. He had the most penetrating brown eyes she'd ever seen. A face made up of intriguing angles. And a smile that could make her knees weak.

In wonder she glanced down at her drink. What was *in* this wine, anyway? The room was starting to feel warm and she was having trouble catching her breath.

The return of Guy Delancey was like an unwelcome slap of cold air. "It's starting," said Guy.

"What is?" murmured Clea.

"The music. Come on, let's sit down."

She focused at last on Guy and saw that he was looking positively grim. "What about Veronica?"

"Don't mention the name to me," he growled.

Now Veronica entered the room, and she came toward them, her gaze pointedly avoiding Guy. "Jordie, *darling,*" she purred, snatching Jordan's arm with ruthless possession. "Let's sit down, shall we?"

With a look of resignation, Jordan allowed himself to be led away to the performance room.

The musicians, a visiting string quartet from London, were already tuning up, and the audience was settled in their seats. Clea and Guy sat on the opposite end of the room from Jordan and Veronica, but the two couples might as well have been seated side by side, for all the barbed looks flying between Guy and Veronica. All during the performance Clea could almost hear the zing of arrows soaring back and forth.

Dvorak was followed by Bartok, Quartet no. 6, and

then Debussy. Through it all, Clea was busy plotting out the evening, wondering how close she could get to the Eye of Kashmir. Hoping that this would be the last evening she'd have to put up with Guy Delancey, with the lies, and with this hideous red hair. She scarcely heard the music. It was only when applause broke out that she realized the program had come to an end.

Refreshments followed, an elegant display of cakes and canapés and wine. A lot of wine. Guy, who'd been barely on the edge of sobriety when he entered the house, now proceeded to drink himself into outright intoxication. It was Veronica's presence that did it. The sight of a lost love flirting with her new escort was just too much for Guy.

Clea watched him reach for yet another glass of wine and decided that things had gone far enough. But how to stop him without making a scene? He was already talking too loudly, laughing too heartily.

That's when Jordan stepped in. She hadn't asked him to, but she'd seen him frowning at Guy, counting the glasses of wine he'd consumed. Now he slipped in beside Guy and said quietly, "Perhaps you should slow down a bit, chap?"

"Slow down what?" demanded Guy.

"That's your sixth, I believe. And you'll be driving the lady home."

"I can handle it."

"Come on, Delancey," Jordan urged. "A little self-control."

"Self-*control?* Who the hell're you to be talking about self-control?" Guy's voice had risen to a bellow, and all around them, conversations ceased. "You take up with another man's wife and you point at *me?*"

"No one's taken up with anyone's wife—"

"At least when I did it, I had the decency to be discreet about it!"

Veronica gave a startled gasp of dismay and ran out of the room.

"Coward!" Guy yelled after her.

"Delancey, please," murmured Jordan. "This isn't the time or place—"

"Veronica!" Guy broke away and pushed his way toward the door. "Why don't you face the bloody music for once! Veronica!"

Jordan looked at Clea. "He's pickled. You can't drive home with him tonight."

"I'll handle him."

"Well, take his keys, at least. Insist on driving yourself."

That was exactly what she'd planned to do. But when she followed Guy outside, she found that he and Veronica were still wrangling away, and loudly, too. Guy was so drunk he was weaving, barely able to stay on his feet. Lying bitch, he kept saying, couldn't trust her, could never trust her. She'd rip your heart in pieces, that's what she'd do, damn her, and he didn't need that. He could find another woman with just the snap of his fingers.

"Then why don't you?" Veronica lashed back.

"I will! I have." Guy swiveled around and focused, bleary-eyed, on Clea. He grabbed her hand. "Come on, let's go!"

"Not in your condition," Clea said, pulling back.

"There's nothing wrong with my condition!"

"Give me the car keys, Guy."

"I can drive."

"No, you can't." She pulled out of his grasp. "Give me the keys."

In disgust he waved her off. "Go on, then. Find your own way home! To hell with both of you! To hell with women!" He stumbled away to his car. With difficulty he managed to open the door and climb in.

"Bloody idiot," muttered Veronica. "He's going to get himself killed."

She's right, thought Clea. She ran to Guy's car and yanked open the door. "Come on, get out."

"Go away."

"You're not driving. I am."

"Go away!"

Clea grabbed his arm. "I'll take you home. You get into the back seat and lie down."

"I don't take orders from any bloody *woman!*" he roared and viciously shoved her away.

Tottering on high heels, Clea stumbled backward and landed in the shrubbery. Stupid man, he was too damn drunk to listen to reason. Even as she struggled to disentangle her necklace from the branches, she could hear him cranking the engine, could hear him muttering about parasitic women. He cursed and slapped the steering wheel as the motor died. Again he cranked the ignition. Just as Clea managed to free her necklace from the shrub, just as she started to sit up, the car's engine roared to life. Without even a farewell glance at her, Guy pulled away.

Idiot, she thought, and rose to her feet.

The explosion slammed her backward. She flew clear over the shrub and landed flat on her back under a tree. She was too stunned to feel the pain of the impact. What she registered first were the sounds: the screams and shouts, the clatter of flying metal hitting the road and then the crackle of flames. Still she felt no pain, just a vague awareness that it was surely to come. She got to her knees and began to crawl like a baby—toward what, she didn't know. Just away from the tree, from the damn bushes. Her brain was starting to work now and it was telling her things she didn't want to know. Her head was starting to hurt, too. Pain and awareness in a simultaneous rush. She thought she was crying, but she wasn't sure; she couldn't even hear her own voice through the roar of noises. She couldn't tell if the warmth streaming down her cheek was blood or tears or both. She kept crawling, thinking, *I'm dead if I don't get away. I'm dead.*

A pair of shoes stood in her way. She looked up and saw a man staring down at her. A man who seemed vaguely familiar, only she couldn't quite figure out why.

He smiled and said, "Let me get you to a hospital."

"No—"

"Come on, you're hurt." He grabbed her arm. "You need to see a doctor."

"No!"

Suddenly the man's hand evaporated and he was gone.

Clea huddled on the ground, the night twirling around her in a carousel of flames and darkness. She heard another voice now—this one familiar. Hands grasped her by the shoulders.

"Diana? *Diana?*"

Why was he calling her that? It wasn't her name. She squinted up into the face of Jordan Tavistock.

And she fainted.

Chapter 5

The doctor switched off the ophthalmoscope and turned on the hospital room light. "Everything appears neurologically intact. But she has had a concussion, and that brief loss of consciousness concerns me. I recommend at least one night in hospital. For observation."

Jordan looked at the pitiful creature lying in bed. Her red hair was tangled with grass and leaves, and her face was caked with dried blood. He said, "I wholeheartedly agree, Doctor."

"Very good. I don't expect there'll be any problems, but we'll watch for danger signs. In the meantime, we'll keep her comfortable and—"

"I can't stay," the woman said.

"Of course you're staying," said Jordan.

"No, I have to get out of here!" She sat up and swung her legs over the side of the bed.

Jordan quickly moved to restrain her. "What the blazes are you doing, Diana?"

"Have to… Have to…" She paused, obviously dizzy, and gave her head a shake.

"You can't leave. Not after a concussion. Now then, let's get back into bed, all right?" Gently but firmly he urged her back under the covers. That attempt to sit up had drained all the color from her face. She seemed as fragile as tissue paper, and so insubstantial she might float away without the weight of the blankets to hold her down. Yet her eyes were bright and alive and feverish with…what? Fear? Grief? Surely she didn't harbor any real feelings for Guy Delancey?

"I'll have a nurse in to help you straightaway," said the doctor. "You just rest, Miss Lamb. Everything will be fine."

Jordan gave her hand a squeeze. It felt like a lump of ice in his grasp. Then, reluctantly, he followed the doctor out of the room.

Down the hall, out of the woman's earshot, Jordan asked, "What about Mr. Delancey? Do you know his condition?"

"Still in surgery. You'd have to inquire upstairs. I'm afraid it doesn't sound hopeful."

"I'm surprised he's alive at all, considering the force of that blast."

"You really think it was a bomb?"

"I'm sure it was."

The doctor glanced at the nurses' station, where a policeman stood waiting for a chance to question the woman. Two cops had grilled her already, and they hadn't been very considerate of her condition. The doctor shook his head. "God, what's the world coming to?

Terrorist bombs going off in *our* corner of the world now…"

Terrorists? thought Jordan. Yes, of course it *would* be blamed on some shadowy villain, some ill-defined evil. Who but a terrorist would plant a bomb in a gentleman's car? It was a miracle that only one person had been seriously hurt tonight. A half dozen other musicale guests had suffered minor injuries—glass cuts, abrasions—and the police were calling this a lucky escape.

For everyone but Delancey.

Jordan rode the lift upstairs to the surgical floor. The waiting room was aswarm with police, none of whom would tell him a thing. He hung around for a while, hoping to hear some news, any news, but all he could learn was that Delancey was still alive and on the operating table. As for whether he would live, that was a matter for God and the surgeons.

He returned to the woman's floor. The policeman was still standing in the nurses' station, sipping coffee and chatting up the pretty clerk. Jordan walked right past them and opened the door to Diana's room.

Her bed was empty.

At once he felt a flicker of alarm. He crossed to the bathroom door and knocked. "Diana?" he called. There was no answer. Cautiously he opened the door and peeked inside.

She wasn't there, either, but her hospital gown was. It lay in a heap on the linoleum.

He yanked open the closet door. The shelves were empty; the woman's street clothes and purse had vanished.

What the hell are you thinking? he wondered. Why

would she crawl out of her hospital bed, get dressed and steal away like a thief into the night?

Because she is a thief, you bloody fool.

He ran out of the room and glanced up and down the hall. No sign of her. The idiot cop was still flirting with the clerk and was oblivious to anything but the buzz of his own hormones. Jordan hurried down the hall, toward the emergency stairs. If the woman was running from the police, then she'd probably avoid the lift, which opened into the lobby. She'd go for the side exit, which led straight to the parking lot.

He pushed into the stairwell. He was on the third floor. When last he'd seen Diana, she'd looked scarcely strong enough to stand, much less run down two flights of stairs. Could she make it? Was she even now lying in a dead faint on some lower landing?

Terrified of what he might find, Jordan started down the stairs.

Her head was pounding mercilessly, the high heels were killing her, but she kept marching like a good soldier down the road. That was how she managed to keep going, left-right-left, some inner drill sergeant screaming commands in her brain. Don't stop, don't stop. The enemy approaches. March or die.

And so she marched, stumbling along on her high heels, her head aching so badly she could scream. Twice she heard a car approaching and had to scramble off the road to hide in the bushes. Both times the cars passed without seeing her, and she crawled back to the road and resumed her painful march. She had only a vague plan of what came next. The nearest village couldn't be more than a few miles away. If she could just get to a train station, she could get out of Buckinghamshire. Out of England.

And then where do I go?

No, she couldn't think that far ahead. All she knew was that she'd failed miserably, that there'd be no more chances and that she was at the very top of Van Weldon's hit list. With new desperation she pushed on, but her feet didn't seem to be working, and the road was weaving before her eyes. *Can't stop,* she thought. *Have to keep going.* But shadows were puddling her vision now, creeping in from the sides. Suddenly nauseated, she dropped to her knees and lowered her head, waiting for the dizziness to pass. Crouching there in the darkness, she vaguely sensed the vibrations through the asphalt. Little by little the sound penetrated the fog clouding her brain.

It was a car, approaching from behind.

Her gaze shot back up the road and she saw the headlights gliding toward her. With a spurt of panic she stumbled to her feet, ready to dash into the bushes, but the dizziness at once assailed her. The headlights danced, blurred into a haze. She discovered she was on her knees, and that the asphalt was biting into her palms. The slam of a car door, the hurried crunch of shoes over gravel told her it was too late. She'd been spotted.

"No," she said as arms closed around her body. "Please, no!"

"It's all right—"

"No!" she screamed. Or thought she had. Her face was wedged against someone's chest, and her cry came out no louder than a strangled whisper. She began to flail at her captor, her fists connecting with his back, his shoulders. The arms only closed in tighter.

"Stop it, Diana! I won't hurt you. *Stop it!*"

Sobbing, she raised her head, and through a mist of tears and confusion she saw Jordan gazing down at her. Her fists melted as her hands reached out to clutch at his jacket. The wool felt so warm, so substantial. Like the man. They stared at each other, her face upturned to his, her body feeling numb and weightless in his arms.

All at once his mouth was on hers, and the numbness gave way to a flood of glorious sensations. With that one kiss he offered his warmth, his strength, and she drank from it, felt its nourishment revive her battered soul. She wanted more, more, and she returned his kiss with the desperate need of a woman who's finally found, in a man's arms, what she'd long been seeking. Not desire, not passion, but comfort. Protection. She clung to him, relinquishing all control of her fate to the only man who'd ever made her feel safe.

Neither of them heard the sound of the approaching car.

It was the distant glare of headlights that forced them to pull apart. Clea turned to look up the road and registered the twin lights burning closer. Instantly she panicked. She jerked out of Jordan's arms and plunged headlong into the bushes.

"Wait!" called Jordan. "Diana?"

Blindly she thrashed through the branches, desperate to flee, but her legs still weren't working right. She heard Jordan right behind her, his footsteps snapping across twigs as he ran to catch up. He snagged her arm.

"Diana—"

"They'll see me!"

"Who?"

"Let me go!"

On the road, the car braked to a stop. They heard the door swing open. At once Clea dropped to the ground and cowered in the shadows.

"Halloa!" called a man's voice. "Everything all right?"

Please, Jordan, Clea prayed. *Cover for me! Don't tell him I'm here....*

There was a pause, then she heard Jordan call back, "Everything's fine!"

"Saw your car had pulled off. Just wanted to check," said the man.

"I'm, er..." Jordan gave a convincingly sheepish laugh. "Answering the call of nature."

"Oh. Well. Carry on, then." The car door slammed shut, and the taillights glided away down the road.

Clea, still shaking, gave a sob of relief. "Thank you," she whispered.

For a moment he stood watching her in silence. Then he reached down and pulled her to her feet. She swayed unsteadily against him.

"Come on," he said gently. "I'll take you back to the hospital."

"No."

"Now see here, Diana. You're in no condition to be wandering around at night."

"I can't go back."

"What are you afraid of, anyway? The police?"

"Just let me *go!*"

"They won't arrest you. You haven't done anything." He paused. Softly he asked, "Have you?"

She wrenched herself free. That one effort cost her what little strength she had left. Suddenly her head was swimming and the darkness seemed to whirl around her like black water. She didn't remember sinking to the ground, didn't remember how she got into his arms, but suddenly she was there, and he was carrying her to the car. She was too tired to struggle, too weak to care anymore what happened to her. She was thrust into the front seat, where she sagged with her head against the door, trying not to faint, fighting the nausea that was beginning to roil her stomach again. *Can't throw up in this nice car,* she thought. *What a shame it would be to ruin his leather upholstery.* She vaguely registered the fact that he was sitting beside her, that the car was now moving. That was enough to nudge fear back into her addled brain.

She reached for his arm, her fingers clutching at his jacket sleeve. "Please," she begged. "Don't take me back to the hospital."

"Relax. I won't force you to go back."

She struggled to focus. Through the darkness of the car, she saw his profile, lean and tense as he stared ahead at the road.

"If you insist, I'll take you to your hotel," he offered. "But you need someone to look after you."

"I can't go there, either."

He frowned at her. Her fear, her desperation, must have registered on her face. "All right, Diana." He sighed. "Just tell me where you want to go."

"The train station."

He shook his head. "You're in no condition to travel."

"I can do it."

"You can scarcely stand up on your own two feet!"

"I have no choice!" she cried. Then, with a desperate sob, she whispered, "I have no choice."

He studied her in silence. "You're not getting on the train," he said at last. "I won't allow it."

"Won't *allow* it?" Sudden rage made her raise her head in defiance. "You have no right. You don't have any idea what I'm facing—"

"Listen to me! I'm taking you to a safe place. You have to trust me on this." He looked at her, a gaze so direct it defied her not to believe him. How simple it would be to hand over her fate to this man, and hope for the best. She wanted to trust him. She *did* trust him. Which meant it was all over for her, because no one who made a mistake that stupid would live long enough to regret it.

I don't have a choice, she thought as another wave of dizziness sent her head lolling to her knees. She might as well wave the white flag. Her future was now out of her hands.

And firmly in the grasp of Jordan Tavistock.

"How is she doing?" asked Richard.

Drained and exhausted, Jordan joined Richard in the library and poured himself a generous shot of brandy. "Obviously scared out of her wits," he said. "But otherwise she seems all right. Beryl's putting her to bed now. Maybe we'll get more out of her in the morning." He drained the brandy in a few gulps, then proceeded to pour himself a well-deserved second shot. He could feel Richard's doubtful gaze on him as he took another sip and sank into the easy chair by the fireplace. Sobriety was normally one of Jordan's virtues. It was unlike him to guzzle a triple brandy in one sitting.

It was certainly not like him to drag home stray females.

Yet that's exactly what he had upstairs at this moment, bundled away in the guest bedroom. Thank God Beryl hadn't bombarded him right off with questions. His sister was good that way; in a crisis she simply did what needed to be done. For the moment the bruised little waif would be well taken care of.

Questions, however, were sure to follow, and Jordan didn't know how to answer them because he himself didn't have the answers. He didn't even know why he'd brought Diana home. All he knew was that she was terrified, and that he couldn't turn his back on her. For some insane reason he felt responsible for the woman.

Even more insane, he *wanted* to feel responsible for her.

He leaned back and rubbed his face with both hands. "What a night," he groaned.

"You've been a very busy fellow," Richard observed. "Car bombs. Runaway females. Why didn't you tell us all this was cooking?"

"I had no idea bombs *would* be going off! I thought all I was dealing with was a cat burglar. Or is it burglaress?" He gave his head a shake to clear away the pleasant fog of brandy. "Theft is one thing. But she never mentioned anything about mad bombers."

Richard moved closer. "My question is," he said quietly, "who was the intended victim?"

"What?" Jordan looked up. He had great respect for his future brother-in-law. Years of working in the intelligence business had taught Richard that one should never accept evidence at face value. One had to examine around it, under it, looking for the twists and turns that might lead to completely different conclusions. Richard was doing that now.

"The bomb was planted in Guy Delancey's car," said Richard. "It could have been a random attack. It could have been aimed specifically at Delancey. Or…"

Jordan frowned at Richard. He saw that they were both considering the same possibility. "Or the target wasn't Delancey at all," Jordan finished softly.

"She was supposed to be riding in the car with him," said Richard. "She would have been killed, as well."

"There's no doubt Diana's terrified. But she hasn't told me what she's afraid of."

"What *do* you know about the woman?"

Jordan shook his head. "All I know is her name is Diana Lamb. Other than that I can't tell you much. I'm not even sure what her real hair color is! One day she's blond, then the next day she transforms into a redhead."

"What about the fingerprints? The ones you got off her glass?"

"I had Uncle Hugh's friend run them through the Scotland Yard computer. No match. Not a surprise, really. Since I'm sure she's a Yank."

"You *have* been busy, haven't you? Why the hell didn't you let me in on this earlier? I could've sent the fingerprints off to American authorities by now."

"I wasn't at liberty to say a thing. I'd promised Veronica, you see."

Richard laughed. "And a gentleman always keeps his promises."

"Well, yes. Except under certain circumstances. Such as car bombs." Jordan stared at his empty brandy snifter and considered pouring another. No, better not. Just look at what drink had done to Guy Delancey. Drink and women—the sole purpose of Delancey's life. And now he lay deprived of both.

Jordan set down the glass. "Motive," he said. "That's what I don't know. Why would someone kill Diana?"

"Or Delancey."

"That," said Jordan, "isn't too difficult to answer. God only knows how many women he's gone through in the past year. Add to that a few angry husbands, and you've probably got a slew of people who'd love to knock him off."

"Including your friend Veronica and her husband."

That possibility made Jordan pause. "I hardly think either one of them would ever—"

"Nevertheless, we have to consider them. Everyone's a suspect."

The sound of footsteps made both men turn. Beryl walked into the library and frowned at her brother and her fiancé. "Who's a suspect?" she demanded.

"Richard wants to include anyone who's had an affair with Guy Delancey," said Jordan.

Beryl laughed. "It'd be easier to start off with who *hasn't* had an affair with the man." She caught Richard's inquiring glance and she snapped, "No, I never have."

"Did I say anything?" asked Richard.

"I saw the look in your eye."

"On that note," cut in Jordan, rising to his feet, "I think I'll make my escape. Good night all."

"Jordan!" called Beryl. "What about Diana?"

"What about her?"

"Aren't you going to tell me what's going on?"

"No."

"Why not?"

"Because," he said wearily, "I haven't the faintest idea." He walked out of the library. He knew he owed Beryl an explanation, but he was too exhausted to repeat the story a second time. Richard would fill her in on the details.

Jordan climbed the stairs and started up the hall toward his bedroom. Halfway there, he stopped. Some compulsion made him turn around and walk, instead, to the bedroom where Diana was staying. He lingered outside the closed door, debating whether he should walk away.

He couldn't help himself; he tapped on the door. "Diana?" he called.

There was no answer. Quietly he entered the room.

A corner lamp had been left on, and the glow spilled softly over the bed, illuminating its sleeping occupant. She lay curled up on her side, her arms wrapped protectively around her chest, her hair rippling in red-gold waves across the pillow. The linen nightgown she wore was Beryl's, and a few sizes too big; the billowing sleeves almost engulfed her hands. He knew he should leave, but he found himself sinking into the chair beside the bed. There he watched her sleep and thought how very small she looked, how defenseless she truly was.

"My little thief," he murmured.

A sigh suddenly escaped her throat and she stirred awake. She looked at him with unfocused eyes, then slowly seemed to comprehend where she was.

"I'm sorry," he said, and rose from the chair. "I didn't mean to wake you. Go back to sleep." He turned to leave.

"Jordan?"

He glanced back at her. She seemed to be lost in a sea of white sheets and goose-down pillows and puffy nightgown linen, and he had the ridiculous urge to pull her out of there before she drowned.

"I…have to tell you something," she whispered.

"It can wait till tomorrow."

"No, I have to tell you now. It's not fair of me, pulling you into this. When you could get hurt."

Frowning, he moved back to the bed. "The bomb. In the car. *Was* it meant for Guy?"

"I don't know." She blinked, and he saw the sparkle of tears on her lashes. "Maybe. Or maybe it was meant for me. I can't be sure. That—that's what makes this so confusing. Not knowing if I'm the one who was supposed to die. I keep thinking…" She looked at him, her eyes full of torment. "I keep thinking it's my fault, what happened to Guy. He never really did anything wrong. I mean, not *seriously* wrong. He just got caught up in a bit of greed. But he didn't deserve…" She swallowed and looked down at the sheets. "He didn't deserve to die," she whispered.

"There's a chance he might live."

"You saw the explosion! Do you really think anyone could survive it?"

After a pause Jordan admitted, "No. To be honest, I don't think he'll survive."

They fell silent for a moment. *Had she cared at all for Delancey?* he wondered. *Or are her tears purely from guilt?* He couldn't help but feel a little guilty himself. After all, he'd invaded the man's house. He'd never really liked Delancey, had thought him laughable. But now the man was at death's door. No one, not even Guy Delancey, deserved such a terrible end.

"Why do you think *you* might have been the target?" he asked.

"Because…" She let out a deep breath. "Because it's happened before."

"Bombs?"

"No. Other things. Accidents."

"When?"

"A few weeks ago, in London, I was almost run down by a taxi."

"In London," he noted dryly, "that could happen to anyone."

"It wasn't the only time."

"You mean there was another accident?"

She nodded. "In the Underground. I was standing on the train platform. And someone pushed me."

He stared at her skeptically. "Are you positive, Diana? Isn't it more likely that someone just bumped into you?"

"Do you think I'm *stupid?*" she cried. "Wouldn't I know it if someone *pushed* me?" With a sob of frustration she buried her face in her hands.

Her unexpected outburst left him stunned. For a moment he could think of nothing to say. Then, gently, he reached for her shoulder. With that one touch, something seemed to leap between them. A longing. Through the flimsy nightgown fabric he felt the warmth of her skin, and with sudden vividness he remembered the taste of her mouth, the sweetness of her kisses earlier that night.

Ruthlessly he suppressed all those inconvenient urges now threatening to overwhelm his sense of reason. He sat beside her on the bed. "Tell me," he said. "Tell me again what happened in the Underground."

"You won't believe me."

"Give me a chance. Please."

She raised her head and looked at him, her gaze moist and uncertain. "I—I fell onto the tracks. The train was just pulling in. If it hadn't been for a man who saw me—"

"A man? Then someone pulled you out?"

She nodded. "I never even learned his name. All I remember is that he reached down and yanked me back onto the platform. I tried to thank him, but he just—just told me to be more careful. And then he was gone." She shook her head in bewilderment. "My guardian angel."

He looked into those glistening brown eyes and wondered if any of this was possible. Wondered how anyone could be cold-blooded enough to push this woman under a train.

"Why would anyone want you dead?" he asked. "Is it something you've done?"

Instantly she stiffened, as though he'd struck her. "What do you mean, is it something I've done?"

"I'm just trying to understand—"

"Do you think I deserve this somehow? That I must be guilty of something?"

"Diana, I'm not accusing you of anything. It's just that murder—attempted murder—generally involves a motive. And you haven't told me what it is."

He waited for an answer, but he realized that he'd somehow lost her. She was huddled in a self-protective embrace, as though to ward off any further attacks he might launch against her.

"Diana," he said gently, "you have to trust me."

"I don't have to trust anyone."

"It would make it easier. If I'm to help you at all—"

"You've already helped me. I can't really ask you for anything more."

"The least you can do is tell me what I've gotten involved in. If bombs are going to be blowing up around here, I'd like to know why."

She sat stubbornly huddled, not responding. In frustration he rose from the bed, paced to the door, then paced back. Damn it all, she *was* going to tell him. Even if he had to use the threat of last resort.

"If you don't tell me," he said, "I really shall have to call the police."

She looked up in astonishment and gave a disbelieving laugh. "The *police?* I'd think they're the last people you'd want to call. Considering."

"Considering what?"

"Delancey's bedroom. The minor matter of a little burglary."

Sighing, he clawed his hair back. "The time has come to set you straight on that. The truth is, I broke into Guy's house as a favor to a lady."

"What favor?"

"She'd written a few…indiscreet letters to him. She wanted the letters back."

"You're saying it was all a gentleman's errand?"

"You could call it that."

"You didn't mention any lady before."

"That's because I'd promised her I'd stay silent. For the sake of her rather tenuous marriage. But now Delancey's been hurt and bombs are exploding. I think it's time to start telling the truth." He gave her a pointed look. "Don't you agree?"

She thought it over for a moment. Then her gaze slid away from his and she said, "All right. I guess it's confession time." She took a deep breath. "I'm not a thief, either."

"Why were you in Delancey's bedroom?"

"I was doing my job. We're trying to collect evidence. An insurance fraud case."

This time Jordan burst out laughing. "You're claiming to be with the police?"

Red faced, she looked up defiantly. "Why is that funny?"

"Which branch do you work for? The local constabulary? Scotland Yard? Interpol, perhaps?"

"I... I work for a private investigator. Not the police."

"Which investigator?"

"You wouldn't know the company."

"I see. And who, may I ask, is the subject of your investigation?"

"He's not English. His name's not important to you."

"How does Guy Delancey fit in?"

Wearily she ran her hand through her hair. In a voice drained of emotion, she said, "A few weeks ago Guy purchased an antique dagger known as the Eye of Kashmir. It was one of several art pieces reportedly carried aboard the *Max Havelaar* last month. That ship later sank off the coast of Spain. Nothing was recovered. The man who owned the vessel—a Belgian—filed a thirty-two-million-dollar insurance claim for the loss of the ship. And for the artwork. He owned it all."

Jordan frowned. "But you say Delancey recently acquired this dagger. When?"

"Three weeks ago. *After* the boat sank."

"Then...the dagger was never aboard the vessel."

"Obviously not. Since Delancey was able to buy it from some private seller."

"And that's the case you're trying to build? Against the owner of the boat? This Belgian fellow?"

She nodded. "He gets reimbursed by the insurance

company for the losses. And he keeps the art to resell. It works out as a sort of double indemnity."

"How did you know Delancey'd acquired the dagger?"

Drained, she sank back against the pillows. "People brag." She sighed. "Delancey did, anyway. He told friends about a seventeenth-century dagger he'd bought from a private source. A dagger with a star corundum—a sapphire—mounted in the hilt. Word got around in the antiques community. From the description, we knew it was the Eye of Kashmir."

"And that's what you were trying to steal from Delancey?"

"Not steal. Confirm its whereabouts. So it can later be confiscated as evidence."

Silently he mulled over this rush of new information. Or was it new fabrication? "You told me earlier tonight that you were stealing something once owned by your family."

She gave a regretful shrug. "I lied."

"Really?"

"I didn't know if I could trust you."

"And you trust me now?"

"You've given me no reason not to." She studied his face, as though looking for some betraying sign that he was not to be trusted, that she'd made a fatal mistake. Slowly she smiled. A coy, almost seductive smile. "And you've been so awfully kind to me. A true gentleman."

Kind? he thought with a silent groan. Was there anything that could dash a man's hopes more brutally than to be called *kind?*

"I *can* trust you," she asked, "can't I?"

He began to pace again, feeling irritated at her, at

himself, at how much he wanted to believe this latest outlandish story. He'd been gazing too long into those doe eyes of hers. It was turning his brain into gullible mush. "Why not trust me?" he muttered in exasperation. "Since I've been so awfully *kind*."

"Why are you angry? Is it because I lied to you before?"

"Shouldn't I be angry?"

"Well, yes. I suppose so. But now that I've come clean—"

"Have you?"

Her jaw squared. It made her even prettier, damn it. He could kick himself for being so susceptible to this creature.

"Yes," she said, her gaze steady. "The Belgian, the *Max Havelaar,* the dagger—it's all *completely* on the level." She paused, then added quietly, "So is the danger."

The bomb is proof enough of that, he thought.

That, and the sight of her curled up in that bed, gazing at him with those liquid brown eyes, was enough to make him accept everything she'd told him. Which meant he was either going out of his mind or he was too exhausted to think straight.

They both needed to sleep.

He knew he should simply say good-night and walk out of the room. But some irresistible compulsion made him lean down and place a kiss on her forehead. The scent of her hair, the sweetness of soap, was intoxicating.

At once he backed away. "You'll be absolutely safe here," he said.

"I believe you," she said. "And I don't know why I should."

"Of course you should. It's the solemn word of a gentleman." Smiling, he turned off the lamp and left the room.

An hour later he still lay awake in bed, thinking about what she'd told him. All that babbling about insurance fraud and undercover investigations was rubbish and he knew it. But he did believe she was in danger. That much he could see in her eyes: the fear.

He considered just how safe she was here. He knew the house was up-to-date when it came to locks and alarm systems. During the years Uncle Hugh had worked with British Intelligence, security had been a priority here at Chetwynd. The grounds had been monitored, the personnel screened, the rooms regularly swept for listening devices. But since his uncle's retirement a few months ago, those precautions had gradually fallen by the wayside. Civilians, after all, did not need the trappings of a fortress. While Chetwynd was still fairly secure, anyone determined to break in could probably find a way.

But first they'd have to learn that the woman was here.

That last thought eased Jordan's fears. No one outside this house could possibly know the woman's location. As long as that fact remained a secret, she was safe.

Chapter 6

Clea waited until the house had fallen completely silent before she climbed out of bed. Her head still pounded, and the floor seemed to wobble under her bare feet, but she forced herself to cross the room and crack open the door.

The hallway was deserted. At the far end a small lamp burned, casting its glow across the carpet runner. Next to the lamp was a telephone.

Noiselessly Clea crept down the hall and picked up the receiver. Shaking off a twinge of guilt, she punched in Tony's number in Brussels. All right, so it was a long-distance call. This was an emergency, and the Tavistocks could surely afford the phone bill.

Four rings and Tony answered. "Clea?"

"I'm in trouble," she whispered. "Somehow they've tracked me down."

"Where are you?"

"Safe for the moment. Tony, Delancey's been hurt. He's in a hospital, not expected to live."

"What? How…"

"A bomb went off in his car. Look, I don't think I can reach the Eye. Not for a while. There'll be hordes of police watching his house."

He didn't answer. She thought for a moment the call had been cut off. Then Tony said, "What do you plan to do?"

"I don't know." She glanced around at the sound of a creak, but saw no one. Just old house noises, she thought, her heart still hammering. She said softly, "If they found me, they could find you, too. Get out of Brussels. Go somewhere else."

"Clea, there's something I have to tell you—"

She spun around at another noise. It came from one of the bedrooms. Someone was awake! She hung up the phone and scurried away up the hall.

Back in her room she stood by the door, listening. To her relief, she heard nothing more. At least she'd had a chance to warn Tony. Now it was time to think about herself. She locked the door and wedged a chair against it for good measure. Then she climbed back into bed.

Her headache was starting to fade; perhaps by morning she'd be as good as new. In which case she'd leave Chetwynd and get the hell away before Van Weldon's people tracked her down again. She'd been lucky up till now, but luck couldn't hold, not against the sort of people she was facing. Another change of appearance was called for. A haircut and a reincarnation as a brunette. Glasses. Yes, that might do it, might allow her to slip unnoticed into the London crowd. Once she got out of England, Van Weldon might lose interest in her. She might have a chance of surviving to a ripe old age.

Might.

Tony dropped the receiver back in the cradle. "She hung up on me," he said, and turned to the other man. "I couldn't keep her on the line."

"It may have been long enough."

"Christ, she sounded scared out of her wits. Can't you people call this off?"

"Not yet. We don't have enough. But we're getting close."

"How do you know?"

"Because Van Weldon's getting close to her. He'll be making another move soon."

Tony watched the other man pull out a cigarette and tap it against his lighter. *Why do people do that, tap their cigarettes?* Just another annoying habit of this fellow. In the past week Tony had gotten to know Archie MacLeod's every tic, every quirk, and he was well-nigh sick of the man. If only there was some other way.

But there wasn't. MacLeod knew all about Tony's past, knew about the years he'd spent in prison. If Tony didn't cooperate, MacLeod and Interpol would have that information broadcast to every antiques buyer in Europe. They'd ruin him. Tony had no choice but to go along with this crazy scheme. And pray that Clea didn't get killed in the process.

"You let Van Weldon get too close this time," Tony observed. "Clea could've been blown up in that car."

"But she wasn't."

"Your man slipped up. Admit it!"

MacLeod exhaled a puff of cigarette smoke. "All

right, so we were taken by surprise. But your cousin's alive, isn't she? We're keeping an eye on her."

Tony laughed. "You don't even know where she is!"

MacLeod's cellular phone rang. He picked it up, listened a moment, then hung up. He looked at Tony. "We know exactly where she is."

"The phone call?"

"Traced to a private residence. A Hugh Tavistock in Buckinghamshire."

Tony shook his head. "Who's that?"

"We're running the check now. In the meantime, she'll be safe. Our field man's been notified of her whereabouts."

Tony sat on the bed and clutched his head. "When Clea finds out about this, she's bloody well going to kill me."

"From what we've seen of your cousin," said MacLeod with a laugh, "she very likely will."

"They have lost her," said Simon Trott.

Victor Van Weldon allowed no trace of alarm to show on his face as he received the news, but he could feel the rage tightening its grip on his chest. In a moment it would pass. In a moment he'd let his displeasure be known. But he must not lose control, not in front of Simon Trott.

"How did it happen?" asked Van Weldon, his voice icy calm.

"It happened at the hospital. She was taken there after the bombing. Somehow she slipped away from our man."

"She was injured?"

"A concussion."

"Then she can't have gotten very far. Track her down."

"They're trying to. They're afraid, though, that…"

"What?"

"She may have enlisted the help of authorities."

Again, that giant fist seemed to close around Van Weldon's chest. He paused for a moment, struggling for air, counting the seconds for the spell to pass. This was a bad one, he thought, and all because of that woman. She'd be the death of him. He took out his bottle of nitroglycerin and slipped two tablets under his tongue. Slowly the discomfort began to fade. I'm not ready to die, he thought. Not yet.

He looked at Trott. "Have we any proof she's contacted the authorities?"

"She's escaped too many times. She must be getting help. From the police. Or Interpol."

"Not Clea Rice. She'd never trust the police." He slipped the nitroglycerin bottle back in his pocket and took a deep breath. The pain was gone.

"She has been lucky, that's all," said Van Weldon. He gave a careless wave of his hand. "Her luck will run out."

She had not meant to sleep so late, but the concussion had left her groggy and the bed was so comfortable and she felt safe in this house—the safest she'd felt in weeks. By the time she finally crawled out of bed, the sun was shining straight through her window and her headache had faded to only a dull soreness.

I'm still alive, she thought in wonder.

From various parts of the house came the sounds of morning stirrings: creaking floorboards, water running through the pipes. Too late to make an escape unnoticed. She would simply have to play the guest for a few hours. Later she'd slip away, make it on foot to the village train station. How far was it, a few miles? She could do it. After all, she'd once trudged ten miles along the Spanish coast. And that was in the dead of night, while sopping wet. But then, she hadn't been wearing high heels.

She surveyed her clothes. Her dress, torn and dirt stained, was draped over a chair. Her stockings were in shreds. Her shoes, those wretched instruments of torture, sat mocking her with their three-inch spike heels. No, she'd rather go barefoot. Or perhaps in bedroom slippers? She spied a pair by the dresser, comfy-looking pink slippers edged with fluff. Wouldn't *that* blend in with the crowd?

She pulled on a silk bathrobe she found in the closet, slid her feet into the pink slippers and pulled away the chair she'd wedged against the door. Then she ventured out of the room.

The rest of the household was already up and about. She went downstairs and spied them through the French doors. They were outside, assembled around a breakfast table on the terrace. It looked like a photo straight from the pages of some stylish magazine, the iron railings traced by climbing roses, the dew-kissed autumn garden, the table with its linen and china. And the people sitting around that table! There was Beryl with her model's cheekbones and glossy black hair. There was Richard Wolf, lean and relaxed, his arm slung possessively around Beryl's shoulders.

And there was Jordan.

If last night had been a trial for him, it certainly didn't show this morning. He was looking unruffled and elegant as ever, his fair hair almost silvery in the morning light, his tweed jacket perfectly molded to his shoulders. As Clea watched them through the glass, she thought how perfect they looked, like thoroughbreds reared on bluegrass. It wasn't envy she felt, but a sense of wonder, as though she were observing some alien species. She could move among them, could even act the part, but the wrong blood would always run in her veins. Tainted blood. Like Uncle Walter's blood.

Too timid to intrude on that perfect tableau, she turned to retreat upstairs. But as she backed away from the French doors she heard Jordan call her name and she knew she'd been spotted. He was waving to her, beckoning her to join them. No chance of escape now; she'd simply have to brazen it out.

She smoothed out the silk robe, ran her fingers through her hair and stepped out onto the terrace. Only then did she remember the pink slippers. The soles made painfully distinct scuffing sounds across the flagstones.

Jordan rose and pulled out a chair for her. "I was about to check on you. Feeling better this morning?"

Uneasily she tugged the edges of the robe together. "I'm really not dressed for breakfast. My clothes are a mess and I didn't know what else—"

"Don't give it a thought. We're a casual bunch here."

Clea glanced at Beryl, flawlessly pulled together in cashmere and jodhpurs, at Jordan in his wool tweed. A casual bunch. Right. Resignedly she sat down in the offered chair and felt like some sort of zoo specimen with fluffy pink feet. While Jordan poured her coffee and dished out a serving of eggs and sausages, she found herself focusing on his hands, on his long fingers, on the golden hairs glittering on the backs of his wrists. An aristocrat's hands, she thought, and remembered with sudden clarity the gentle strength with which those hands had reached for her in the road last night.

"Don't you care for eggs?"

She blinked at her plate. Eggs. Yes. Automatically she picked up the fork and felt all eyes watching her as she took her first bite.

"I did try to leave you some fresh clothes this morning," Beryl explained. "But I couldn't seem to get in your door."

"I had a chair in front of it," said Clea.

"Oh." Beryl gave a sheepish smile, as though to say, *Well, of course. Doesn't everybody barricade their door?*

No one seemed to know how to respond, so they simply watched Clea eat. Their gazes were not unfriendly, merely...puzzled.

"It's just a habit I picked up," Clea said as she poured cream in her coffee. "I don't trust locks, you see. It's so easy to get past them."

"Is it?" said Beryl.

"Especially bedroom doors. One can bypass your typical bedroom lock in five seconds. Even the newer ones with the disk tumblers."

"How very useful to know that," Beryl murmured.

Clea looked up and saw that everyone was watching her with fascination. Face flushing, she quickly dropped her gaze back to the eggs. *I'm babbling like an idiot,* she thought.

She flinched when Jordan reached for her hand.

"Diana, I've told them."

She stared at him. "Told them? You mean...about..."

"Everything. The way we met. The attempts on your life. I *had* to tell them. If they're to help you, then they need to know it all."

"Believe me, we *do* want to help," said Beryl. "You can trust us. Every bit as much as you trust Jordie."

Clea's hands were unsteady. She dropped them to her lap. *They're asking me to trust them,* she thought in misery. *But I'm the one who hasn't been telling the truth.*

"We have resources that might prove useful," said Jordan. "Connections with Intelligence. And Richard's firm specializes in security. If you need any help at all…"

The offer was almost too tempting to resist. For weeks she'd been on her own, had hopscotched from hotel to hotel, never sure whom she could trust, or where she would go next. She was so very tired of running.

And yet she wasn't ready to put her life in anyone's hands. Not even Jordan's.

"The only favor I ask," she said quietly, "is a ride to the train station. And perhaps…" She glanced down at the pink slippers and gave a laugh. "A change of clothes?"

Beryl rose to her feet. "That I can certainly arrange." She tugged on her fiancé's arm. "Come on, Richard. Let's go rummage around in my closet."

Clea was left sitting alone with Jordan. For a moment they sat in silence. Up in the trees, doves cooed a lament to the passing of summer. The clouds drifted across the sun, tarnishing the morning to gray.

"Then you'll be leaving us," said Jordan.

"Yes." She folded her napkin and carefully laid it on the table. Though she remained focused on that small

square of cream linen, she couldn't shut out her awareness of the man. She could almost feel the warmth of
his gaze. All her senses were conspiring against her
efforts at indifference. Last night, with that first kiss,
they'd crossed some invisible threshold, had wandered
into territory with no boundaries, where the possibilities seemed limitless.

That's all they are, she reminded herself. *Possibilities.* Fantasies winking in the murk of half-truths. She
had told him so many lies, had changed her story so
many times. She still hadn't told him the worst truth of
all. Who she was, what she was.

What she had been.

Better to leave him with the fantasy, she thought. Let
him assume the best about me. And not know the worst.

She looked up and found he was watching her with
a gaze both puzzled and thoughtful. "Where will you
go next?" he asked.

"London. It's clear I can't handle this alone. My...as-
sociates at the agency will carry on the investigation."

"And what will you do?"

She gave a shrug, a smile. "Take an easier case.
Something that doesn't involve exploding cars."

"Diana, if you ever need my help—anything at all—"

Their gazes met and she saw in his eyes the offer
of more than just assistance. She had to fight off the
temptation to confess everything, to draw him into this
dangerous mess.

She shook her head. "I have some very capable col-
leagues. They'll see I'm taken care of. But thanks for
the offer."

He gave a curt nod of the head and said no more
about it.

* * *

Seated on a bench on the train platform, a gray-suited man read his newspapers and watched the passengers gather for the twelve-fifteen to London. It was the fourth train of the day, and so far he hadn't spotted Clea Rice. The bench was occupied by three other women and a bouncy child who kept knocking at the newspaper, and the man was ready to give the brat a whack out of frustration. He'd been so sure Clea Rice would choose the train; now it looked as if she'd managed to sneak out of town some other way. Yes, she was definitely getting better at the game—a quick study at doing the unexpected. He still didn't know how she'd managed to slip away from the hospital last night. That would have been a far easier place to finish it, a private room, the patient under sedation. He had passed for a doctor once before, on a previous job. He certainly could have repeated the ruse.

A pity she hadn't cooperated.

Now he'd have to track her down again, before she vanished into the teeming masses of London.

"Other people 'ere could use the bench, y'know," said a woman.

He looked sideways and saw a steel-haired lady toting a shopping bag. "It's occupied," he said, and snapped his newspaper taut.

"Decent man'd leave it to folks wi' difficulties," said the woman.

He kept reading his newspaper, his fingers suddenly itching for the automatic in his shoulder holster. A hole right between the old biddy's eyes, that's what he'd like to do, just to shut her up. She was nattering on and on now about the dearth of gentlemen in this world, saying it to no one in particular, but loudly enough to draw the attention of people standing nearby. This was not good.

He stood, shot a poisonous look at the old hag, and surrendered his spot on the bench. She claimed it with a grunt of satisfaction. Folding up his newspaper, he wandered to the other end of the platform.

That's when he spotted Clea Rice.

She'd just emerged from the loo. She was wearing a houndstooth skirt and jacket, both a few sizes too large. Her hair was almost completely concealed by a scarf, but a few tendrils of red bangs peeked out. That, plus the way she moved—her gaze darting around, her circuitous route keeping her well away from the platform's edge—told him it was her.

This was not the place to do it.

He decided he'd let her board and would follow her onto the train. There he could keep an eye on her. Perhaps when she got off again...

He had his ticket ready. He stepped forward and joined the crowd of passengers waiting to board.

So Clea Rice was taking the twelve-fifteen to London. Not the wisest move she could make, thought Charles Ogilvie as he stood in line behind her at the ticket office. He'd had no trouble tailing her from Chetwynd. Jordan Tavistock's champagne gold Jaguar wasn't exactly easy to miss. If he had been able to stay on their trail, surely someone else could do it, as well.

And now the woman was about to board a train in broad daylight.

Ogilvie reached the head of the line and quickly purchased his ticket. Then he followed the woman onto the platform. She vanished into the women's loo. He waited. Only as the train approached the station did she reemerge. There were about two dozen people standing on the platform, a mingling of business types and housewives, any one of whom could prove lethal. Ogilvie allowed his gaze to drift casually across the faces, trying to match one of them with a face he might have seen before.

At the far edge of the crowd he spotted someone who seemed familiar, a man in a gray suit and carrying a newspaper. His face, while not in any way distinctive, still struck a memory chord. Where had he seen him before?

The hospital. Last night, in the lobby. The man had been buying a paper from the hall newsstand.

Now he was boarding the twelve fifteen to London. Right behind Clea Rice.

A surge of adrenaline pumped through Ogilvie's veins. If something was going to happen, it'd be soon. Perhaps not here in the crowd, but on the train, or at the next stop. All it took was a gun barrel to the back of the head. Clea Rice would never see it coming.

The man in the gray suit was edging closer to the woman.

Ogilvie pushed forward. Already he had his jacket unbuttoned, his shoulder holster within easy reach. His gaze stayed focused on Mr. Gray Suit. At the first sign of attack, he'd bloody well better be ready. He was Clea Rice's only lifeline.

And there'd be no second chances.

Almost there. Almost there.

Clea clutched the ticket like a good-luck charm as she waited for the train to glide to a stop. She hung back a bit, allowing everyone else to press forward first. The memory of that incident in the London Underground was still too fresh; never again would she stand at any platform edge while a train pulled in. All it took was one push from behind. No, it was better to hang back where she could see trouble coming.

The train had pulled to a stop. Passengers were starting to board.

Clea eased into the gathering. Her headache had come throbbing back with a vengeance, and she longed for the relative privacy of a train compartment. A few more steps, and she'd be on her way back to London. To anonymity. It was the best choice, after all—to simply drop out of sight. She'd been insane to think she could match wits with Van Weldon, an opponent who'd met her every thrust with a deadlier parry, who had every reason, and every resource, to crush her. Call it surrender, but she was ready to yield. Anything to stay alive.

She was so focused on getting aboard that she didn't notice the disturbance behind her. Just as she climbed onto the first step, a hand gripped her by the arm and tugged her back onto the platform.

She spun around, every nerve instantly wired for attack, her fingers arcing to claw across her assailant's face. An instant before striking flesh, she froze.

"Jordan?" she said in astonishment.

He grabbed her wrist. "Let's get out of here."

"What are you doing?"

"I'll explain later. Come on."

"But I'm leaving—"

He tugged her away, out of the line of passengers. She tried to yank free but he caught her by the shoulders and pulled her close to him. "Listen to me," he whispered. "Someone's followed us here, from Chetwynd. You can't get on the train."

Instantly she stiffened. His breath felt hot in her hair, and her awareness of his scent, his warmth, had never been more acute. Even through the tweed jacket she could feel the thudding of his heart, the tension in his arms. Without a word she nodded, and the arms encircling her relaxed their hold. Together they turned away from the train and took a step back up the platform.

A man seemed to appear from nowhere. He materialized directly in their path, a man in a gray suit. His face was scarcely worth noting; it was the gun in his hand that drew Clea's stunned gaze.

She was already pivoting away to the left when the first shot rang out. Something slammed into her shoulder, shoving her away. Jordan. In what seemed like slow motion she caught a flash of Jordan's tweed jacket as he lunged against her, and then she was stumbling sideways, falling to her knees onto the platform. The impact of the pavement sent a shock wave straight up her spine. The pain in her head was almost blinding.

Screams erupted all around her. She scrambled back to her feet, at the same time twisting around to locate the attacker. The platform was a melee of panicked bodies scattering in every direction. Jordan still shielded her from a clear view, but over his shoulder she caught a glimpse of the gunman.

Just as he caught a glimpse of her. He raised his pistol.

The shot was like a thunderclap. Clea flinched, but she felt no pain, no impact, nothing but astonishment that she was still alive.

On the gunman's face was registered equal astonishment. He stared down at his chest, where the crimson stain of blood was rapidly blossoming across his shirt. He wobbled, dropped to his knees.

"Get out of here!" barked a voice somewhere off to the side.

Clea turned and saw a second man with a gun standing a few yards away. Frantically he waved at her to get moving.

The man in the gray suit was crawling on hands and knees now, gurgling, cursing, still refusing to drop his pistol. It took a firm push from Jordan to propel Clea forward. Suddenly her legs were working again. She began to run along the edge of the platform, every pounding footstep like another nail being driven into her aching head. She could hear Jordan right behind her, could hear the shouts of confusion echoing in their wake. They reached the rear of the train, leapt off onto the tracks and dashed across to the opposite platform.

Clea scrambled up first. Jordan seemed to be lagging behind. She paused to grab his hand and haul him up from the tracks.

"Don't wait for me," he gasped as they sprinted for the steps. "Just go—the parking lot—"

"I have to wait for you! You have the bloody car keys!"

The Jaguar was double-parked near the station gate. Jordan tossed Clea his keys. "You'd better drive," he said.

She didn't stop to argue. She slid in behind the wheel and threw the car into gear. They screeched out of the lot.

Farther up the road the sound of sirens drew close.

The police were headed for the station, thought Clea; they weren't interested in *her*.

She was right. Two police cars sped right past them and kept going.

Clea glanced in the rearview mirror and saw that the road behind them was empty. "No one seems to be following us. I think we're all right."

"For now."

"You said we were tailed from Chetwynd. How did you know?"

"I wasn't sure at first. I kept seeing a black MG on the road behind us. Then it dropped out of sight. That's why I didn't mention it. I thought it was gone."

"But you came back to get me."

"On the way out of the gate I saw the MG again. It was pulling in to a parking space. That's when I realized..." Grimacing, he shifted in his seat. "Are you going to tell me what the hell's going on?"

"Someone just tried to kill us."

"That I think I knew. Who was the gunman?"

"You mean his name?" She shook her head. Just that movement brought the throbbing back to her skull. "No idea."

"And the other man? The one who just saved our lives?"

"I don't know his name, either. But..." She paused. "I think I've seen him before. In London. The Underground."

"Your guardian angel?"

"But this time *you* saw him. So I guess he's not an angel at all." She glanced in the mirror. Still no one following them. Breathing more easily, she thought ahead to what came next. Chetwynd?

As if he'd read her mind, he said, "We can't go back to Chetwynd. They'll be expecting that."

"*You* could go back."

"I'm not so sure."

"You're not the one they want."

"Are you going to tell me who *they* are?"

"The same people who blew up Guy Delancey's car."

"These people—are they connected with this mysterious Belgian? Or was that just another fable?"

"It's the truth. Sort of."

He groaned. "Sort of?"

She glanced sideways and she noticed that his jaw was tightly squared. *He must be as terrified as I am,* she thought.

"I think I have the right to know the whole truth," he said.

"Later. When I've carved us out some breathing space." She nudged the accelerator. The Jaguar responded with a quiet purr and a burst of speed. "Right now, I just want to get the hell out of this county. When we hit London—"

"London?" He shook his head. "You think it'll be that easy? Just cruise down the highway? If they're as dangerous as you say, they'll have the main roads covered."

And a pale gold Jaguar wasn't a car they'd be likely to miss, she realized. She'd have to ditch the Jag. And maybe the man, as well. He'd be better off without her. Trouble seemed to attach itself to her like iron filings to a magnet, and when the next crisis hit, she didn't want Jordan caught in the cross fire. She owed him that much.

"There's a turnoff coming up," he said. "Take it."

"Where does it go?"

"Back road."

"To London?"

"No. It'll take us to an inn. I know the proprietors. There's a barn where we can hide the car."

"And how do I get to London?"

"We don't. We stay put for a while and get our bearings. Then we figure out our next move."

"I say our next move is to keep going! On foot if we have to! I won't hang around this neighborhood any longer than—"

"But I'm afraid I'll have to," he murmured.

She glanced sideways again. What she saw almost made her swerve off the road in horror.

He had pulled back the edge of his jacket and was staring down at his shirt. Bright splotches of blood stained the fine linen.

Chapter 7

"Oh, my god," said Clea. "Why didn't you tell me?"

"It's not serious."

"How the hell can you tell?"

"I'm still breathing, aren't I?"

"Oh, that's just *wonderful*." She spun the wheel and sent the Jag in a dizzying U-turn. "We're going to a hospital."

"No." He reached over and grabbed her hand. "They'd be on you in a flash."

"What am I supposed to do? Let you bleed to death?"

"I'm all right. I think it's stopped." He looked down again at his shirt. The stains didn't seem to be spreading. "What's the cliché? 'It's only a flesh wound'?"

"What if it isn't? What if you're bleeding internally?"

"I'll be the first to beg for help. Believe me," he added with a pained smile, "I'm truly a coward at heart."

A coward? she thought. Not this man. He was the least cowardly man she knew.

"Go to the inn," he insisted. "If this is really serious, I can call for help."

Reluctantly she made another U-turn and headed back the way they'd been going. The turnoff brought them onto a narrow road lined by hedgerows. Through gaps in the foliage she spied a patchwork of fields and stone walls. The hedgerows gave way to a graveled driveway, and they pulled up at last in front of the Munstead Inn. A cottage garden, its blossoms fading into autumn, lined the front walk.

Clea scrambled out of the car to help Jordan to his feet.

"Let me walk on my own," he said. "Best to pretend nothing's wrong."

"You might faint."

"I'd never do anything so embarrassing." Grunting, he managed to slide out of the car and stand without her assistance. He made it on his own power through the garden and up the front steps.

Their knock on the door was answered by an elderly gentleman whose peat-colored trousers hung limp on his bony frame. He peered at them through bifocals, then exclaimed in pleasure, "Why, if it isn't young Mr. Tavistock!"

Jordan smiled. "Hello, Munstead. Any rooms available?"

"For friends o' yours, anytime!" The old man stepped aside and waved them into the front hall. "Chetwynd's full up, then?" he asked. "No room for guests?"

"Actually, this room would be for me and the lady."

"You and…" Munstead turned and regarded Jordan

with surprise. A sly grin spread across his face. "Ah, it's a bit of a hush thing, is it?"

"Just between us."

Munstead winked. "Gotcha, sir."

Clea didn't know how Jordan managed to hold up his end of the banter. As the old man rummaged for a key, Jordan politely inquired as to Mrs. Munstead's health, asked how the garden was this summer and were the children coming to visit at Christmas? At last they were led upstairs to the second floor. Under better circumstances Clea might have appreciated the romantic touches to the place, the flocked wallpaper, the lace curtains. Now her only focus was to get Jordan into a bed and his wound checked.

When they were safely behind closed doors, Clea practically forced Jordan down onto the mattress. He sat there, his face screwed up in discomfort, as she pulled off the tweed jacket. The droplets of blood staining his shirt led a trail under his right arm.

She unbuttoned the shirt. The blood had dried, adhering the fabric to his skin. Slowly, gently she peeled the shirt off, revealing a broad chest with tawny hair, some of it caked with blood. What she saw looked more like a slash than a bullet wound, as though a knife blade had caught him just in front of the armpit and sliced straight back along his right side.

She gave a sigh of relief. "It looks like just a graze. Caught you in passing. It could just as easily have gone straight through your chest. You're lucky."

He stared down at his wound and frowned. "Maybe it's more a case of divine intervention than luck."

"What?"

"Hand me my coat."

Perplexed, she passed him the tweed jacket. The bullet's entry was easy to locate. It cut a hole through the fabric over the right chest. Jordan reached inside the inner pocket and pulled out a handsome watch attached to a chain. Clearly stamped on the gold watch cover was an ugly dent.

"A helping hand from beyond the grave," he said, and handed Clea the watch.

She flipped open the dented cover. Inside was engraved the name Bernard Tavistock.

"My father's," said Jordan. "I inherited it on his death. It seems he's still watching out for me."

"Then you'd better keep it close by," she said, handing it back. "So it can ward off the next bullet."

"I sincerely hope there won't *be* a next bullet. This one's bloody uncomfortable as it is."

She went into the bathroom, soaked a towel in warm water and wrung it out. When she came back to the bed, he was looking almost sheepish about all the fuss. As she bent to clean the wound, their heads brushed, and she inhaled a disturbingly primal mingling of scents. Blood and sweat and after-shave. His breath warmed her hair, and that warmth seemed to seep into her cheeks. Desperately trying to ignore his effect on her, she kept her gaze focused on his wound.

"I had no idea you'd been hurt," she said softly.

"It was the first shot. I sort of stumbled into it."

"Stumbled, hell! You pushed me away, you idiot."

He laughed. "Chivalry goes unappreciated."

Without warning she planted both hands on either side of his face and lowered her mouth to his in a fierce kiss. She knew at once it was a mistake. Her stomach seemed to drop away inside her. She felt his lips

press hard against hers, heard his growl of both longing and satisfaction. Before he could tug her against
him, she pulled away.

"You see, you're wrong," she whispered. "Chivalry
is most definitely appreciated."

"If that's my reward, I may just do it again."

"Well, don't. Once is chivalry. Twice is stupidity."

Breathing hard, she focused her attention back on
his wound. She could feel him watching her, could still
taste the tang of his lips on hers, but she stubbornly refused to meet his gaze. If she did, they'd only kiss again.

She wiped up the last dried flecks of blood and
straightened. "How are we going to dress it?"

"I've a first aid kit in the car. Bandages and such."

"I'll get it."

"Park the car in the barn, while you're at it. Get it
out of sight."

With almost a sense of relief, she fled the room and
hurried down the stairs. Once outside, she felt she could
breathe again, felt she was back in control.

She walked deliberately to the Jaguar, started the
engine and parked it inside the barn. After fetching the
first aid kit out of the trunk, she stood by the car for a
moment, taking deep, calming breaths of hay-scented
air. At last her headache was all but gone and she could
think clearly again. *Must concentrate,* she thought. *Remember what it is I'm facing. I can't afford to be dis-
tracted. Even by someone as distracting as Jordan.*

With first aid kit in hand, she returned to the room.
The instant she stepped inside she felt her hard-won
composure begin to crack around the edges. Jordan was
standing at the window, his broad back turned to her,
his gaze focused somewhere on the garden outside. She

suppressed the impulse to go to him, to slide her hands down that expanse of naked skin.

"I hid the car," she said.

She thought he nodded, but he didn't answer.

After a pause she asked, "Is something wrong?"

He turned to look at her. "I called Chetwynd."

She frowned, trying to understand why, with that one call, his whole demeanor should change. "You called? Why?"

"To tell them what's happened. We're going to need help."

"It's better if they don't know. Safer if we don't—"

"Safer for whom?"

"For everyone. They might talk to the wrong people. Reveal things they shouldn't—"

She couldn't read his expression against the glare of the window. But she could hear the anger in his voice. "If I can't count on my own family, who *can* I count on?"

Stung by his tone, she sat on the bed and stared dully at the first aid kit in her lap. "I envy you your blind faith," she said softly. She opened the kit. Inside were bandages, adhesive tape, a bottle of antiseptic. "Come here. I'd better dress that wound."

He came to the bed and sat beside her. Neither of them spoke as she opened packets of gauze and snipped off lengths of tape. She heard him suck in a startled gasp of air when she dabbed on the antiseptic, but he said nothing. His silence frightened her. Something had changed between them since she'd left the room, something about that phone call to Chetwynd. She was afraid to ask about it, afraid to cut what few threads of connection still remained between them. So she said nothing, but simply finished the task, the whole time fighting off a sense of panic that she'd lost him. Or even worse, that he'd turned against her.

Her worst suspicions seemed confirmed when he said, as she was pressing the last strip of tape to his chest, "Richard's on his way."

She sat back and stared at him. "You told him where we are?"

"I had to."

"Couldn't you just say you're alive and well? Leave it at that?"

"He has something to tell me."

"He could have said everything over the phone."

"It has to be face-to-face." Jordan paused, then he added quietly, "It has to do with you."

She sat clutching the roll of tape, her gaze frozen on his face. *He knows,* she thought. She felt sick to her stomach, sick of herself and her sorry past. Whatever attraction Jordan had felt for her was obviously gone now, destroyed by some revelation gleaned from a phone call.

She swallowed and looked away. "What did he tell you?"

"Only that you haven't been entirely honest about who you are."

"And…" She cleared her throat. "How did he find out?"

"Your fingerprints."

"What fingerprints?"

"The polo field. You left them on your glass in the refreshment tent."

It took her a moment for the implications to sink in. "Then you—*you're* the one who—"

He nodded. "I picked up your glass. Your fingerprints weren't on record at Scotland Yard. So I asked Richard to check with American authorities. And they had the prints on file."

She shot to her feet and backed away from the bed. "I trusted you!"

"I never meant to hurt you."

"No, you just prowled around behind my back."

"I knew you weren't being straight with me. How else could I find out? I had to know."

"Why? What difference would it make to you?" she cried.

"I wanted to believe you. I wanted to be absolutely sure of you."

"So you set out to prove I'm a fraud."

"Is that what I've proved?"

She shook her head and laughed. "What else would I be but a fraud? It's what you looked for. It's what you expected to find."

"I don't know what I expected to find."

"Maybe that I'd be some—some princess in disguise? Instead you learn the truth. A frog instead of a princess. Oh, but you must be *so* disappointed! *I* find it disappointing that I can't ever outrun my past. No matter how hard I try, it follows me around like one of those little cartoon rain clouds over my head." She looked down at the flowered rug. For a moment she studied the pattern of its weave. Then, wearily, she sighed. "Well, I do thank you for your help. You've been more of a gentleman than any man has ever been to me. I wish… I'd hoped…" She shook her head and turned to the door.

"Where are you going?"

"It's a long walk to London. I think I'll get started."

In an instant he was on his feet and crossing toward her. "You can't go."

"I have a life to get on with."

"And how long will it last? What happens at the next train station?"

"Are you volunteering to take another bullet?"

He caught her arm and pulled her against him. As she collided with his chest, she felt her whole body turn liquid against his heat.

"I'm not sure what I'm volunteering for," he murmured. "But I think I've already signed up…"

The kiss caught them both off-balance. The instant their lips met, Clea felt herself swaying, tilting. He pressed her to the wall, his lips on hers, his body a warm and breathing barrier to escape. Their breaths were coming so loud and fast, their sighs so needy, that she didn't hear the footsteps creaking on the stairs, didn't hear them approach their room.

The knock on the door made them both jerk apart. They stared at each other, faces flushed with passion, hair equally tousled.

"Who is it?" Jordan called.

"It's me."

Jordan opened the door.

Richard Wolf stood in the hall. He glanced at Clea's reddened cheeks, then looked at Jordan's bare chest. Without comment he stepped into the room and locked the door behind him. Clea noticed he had a file folder stuffed with papers.

"You weren't followed?" asked Jordan.

"No." Richard looked at Clea, and she almost felt like slinking away, so cool was that gaze of his. *So now the truth will be spilled. He knows all, of course.* That must be what he had in that folder—the proof of her identity. Who and what she'd been. He would lay it all out for Jordan, and she wouldn't be able to deny it. And how would Jordan react? With anger, disgust?

Feeling defeated beyond words, she went to the bed and sat down. She wouldn't look at either one of the men; she didn't want to see their faces as they shared the facts about Clea Rice. She would just sit here and passively confirm it all. Then she would leave. Surely Jordan wouldn't bother to stop her this time. Surely he'd be happy to see her go.

She waited on the bed and listened as the truth was finally told.

"Her name isn't Diana Lamb," said Richard. "It's Clea Rice."

Jordan looked at the woman, half expecting a protest, a denial, *some* sort of response, but she said nothing. She only sat with her shoulders hunched forward, her head drooping with what looked like profound weariness. It was almost painful to look at her. This was not at all the brash Diana—correction, Clea—he knew. But then, he'd never really known her, had he?

Richard handed the folder to Jordan. "That was faxed to me just an hour ago from Washington."

"From Niki?"

Richard nodded. Nikolai Sakaroff was his partner in Sakaroff and Wolf, Security Consultants. Formerly a colonel with the KGB and now an enthusiastic advocate of capitalism, Sakaroff had turned his talents for intelligence gathering to more profitable uses. If anyone could dig up obscure information, it was Niki.

"Her fingerprints were on file with the Massachusetts police," said Richard. "Once that fact was established, the rest of it came easy."

Jordan opened the folder. The first page he saw was a grainy reproduction of a mug shot, a frontal and two profiles. The faxing process had blurred the details, but he could still tell it was a younger version of Clea. The subject gazed unsmiling at the camera, her dark eyes wide and bewildered, her lips pressed tightly together. Her hair, free flowing about her shoulders, appeared to be blond. Jordan glanced once again at the live woman. She hadn't moved.

He turned to the next page.

"Three years ago she was convicted of harboring a felon and destruction of evidence," said Richard. "She served ten months in the Massachusetts State Penitentiary, with time off for good behavior."

Jordan turned to Clea. "Is this true?"

She gave a low and bitter laugh. "Yes. In prison I was *very* well behaved."

"And the rest of it? The conviction? The ten months served?"

"You have it all there. Why are you asking me?"

"Because I want to know if it's true."

"It's true," she whispered, and her head seemed to droop even lower.

She seemed in no mood to elaborate, so Jordan turned back to Richard. "Who was the felon? The one she aided?"

"His name's Walter Rice. He's still serving time in Massachusetts."

"Rice? Is he a relative?"

"He's my uncle Walter," said Clea dully.

"What crime did this uncle Walter commit?"

"Burglary. Fraud. Trafficking in stolen goods." She shrugged. "Take your pick. Uncle Walter had a long and varied career."

"Of which Clea was a part," said Richard.

Clea's chin shot up. It was the first spark of anger she'd displayed. "That's not true!"

"No? What about your juvenile record?"

"Those were supposed to be sealed!"

"Sealed doesn't mean nonexistent. At age twelve, you were caught trying to pawn stolen jewelry. At age fourteen, you and your cousin burglarized half a dozen homes on Beacon Hill."

"I was only a child! I didn't know what I was doing!"

"What did you *think* you were doing?"

"Whatever Uncle Walter told us to do!"

"Did Uncle Walter have such power over you that you didn't know right from wrong?"

She looked away. "Uncle Walter was…he was the one I looked up to. You see, I grew up in his house. It was just the three of us. My cousin Tony and my uncle and me. I know what we did was wrong. But the burglaries—they didn't seem real to me, you know. It was more of a…a game. Uncle Walter used to dare us. He'd say, 'Who's clever enough to beat *that* house?' And we'd feel cowardly if we didn't take him up on the dare. It wasn't the money. It was never the money." She looked up. "It was the challenge."

"And what about that issue of right and wrong?"

"That's why I stopped. I was eighteen when I moved out of Uncle Walter's house. For eight years I stayed on the straight and narrow. I swear it."

"In the meantime, your uncle went right on robbing houses. The police say he was responsible for dozens of burglaries in Boston's wealthiest neighborhoods. Luckily, no one was ever hurt."

"He'd never hurt anyone! Uncle Walter didn't even own a gun."

"No, he was just a virtuous thief."

"He swore he never took from people who couldn't afford it."

"Of course not. He went where the money was. Like any smart burglar."

She stared down again at her knotted hands. A convicted criminal, thought Jordan. She hardly looked the part. But she had managed to deceive him from the start, and he knew now he couldn't trust his own eyes, his own instincts. Not where she was concerned.

He refocused his attention on the file. There were a few pages of notes written in Niki Sakaroff's precise hand, dates of arrest, conviction, imprisonment. There was a copy of a news article about the career of Walter Rice, whose exploits had earned legendary status in the Boston area. As Clea had said, old Walter never actually hurt anyone. He just robbed and he did it with style. He was known as the Red Rose Thief, for his habit of always leaving behind his calling card: a single rose, his gesture of apology to the victims.

Even the most skillful thief, however, eventually meets with bad luck. In Walter's case it took the form of an alert homeowner with a loaded pistol. Caught in the act, with a bullet in his arm, Walter found himself scrambling out the window for his life.

Two days later he was arrested in his niece's apartment, where he'd sought refuge and first aid.

No wonder she did such a good job of dressing my wound, thought Jordan. *She's had practice.*

"It seems to be a Rice family trait," observed Richard. "Trouble with the law."

Clea didn't refute the statement.

"What about this cousin Tony?" asked Jordan.

"He served six years. Burglary," said Richard. "Niki hears through the grapevine that Tony Rice is somewhere in Europe, working as a fence in black market antiques. Am I right, Miss Rice?"

Clea looked up. "Leave Tony out of this. He's clean now."

"Is he the one you're working with?"

"I'm not working with anyone."

"Then how were you planning to fence the loot?"

"What loot?"

"The items you planned to steal from Guy Delancey?"

She reacted with a look of hopeless frustration. "Why do I bother to answer your questions?" she said. "You've already tried and convicted me. There's nothing left to say."

"There's plenty left for you to say," said Jordan. "Who's trying to kill you? And maybe pop me off in the process?"

"He won't bother with you, once I'm gone."

"*Who* won't?"

"The man I told you about." She sighed. "The Belgian."

"You mean that part of the story was true?"

"Yes. Absolutely true. So was the part about the *Max Havelaar*."

"What Belgian?" asked Richard.

"His name is Van Weldon," said Clea. "He has people working for him everywhere. Guy was just an accidental victim. *I'm* the one Van Weldon wants dead."

There was a long silence. Richard said slowly, "Victor Van Weldon?"

A glint of fear suddenly appeared in Clea's eyes. She was staring at Richard. "You...know him?"

"No. I just heard the name. A short time ago, in fact." He was frowning at Clea, as though seeing some new aspect to her face. "I spoke to one of the constables about the man shot at the railway station."

"The one who tried to kill us?" said Jordan.

Richard nodded. "He's been identified as a George Fraser. English, with a London address. They tried to track down his next of kin, but all they came up with was the name of his employer. He's a service rep for the Van Weldon Shipping Company."

At the mention of the company's name, Jordan saw Clea give an involuntary shudder, as though she'd just been touched by the chill hand of evil. Nervously she rose to her feet and went to the window, where she stood hugging herself, staring out at the afternoon sunlight.

"What about the other gunman?" asked Jordan.

"No sign of him. It seems he managed to slip away."

"My guardian angel," murmured Clea. "Why?"

"You tell us," said Richard.

"I know why someone's trying to kill me. But not why anyone wants to keep me *alive*."

"Let's start with what you do know," said Jordan. He went to her, placed his hand gently on her shoulder. She felt so small, so insubstantial to his touch. "Why does Victor Van Weldon want you dead?"

"Because I know what happened to the *Max Huve-laar*."

"Why it sank, you mean?"

She nodded. "There was nothing valuable aboard that boat. Those insurance claims were false. And the crew was considered expendable."

"How do you know all this?"

"Because I was there." She turned and looked at him, her eyes haunted by some vision of horror only she could see. "I was aboard the *Max Havelaar* the night it went down."

Chapter 8

"It was my first trip to Naples," she said. "My first year ever in Europe. I was desperate to escape all those bad memories from prison. So when Tony wrote, inviting me to Brussels, I leapt at the chance."

"That's your cousin?" asked Richard.

Clea nodded. "He's been in a wheelchair since his accident on the autobahn last year. He needed someone he could trust to serve as his business representative. Someone who'd round up buyers for the antiques he sells. It's a completely legitimate business. Tony's no longer dealing in the black market."

"And that's why you were in Naples? On your cousin's behalf?"

"Yes. And that's where I met my two Italian sailors." She looked away again, out the window. "Carlo and Giovanni…"

They were the first mate and navigator aboard a boat docked in the harbor. Both men had liquid brown eyes and ridiculously long lashes and a penchant for innocent mischief. Both adored blondes. And although they'd flirted and made eyes at her, Clea had known on some instinctive level that they were absolutely harmless. Besides, Giovanni was a good friend of Tony's, and in Italy the bond of trust between male friends overrode even the Italian's finely honed mating instinct. Much as they might be tempted, neither man would dream of crossing the line with Clea.

"We spent seven evenings together, the three of us," murmured Clea. "Eating in cafés. Splashing in fountains. They were so sweet to me. So polite." She gave a soft laugh. "I thought of them as younger brothers. And when they came up with this wild idea of taking me to Brussels aboard their ship, I never thought to be afraid."

"You mean as a passenger?" asked Jordan.

"More as an honored stowaway. It was a little escapade we hatched over Campari and pasta. Their ship was sailing in a few days, and they thought, wouldn't it be fun if I came along? Their captain had no objections, as long as I stayed below and out of sight until they left the harbor. He didn't want any flack from the ship's owner. I could come out on deck once we were at sea. And in Brussels they'd sneak me off again."

"You trusted them?"

"Yes. It sounds crazy now, but I did. They were so... harmless." Clea smiled at the memory. "Maybe it was all that Campari. Maybe I was just hungry for a bit of adventure. We had it all planned out, you see. The wine we'd bring aboard. The meals I'd whip up for everyone. They told me it was a large boat, and the only cargo was a few crates of artwork bound for an auction house in Brussels. There'd be plenty of room for a crew of eight. And me.

"So that night I was brought aboard. While the men got ready to leave, I waited below in the cargo hold. Giovanni brought me hot tea and chocolate biscuits. He was such a nice boy…"

"It was the *Max Havelaar* you boarded?" asked Richard softly.

She swallowed. "Yes. It was the *Max Havelaar.*" She took a deep breath, mustering the strength to continue. "She was an old boat. Everything was rusted. Everything seemed to creak. I thought it odd that a vessel that large would carry as its only cargo a few crates of artwork.

"I saw a manifest sheet hanging on one of the crates in the hold. I looked it over. And that's when I realized there was a fortune's worth of antique art in those crates."

"Was the owner listed?"

"Yes. It was the Van Weldon company. They were the shipping agent, as well."

"What did you do then?"

"I was curious, of course. I wanted to take a peek, but all the crates were nailed shut. I looked around for a bit, and finally found a knothole in one of the boards. It was big enough to shine a penlight through. What I saw inside didn't make sense."

"What was there?"

"Stones. The bottom of the crate was lined with stones."

She turned from the window. The two men were

staring at her in bewilderment. No wonder. She, too, had been just as bewildered.

"Did you speak to the crew about this?" asked Richard.

"I waited until we'd left the dock. Then I found Giovanni. I asked him if he realized they were carrying crates of rocks. He only laughed. Said I must be seeing things. He'd been told the crates were valuable. He'd seen them loaded aboard himself."

"Who loaded them?"

"The Van Weldon company. They came in a truck directly from their warehouse."

"What did you do then?"

"I insisted we speak to Vicenzo. The captain. He laughed at me, too. Why would a company ship rocks, he kept asking me. And he had other concerns at the time. The southern coast of Sardinia was coming up, and he had to keep a watch out for other ships. He told me he'd check the cargo later.

"It wasn't until we'd passed Sardinia that I was able to drag them below decks to look. They finally pried open one of the crates. There was a layer of wood shavings on top. Typical packing material. I told them to keep digging. They went through the shavings, then through a layer of newspapers. They kept going deeper and deeper, expecting to find the artwork that was on the manifest. All they found were stones."

"The captain must have believed you then?"

"Of course. He had no choice. He decided to radio Naples, to find out what was going on. So we climbed up the steps to the bridge. Just as we got there, the engine room exploded."

Richard and Jordan said nothing. They only watched

her in grim silence as she told them about the last moments of the *Max Havelaar.*

In the panic that followed the explosion, as Giovanni radioed his last SOS, as the crew—what remained of the crew—scrambled to lower the lifeboat, the rocks in the cargo hold were forgotten. Survival was all that mattered. The flames were spreading rapidly; the *Max Havelaar* would be a floating inferno.

They lowered the lifeboat onto the swells. There was no time to climb down the ladder; with the flames licking at their backs, they leapt into the dark Mediterranean.

"The water was so cold," she said. "When I surfaced, I could see the *Havelaar* was all in flames. The lifeboat was drifting about a dozen yards away. Carlo and the second mate had already managed to crawl in, and they were leaning over the gunwale, trying to haul aboard Vicenzo. Giovanni was still in the water, struggling just to keep his head up.

"I've always been a strong swimmer. I can stay afloat for hours if I have to. So I yelled to the men that they should get the others to climb aboard first. And I treaded water..." She'd felt strangely calm, she remembered. Almost detached from the crisis. Perhaps it was the rhythmic motion of her limbs stroking the liquid darkness. Perhaps it was the sense of dreamlike unreality. She hadn't been afraid. Not yet.

"I knew the Spanish coast was only two miles or so to the north. By morning we could've paddled the lifeboat to land. Finally, all the men were hauled aboard. I was the only one left in the water. I swam over to the lifeboat and had just reached up for a hand when we all heard the sound of an engine."

"Another boat?" asked Jordan.

"Yes. A speedboat of some kind. Suddenly the men all were shouting, waving like crazy. The lifeboat was rocking back and forth. I was behind the gunwale and couldn't see the other boat as it came toward us. They had a searchlight. And I heard a voice calling to us in English. Some sort of accent—I'm not sure what kind. He identified their boat as the *Cosima*.

"Giovanni reached down to help me climb aboard. He'd just grabbed my hand when..." She paused. "When the *Cosima* began to fire on us."

"On the *lifeboat?*" asked Jordan, appalled.

"At first I didn't understand what was happening. I could hear the men crying out. And my hand slid away from Giovanni's. I saw that he was crumpled against the gunwale, staring down at me. I didn't understand that the sound was gunfire. Until a body fell into the water. It was Vicenzo's," she whispered, and looked away.

"How did you escape?" asked Jordan, gently.

Clea took an unsteady breath. "I dove," she said softly. "I swam underwater as far as my lungs would carry me. As fast as I could stroke away from that searchlight. I came up for air, then dove again and kept swimming. I thought I heard bullets hitting the water around me, but *Cosima* didn't chase after me. I just kept swimming and swimming. All night. Until I reached the coast of Spain."

She stood for a moment with bowed head. Neither man spoke. Neither man broke the silence.

"They killed them all," she whispered. "Giovanni. The captain. Six helpless men in a lifeboat. They never knew there was a witness."

Jordan and Richard stood watching her. They were

both too shocked by her story to say a word. She didn't know if they believed any of it; all she knew was that it felt good to finally tell it, to share the burden of horror.

"I reached the coast around dawn," she continued. "I was cold. Exhausted. But mostly I was desperate to reach the police." She shook her head. "That was my mistake, of course. Going to the police."

"Why?" asked Jordan gently.

"I ended up in some village police station, trying to explain what had happened. They made me wait in a back room while they checked the story. It turns out they called the Van Weldon company, to confirm their boat was missing. It made sense, I suppose. I can't blame the police for checking. So I waited three hours in that room for some representative from Van Weldon to arrive. Finally he did. I heard his voice through the door. I recognized it." She trembled at the memory. "It was the voice from the *Cosima*."

"You mean the killers were working for Van Weldon?" said Jordan.

Clea nodded. "I was climbing out that window so fast I must have left scorch marks. I've been running ever since. I found out later that *Cosima*'s registered owner is the Van Weldon Shipping Company. They sabotaged the *Havelaar*. They murdered its crew."

"And then claimed it as a giant loss," said Richard. "Artwork and all."

"Only there *wasn't* any artwork aboard," said Clea. "It was a dummy shipment, meant to go down on a boat they didn't need anymore. The real art's being stored somewhere. I'm sure it will be sold, piece by piece, on the black market. A double profit, counting the insurance."

"Who carried the policy?"

"Lloyd's of London."

"Have you contacted them?"

"Yes. They were skeptical of my story. Kept asking me what I wanted out of this, whether I had a grudge against the Van Weldon company. Then they learned about my prison record. After that, they didn't believe anything I said." Sighing, she went to the bed and sat down. "I told my cousin Tony to drop out of sight—he's the obvious person they'd use to track me down. He's in a wheelchair. Vulnerable. He's hiding out somewhere in Brussels. I can't really expect much help from him. So I'm floundering around on my own."

A long silence passed. When at last she found the courage to look up, she saw that Jordan was frowning at the wall, and that Richard Wolf was obviously not convinced of her story.

"You don't believe me, do you, Mr. Wolf?" she said.

"I'll reserve judgment for later. When I've had a chance to check the facts." He turned to Jordan. "Can we talk outside?"

Jordan nodded and followed Richard out of the room.

From the window Clea watched the two men standing in the garden below. She couldn't hear what they were saying, but she could read their body language— the nods, the grim set of Jordan's face. After a few moments Richard climbed in his car and drove away. Jordan reentered the building.

Clea stood waiting for him. She was afraid to face him, afraid to confront his skepticism. Why should he believe her? She was an ex-con. In the past month she had told so many lies she could scarcely keep them all straight. It was too much to ask that he would take her word for it this time.

The door opened and Jordan entered, his expression unreadable. He studied her for a moment, as though not certain just what to do with her. Then he let out a deep breath.

"You certainly know how to throw a fellow for a loop," he said.

"I'm sorry" was all she could think of saying.

"Sorry?"

"I never meant to drag you into this. Or your family either. It would be easier all around if you just go home. Somehow I'll get to London."

"It's a little late in the game, isn't it? To be casting me off?"

"You'll have no problems. Van Weldon isn't interested in *you*."

"But he is."

"What?"

"That's what Richard wanted to tell me. On his way to meet us, he was followed. Someone's watching Chetwynd, monitoring everyone's comings and goings."

Clea stiffened with alarm. "They followed him here?"

"No, he lost them."

"How can he be sure?"

"Believe me, Richard's an old hand at this. He'd know if he was followed."

Heart racing, she began to pace the room. She didn't care how skilled Richard Wolf might be—the chances were, he would underestimate Van Weldon's power, his resources. She'd spent the past month fighting for her life. She'd made it her business to learn everything she could about Van Weldon, and she knew, better than anyone, how far his tentacles reached. He had already discovered the link between her and the Tavistocks. It was just a matter of time before he used that knowledge to track her down.

She stopped pacing and looked at Jordan. "What next? What does your Mr. Wolf have in mind?"

"A fact-finding mission. Some discreet inquiries, a chat with Lloyd's of London."

"What do we do in the meantime?"

"We sit tight and wait right here. He'll call us in the morning."

She nodded and turned away. *In the morning,* she thought, *I'll be gone.*

Victor Van Weldon was having another attack, and this was a severe one, judging by the pallor of his face and the tinge of blue around his lips. Van Weldon was not long for this world, thought Simon Trott—a few months at the most. And then he'd be gone and the path would be clear for his appointed successor—Trott himself.

If Van Weldon didn't sack him first, a possibility that was beginning to seem likely since the latest news had broken.

"How can this be?" Van Weldon wheezed. "You said it was under control. You said the woman was ours."

"A third party stepped in at the last moment. He ruined everything. And we lost a man."

"What about this family you mentioned—the Tavistocks?"

"The Tavistocks are a distraction, nothing more. It's not them I'm worried about."

"Who, then?"

Trott paused, reluctant to broach the possibility. "Interpol," he said at last. "It seems the woman has attracted their attention."

Van Weldon reacted with a violent spasm of coughing. When at last he'd caught his breath again, he turned his malevolent gaze to Trott. "You have brought us to disaster."

"I'm sure it can be remedied."

"You left the task to fools. And so," he added ironically, "did I."

"The police have nothing. Our man is dead. He can't talk."

"Clea Rice can."

"We'll find her again."

"How? Every day she grows more and more clever. Every day we seem to grow more and more stupid."

"Eventually we'll have a lead. Our contact in Buckinghamshire—"

Van Weldon gave a snort. "That contact is a liability! I want the connection severed. And there must be a consequence. I will not tolerate such treachery."

Trott nodded. Consequences. Penalties. Yes, he understood their necessity.

He only hoped that he would not someday be on the receiving end.

It was well after dark when Richard Wolf finally drove in through the gates of Chetwynd. As he passed between the stone pillars his gaze swept the road, searching for a telltale silhouette, a movement in the bushes. He knew he was being watched, just as he knew he'd been followed earlier today. Even if he didn't quite believe Clea Rice's story, he did believe that she was in real danger. Her fear had infected him as well, had notched up his alertness to the point he was watching every shadow. He was glad Beryl had gone off to London for a few days. He'd call her later and suggest she stay longer—anything to keep her well away from this Clea Rice mess.

A car he didn't recognize was parked in the driveway.

Richard pulled up beside it. Cautiously he got out and circled around the Saab, glanced through the window at the interior. Inside were a few folded newspapers, nothing to identify the driver.

He went up the steps to the house.

Davis greeted him at the front door and helped him off with his raincoat. "You have a visitor, Mr. Wolf."

"So I've noticed. Who is it?"

"A Mr. Archibald MacLeod. He's in the library."

"Did he mention the purpose of his visit?"

"Some sort of police business."

At once Richard crossed the hall to the library. A man—brown haired, short but athletic build—stood beside the far bookcase, examining a leather-bound volume. He looked up as Richard entered.

"Mr. MacLeod? I'm Richard Wolf."

"Yes, I know. I've made inquiries. I've just spoken to an old colleague of yours—Claude Daumier, French Intelligence. He assures me I can have complete confidence in you." MacLeod closed the book and slid it back on the shelf. "I'm from Interpol."

"And I'm afraid I'm quite in the dark."

"We believe you and Mr. Tavistock have stumbled into a somewhat hazardous situation. I'm anxious to see that no one gets hurt. That's why I'm here to ask for your cooperation."

"In what matter?"

"Tell me where I can find Clea Rice."

Richard hoped his alarm didn't show on his face. "Clea Rice?" he asked blankly.

"I know you're familiar with the name. Since you requested an ID of her fingerprints. And a copy of her criminal record. The American authorities alerted us to that fact."

The man really must be with the police, Richard concluded. Nevertheless, he decided to proceed cautiously. Just because MacLeod was a cop didn't mean he could be trusted.

Richard crossed to the fireplace and sat down. "Before I tell you anything," he said, "I'd like to hear the facts."

"You mean about Clea Rice?"

"No. About Victor Van Weldon."

"Then will you tell me how to find Miss Rice?"

"Why do you want her?"

"We've decided it's time to move on her. As soon as possible."

Richard frowned. "You mean—you're arresting her?"

"Not at all." MacLeod faced him squarely. "We've used Miss Rice long enough. It's time to bring her into protective custody."

A soft drizzle was falling as Clea stepped out the front door of the Munstead Inn. It was past midnight and all was dark inside, the other occupants having long since retired. For a full hour she had lain awake beside

Jordan, waiting until she was certain he was asleep. Since the revelations of that afternoon, mistrust seemed to loom between them, and they had staked out opposite sides of the bed. They'd scarcely spoken to each other, much less touched.

Now she was leaving, and it was all for the better. The break was cleaner this way—no sloppy emotions, no uneasy farewells. He was the gentleman. She was the ex-con. Never the twain could meet.

The back gate squealed as she opened it. She froze, listening, but all she heard was the whisper of drizzle on tree leaves and, in the distance, the barking of a dog. She pulled her jacket tightly against the moist chill and began to trudge down the road.

It would be an all-night walk; by daybreak she could be miles from here. If her feet held out. If she wasn't spotted by the enemy.

Ahead stretched the twin hedgerows lining both sides of the road. She debated whether or not to walk on the far side of the hedge, where she would be hidden from the road, but after a few steps in the mud she decided the pavement was worth the risk. She wouldn't get far in this sucking mire. Chances were, no one would be driving this late at night, anyway. She slogged back around the hedge and clambered onto the road. There she froze.

The silhouette of a man was standing before her.

"You could have told me you were leaving," said Jordan.

Relieved it was him, she found her breath again. "I could have."

"Why didn't you?"

"You would have stopped me. And I can't afford any more delays. Not when I know they're one step behind."

"You'll be safer with me than without me."

"No, I'm safer on my own. I'm getting good at this, you know. I may actually survive to see the ripe old age of thirty-one."

"As what, a fugitive? What kind of life is that?"

"At least it's a life."

"What about Van Weldon? He gets off with murder?"

"I can't do anything about that. I've tried. All it's earned me is a bunch of thugs on my tail and a head of peroxide-damaged hair. I give up, okay? He wins. And I'm out of here." She turned and began to walk away, down the road.

"Why did you come to England, anyway? Was it really the dagger you were after?"

"Yes. I thought, if I could steal it back, I'd have my evidence. I could prove to everyone that Van Weldon was lying. That he'd filed a false claim. And maybe— maybe someone would believe me."

"If what you're saying is true—"

"*If* it's true?" She turned in disgust and continued walking up the road. Away from him. "I suppose I made up the guy with the gun, too."

He followed her. "You can't keep running. You're the only witness to what happened to the *Havelaar*. The only one who can nail Van Weldon in court."

"If he doesn't nail me first."

"The police need your testimony."

"They don't believe me. And they won't without solid evidence. I wouldn't trust the police, anyway. You think Van Weldon got rich playing by the rules? Hell, no. I've checked into him. He has a hundred lawyers who'll pull strings to get him off. And probably a hundred cops in his pocket. He owns a dozen ships, fourteen hotels and three casinos in Monaco. Okay, so last year he didn't do so well. He got overextended and lost a bundle. That's why he ditched the *Havelaar* to—pardon the pun—keep his head above water. He's a little desperate and a little paranoid. And he'll squash anyone who gets in his way."

"I'll get you help, Clea."

"You have a nice mansion and a CIA-in-law. That's not enough."

"My uncle worked for MI6. British Intelligence."

"I suppose your uncle's chummy with a few members of Parliament?"

"Yes, he is."

"So is Van Weldon. He makes friends everywhere. Or he buys them."

He grabbed her arm and pulled her around to face him. "Clea, eight men died on the *Havelaar*. You saw it happen. How can you walk away from that?"

"You think it's easy?" she cried. "I try to sleep at night, and all I see is poor Giovanni slumping over the lifeboat. I hear gunfire. And Vicenzo moaning. And I hear the voice of that man. The one on the *Cosima*. The one who ordered them all killed…" She swallowed back an unexpected swell of tears. Angrily she wiped them away. "So, no, it ain't easy. But it's what I have to do if I want—"

Jordan cut her off with a sharp tug on her arm. Only at that instant did Clea notice the flicker of light reflected in his face. She spun around to face the road.

In the distance a car was approaching. As it rounded a curve, its headlights flitted through the hedgerow branches.

At once Jordan and Clea were dashing back the way they'd come. The hedges were too high and thick to cross; their only escape route was along the road. Rain had left the pavement slippery, and Clea's every step was bogged down by the mud still clinging to her shoes. Any second they'd be spotted.

Jordan yanked her sideways, through a gap in the hedge.

They tumbled through and landed together in a bed of wet grass. Seconds later the car drove past and continued on, toward the Munstead Inn. Through the stillness of the night they heard the engine's growl fade away. Then there was nothing. No car doors slamming, no voices.

"Do you think they've gone on?" whispered Clea.

"No. It's a dead-end road. There's only the inn."

"Then what are they doing?"

"Watching. Waiting for something."

For us, she thought.

Suddenly she was frantic to get away, to escape the threat of that car and its faceless occupants. This time she didn't dare use the road. Instead she headed across the field, not knowing where she was going, knowing only that she had to get as far away from the Munstead Inn as she could. The mud sucked at her shoes, slowing every step, making her stumble again and again, until she felt as if she was trapped in that familiar nightmare of pursuit, her legs refusing to work. She was panting so hard she didn't hear Jordan following at her heels. Only when she fell to her knees and he reached down for her did she realize he was right beside her.

He pulled her back to her feet. She stood swaying, her legs shaky, her breath coming in gasps. Around them stretched the dark vastness of the field. Overhead the sky was silvery with mist and rain.

"We're all right," he panted, struggling to catch his breath, as well. "They're not following us."

"How did they know where to look for us?"

"It couldn't have been the Munsteads."

"Then it was Richard Wolf."

"No," said Jordan firmly. "It wasn't Richard."

"They could've followed him—"

"He said he wasn't followed."

"Then he was wrong!" She pulled away. "I should never have trusted you. Any of you. Now it's going to get me killed." She turned and struggled on through the mire.

"Clea, wait."

"Go home, Jordan. Go back to being a gentleman."

"Can you keep on running?"

"Damn right I can! I'm getting as far away as possible. I yanked on the tiger's tail. I was lucky to live through it."

"You think Van Weldon will let you go? He'll hunt you down, Clea. Wherever you run, you'll be looking over your shoulder. You're a constant threat to him. The one person who could destroy him. Unless he destroys you first."

She turned. In the darkness of the field his face was a black oval against the silver of the night clouds. "What do you want me to do? Fight back? Surrender?" She gave a sob of desperation. "Either way, Jordan, I'm lost. And I'm scared." She hugged herself in the rain. "And I'm freezing to death."

At once his arms came around her, pulling her into his embrace. They were both damp and shivering, yet

even through their soaked clothes she felt his warmth
seep toward her. He took her face in his hands, and the
kiss he pressed to her lips was enough to sweep away,
just for a moment, her discomfort. Her fear. As the
rain began to beat down on the fields and the clouds
swept across the moon, she was aware only of him, the
salty heat of his mouth, the way his body molded itself
around hers.

When at last she'd caught her breath again, and they
stood gazing at each other in the darkness, she found
she was no longer shaking from fear, but from longing.

For him.

He said softly, "I know a place we can go tonight.
It's a long walk. But it will be warm there, and dry."

"And safe?"

"And safe." Again he framed her face in his hands
and kissed her. "Trust me."

I have no choice, she thought. *I'm too tired to think
of what I should do. Where I should go.*

He took her hand. "We cross this field, then follow
the roads," he said. "On pavement, so they won't be able
to track our footprints."

"And then?"

"It's a three-, four-mile walk. Think you can make
it?"

She thought about the men in the car, waiting outside the Munstead Inn. She wondered if somewhere, in
the cylinder of one of their guns, there lurked a bullet
with her name on it.

"I can make it," she said, her pace quickening. "I'll do
anything," she added under her breath, "to stay alive."

Chapter 9

A few taps of a rock and the window shattered.

Jordan broke away the jagged edges and climbed in. A moment later he reappeared at the cottage's front door and motioned for Clea to enter.

She stepped inside and found herself standing in a quaint room furnished with rough-hewn antiques and pewter lamps. Massive ceiling beams, centuries old, ran the length of the room, and all around her, burnished wainscoting gleamed against the whitewashed walls. It would have been a cozy room were it not so cold and drafty. The English, thought Clea, must have thermally insulated hides.

Jordan, soaked as he was, looked scarcely discomfited as he moved about the room, closing shutters. "I'll have to make it up to old Monty, that broken window. He'll understand. Doesn't much use this cottage except in the summer. In fact, I believe he's in Moritz at the moment. Trying to land the next Mrs. Montgomery Dearborn."

How many Mrs. Dearborns are there? Clea wanted to ask, but she couldn't get out the question; her teeth were chattering too hard. What feeling she had left in her limbs was quickly fading to numbness. She knew she should strip off her wet clothes, should try to start a fire in the hearth, but she couldn't seem to make her body move. She could only stand there, water dripping from her clothes onto the wood floor.

Jordan turned on a lamp. By the light's glow he caught his first real look at her. "Good Lord," he said, touching her face. "You're like an ice cube."

"Fire," she whispered. "Please, start a fire."

"That'll take too long. You need to get warmed up now." He pulled her down a hall and into the bathroom. Quickly he turned on the shower spigot. As water hissed out in a sputtering stream he began to peel off her sopping wool jacket.

"Electric coil heater," said Jordan. "It'll warm up in a minute." He tossed her jacket aside and unzipped her skirt. She was too cold to care about anything so trivial as modesty; she let him pull her skirt off, let the fabric drop in a pile on the floor. The water was steaming now; he tested the temperature, then thrust her, underwear and all, into the shower.

Even with hot water streaming over her body, it seemed to take forever for her to stop shaking. She huddled, dazed, under the spigot. Slowly the heat penetrated her numbness and she could feel her blood start to circulate again, could feel the flush of warmth at last seeping toward her core.

"Clea?" she heard Jordan say.

She didn't answer. She was too caught up in the pleasure of being warm again. Sighing, she shifted around
to let the stream roll down her back. Vaguely, through
the rattle of water, she heard Jordan call.

"Are you all right?"

Before she could answer, the shower curtain was
abruptly pushed aside. She found herself gazing up at
Jordan's face.

As he was gazing at hers.

For a moment they said nothing. The only sound
was the pounding of the shower. And the pulsing of her
heartbeat in her ears. Though she was barely clothed,
though her transparent undergarments clung to her skin,
Jordan's gaze never wavered from her face. He seemed
mesmerized by what he saw there. Drawn by the longing he surely recognized in her eyes.

She reached out and touched his face. His cheek felt
rough and chilled under her hot fingertips. Just that
one contact, that brush of her skin against his, seemed
to melt all the barriers between them. She felt another
kind of heat ignite within her. She pulled his face down
to hers and met his lips in a kiss.

At once they were both clinging to each other.
Whimpering. Hot water streamed across their shoulders, hers bare, his still clothed in the shirt. Through the
curls of steam, she saw in his face the long-suppressed
desire that had been throbbing between them since the
night they'd met.

She pressed even more eagerly against him and gave
a soft sigh of pleasure, of triumph, at the burgeoning
response of his body.

"Your clothes," she murmured, and reached up feverishly to pull off his shirt. He shrugged it off onto the bathroom floor, baring his chest, so recently bandaged. The golden hairs were damp and matted from the shower. They were both breathing in gasps now, both working frantically at his belt.

Somehow they got the water shut off. Somehow they managed to find their way out of the shower, out of the bathroom with its obstacle course of wet clothes littering the tiles. They left a trail of still more wet clothes, lying where they'd dropped, his trousers near the bathroom door, her bra in the hallway, his undershorts at the threshold of the bedroom. By the time they reached the bed, there were no more clothes to shed. There was only damp flesh and murmurs and the yearning to be joined.

The bedroom was cold and they slid, shivering, beneath the goose-down duvet. As they lay with limbs intertwined, mouths exploring, tasting, the heat of their bodies warmed the bed. Her shivering ceased. The room's chill was forgotten in the rush of sensations now flooding through her, the sweet ache between her thighs, the sharp darts of pleasure as his mouth found her breasts, drawing her nipples to almost agonizing tautness.

She rose above him and returned the torment with a vengeance. Her mouth traced down the plane of his chest, grazed his belly, seeking ever more sensitive flesh. Groaning, he gripped her shoulders, and his body twisted off the mattress, rolling her onto the pillow. Suddenly she was lying beneath him, his body hard atop hers, his hands cupping her face.

Their gazes met, held. They never stopped looking at each other, even as he slid inside her, filled her. Even as she cried out with the pleasure of his penetration.

He moved slowly, gently. Their gazes held.

His breaths came faster, his hands clutching more tightly at her face. Still they looked at each other, joined in a bond that went deeper than flesh.

Only when she felt that exquisite ache build to the first ripples of release did she close her eyes and surrender to the sensations flooding through her. A soft cry floated from her throat, a sound both foreign and wonderful. It was matched, seconds later, by his groan. Through the ebbing waves of her own pleasure she felt his last frantic thrusts, and then he pulsed deep within her. With a shuddering sigh his spent body came to rest and fell still.

She cradled his head against her shoulder. As she pressed a kiss to his damp hair, she felt a wave of tenderness so overpowering it frightened her.

We made love. What does it mean?

They'd enjoyed each other's bodies. They'd given each other satisfaction and, for a few moments, even happiness.

But what does it mean?

She pressed another kiss to the damp tendrils and felt again that twinge of affection, so intense this time it brought tears to her eyes. Blinking them away, she turned her face from him, only to feel his hand cradle her cheek and nudge her gaze back to his.

"You are the most surprising woman I've ever met," he said.

She swallowed. And laughed. "That's me. Full of surprises."

"And delights. I never know what to expect from you. And it's starting to drive me quite mad." He lowered his mouth and tenderly brushed his lips against hers, tasting, nibbling. Enjoying. Already she could feel the rekindling of his arousal, could feel his heaviness stirring against her thigh.

She slid her hand between their hips and with a few silken strokes she had him hard and throbbing again. "You're full of surprises yourself," she murmured.

"No, I'm quite…" he gave a sigh of delight "…conventional."

"Are you?" She lowered her mouth to his nipple and traced a circle of wetness with her tongue.

"Some would even call me—" he dropped his head back and groaned "—damned predictable."

"Sometimes," she whispered, "predictable is good."

With her tongue she began to trace a wet line across his chest to his other nipple. He was breathing hard, struggling to check his rising tide of passion.

"Wait. Clea…" He caught her face. Gently he tilted it up toward him and looked at her. "I have to know. Why were you crying?"

"I wasn't."

"You were. A moment ago."

She studied him, hungrily devouring every detail. The way the light played on his ruffled hair. The crescent shadows cast by his eyelashes. The way he looked at *her,* so quietly, intently. As though she was some strange, unknowable creature.

"I was thinking," she said, "how different you are from any man I've known."

"Ah. No wonder you were crying."

She laughed and gave him a playful slap. "No, silly. What I meant was, the men I've known were always… after something. Wanting something. Planning the next take."

"You mean, like your uncle Walter?"

"Yes. Like my uncle Walter."

The mention of her past, her flawed childhood, suddenly dampened her desire. She pulled away from him. Sitting up, she hugged her knees. If only she could make that part of her life drop away. If only she could be born anew. Without shame.

"I'm embarrassed to admit he's my relative," she said.

He laughed. "I'm embarrassed by my relatives all the time."

"But none of yours are in prison…are they?"

"Not as of this moment, no."

"Uncle Walter is. So was my cousin Tony." She paused and added softly, "So was I."

He reached for her hand. He didn't say anything. He just watched her, and listened.

"It was so ironic, really. For eight years I went perfectly straight. And suddenly Uncle Walter pops up outside my apartment. Bleeding all over my front porch. I couldn't turn him in. And he wouldn't let me take him to the hospital. So there I was, stuck with him. I burned his clothes. Tossed his lock picks in a Dumpster across town. And then the police showed up." She gave a shrug, as though that last detail was scarcely worth mentioning. "The funny thing is," she said, "I don't hate him for it. Not a bit. You can't hate Uncle Walter. He's so damn…" She gave a sheepish shrug. "Lovable."

Laughing, he pressed her palm to his lips. "You have a most unique take on life. Like no other woman I've known."

"How many ex-cons have you slept with?"

"You, I must admit, are my first."

"Yes, I imagine you'd normally prefer a proper lady."

He frowned at her. "What's this rubbish about *proper* ladies, anyway?"

"Well, I don't exactly qualify."

"*Proper* is dull. And you, my dear Miss Rice, are not dull."

She tossed her head back and laughed. "Thank you, Mr. Tavistock, for the compliment."

He tugged her toward him. "And as for your notorious uncle Walter," he whispered, pulling her down on top of him, "if he's related to you, he must have some redeeming features."

She smiled down at him. "He *is* charming."

He cupped her face and kissed her. "I'm sure."

"And clever."

"I can imagine."

"And the ladies say he's quite irresistible..."

Again Jordan's mouth found hers. His kiss, deeper, harder, swept all thoughts of Uncle Walter from her mind.

"Quite irresistible," murmured Jordan, and he slid his hand between her thighs.

At once she was lost, needing him, crying out for him. She bared her warmth and he took it tenderly. And when it was over, when exhaustion finally claimed him, he fell asleep with his head on her breast.

She smiled down at his tousled hair. "You will remember me fondly some day, won't you, Jordan?" she whispered.

And she knew it was the best she could hope for.

It was all she dared hope for.

He awakened to the subtle perfume of a woman's scent, to the tickle of hair against his face. He opened his eyes and by the gray light slanting in through the shutters he saw Clea asleep beside him. Without a trace of makeup, and her hair lushly tangled across the pillow, she looked like some fairy princess over whom a spell of deathless repose had been cast. Unarousable, untouchable. Not altogether real.

How real she'd felt to him last night! Not a princess at all, but a temptress, full of sweet mischief and even sweeter fire.

Even now he couldn't resist her. He reached for her and kissed her on the mouth.

Her reaction was abrupt and startling. She gave a shudder of alarm and jerked up from the pillow.

"It's all right," he soothed. "It's only me."

She stared for a moment, as though not recognizing him. Then she gave a soft gasp and shook her head. "I—I haven't been sleeping very well. Needless to say."

He watched her huddle beneath the duvet and wondered how she had maintained her sanity through those weeks of running and hiding. He couldn't help but feel a rush of pity for her. It was mingled with admiration for her strength. Her will to live.

She glanced at the window and saw daylight gleaming through the closed shutters. "They'll be searching for us. We can't stay here much longer."

"We can't exactly stroll away, either. Not without help."

"Oh, no. No more calling on friends and family. I'm sure that's how they found us last night. Your Richard Wolf must have told someone."

"He'd never do that."

"Then they followed him. Or they've tapped your phone. Something." Abruptly she climbed out of bed and snatched up her underwear. Finding it still damp, she tossed it in disgust onto a chair. "I'm going to have to leave naked."

"Then you'll most certainly catch someone's eye."

"You're not much help. Can't you get out of bed, at least?"

"I'm thinking. I think best in bed."

"Bed is where most men don't think at all." She picked up her bra. It, too, was damp. She looped it over the doorknob and glanced around the room in frustration. "You say the man who owns this place is a bachelor?"

"In between states of wedded bliss."

"Does he have any women's clothes?"

"I've never thought to ask Monty such a personal question."

"You know what I mean."

He rose from the bed and went to open the wardrobe door. Inside hung two summer suits, a raincoat and a few neatly pressed shirts. On Jordan they'd all fit nicely. On Clea they'd look ridiculous. He took out a bathrobe and tossed it to her.

"Unless we can turn you into a six-foot man," he said, "this wardrobe won't work. And even if we did find women's clothes in here, there's still the matter of your hair. That flaming red isn't the most subtle color."

She snatched a lock of her hair and frowned at it. "I hate it, anyway. Let's cut it off."

He eyed those lustrous waves and was forced to give a regretful nod. "Monty always keeps a bottle of hair dye around to touch up his graying temples. We could darken what's left of your hair."

"I'll find some scissors."

"Wait. Clea," he said. "We have to talk."

She turned to him, her jaw set with the determination of what had to be done. "About what?"

"Even if we do change your appearance, running may not be your best option."

"I think it's my only option."

"There's still the authorities."

"They didn't believe me before. Why should they believe me now? My word's nothing against Van Weldon's."

"The Eye of Kashmir would change that."

"I don't have it."

"Delancey does."

She shook her head. "By now, Van Weldon must have realized what a mistake it was to sell the Eye so soon. His people will be trying to get it back."

"What if they haven't? It may still be in Delancey's house, waiting to be snatched. By us."

She went very still. "Us?" she asked quietly.

"Yes, us." He smiled at her, a smile that did not seem to inspire much confidence, judging by her expression. "Congratulations. Meet your new partner in crime," he said.

"That's supposed to make me feel better?"

"Doesn't it?"

"I'm just thinking about your last burglary attempt. And how close you came to getting us both handcuffed."

"That was inexperience. I'm now fully seasoned."

"Right. And ready for the frying pan."

"What is this, a crisis of confidence? You told me you used to burglarize houses just for the challenge of it."

"I didn't know better then. I was a kid."

"And now you're experienced. Better at the art."

Letting out a breath, she began to pace a line back and forth in the carpet. "I know I could break in again. I'm *sure* I could. But I don't know where to look. The dagger could be anywhere upstairs. The bedroom, the guest rooms. I'd need time."

"Together, we could do it in half the time."

"Or get caught twice as fast," she muttered. And she left the room.

He followed her into the kitchen, where he found her rummaging through drawers for the scissors. "There's always the other option," he said. "The logical one. The reasonable one. We go to the police."

"Where they'll laugh in my face, the way they did before. And Van Weldon will know exactly where to find me."

"You'll be under protection. I promise."

"The safest place for me, Jordan, is out where I can run. A moving target's not so easy to hit." She found the scissors and handed them to him. "Especially when the target keeps changing its appearance. Go ahead, do it."

He looked down at the scissors, then looked at that beautiful mane of hair. The task was almost too painful, but he had no choice. Regretfully he took a handful of cinnamon red hair. Just the scent of those silky strands was enough to reawaken all the memories of last night. The way her body had fitted against his. The way she'd moved beneath him, not a docile release but the joyous shudders of a wild creature.

That's what she was. A wild thing. Sensuous. Unpredictable. In time she would drive him crazy.

Already he was losing his long-practiced sense of self-control. All it took was a few whiffs of her hair, the touch of silk in his palm, and he was ready to drag her back to bed.

He gave his head a shake to clear away those inconvenient images. Then he lifted the scissors and calmly, deliberately, began to snip off her hair.

By the gray morning light, they followed the footprints in the mud—a pair of them, one large set, one smaller set, veering away from the road. The prints headed west across the field. It had rained heavily last night, and the tracks were easy to follow for about three hundred yards or so, until they connected up with another road. Then, after a few muddy imprints on the pavement, the footprints faded.

They could be anywhere by now.

Archie MacLeod gazed out over the field and cursed. "I should've known she'd do this. Probably got one inkling we were on her trail and off she goes. Like a bloody she-fox, that one."

"You can hardly blame her," said Richard. "Of course she'd expect the worst. How did your people fumble this one? They were supposed to bring her into custody. Instead they managed to chase her underground."

"Their orders were to do it quietly. Somehow she got wind of them."

"Or Jordan did," said Richard. "I should have contacted him last night. Told him what was coming down. Now he'll wonder."

"You don't think he doubts *you?*"

"No. But he'll be cautious now. He'll assume Van Weldon's got me covered, that it won't be safe to contact me. That's what I'd assume in his place."

"So how do we find them now?"

"We don't." Richard turned to his car and slid in behind the wheel. "And we hope Van Weldon doesn't, either."

"I'm not so confident of that."

"Jordan's clever. So is Clea Rice. Together they may do all right."

MacLeod leaned in the car window. "Guy Delancey died this morning."

"I know," said Richard.

"And we've just heard rumors that Victor Van Weldon's upped the price on Clea Rice to two million. Within twenty-four hours this area will be swarming with contract men. If they get anywhere near Clea Rice, she won't stand a chance. Neither will Tavistock."

Richard stared at him. "Why the hell did you wait so long to bring her into custody? You should have locked her under guard weeks ago."

"We didn't know whether to believe her."

"So you waited for Van Weldon to make a move, was that the strategy? If he tried to kill her, she must be telling the truth?"

MacLeod slapped the car door in frustration. "I'm not defending what we've done. I'm just saying we're now convinced she's told the truth." He leaned forward. "Jordan Tavistock is your friend. You must have an idea where he'd go."

"I'm not even sure he's the one calling the shots right now. It might be the woman."

"You let me know if you come up with any ideas. Anything at all about where they might go next."

Richard started the car. "I know where *I'd* go if I were them. I'd get away from here. I'd run as fast as I could. And I'd damn well get lost in a crowd."

"London?"

Richard nodded. "Can you think of a better place to hide?"

"That woman must have nine lives. And she's used up only three of them," said Victor Van Weldon. He was wheezing again. His breathing, which was normally labored even on the best of days, had the moist rattle of hopelessly congested lungs.

Soon, thought Simon Trott. Victor was a dying man. What a relief it would be when it was over. No more of these distasteful audiences, these grotesque scenes of a virtual corpse fighting to hang on. If only the old man would just get it over with and die. Until then, he'd have to stay in the old man's good graces. And for that, he'd have to take care of this Clea Rice problem.

"You should have seen to this yourself," said Victor. "Now we've lost our chance."

"We'll find her again. We know she's still with Tavistock."

"Has he surfaced yet?"

"No. But eventually he'll turn to his family. And we'll be ready."

Van Weldon exhaled a deep sigh. His breathing seemed clearer, as though the assurances had eased the congestion in his lungs. "I want you to see to it personally."

Trott nodded. "I'll leave for London this evening."

Crouched behind the yew hedge of Guy Delancey's yard, Jordan and Clea waited in the darkness for the house lights to go out. Whitmore's nightly habit was as it had always been, the checking of the windows and doors at nine o'clock, the pause in the kitchen to brew a pot of tea, then the retreat upstairs to his room in the servants' wing. How many years has the fellow clung to that petrified routine of his? Clea wondered. What a shock it must be to him, to know that all would soon change.

Clea and Jordan had heard it on the radio that morning: Guy Delancey was dead.

Soon others would come to claim this house. And old Whitmore, a relic from the dinosaur age, would be forced to evolve.

The lights in the servants' wing went out.

"Give him half an hour," whispered Jordan. "Just to make sure he's asleep."

Half an hour, thought Clea, shivering. She'd freeze by then. She was dressed in Monty's black turtleneck and a baggy pair of jeans, which she'd shortened with a few snips of the scissors. It wasn't enough protection against this chill autumn night.

"Which way do we enter?" asked Jordan.

Clea scanned the house. The French door leading from the terrace was how she'd broken in the last time. No doubt that particular lock had since been replaced. So, undoubtedly, had the locks on all the ground-floor doors and windows.

"The second floor," she said. "Balcony off the master bedroom."

"That's how I got in the last time."

"And if *you* managed to do it," she said dryly, "it must have been a piece of cake."

"Oh, right, insult your partner. See where it gets you."

She glanced at him. His blond hair was concealed under a watch cap, and his face was blackened with grease, In the darkness only the white arc of his teeth showed in a Cheshire-cat grin.

"You're sure you're up to this?" she asked. "It could get sticky in there."

"Clea, if things do go wrong, promise me."

"Promise you what?"

"You'll run. Don't wait for me. And don't look back."

"Trying to be chivalrous again? Something silly like that?"

"I just want to get things straight now. Before things go awry."

"Don't say that. It's bad luck."

"Then this is for good luck." He took her arm, pulled her against him and kissed her. She floundered in his embrace, torn between wanting desperately to get kissed again, and wanting to stay focused on the task that lay ahead. When he finally released her, they stared at each other for a moment. Only the gleam of his eyes and teeth were visible in the darkness.

That was a farewell kiss, she realized. In case things went wrong. In case they got separated and never saw each other again. A chill wind blew and the trees creaked overhead. As the moments passed, and the night grew colder, she tried to commit every detail to memory. Because she knew, as he did, that every step they took could end in disaster. She had not counted on this complication, had not wanted this attraction. But here it was, shimmering between them. The fact it couldn't last, that any feelings they had for each other were doomed by who she was, and who he was, only made those feelings all the sweeter. *Will you miss me someday, Jordan Tavistock?* she wondered. *As much as I'll miss you?*

At last he turned and looked at the house. "I think it's time," he said softly.

She, too, turned to face the house. The wind swept the lawn, bringing with it the smell of dead leaves and chill earth. The scent of autumn, she thought. Too soon, winter would be upon them…

She eased away from the hedge and began to move through the shadows. Jordan was right behind her.

They crossed the lawn, their shoes sinking into wet grass. Beneath the bedroom balcony they crouched to reassess the situation. They heard only the wind and the rustle of leaves.

"I'll go first," he said.

Before she could protest, he was scrambling up the wisteria vine. She winced at the rattle of branches, expecting at any moment that the balcony doors would fly open, that Whitmore would appear waving a shotgun. Lucky for them, old Whitmore still seemed to be a sound sleeper. Jordan made it all the way up without a hitch.

Clea followed and dropped noiselessly onto the balcony.

"Locked," said Jordan, trying the doorknob.

"Expected as much," she whispered. "Move away."

He stepped aside and watched in respectful silence as she shone a penlight on the lock. "This should be even easier than the one downstairs," she whispered and gently inserted the makeshift L-pick she'd fashioned that afternoon using a wire hanger and a pair of pliers. "Circa 1920. Probably came with the house. Let's hope it's not so rusty that it bends my…" She gave a soft chuckle of satisfaction as the lock clicked open. Glancing at Jordan she said wryly, "There's nothing like a good stiff tool."

He answered, just as wryly, "I'll remember to keep one on me."

The room was as she'd remembered it, the medieval curtained bed, the wardrobe and antique dresser, the desk and tea table near the balcony doors. She'd searched the desk and dresser before; now she'd take up where she had left off.

"You search the wardrobe," she whispered. "I'll do the nightstands."

They set to work. By the thin beam of her penlight she examined the contents of the first nightstand. In the drawers she found magazines, cigarettes and various other items that told her Guy Delancey had used this bed for activities beyond mere sleeping. A flicker of movement overhead made her aim the penlight at the ceiling. There was a mirror mounted above the bed. To think she had actually considered a romp in this bachelor playpen! Turning her attention back to the nightstand, she saw that the magazines featured naked ladies galore, and not very attractive ones. Entertainment, no doubt, for the nights Guy couldn't find female companionship.

She searched the second nightstand and found a similar collection of reading material. So intent was she on poking for hidden drawers, she didn't notice the creak of floorboards in the hallway. Her only warning was a sharp hiss from Jordan, and then the bedroom door flew open.

The lights sprang on overhead.

Clea, caught in midcrouch beside the bed, could only blink in surprise at the shotgun barrel pointed at her head.

Chapter 10

The gun was wavering ominously in Whitmore's unsteady grasp. The old butler looked most undignified in his ratty pajamas, but there was no mistaking the glint of triumph in his eyes.

"Gotcha!" he barked. "Thinkin' to rob a dead man, are you? Think you can get away with it again? Well, I'm not such an old fool!"

"Apparently not," said Clea. She didn't dare glance in Jordan's direction, but off in her peripheral field of vision she spied him crouched beside the wardrobe, out of Whitmore's view. The old man hadn't yet realized there were two burglars in the room.

"Come on, come on! Out from behind that bed! Where I can see you!" ordered Whitmore.

Slowly Clea rose to her feet, praying that the man's trigger finger wasn't as unsteady as his grip. As she straightened to her full height, Whitmore's gaze widened. He focused on her chest, on the unmistakable swell of breasts.

"Ye're only a woman," he marveled.

"Only?" She gave him a wounded look. "How insulting."

At the sound of her voice, his eyes narrowed. He scanned her grease-blackened face. "You sound familiar. Do I know you?"

She shook her head.

"Of course! You come to the house with poor Master Delancey! One of his lady friends!" The grip on the shotgun steadied. "Come 'ere, then! Away from the bed, you!"

"You're not going to shoot me, are you?"

"We're going to wait for the police. They'll be here any minute."

The police. There wasn't much time. Somehow they had to get that gun away from the old fool.

She caught a glimpse of Jordan, signaling to her, urging her to shift the butler's gaze toward the left.

"Come on, move out from behind the bed!" ordered Whitmore. "Out where I can get a clear shot if I have to!"

Obediently she crawled across the mattress and climbed off. Then she took a sideways step, causing Whitmore to turn leftward. His back was now squarely turned to Jordan.

"I'm not what you think," she said.

"Denying you're a common thief, are you?"

"Certainly not a *common* one, anyway."

Jordan was approaching from the rear. Clea forced

herself not to stare at him, not to give Whitmore any clue of what was about to happen…

What *was* about to happen? Surely Jordan wouldn't bop the old codger on the head? It might kill him.

Jordan raised his arms. He was clutching a pair of Guy Delancey's boxer shorts, was going to pull them like a hood over old Whitmore's head. Somehow Clea had to get that gun pointed in another direction. If startled, Whitmore might automatically let fly a round.

She gave a pitiful sob and fell to her knees on the floor. "You can't let them arrest me!" she wailed. "I'm afraid of prison!"

"Should've thought of that before you broke in," said Whitmore.

"I was desperate! I had to feed my children. There was no other way…" She began to sob wretchedly.

Whitmore was staring down at her, astonished by this bizarre display. The shotgun barrel was no longer pointed at her head.

That's when Jordan yanked the boxer shorts over Whitmore's face.

Clea dived sideways, just as the gun exploded. Pellets whizzed past. She scrambled frantically back to her feet and saw that Jordan already had Whitmore's arms restrained, and that the gun had fallen from the old man's grasp. Clea scooped it up and shoved it in the wardrobe.

"Don't hurt me!" pleaded Whitmore, his voice muffled by the makeshift hood. The boxer shorts had little red hearts. Had Delancey really pranced around in little red hearts? "Please!" moaned Whitmore.

"We're just going to keep you out of trouble," said Clea. Quickly she bound the butler's hands and feet with Delancey's silk ties and left him trussed on the bed. "Now you lie there and be a good boy."

"I promise!"

"And maybe we'll let you live."

There was a pause. Then Whitmore asked fearfully, "What do you mean by *maybe?*"

"Tell us where Delancey keeps his weapons collection."

"What weapons?"

"Antique swords. Knives. Where are they?"

"There's not much time!" hissed Jordan. "Let's get out of here."

Clea ignored him. *"Where are they?"* she repeated.

The butler whimpered. "Under the bed. That's where he keeps them!"

Clea and Jordan dropped to their knees. They saw nothing beneath the rosewood frame but carpet and a few dust balls.

Somewhere in the night, a siren was wailing.

"Time to go," muttered Jordan.

"No. Wait!" Clea focused on an almost imperceptible crack running the length of the bed frame. A seam in the wood. She reached underneath and tugged.

A hidden drawer glided out.

At her first glimpse of the contents, she gave an involuntary gasp of wonder. Jewels glittered in hammered-gold scabbards. Sword blades of finely tempered Spanish steel lay in gleaming display. In the deepest corner were stored the daggers. There were six of them, all exquisitely crafted. She knew at once which dagger was the Eye of Kashmir. The star sapphire mounted in the hilt gave it away.

"They were his pride and joy," moaned Whitmore. "And now you're stealing them."

"I'm only taking one," said Clea, snatching up the Eye of Kashmir. "And it didn't belong to him, anyway."

The siren was louder now and closing in.

"Let's *go!*" said Jordan.

Clea jumped to her feet and started toward the balcony. "Cheerio!" she called over her shoulder. "No hard feelings, right?"

"Bloody unlikely!" came the growl from under the boxer shorts.

She and Jordan scrambled down the wisteria vine and took off across the lawn, headed at a mad dash for the woods fringing the property. Just as they reached the cover of trees, a police car careened around the bend, siren screaming. Any second now the police would find Whitmore tied up on the bed and then all hell would break loose. The threat of pursuit was enough to send Jordan and Clea scrambling deep into the woods. Replay of the night we met, thought Clea. Hanging around Jordan Tavistock must be bad luck; it always seemed to bring the police on her tail.

The sting of branches whipping her face, the ache of her muscles, didn't slow her pace. She kept running, listening for sounds of pursuit. A moment later she heard distant shouting, and she knew the chase had begun.

"Damn," she muttered, stumbling over a tree root.

"Can you make it?"

"Do I have a choice?"

He glanced back toward the house, toward their pursuers. "I have an idea." He grabbed her hand and tugged her through a thinning copse of trees. They stumbled into a clearing. Just ahead, they could see the lights of a cottage.

"Let's hope they don't keep any dogs about," he said and started toward the cottage.

"What are you doing?" she whispered.

"Just a small theft. Which, I'm sorry to say, seems to be getting routine for me."

"What are you stealing? A car?"

"Not exactly." Through the darkness his teeth gleamed at her in a smile. "Bicycles."

In The Laughing Man Pub, Simon Trott stood alone at the bar, nursing a mug of Guinness. No one bothered him, and he bothered no one, and that was the way he liked it. None of the usual poking and prodding of a stranger by the curious locals. The villagers here, it seemed, valued a man's privacy, which was all to the better, as Trott had no tolerance tonight for even minor annoyances. He was not in a good mood. That meant he was dangerous.

He took another sip of stout and glanced at his watch. Almost midnight. The pub owner, anxious to close up, was already stacking up glasses and darting impatient looks at his customers. Trott was about to call it a night when the pub door opened.

A young policeman walked in. He sauntered to the bar where Trott stood and called for an ale. A few moments went by, no one saying a word. Then the policeman spoke.

"Been some excitement around 'ere tonight," he said to no one in particular.

"What sort?" asked the bartender.

"'Nother robbery, over at Under'ill. Guy Delancey's."

"Thieves gettin' bloody cheeky these days, if you ask me," the bartender said. "Goin' for the same 'ouse twice."

"Aren't they, though?" The policeman shook his head. "Makes you wonder what's become of society these days." He drained his mug. "Well, I best be gettin' 'ome. 'Fore the missus gets to worryin'." He paid the tab and walked out of the pub.

Trott left, as well.

Outside, in the road, the two men met. They walked across the village green, stepping in and out of shadows.

"Anything stolen from Underhill tonight?" asked Trott.

"The butler says just one item was taken. Antique weapon of some sort."

Trott's head lifted in sudden interest. "A dagger?"

"That's right. Part of a collection. Other things weren't touched."

"And the thieves?"

"There were two of them. Butler only saw the woman."

"What did she look like?"

"Couldn't really tell us. Had some sort of black grease on 'er face. No fingerprints, either."

"Where were they last seen?"

"Escaped through the trees. Could've gone in any direction. I'm afraid we lost 'em."

Then Clea Rice had not left Buckinghamshire, thought Trott. Perhaps she was right now in this very village.

"If I 'ear more, I'll let you know," said the policeman.

Their conversation had come to an end. Trott reached into his jacket and produced an envelope stuffed with five-pound notes. Not a lot of money, but enough to help keep a young cop's family clothed and fed.

The policeman took the envelope with an odd reluctance. "It's only information you'll be wantin', right? You won't be expecting more?"

"Only information," Trott reassured him.

"Times are…difficult, you see. Still, there are things I don't—won't—do."

"I understand." And Trott did. He understood that even upright cops could be tempted. And that for this one, the downhill slide had already begun.

After the two men parted, Trott returned to his room in the inn and called Victor Van Weldon.

"As of a few hours ago, they were still in the area," said Trott. "They broke into Delancey's house."

"Did they get the dagger?"

"Yes. Which means they've no reason to hang around here any longer. They'll probably be heading for London next."

Even now, he thought, Clea Rice must be wending her way along the back roads to the city. She'll be feeling a touch of triumph tonight. Perhaps she's thinking her ordeal will soon end. She'll sense hope, even victory whenever she looks at that dagger. The dagger she calls the Eye of Kashmir.

How wrong she will be.

The sounds of London traffic awakened Clea from a sleep so heavy she felt drugged. She rolled onto her back and peered through slitted lids at the daylight shining in through the ratty curtains. How long had they slept? Judging by her grogginess it might have been days.

They'd checked in to this seedy hotel around six

in the morning. Both of them had stripped off their clothes and collapsed on the bed, and that was the last she remembered. Now, as her brain began to function again, the events of last night came back to her. The endless wait at the station for the 4:00 a.m. train out of Wolverton. The fear that, lurking among the shadows on the platform, was someone who'd been watching for them. And then, during the train ride to London, the anxiety that they'd be robbed, that they'd lose their precious cargo.

She reached under the bed and felt the wrapped bundle. The Eye of Kashmir was still there. With a sigh of relief she settled back on the bed, next to Jordan.

He was asleep. He lay with his face turned toward her, his bare shoulder tanned a warm gold against the linen, his wheat-colored hair boyishly tousled. Even in sleep he looked every inch the aristocrat. Smiling, she stroked his hair. *My darling gentleman,* she thought. *How lucky I am to have known you. Someday, when you're married to some proper young lady, when your life has settled in according to plan, will you still remember your Clea Rice?*

Sitting up, she stared at her own reflection in the dresser mirror. Right, she thought.

Suddenly depressed, she left the bed and went to take a shower. Later, as she inspected her latest hair color—this time a nut brown, courtesy of Monty's bottle of hair dye—she felt resentment knot up in her stomach. She was not a lady, nor was she proper, but she damn well had her assets. She was bright, she could think fast on her feet and, most important, she could take care of herself. What possible use did *she* have for a gentleman? He'd be a nuisance, really, dragging her off all the time to soirees. Whatever those were. She'd never fit into his world. He'd never fit into hers.

But here, in this room with the mangy carpet and mildewed towels, they could share a temporary world. A world of their own making. She was going to enjoy it while it lasted.

She went back to the bed and climbed in next to Jordan.

At the touch of her damp body, he stirred and murmured, "Is this my wake-up call?"

She answered his question by sliding her hand under the covers and stroking slowly down the length of his torso. He sucked in a startled gasp as she found exquisitely tender flesh and evoked the hoped-for response.

"If that was my wake-up call," he groaned, "I think it worked."

"Maybe now you'll get up, sleepyhead," she said, laughing, and rolled away.

He caught her arm and hauled her right back. "What about this?"

"What about what?"

"This."

Her gaze traveled to the distinct bulge under the sheets. "Shall I take care of that for you?" she whispered.

"Seeing as you're the reason it's there in the first place…"

She rolled on top of him, fitting her hips to his. He was at her mercy now, and she intended to make him beg for his pleasure. But as their bodies moved together, as she felt him grasp her hips in both hands and pull her down against him, it was she who was at his mercy, she who was begging for release. He gave it to her, in wave after glorious wave, and through the roar of her pulse in her ears she heard him say her name aloud. Once, twice, in a murmur of delight.

Yes, I'm the one he's making love to, she thought. *Me. Only me.*

For these few sweet moments, it was enough.

Anthony Vauxhall was a starched little prig of a man with a nose that always seemed to be tilted up in distaste of mere mortals. Jordan had met him several times before, on matters relating to his late parents' estate. Their conversations had been cordial, and he hadn't formed much of an opinion of the man either way.

He was forming an opinion of Anthony Vauxhall now, and it wasn't a good one.

It was nearly 4:00 p.m., and they were seated in Vauxhall's office in the Lloyd's of London building on Leadenhall Street. In the past hour and a half Jordan and Clea had managed to purchase decent clothes, grab a bite to eat and scurry downtown to Lloyd's before the offices closed. Now it appeared that their efforts might prove futile. Vauxhall's response to Clea's story was one of obvious skepticism.

"You must understand, Miss Rice," said Vauxhall, "Van Weldon Shipping is one of our most distinguished clients. One of our oldest clients. Our relationship goes back three generations. For us to accuse Mr. Van Weldon of fraud is, well..." He cleared his throat.

"Perhaps you weren't listening to Miss Rice's story," said Jordan. "She was *there*. She was a witness. The loss of the *Max Havelaar* wasn't an accidental sinking. It was sabotage."

"Even so, how can we assume Van Weldon is responsible? It could have been another party. Pirates of some kind."

"Doesn't a multimillion-dollar claim concern your firm?"

"Well, naturally."

"Wouldn't your underwriters want to know if they've paid out to a company that staged its own losses?"

"Of course, but—"

"Then why aren't you taking these accusations seriously?"

"Because—" Vauxhall took a deep breath. "I spoke to Colin Hammersmith about this very matter. Right after I got your call earlier today. He's in charge of our investigations branch. He'd heard this rumor a few weeks back and his advice was, well…" Vauxhall shifted uneasily. "To consider the source," he said at last.

The source. Meaning Clea Rice, ex-con.

Jordan didn't need to look at her; he could feel her pain, as surely as if the blow had landed on his own shoulders. But when he did look at her, he was impressed by how well she was taking it, her chin held high, her expression calm and focused.

Ever since that long red hair had been cut away, her face had seemed even more striking to him, her sculpted cheeks feathered by wisps of brown hair, the dark eyes wide and gamine. He had known Clea Rice as a blonde, then a redhead and now a brunette. Though he'd found each and every version of her fascinating, of all her incarnations, this one he liked the best. Perhaps it was the fact he could actually focus on her face now, without the distraction of all that hair. Perhaps it matched her personality, those elfin tendrils wisping around her forehead.

Perhaps he was beyond caring about details as inconsequential as hair because he was falling in love with her.

That's why this insult by Vauxhall so enraged him.

He said, none too civilly, "Are you questioning Miss Rice's integrity?"

"Not...not exactly," said Vauxhall. "That is—"

"What *are* you questioning, then?"

Vauxhall looked miserable. "The story, it just appears— Oh, let's be frank, Mr. Tavistock. A slaughter at sea? Sabotage of one's own vessel? It's so shocking as to be—"

"Unbelievable."

"Yes. And when the accused is Victor Van Weldon, the story seems even more farfetched."

"But I saw it," insisted Clea. "I was there. Why won't you believe me?"

"We've already looked into it. Or rather, Mr. Hammersmith's department did. They spoke to the Spanish police, who assert that it was most probably an accident. An engine explosion. No bodies were ever found. Nor did they find evidence of murder."

"They wouldn't," said Clea. "Van Weldon's people are too clever."

"And as for the wreckage of the *Havelaar,* it went down in deep water. It's not easily salvageable. So we have nothing on which to base an accusation of sabotage."

Throughout Vauxhall's almost disdainful rebuttal, Clea had maintained her composure. She had regarded the man with almost regal calm. Jordan had watched in fascination as she took it all without batting an eyelash. Now he recognized the glimmer of triumph in her eyes. She was going to unveil the evidence.

Clea reached into her purse and withdrew the cloth-wrapped bundle that she'd so carefully guarded for the past sixteen hours. "You may find it difficult to take my word," she said, laying the bundle on his desk. "I understand that. After all, who am I to walk in off the street and tell you some fantastic tale? But perhaps this will change your mind."

Vauxhall frowned at the bundle. "What is that?"

"Evidence." Clea removed the cloth wrapping. As the last layer fell away, Vauxhall sucked in an audible gasp of wonder. A jeweled scabbard lay gleaming in its undistinguished bed of muslin cloth.

Clea slid the dagger out of the scabbard and laid it down, razor tip pointed toward Vauxhall. "It's called the Eye of Kashmir. Seventeenth century. The jewel in the hilt is a blue star sapphire from India. You'll find a description of it in your files. It was part of Victor Van Weldon's collection, insured by your company. A month ago it was being transported from Naples to Brussels aboard a vessel which, coincidentally, was also insured by your company. The *Max Havelaar*."

Vauxhall glanced at Jordan, then back at Clea. "But that would mean…"

"This dagger should be on the ocean floor right now. But it isn't. Because it was never aboard the *Havelaar*. It was kept safely in storage somewhere, then sold on the black market to an Englishman."

"How did *you* get it?"

"I stole it."

Vauxhall stared at her for a moment, as though not

certain she was being serious. Slowly he reached for his intercom button. "Miss Barrows," he murmured, "could you ring Mr. Jacobs, down in appraisals? Tell him to come up to my office. And have him bring his loupe or whatever it is he uses to examine gems."

"I'll ring him at once."

"Also, could you fetch the Van Weldon company's file for me? I want the papers for an antique dagger known as the Eye of Kashmir." Vauxhall sat back in his chair and regarded Clea with a troubled look. "This puts a new complexion on things. Mr. Van Weldon's claims, if I recall correctly, were in the neighborhood of fifteen million pounds for the art collection alone. This—" he waved at the dagger "—would call his claims into question."

Jordan looked at Clea and recognized her look of relief. *It's over,* he read in her eyes. *This nightmare is finally over.*

He took her hand. It was clammy, shaking, as though in fear. Of all the frightening events this past week, this moment must have been one of the most harrowing, because she had traveled so long and hard to reach it. She was too tense to smile at him, but he felt her fingers tighten around his. When this is over, he thought, well and truly over, we're going to celebrate. We're going to check in to a hotel suite and have all our meals delivered. And we're going to make love day and night until we're too exhausted to move. Then we'll sleep and start all over again…

They continued to cast knowing looks back and forth even as Vauxhall's secretary entered to deliver Van Weldon's files, even as Mr. Jacobs arrived from appraisals to examine the dagger. He was a distinguished-looking gentleman with a full mane of silver hair. He studied the Eye for what seemed like an eternity. At last he looked up and said to Vauxhall, "May I see the policy appraisal?"

Vauxhall handed it over. "There's a photo, as well. It seems to be identical."

"Yes. It does." Mr. Jacobs squinted at the photo, then regarded the dagger again. This time he focused his attention on the star sapphire. "Quite excellent work," he murmured, peering through the jeweler's loupe. "Exquisite craftsmanship."

"Don't you think it's time to call the authorities?" asked Jordan.

Vauxhall nodded and reached for the telephone. "Even Victor Van Weldon can't argue away the Eye of Kashmir, can he?"

Mr. Jacobs looked up. "But this isn't the Eye of Kashmir," he said.

The room went absolutely silent. Three pairs of eyes stared at the elderly appraiser.

"What do you mean, it's not?" demanded Vauxhall.

"It's a reproduction. A synthetic corundum. An excellent one, probably made using the Verneuil method. But as you'll see, the star is rather more pronounced than you'd find in a natural stone. It's worth perhaps two, three hundred pounds, so it's not entirely without value. But it's not a true star sapphire, either." Mr. Jacobs regarded them with a calm, bespectacled gaze. "This is not the Eye of Kashmir."

Clea's face had drained of color. She sat staring at the dagger. "I don't...don't understand..."

"Couldn't you be mistaken?" asked Jordan.

"No," said Mr. Jacobs. "I assure you, it's a reproduction."

"I demand a second opinion."

"Certainly. I'll recommend a number of gemologists—"

"No, we'll make our own arrangements," said Jordan.

Mr. Jacobs reacted with a look of injured dignity. He slid the dagger to Jordan. "Take it to whomever you wish," he said, and rose to leave.

"Mr. Jacobs?" called Vauxhall. "We hold the policy on the Eye of Kashmir. Shouldn't we retain this dagger until this matter is cleared up?"

"I see no reason to," snapped Mr. Jacobs. "Let them keep the thing. After all, it's nothing but a fake."

Chapter 11

Nothing but a fake.

Clea clutched the wrapped bundle in both hands as she and Jordan rode the elevator to the first floor. They walked out into the fading sunlight of late afternoon.

Nothing but a fake.

How could she have been so wrong?

She tried to reason out the possibilities, but her brain wouldn't function. She was operating on autopilot, her feet moving mechanically, her body numb. She had no evidence now, nothing to back up her story. And Van Weldon was still in pursuit. She could change her name a hundred times, dye her hair a hundred different shades, and still she'd be looking over her shoulder, wondering who might be moving in for the kill.

Victor Van Weldon had won.

It would almost be easier just to walk into his office,

meet him face-to-face and tell him, "I give up. Just get it over with quick." She wouldn't last much longer, anyway. Even now she was scarcely aware of the faces on the street, much less able to watch for signs of danger. Only the firm guidance of Jordan's hand kept her moving in any sort of purposeful direction.

He pulled her into a taxi and directed the driver to Brook Street.

Gazing out dully at the passing traffic, she asked, "Where are we going?"

"To get that second opinion. There's a chap I know, has a shop in the area. He's done some appraisals for Uncle Hugh in the past."

"Do you think Mr. Jacobs could be wrong?"

"Wrong. Or lying. At this point, I don't trust anyone."

Does he trust me? she wondered. *The dagger's a fake. Maybe he thinks I am, as well.*

The taxi dropped them off at a shop in the heart of Mayfair. From the exterior it did not look like the sort of establishment any family as lofty as the Tavistocks would patronize. A sign in the window said Clocks and Jewellery—Bought and Sold. Behind the dusty plate glass was arranged a selection of rings and necklaces that were obviously paste.

"This is the place?" asked Clea.

"Don't be fooled by appearances. If I want a straight answer, this is the man I ask."

They stepped inside, into a dark little cave of a room. On the walls were hung dozens of wooden cuckoo clocks, all of them ticking away. The counter was deserted.

"Hello?" called Jordan. "Herr Schuster?"

A door creaked open and an elderly gnome of a

man shuffled out from a back room. At his first glimpse of Jordan, the man gave a cackle of delight.

"It's young Mr. Tavistock! How many years has it been?"

"A few," admitted Jordan as he shook the man's hand. "You're looking very well."

"Me? Bah! I am twenty years on borrowed time. To be alive is enough. And your uncle, he is retired now?"

"As of a few months ago. He's enjoying it immensely." Jordan slid an arm around Clea's shoulders. "I'd like you to meet Miss Clea Rice. A good friend of mine. We've come to ask you for some help."

Herr Schuster shot a sly glance at Clea. "Would this perhaps be for an engagement ring?"

Jordan cleared his throat. "It's rather…your expert opinion we need at the moment."

"On what matter?"

"This," said Clea. She unwrapped the bundle and handed him the dagger.

"The star sapphire in the hilt," said Jordan. "Is it natural or man-made?"

Gingerly Herr Schuster took the dagger and weighed it in his hands, as though trying to divine the answer by its touch. He said, "This will require some time."

"We'll wait," said Jordan.

The old jeweler retreated into the back room and shut the door behind him.

Clea looked doubtfully at Jordan. "Can we trust his opinion?"

"Absolutely."

"You're that sure of him?"

"He used to be the leading authority on gemstones in East Berlin. In the days before the wall came down. He also happened to work as a double agent for MI6. You'd be amazed how much one can learn from chats with the wives of high Communist officials. When things got dangerous, Uncle Hugh helped him cross over."

"So that's why you trust him."

"It's a debt he owes my uncle." Jordan glanced at the door to the back room. "Old Schuster's been keeping a low profile here in London ever since. Touch of paranoia, I suspect."

"Paranoia," said Clea softly. "Yes, I know exactly how he's lived." She turned to the window and stared out through the dusty glass at Brook Street. A bus rumbled past, spewing exhaust. It was early evening now, and the afternoon crowd had thinned out to a few shop girls straggling home for the night and a man waiting at the bus stop.

"If it is a fake," she said, "will you...still believe me, Jordan?"

He didn't answer at first. That brief silence was enough to send despair knifing through her. He said at last, "Too much has happened for me *not* to believe you."

"But you have doubts."

"I have questions."

She laughed softly. Bitterly. "That makes two of us."

"Why, for instance, would Delancey have bought a replica? He certainly had the money to spend. He would have insisted on the genuine item."

"He might have been misled. Believed it was the real Eye of Kashmir."

"No, Guy was a discerning collector. He'd get an expert's advice before he bought it. You saw how easily

Mr. Jacobs identified that stone as man made. Guy would have learned that fact just as easily."

She gave a sigh of frustration. "You're right, of course. He would have had it looked at. Which means whoever appraised it was either crooked or incompetent or…" Suddenly she turned to him. "Or he was right on the money."

"I told you, Guy would never buy a reproduction."

"Of course he wouldn't. He bought the real Eye of Kashmir."

"Then how did he wind up with a fake?"

"Someone switched it for the real one. *After* Guy bought it." She was moving around the room now, her mind racing. "Think about it, Jordan. Before you buy a painting or antique, aren't you very careful to confirm it's genuine?"

"Naturally."

"But after you've bought it—say, a painting—and you've had it hanging on your wall for a while, you don't bother to have it reauthenticated."

Slowly Jordan nodded. "I think I'm beginning to understand. The dagger was replaced sometime after Guy bought it."

"And he didn't realize! He has so many collectibles in that house. He'd never notice that one little dagger wasn't quite the same."

"All right, time for a reality check here. You're saying that our theoretical thief commissioned an exact replica. And then he managed to switch daggers without Guy's knowledge? That would require a hell of a lot of inside knowledge. Remember how much trouble we had, locating the Eye? Without Whitmore's help, we never would've found that hiding place."

"You're right, of course," she admitted with a sigh. "A thief would have to know exactly where it was hidden. Which means it had to be someone very close to Delancey."

"And that would eliminate an outside thug. Van Weldon's or otherwise." He shook his head. "I don't want to say 'the butler did it.' But I think the list of suspects is rather short."

"What about Guy's family?"

"Estranged. None of them even live in the neighborhood."

"One of his lovers, then?"

"He did have a few." He aimed an inquiring glance her way.

"I wasn't one of them," she snapped. "So who *has* Guy romanced in the last month?"

"Only one woman I'm aware of. Veronica Cairncross."

There was a long silence. "You're the one who knows her, Jordan," said Clea. "You two are friends…"

He frowned, troubled by the possibilities. "I've always considered her a bit wild. Impulsive. And not altogether moral. But a thief…"

"She's someone to consider. There's the household staff, as well. Come to think of it, anyone could've slipped into that bedroom. I got in. So did you. If it hadn't been for old Whitmore, we would have slipped out without anyone being the wiser."

Jordan went very still. "Whitmore," he said.

"What about him?"

"I'm thinking."

She watched in bewilderment as he muttered the

name again, more softly. With sudden comprehension he looked at her. "Yes, Whitmore's the key."

She laughed. "You're not back to saying the butler did it?"

"No, it's the fact he was *home* that night! Veronica assured me it was Whitmore's night off. That the house would be empty. But when I broke in, he was right there. All this time I assumed she'd made a mistake. But what if it wasn't a mistake? What if she *wanted* the butler home?"

"Why on earth would she?"

"To raise the alarm. And notify the police."

"What would be the point?"

"There'd be an official record of a break-in. If Guy ever discovered the real Eye of Kashmir was gone, he'd assume the theft occurred that night. The night Whitmore raised the alarm."

"A night Veronica had an airtight alibi. Your sister's engagement party."

Jordan nodded. "It'd never occur to him that the switch was made earlier. *Before* that night. By an acquaintance so intimate she knew exactly where the Eye was hidden. An acquaintance who'd been in and out of that bedroom." Jordan slapped his temple in frustration. "All this time I thought *she* was the thick one. *I'm* the idiot."

Clea shook her head. "You're giving Veronica an awful lot of credit. How would she manage to commission such an accurate replica? It would take time. The forger would need to work from the original. I hardly think Guy would let her borrow it for a week. So where would this replica come from?"

"There's always the previous owner," said Jordan.

Clea's mouth went dry. *Van Weldon. The previous owner was Van Weldon.*

She went to stand beside him, close enough to lean her cheek against the fine wool of his jacket. Softly she said, "Veronica. Van Weldon. Could there be a link?"

"I don't know. She's never mentioned Van Weldon's name."

"He has connections everywhere. People who owe him. People who are afraid of him."

"It seems unlikely."

"But how well do you really *know* her, Jordan? How well do we really know anyone?"

He said nothing. He stood very still, not reaching for her, not even looking at her. Aching, she thought, *Oh, Jordan. How well do I really know you? And what little you know of me is the very worst....*

They stood just inches apart, yet she felt cold and alone as they both gazed out at that street where the shadows crept toward dusk. She reached out to him. His shoulder was rigid. Unresponsive to her touch.

"Clea," he said softly. "I want you to go into the back room. Ask Herr Schuster if there's a rear door."

"What?"

"There's a man standing at the bus stop. See him?"

She focused on the street. And on the man standing there. He wore a brown suit and carried a black umbrella, and every so often he glanced at his watch, as though late for some appointment. No wonder. He'd been waiting for his bus a long time now.

Slowly Clea backed away from the window.

Jordan didn't move, but continued to gaze out calmly at the street. "He's let two go past now," he said. "I don't think he's waiting for a bus."

She fought the impulse to run headlong through that rear door. She had no idea if the man could see them through those dusty front windows. She managed to stroll casually to the rear of the shop, then she pushed through the door, into the workshop.

Herr Schuster was at his jeweler's bench. "I am afraid the news is disappointing. The star sapphire—"

"Is there a back way out?" she asked.

"Excuse me?"

"Another exit?"

Jordan stepped in behind Clea. "There's a man following us."

Herr Schuster rose to his feet in alarm. "I have a back door." At a frantic shuffle, he led them through the workshop's clutter and opened the door to what looked like a closet. Dusty coats hung inside. He shoved the old garments aside. "There is a latch at the rear. The door leads to the alley. Around the corner is South Molton. You wish me to call the police?"

"No, don't. We'll be fine," said Jordan.

"The man—he is dangerous?"

"We don't know."

"The dagger—do you want it back?"

"It's not genuine?"

Regretfully Herr Schuster shook his head. "The sapphire is synthetic corundum."

"Then keep it as a souvenir. But don't show it to anyone."

A buzzer suddenly rang in the workshop. Herr Schuster glanced toward the front room. "Someone has come in the door. Hurry, go!"

Jordan grabbed Clea's hand and pulled her into the closet. Instantly the coats were slid back in place and the door shut on them. In the sudden darkness they blindly fumbled along the rear door for the latch and pushed.

They stumbled out into an alley. At once they tore around the corner onto South Molton Street. They didn't stop running until they'd reached the Bond Street Underground.

Aboard the train to Tottenham Court Road, Clea sat in stunned silence as the blackness of the tunnel swept past her window. Only when Jordan had taken her hand in his did she realize how chilled her fingers were, like icicles in the warmth of his grasp.

"He won't give up," she said. "He'll never give up."

"Then we have to stay one step ahead."

Not we, she thought. *I'm the one Van Weldon wants. The one he'll kill.*

She stared down at the hand now holding hers. A hand with all the strength a woman could ever need, could ever want. In a few short days she'd come to trust Jordan in a way she'd never trusted anyone. And she understood him well enough by now to know the gentleman's code of honor by which he operated—an absurd concept under these brutal circumstances. He would never abandon a woman in need.

So she would have to abandon him.

She chose her words carefully. Painfully. "I think it would be better if…" The words caught in her throat. She forced herself to stare ahead. Anywhere but at Jordan. "I think I would be better off on my own. I can move faster that way."

"You mean without me."

"That's right." Her chin slanted up as she found the courage to keep talking. "I can't afford to spend my time worrying about you. You'll be fine holed up in Chetwynd."

"And where will you go?"

She smiled nonchalantly. "Some place warm. The south of France, maybe. Or Sicily. Anywhere I can be on a beach."

"If you live long enough to climb into a bathing suit."

The train pulled in to the next stop. Abruptly he pulled her to her feet and snapped, "We're getting off."

She followed him off the train and up the station steps to Oxford Street. He was silent, his shoulders squared in anger. So much for self-sacrifice, she thought. All she'd managed to do was turn him against her. And why the hell was he mad at her, anyway? It wasn't as if she'd rejected him. She'd simply offered him the chance to leave.

The chance to live.

"I was only thinking of *you,* you know," she said.

"I'm quite aware of that."

"Then why are you ticked off at me?"

"You don't give me much credit."

"There's nothing more you can do for me. You have to admit, it doesn't make sense for both of us to get our heads blown off. If we split up, they'll forget all about you."

"Will *you* forget all about me?"

She halted on the sidewalk. "Does it matter?"

"Doesn't it?" He turned to face her. They stood looking at each other, an obstruction to all the pedestrians moving along the sidewalk.

"I don't know what you're getting at," she said. "I'm sorry it has to end this way, Jordan. But I have to look out for number one. Which means I can't have you around. I don't *want* you around."

"You don't know what the hell you want."

"All right, maybe I don't. But I do know what's best for *you*."

"So do I," he said, and reached for her. His arms went around her back and his mouth came down on hers in a branding kiss that held no gentleness, brooked no resistance.

Far from protesting, she welcomed the assault, thrilled to the surge of his tongue into her mouth, the hungry roving of his hands up and down her back. She could not hide her desire from him, nor could he from her. They were both helpless and hopeless, lost to the crazy yearnings that always burst forth whenever they touched. It had been this way from the start. It would always be this way. A look, a touch, and suddenly the tension would be sizzling between them.

His lips slid to her cheek, then her ear, and the tickle of his hot breath sent a tremor of delight down her spine. "Have I made myself clear?" he whispered.

She moaned. "About what?"

"About staying together."

The need was still too strong between them. She pulled away and took a step back, fighting the urge to touch him again. *You and your crazy sense of honor,* she thought, staring up at his face. *It will get you killed. And I couldn't stand that.*

"I'm not exactly helpless, you know," she said.

He smiled. "Still, you have to admit I've come in handy on occasion."

"On occasion," she agreed.

"You need me, Clea. To beat Van Weldon."

She shook her head. "I've already tried. Now there's nothing else I can do."

"Yes, there is."

"The dagger's gone. I have no evidence. I can't see any way to get at him."

"There is a way." He moved closer. "Veronica Cairn-cross."

"What about her?"

"I've been trying to piece it all together. And I think you're right. She could be the key to all this. I've known Ronnie for years. She's a jolly girl, great fun to be around. But she's a gambler. And a big spender. Over the last few years she's run up a fortune in debts. A scam like this could've saved her skin."

"But now we're back to the problem of how she commissioned that reproduction," said Clea. "How'd she get her hands on the original? It belonged to Van Weldon. Did she buy it from him? Borrow it from him?"

"Or steal it from him?"

Clea shuddered at the thought. "No one's stupid enough to cross Van Weldon."

"Somehow, though, that dagger found its way from Van Weldon into Delancey's hands. Veronica could be the link between them. That's what we have to find out." Jordan paused, thinking. "She and Oliver have a town house here in London. They spend their weekdays here. Which means they'd be in town now."

Clea frowned at him. She didn't like this new shift of conversation. "What, exactly, are you thinking?"

He eyed her hair. "I'm thinking," he said, "that it's time for you to try a wig."

Archie MacLeod hung up the phone and looked at Richard Wolf and Hugh Tavistock. "They're in London. My man just spoke to an official from Lloyd's. Jordan and Clea Rice paid a visit there around four o'clock today. Unfortunately the man they met with—an Anthony Vauxhall—wasn't aware of the investigation. He just happened to mention their visit to his superior. By the time we found out, Jordan and Clea Rice had already left."

"So we know they're still alive," said Hugh.

"As of this afternoon, anyway."

They were sitting in Chetwynd's library, the room they'd turned into a crisis headquarters. Hugh had hurried back to Chetwynd that morning, and all day the three of them had sat waiting for word from their police contacts.

This last news was good. Jordan had made it safely to London.

Not that Richard was surprised. In the few months he'd known his future brother-in-law, he'd come to appreciate Jordan's resourcefulness. In a pinch there were few men Richard would rather have at his side.

Clea Rice, too, was a survivor. Together, they might just stay alive.

Richard looked at Hugh. The older man was looking drained and weary. The worry showed plainly in Hugh's round face. "That price on Clea Rice's head will be drawing every contract man in Europe," said Richard.

"Surely, Lord Lovat," said MacLeod, "you can marshal some help from your intelligence contacts. We have to find them."

Hugh shook his head. "My Jordan was reared in the lap of the intelligence business. All these years he's been listening. Learning. He's probably picked up a trick or two. Even with help, it won't be easy to track him down. Which means it won't be easy for Van Weldon to track him down, either."

"You don't know Victor Van Weldon the way I do," said MacLeod. "At this point, he'll be willing to pay a fortune to get rid of Clea Rice. I'm afraid money is the world's best motivator."

"Not money," said Richard. "Fear. That's what will keep Jordan alive."

"Blast it all," said Hugh. "Why do we know so little about this Victor Van Weldon, anyway? Is he so untouchable?"

"I'm afraid he is," admitted MacLeod. He sank into a chair by the fireplace. "Victor Van Weldon has always operated on the fringes of international law. Never quite crossing the boundaries into illegality. At least, never leaving any evidence of it. He hides behind a regiment of lawyers. Keeps homes in Gstaad, Brussels and probably a few places we haven't found out about. He's like some rare bird, almost never sighted, but very much alive."

"You can't dredge up any evidence against him?"

"We know he's involved in international arms shipments. Dabbles in the drug trade. But every time we think we have hard evidence, it disintegrates in our hands. Or a witness dies. Or documents vanish. For years it's been a source of frustration for me, how he manages to elude me. Only recently did I realize how many friends in high places he has, keeping him apprised of my every move. That's when I changed tactics. I picked out my own team of men. An independent team. We've spent the past six months gathering information on Van Weldon, ferreting out his Achilles' heel. We know he's sick—emphysema and heart failure. He hasn't much longer to live. Before he dies, I want him to face a little earthly justice."

"You sound like a man on crusade," said Richard.

"I've lost…people. Van Weldon's work." MacLeod looked at him. "It's something one doesn't forget. The face of a dying friend."

"How close are you now to building a case?"

"We have the foundations. We know Van Weldon took big losses last year. The European economy—it's affected even him. With his empire on the brink of ruin, he was bound to try something desperate. That's when the *Havelaar* went down. Eight men dead, a fortune lost at sea—all of it fully insured. I couldn't convince the Spanish authorities to foot the bill for a proper investigation. It would've required a salvage crew, ships and equipment. Van Weldon, we thought, had slipped away again. Then we heard about Clea Rice." MacLeod sighed. "Unfortunately, Miss Rice is not the sort of witness to base any prosecution on. Prison record. Family of thieves. Here we finally find a weapon against Van Weldon, and it's one that could backfire in court."

"So you can't use her as the basis of any legal case," said Hugh.

"No. We need something tangible. For instance, the artwork listed on the *Havelaar*'s manifest. We know bloody well it didn't go down with the ship. Van Weldon's stashed it somewhere. He's waiting for an opportunity to sell it off piece by piece. If we just knew where he's hidden it."

"It was supposedly shipped from Naples."

"We searched his Naples warehouse. We also searched— not always legally, mind you—every building we know he owns. We're talking about large items, not things you can just hide in a closet. Tapestries and oil paintings and even a few statues. Wherever he's keeping it, it's a large space."

"There must be a warehouse you don't know about yet."

"Undoubtedly."

"Interpol's not authorized to handle this alone," said Hugh. "You're going to need assistance." He reached for the telephone and began to dial. "It's not the customary way of doing things. But with Jordan's life at stake..."

Richard listened as Hugh made the contacts, called in old favors from Scotland Yard's Special Branch, as well as MI5—domestic intelligence. After he hung up, Hugh looked at Richard.

"Now I suggest we get to work ourselves," said Hugh.

"London?"

"Jordan's there. He may try to reach us. I want to be ready to respond."

"What I don't understand," said MacLeod, "is why he hasn't called you already."

"He's cautious," said Richard. "He knows the one thing Van Weldon expects him to do is contact us for help. Under the circumstances, Jordan's best strategy is to keep doing the *unexpected*."

"Precisely the way Clea Rice has operated all these weeks," observed MacLeod. "By doing the unexpected."

Van Weldon was waiting for the call. He picked up the receiver. "Well?"

"They're here," said Simon Trott. "They were spotted leaving Lloyd's of London, as you predicted."

"Is the matter concluded?"

There was a pause. "Unfortunately, no. They vanished off Brook Street—a jewelry store. The proprietor claims ignorance."

The news made Van Weldon's chest ache. He paused a moment to catch his breath, the whole time silently cursing Clea Rice. In all his years he'd never known such a tenacious opponent. She was like a thorn that couldn't be plucked out, and she seemed to keep burrowing ever deeper.

When he'd managed to catch his breath again, he said, "So she did go to Lloyd's. Did she take the dagger?"

"Yes. She must have been rather peeved to learn it was a fake."

"And the real Eye of Kashmir?"

"Safely back where it belongs. Or so I've been assured."

"The Cairncross woman brought us to the brink of disaster. She cannot go unpunished."

"I quite agree. What do you have in mind?"

"Something unpleasant," said Van Weldon. Veronica Cairncross was an opportunistic bitch. And a fool as well to think she could slip one over on them. Her greed had taken her too far this time, and she was going to regret it.

"Shall I see to Mrs. Cairncross myself?" asked Trott.

"Wait. First confirm the collection is safe. It must go on the market within the month."

"So soon after the *Havelaar?* Is that wise?"

Trott raised a good point. It was risky to release the artwork onto the market. To think of all those assets bundled away, untouchable, just when he needed them most! Last year he had overextended himself, had made a few too many commitments to a few too many cartels. Now he needed cash. Lots of it.

"I cannot wait," said Van Weldon. "It must be sold. In Hong Kong or Tokyo, we could fetch excellent prices, and without much notice. Buyers are discreet in Tokyo. See that the collection is moved."

"When?"

"The *Villafjord* is scheduled to dock in Portsmouth tomorrow. I will be on board."

"You…are coming here?" There was an undertone of dismay in Trott's voice. He *should* be dismayed. What had started as a minor difficulty had ballooned into a crisis, and Van Weldon was disgusted with his heir apparent. If Trott could not handle such simple matters as Veronica Cairncross and Clea Rice, how could he hope to assume the company's helm?

"I will see to the shipment myself," said Van Weldon. "In the meantime, I expect you to find Clea Rice."

"We have the Tavistocks under surveillance. Sooner or later, Jordan and the woman will surface."

Perhaps not, thought Van Weldon as he hung up. By now Clea Rice would be weary, demoralized. Her instinct would be to run as far and as fast as she could. That would take care of the problem—temporarily, at least.

Van Weldon felt better. He decided there was really no need to worry about Clea Rice. By now she'd be long gone from London.

It's what any sensible woman would do.

Chapter 12

At twelve-fifteen Veronica Cairncross left her London flat, climbed into a taxi and was driven to Sloane Street where she had lunch at a trendy little café. Afterward she strolled on foot toward Brompton Road, in the general direction of Harrods. She took her sweet time in one shop to purchase lingerie, and in another shop to try on a half-dozen pairs of shoes.

A disguised Clea observed all of this from a distance and with a growing sense of exasperation. Not only did this exercise seem more and more pointless, but also her long black wig was itchy, her sunglasses kept slipping down the bridge of her nose and her new short-heeled pumps were killing her. Perhaps she should have slipped into that same shoe shop where Veronica had spent so much time and picked up a pair of sneakers for herself. Not that she could have afforded anything in there. Veronica clearly frequented only the priciest establishments. *What is it like to be so idle and so rich?* Clea wondered as she trailed the elegant figure up Brompton Road. *Doesn't the woman ever get tired of constant partying and shopping?*

Oh, sure. The poor thing must be bored to tears.

She followed Veronica into Harrods. Inside she lingered a discreet distance away and watched Veronica sample perfumes, browse among scarves and handbags. Two hours later, loaded down with purchases, Veronica strolled out and hailed a taxi.

Clea scurried out after her and after a few frantic glances, spotted another taxi, this one with tinted windows. She climbed in.

Jordan was waiting in the back seat.

"There she goes," said Clea. "Stay with her."

Their driver, a grinning Sikh whom Jordan had hired for the day, expertly threaded the taxi into traffic and maintained a comfortable two-car distance behind Veronica's vehicle.

"Anything interesting happen?" asked Jordan.

"Not a thing. Lord, that woman can shop. She's way out of my league. Any trouble staying with me?"

"We were right behind you."

"I don't think she noticed a thing. Not me or the taxi." Sighing, Clea sat back and pulled off the wig. "This is getting us nowhere. So far all we've found out is that she has time and money on her hands. And a lot of both."

"Be patient. I know Ronnie, and when she gets nervous, she spends money like water. It's her way of blowing off stress. Judging by all the packages she was carrying, she's under a lot of stress right now."

Veronica's taxi had turned onto Kensington. They followed, skirting Kensington Gardens, and headed southwest.

"Now where's she going?" Clea sighed.

"Odd. She's not headed back to the flat."

Veronica's taxi led them out of the shopping district, into a neighborhood of business and office buildings. Only when the taxi stopped and let Veronica off at the curb did Jordan give a murmur of comprehension.

"Of course," he said. "Biscuits."

"What?"

"It's Oliver's company. Cairncross Biscuits." Jordan nodded at the sign on the building. "She's here to see her husband."

"Hardly a suspicious thing to do."

"Yes, it seems quite innocent, doesn't it?"

"Are you implying otherwise?"

"I'm just thinking about Oliver Cairncross. The firm's been in his family for generations. Appointment to the queen and all that…"

She studied Jordan's finely chiseled face as he mulled it over. *Such eyelashes he has,* she thought. No man had a right to such long eyelashes. Or such a kissable mouth. She could watch him for hours and never tire of the way his face crooked up on one side when he was thinking hard. *Oh, Jordan. How I'm going to miss you when this is over….*

"Cairncross biscuits are internationally known," said Jordan. "They're shipped all over the world."

"So?"

"So I wonder which firm is used to transport all those cookie crates. And what's really inside them."

"Uzis, you mean?" Clea shook her head. "I thought Oliver was supposed to be the innocent party. The cuckolded husband. Now you're saying *he's* the one in league with Van Weldon? Not Veronica?"

"Why not both of them?"

"She comes out again," said their driver.

Sure enough, Veronica had reappeared. She climbed back into her taxi.

"You wish me to follow her?" asked the Sikh.

"Yes. Don't lose her."

They didn't. They stayed on Veronica's tail all the way to Regent's Park. There Veronica alighted from the taxi and began to walk across Chester Terrace, toward the Tea House.

"Back into action." Clea sighed. "I hope it's not another two-hour hike." She pulled on a new wig—this one shoulder length and brown—and climbed out of the cab. "How do I look?"

"Irresistible."

She leaned inside and kissed him on the mouth. "You, too."

"Be careful."

"I always am."

"No, I mean it." He pulled her around by the wrist. His grip was insistent, reluctant to let go. "If there was any other way I could do it instead of you, I would —"

"She knows you too well, Jordan. She'd spot you in a second. Me, she'd scarcely recognize."

"Just don't let your guard down. Promise me."

She gave him a breezy grin that masked all the fears she had rattling inside. "And you promise not to vanish."

"I'll keep you right in view."

Still grinning, Clea turned and crossed Chester Terrace.

Veronica was well ahead of her. She seemed to be merely wandering, strolling toward Queen Mary's Rose

Garden, its season of bloom now past. There she lingered, every so often glancing at her watch. Oh, Lord, not waiting for another lover, Clea thought.

Without warning Veronica turned and began walking in Clea's direction.

Clea ducked under an arbor and pretended to inspect the label on the climbing rose. Veronica didn't even glance her way, but headed toward the Tea House.

After a moment Clea followed her.

Veronica had seated herself at a table, and she had a menu propped open in front of her. Clea took a seat two tables behind Veronica and sat facing the other way. At this hour the Tea House was relatively quiet, and she could hear Veronica's whiney voice ordering a pot of Darjeeling and iced cakes. *Now I'll waste another hour,* thought Clea, *waiting for that silly woman to have her tea.*

She glanced toward Cumberland Terrace. Sure enough, there was Jordan sitting on a bench, his face hidden behind a newspaper.

The waiter approached. Clea ordered a pot of Earl Grey and watercress sandwiches. Her tea had just arrived when a man crossed the dining terrace toward Veronica.

Clea caught only a glimpse of him as he moved past her table. He was fair haired, blonder than Jordan, with wide shoulders and a powerful frame—just the sort of hunk Veronica would probably go gaga over. Clea felt a spurt of irritation that yet another hour would be wasted while Veronica made cow eyes at her latest admirer.

"Mr. Trott," Veronica said crossly. "You're late. I've already ordered."

Clea heard the man's voice, speaking behind her, and in the midst of pouring tea, her hand froze.

"I have no time for tea," he said. "I came only to confirm the arrangements."

That was all he said, but his tone of command, the English coarsened by some unidentifiable accent, was enough to make Clea suck in a breath in panic. She didn't dare glance back over her shoulder; she didn't dare let him see her face.

She didn't need to see *his;* his voice was all she needed to recognize him.

She'd heard it before, floating above the sound of lapping Mediterranean waves and the growl of a boat's engine. She remembered how that same voice had cut through the darkness. Just before the bullets began to fly.

All her instincts were screaming at her to lurch from this table and flee. *But I can't,* she thought. *I can't do anything to draw his attention.*

So she sat unmoving, her hands gripping the table-cloth. So acutely did she sense the man's presence behind her, she was surprised that he didn't seem at all aware of *her.*

Her heartbeat thudding, she sat motionless at the table.

Trott watched Veronica light a cigarette and take in an unhurried drag of smoke. She seemed not in the least bit worried, which only proved what a stupid bitch she was, he decided. She thinks she's untouchable. She thinks her husband's too important to our operations. What she doesn't know is that we've already found a replacement for Oliver Cairncross.

Casually she exhaled a cloud of smoke. "The cargo's all there. Nothing missing. I told you it would be, didn't I?"

"Mr. Van Weldon is not pleased."

"Why, because I borrowed one of his precious little trinkets? It was only for a few weeks." Calmly she exhaled another cloud of smoke. "We've been stuck with your bloody crates for months now—at no small risk to ourselves. Why shouldn't I borrow what's in them? I got the dagger back, didn't I?"

"This is not the time or place to speak of it," cut in Trott. He passed a newspaper across the table to Veronica. "The information is circled. We'll expect it to be ready and waiting."

"At your beck and call, your highness," said Veronica, her voice dripping with mockery.

Trott pushed his chair back, preparing to leave. "What about compensation?" asked Veronica. "For all our trouble?"

"You'll have it. After all items are accounted for."

"Of course they will be," said Veronica. She blew out another cloud of smoke. "We're not fools, you know."

Clea heard the man's chair scrape back. He was rising to his feet. Instinctively she huddled closer to the table, afraid to be noticed. She forced herself to take a sip of tea, to pretend no interest whatsoever in the monster standing behind her.

When she heard him walk away, she went almost limp with relief. She glanced back.

Veronica was still sitting at the table, gazing down at a newspaper. After a moment she ripped off half a page, folded it and stuffed it in her purse. Then she, too, rose and left.

It took a while before Clea's nerves steadied enough for her to stand. Veronica was already walking out of the park. Clea started to follow, but her legs were shaking too hard. She took a few steps, faltered and stopped.

By then Jordan had realized something was wrong. She heard his footsteps, and then his arm was around her waist, supporting her, steadying her.

"We can't stay here," she whispered. "Have to hide—"

"What happened?"

"It was him—"

"Who?"

"The man from the *Cosima!*" Wildly she glanced around, her gaze sweeping the park for sight of the blond man.

"Clea, what man?"

She focused at last on Jordan. His gaze seemed to steady her. He held her face in his hand, the pressure of his fingers warming through her numbness.

"Tell me," he said.

She swallowed. "I've heard his voice before. The night the *Havelaar* went down. I was in the water, swimming alongside the lifeboat. He was the one who—the one who—" She blinked, and tears spilled down her face. Softly she finished, "The one who ordered his men to shoot."

Jordan stared at her. "The man with Veronica? You're absolutely certain?"

"He passed by my table. I recognized his voice. I'm sure it was him."

Jordan gave a quick glance around the park. Then he

pulled Clea close, wrapping his arm protectively around her shoulder. "Let's get into the car."

"Wait." She went back to Veronica's table and snatched up the discarded newspaper.

"What's that for?" asked Jordan.

"Veronica left it. I want to see what she tore out."

Their taxi was waiting. As soon as they climbed in the back seat, Jordan ordered, "Move. See that we're not followed."

The Sikh driver grinned at them in the mirror. "A most interesting day," he declared, and sent the cab screeching into traffic.

Jordan draped his jacket over Clea's shoulders and took her hands in his. "All right," he coaxed gently. "Tell me what happened."

Clea took a shaky breath and sank back against the seat. No one was following them. Jordan's hand, warm and steady, seemed to radiate enough courage for them both.

"Did you hear what they were saying?"

"No. They were speaking too softly. And I was afraid to get any closer. After I realized who he was..." She shuddered, thinking of the man's voice. In her nightmares she'd heard that same voice drifting across the black Mediterranean waters. She'd remember the explosion of gunfire. And she'd remember Giovanni, slumping across the lifeboat...

Her head came up. "I do remember something. Veronica called him by name. Mr. Trott."

"You're sure that was it? Trott?"

She nodded. "I'm sure."

Jordan's grip tightened around hers. "Veronica. If I ever get my hands around her elegant little neck..."

"At least now we know. She's the link to Van Weldon. Delancey paid for the Eye. She stole it back. Someone earned a nice profit. And the only loser was Guy Delancey."

"What about the newspaper?"

Clea looked down at the folded pages. "I saw Veronica tear something out."

Jordan glanced at the newspaper's date, then tapped their taxi driver on the shoulder. "Excuse me. You wouldn't happen to have a copy of today's *Times?*"

"But of course. And the *Daily Mail,* as well."

"Just the *Times* will do."

The driver reached over and pulled out a slightly mangled newspaper from the glove compartment. He handed it back to Jordan.

"The top of page thirty-five and six," said Clea. "That's what she's torn out."

"I'm looking for it." Jordan thumbed quickly through the driver's copy. "Here it is. Top of page thirty-five. Article about the Manchester slums. Building renovations. Another about horse breeding in Ireland."

"Try the other side."

Jordan flipped the page. "Let's see. Scandal in some ad agency. Drop-off in the fishing harvest. And..." He paused. "Today's shipping schedule for Portsmouth." He looked at Clea.

"That's it! That has to be it. One of their ships must be arriving in port."

"Or leaving." He sat back, deep in thought. "If Van Weldon has a vessel in Portsmouth, then it's here for either a delivery..."

"Or a pickup," she finished for him.

They looked at each other, both struck by the same startling thought.

"It's taking on cargo," she said. "It must be."

"It could be purely legitimate cargo."

"But there's the chance…" She glanced up as they pulled in front of their hotel. At once she was climbing out the door. "We have to call Portsmouth. Check which vessels are Van Weldon's."

"Clea, wait—"

But she was already hurrying into the building.

By the time he'd settled with their driver and followed her up to the room, Clea was already on the phone. A moment later she hung up and turned to Jordan in triumph.

"There's a *Villafjord* scheduled to dock at five this afternoon. She sails again at midnight. And she's registered to the Van Weldon company."

For a moment he stared at her without speaking. Then he said flatly, "I'm going to call the police." He reached for the phone.

She grabbed his hand. "Don't! Jordan."

"We have to alert the authorities. It could be the best chance they'll have to nail Van Weldon."

"That's why we can't blow it! What if we're wrong? What if his ship's here to take on a cargo of—of undies or something? We'll look like a pair of idiots. So will the police." She shook her head. "We can't tell them until we know *exactly* what's on board."

"But the only way to learn that is…" He froze in the midst of that thought. "Don't you even dare suggest it."

"Just one little tiny peek inside."

"*No.* This is the perfect time to call in Richard. Let him—or someone else—handle it."

"But I don't trust anyone else!"

Again he reached for the phone.

Again she grabbed his hand and held on tightly. "If we let too many people in on this," she said, "I guarantee there'll be a leak. Van Weldon will hear about it, and that'll be it for our big chance. Jordan, we have to wait till the last minute. And we have to be sure of what they'll find."

"You don't really think you can stroll aboard that ship and have a look around, do you?"

"When it comes to making unauthorized entries, I had the world's best teacher."

"Uncle Walter? He got caught, remember?"

"*I* won't get caught."

"Because you're not going anywhere *near* the *Villafjord*." He shook off her hand and began to dial the telephone.

Desperately she snatched away the receiver. "You're not doing this!" she cried.

"Clea." He heaved a sigh of frustration. "Clea, you have to trust me on this."

"No, you have to trust *me*. Trust *my* judgment. *I'm* the one with everything to lose!"

"I know that. But we're both tired. We're going to make mistakes. Now's the time to call the police and put an end to all this. To get back to our lives—our *real* lives. Don't you see?"

She looked into his eyes. *Yes, I see,* she thought. *You've had enough of running. Enough of me. You want your own life back, and I don't blame you.*

Defiantly she raised her chin. "I want to go home, too. I'm sick of hotels and strange beds and dyed hair.

I want this all to be over with just as much as you do. That's why I say we do it *my* way."

"Your way's too bloody risky. The police—"

"I told you, I don't trust them!" Agitated, she paced over to the window, paced back. "I've survived this long only because I didn't trust anyone. *I'm* the only one I can count on."

"You can count on me," he said quietly.

She shook her head and laughed. "In the real world, darling, it's every man for himself. Remember that. You can't trust anyone." She turned and looked at him. "Not even me."

"But I do."

"Then you're crazy."

"Why? Because you're an ex-con? Because you've made a few mistakes in your life?" He moved toward her and took her by the shoulders. "Are you *afraid* to have me believe in you?"

She gave a nonchalant toss of her head. "I'd hate to disappoint anyone."

He cupped her face in his hands and lowered his mouth to hers. "I have complete faith," he whispered. "And so should you."

His kiss was sweet enough to break her heart. And that frightened her, because she knew now there could be no clean parting between them, no easy goodbyes. The break would be painful and haunting and bitter.

And inevitable.

He pulled back. "I'm going to have to trust you now, Clea. To do as I ask. To stay in this room and let me take care of this."

"But I—"

He silenced her by pressing a finger to her lips. "No

arguments, I'm going to assert a little male authority here. Something I damn well should have done ages ago. You're going to wait for me. Here, in this room. Understood?"

She looked at his unyielding expression. Then she gave a sigh. "Understood," she said meekly.

He smiled and kissed her.

She smiled, too, as he walked out of the room. But when she went to the window and watched him leave the building, her smile faded. *What makes you think I'm so damn trustworthy?* she thought.

Turning, she saw Jordan's jacket, which she'd left draped over a chair. Impulsively she thrust her hand in the pocket and pulled out the gold watch. She flipped open the dented cover and looked at the name engraved inside: Bernard Tavistock.

And she thought, This will end it. Here and now. It's going to end anyway, and I might as well do it sooner than later. If I take this watch, something he treasures, I'll cut the ties. Cleanly. Decisively. After all, that's what I am. A thief. An ex-con. He'll be relieved to see me go.

She thrust the watch into her own pocket. Maybe she'd mail it back to him someday. When she was good and ready. When she could think of him without feeling that painful twist of her heart.

Glancing out the window, she saw that Jordan was nowhere in sight. *Goodbye,* she thought. *Goodbye, my darling gentleman.*

A moment later she, too, left the room.

Chapter 13

Richard Wolf was on the telephone to Brussels when the doorbell rang. He paid it no attention—the butler would see to any visitors. Only when he heard Davis's polite knock on the study door did Richard break off his conversation.

The butler, looking oddly uncertain, stood in the doorway. It was something Richard hadn't gotten the hang of, dealing with all these servants. His Yankee sense of privacy was always being violated by all the maids and butlers and underbutlers whom the Tavistocks insisted upon keeping underfoot.

"Pardon the interruption, Mr. Wolf," said Davis. "But there's a foreign gentleman at the door. He insists upon speaking to you at once."

"Foreign?"

"A, er, Sikh, I believe." Davis made a whirling gesture over his head. "Judging by the turban."

"Did he say what his business was?"

"He said he would speak only to you."

Richard cut the call short and followed Davis to the front door.

There was indeed a Sikh waiting on the front step, a short, pleasant-looking fellow with a trim beard and a gold tooth. "Mr. Wolf?" he inquired.

"I'm Richard Wolf."

"You called for a taxi."

"I'm afraid I didn't."

Without a word the Sikh handed an envelope to Richard.

Richard glanced in the envelope. Inside was a single gold cuff link. It was inscribed with the initials J.C.T.

Jordan's.

Calmly Richard nodded and said, "Oh, right. Of course. I'd forgotten all about that appointment. Let me get my briefcase."

While the Sikh waited on the doorstep, Richard ducked back into the study, slid a 9 mm automatic into his shoulder holster and reemerged carrying an empty briefcase.

The Sikh directed him to a taxi at the curb.

Neither of them said a thing as the car moved through traffic. The Sikh drove exactly the way one expected of a cab driver—calmly. Recklessly.

"Are we going some place in particular?" asked Richard.

"Harrods. You will stay there half an hour. Visit all the floors. Perhaps make a purchase. Then you'll return to my taxi. You will recognize it by the number—twenty-three. I will wait for you at the curb."

"What am I to expect?"

The Sikh grinned in the rearview mirror. "I do not know. I am only the driver." He paused. "We are being followed."

"I know," said Richard.

At Harrods Richard got out and entered the store. Inside he did as instructed, wandering about the various departments. He bought a silk scarf for Beryl and a tie for his father back in Connecticut. He was aware of two men lingering nearby, a short man and a blond man. They were good—it was a full five minutes before he noticed them, and only because he'd glimpsed them in a mirror as he tried on top hats. He lost them briefly in the gourmet foods section, but picked them up again in housewares. If Jordan hoped to make contact, it was going to be difficult. Richard knew he could shake these guys if he wanted to. But then he'd probably shake Jordan, as well.

A half hour later he walked out of Harrods. He spotted taxi number twenty-three parked across the street, the Sikh driver still sitting patiently behind the wheel.

He crossed the street and climbed in the back seat of the taxi. "No luck," he said. "I was watched the whole time. Is there a backup plan?"

"This *is* the plan," said a familiar voice.

Richard glanced up in surprise at the rearview mirror, at the face of the bearded, turbaned driver. Jordan's brown eye winked back at him.

"Gotcha," said Jordan, and pulled the taxi into traffic.

"What the hell's going on?"

"Little game of wits. How am I doing so far?"

"Splendidly. You outsmarted me." Richard glanced back and spotted the same car following them.

"I see them," said Jordan.

"Where's Clea Rice?"

"A safe place. But things are coming to a head. We need help."

"Jordan, Interpol's already stepped in. They want Van Weldon's head. They'll arrange for the woman's safety."

"How do I know we can trust them?"

"They'd been watching over her for weeks. Until you two shook them off."

"Veronica's working for Van Weldon. Oliver may be, as well."

Richard, stunned, fell momentarily silent.

"You see, it reaches all levels," said Jordan. "It's like an octopus. Tentacles everywhere. The only people I can really count on are you, Beryl and Uncle Hugh. And you may regret hearing from me at all."

"We've been waiting for you to contact us. Hugh's calling in old favors. You'll be in good hands, I'll see to it myself. MacLeod's just waiting for the chance to move on Van Weldon."

"MacLeod?"

"Interpol. That was his man on the train platform. The one who saved your lives."

Jordan chewed on that piece of information for a moment. "If we come in, how will it be arranged?"

"Through your uncle. Scotland Yard will oversee. Whenever you're ready."

Jordan was silent as he dodged around a tight knot of traffic. "I'm ready," he said at last.

"And the woman?"

"Clea'll take some convincing. But she's tired. I think she's ready to come in, too."

"How shall we do it, then?"

"Sloane Square, the Underground. Make it an hour from now—eight-thirty."

"I'll let Hugh know."

They were coming up on the Tavistocks' London residence, one in a row of elegant Georgian town houses. The car was still following them.

Jordan pulled over to the curb. "One more thing, Richard."

"Yes?"

"There's a ship docking this afternoon in Portsmouth. The *Villafjord*."

"Van Weldon's?"

"Yes. My guess is, she'll be taking on cargo tonight. I suggest the police perform a little unannounced inspection before she leaves port."

"What's the cargo?"

"It'll be a surprise."

Richard stepped out and made a conspicuous point of paying for the ride. Then he walked up the steps and entered the house. As Jordan drove off, Richard saw that the car that had followed them remained parked outside the Tavistock residence. It was just as he'd expected. The men were assigned to watch him; they had no interest in any Sikh driver.

All the tension suddenly left his body. Only then did he realize how edgy he'd been.

And how close to the precipice they'd been dancing.

Back at the hotel, Jordan parked the taxi a block away, and sat for a moment in the driver's seat, watching to see if any cars had followed him. When he saw nothing suspicious, he stripped off his beard and turban, got out and headed for the building.

Trust me, he thought as he climbed the stairs. *You have to learn to trust me.* He knew it would be a long, slow process, one that might take a lifetime. Perhaps it was too late. Perhaps all the damage done in childhood had robbed Clea forever of her faith in other people. Could they live with that?

Could she?

Only then did he realize that, lately, all his thoughts of the future seemed to include *her.*

Sometime in the past week, the shift had occurred. Where once he would have thought *I,* now he thought *we.* That's what came of sharing so much, so intensely. It was both the reward and the consequence, this link between them.

Trust me, he thought, and opened the door.

The room was empty.

He stood staring at the bed, suddenly, painfully aware of the silence. He went into the bathroom; it was empty, as well. He paced back to the bedroom and saw that her purse was gone. And he saw his jacket, lying draped across a chair.

He picked up the jacket and noticed at once that it was lighter than usual. That something was missing. Reaching into the pocket, he discovered that his father's gold watch was missing.

In its place was a note.

"It was fun while it lasted. Clea."

With a groan of frustration, he crumpled the paper in his fist. Blast the woman! She'd picked his pockets! And then she'd headed for…where?

The answer was only too frightening.

It was eight o'clock. She'd had a solid three hours' head start.

He ran back down the stairs to the taxi. First he'd swing past Sloane Square, to pick up some Scotland Yard assistance. And then it'd be on to Portsmouth, where a certain little burglar was, at this moment, probably sneaking up the gangplank of a ship.

If she wasn't already dead.

The fence was higher than she'd expected. Clea crouched in the thickening gloom outside the Cairn-cross Biscuits complex and stared up in dismay at the barbed wire lacing the top of the chain link. This was not the usual penny ante security one expected for a biscuit warehouse. What were they afraid of? An attack by the Cookie Monster? The fence ringed the entire complex, interrupted only by the main gate, which was padlocked for the night. Floodlights shone down on the perimeter, leaving only intermittent patches of shadow. Judging by the fortune invested in security, there was more than just biscuits being stored in that warehouse.

Right on the money, she thought. *Something else is going on in there besides the manufacture of teatime treats.*

It had required only a small leap of logic to lead her to the Cairncross warehouse on the outskirts of London. If Van Weldon's ship was taking on illicit cargo tonight, then here was the obvious holding place for that cargo. Legitimate trucks were probably in and out of here all the time, pulling up to that handy warehouse platform. If a truck showed up tonight to pick up a load of crates, no one in the neighborhood would bat an eyelash.

Very clever, Van Weldon, she thought. *But this time I'm one step ahead of you.*

She'd be ahead of the authorities, as well. By the time Jordan and his precious police converged on that Portsmouth dock, there'd be no telling how many people would know about the forthcoming raid. Or how much warning Van Weldon would have. Now was the time to view the evidence—before Van Weldon had a chance to change plans.

The sound of someone whistling sent Clea scrambling for the cover of bushes. From her hiding place she watched a security guard stroll past, inside the fence. He had a gun strapped to his hip. He moved at a leisurely pace, pausing to flick away a cigarette and crush the butt with his shoe. Then, lighting up another, he continued his circuit.

Clea timed the gap between his appearances. Seven minutes. She waited, let him go around again. This time it was six minutes. Six minutes, max, to get through the fence and into the building. The fence was no problem; a few snips of the wire cutter she'd brought and she'd be in the complex. It was the warehouse that worried her. Those locks might take a while to bypass, and if the guard circled around too early, she'd be trapped.

She had to take the chance.

She snipped a few links in the fence, then hid as the guard came around. The instant he vanished around the corner she cut the last link, scrambled under with her knapsack and dashed across the expanse of pavement to the warehouse side door.

One glance at the lock told her she was in for some trouble. It was a brand-new pin tumbler, and six minutes might not be enough to bypass it. She set her watch alarm for five minutes. Holding a penlight in her teeth, she set to work.

First she inserted an L-shaped tension wrench and gently applied pressure to slide apart the plug and cylinder plates. Next she inserted a lifter pick, with which she gingerly lifted the first lock pin. It slid up with a soft click.

One down, six pins to go.

The next five pins were a piece of cake. It was the seventh one—the last—that kept tripping her up. She felt the minutes tick by, felt the sweat beading on her upper lip as she struggled to lift that seventh pin. Just one more click and she'd be in the door. Interrupt the effort now, and she'd be back to square one.

Her watch alarm gave a beep.

She kept working, gambling on the chance she'd conquer that last pin in the seconds that remained. She was so close, so close.

Too late, she heard the sound of whistling again. The guard was approaching her corner of the building!

She'd never make it back under the fence in time. Neither was there any cover along the building. She had only one route of escape.

Straight up.

Sheer panic sent her clambering like a monkey up a flimsy-looking drainpipe, seeking the cover of the shadows above.

As the guard rounded the corner, she pressed herself to the wall, afraid to move a muscle, afraid even to breathe. A few feet below, the guard stopped. Pulse hammering, Clea watched as he lighted a fresh cigarette and inhaled deeply. Then, with a satisfied sigh, he continued his circuit. He rounded the next corner without a backward glance.

Clea had to make a quick choice: should she try that bloody lock again or keep climbing? Glancing up, she traced the course of the drainpipe to the three-story-high roofline. There might be another way in from there. Though the drainpipe looked flimsy, so far it had supported her weight.

She began to climb.

Seconds later she scrambled up over the edge and dropped onto the rooftop.

A shadowy expanse of asphalt tile lay before her. She started across it, moving past the whirring fans of vents. At last she came to a rooftop door—locked, of course. Another pin tumbler. She set to work with her tension wrench and lifter pick.

In two minutes flat she had the door open.

At her feet a narrow stairway dropped away into the darkness. She descended the stairs, pushed through another door and entered the vast cavern of the warehouse. Here the area was lighted, and she could see rows of crates. All of them were stamped Cairncross Biscuits, London.

She grabbed a crowbar from a tool bin and pried open one of the crates, releasing the fragrant waft of cookies. Inside she found tins with the distinctive red-and-yellow Cairncross logo. The crate did, indeed, contain biscuits.

Frustrated, she glanced around at the other crates. She'd never be able to search them all! Only then did she spot the closed double doors in the far wall.

With mounting excitement she approached the doors.

They were locked. There were no windows, so it was unlikely there was an office beyond.

She picked the lock.

A rush of cooled air spilled out the open door. Air-conditioned, she thought. Climate control? She found the light switch and flicked it on.

The room was filled with crates, each stamped with the Cairncross Biscuits logo. These crates, however, were a variety of sizes. Several were huge enough to house a standing man.

With the crowbar she pried off one of the lids and discovered a fluffy mound of wood shavings. Plunging both arms into the packing, she encountered something solid buried within. She dug into the shavings and the top of the object emerged, its marble surface smooth and gleaming under the lights.

It was the head of a statue, a noble youth with a crown of olive leaves.

Clea, her hands shaking with excitement, pulled a camera from her knapsack and began to snap photos. She took three shots of the statue, then reclosed the lid. She pried open a second crate.

Somewhere in the building, metal clanged.

She froze, listening, and heard the growl of a truck, the protesting squeal of a bay door being shoved open along its tracks. At once she killed the room lights. Opening the door a crack, she peered out into the warehouse.

The loading gate was wide open. A truck had backed up to the platform, and the driver was swinging open the rear doors.

Veronica and the blond man were walking in Clea's direction.

Clea jerked back and shut the door. Frantically she waved her penlight around the room. No other exit. No place to hide except…

Voices were speaking right outside the door.

She grabbed her knapsack, scrambled into the open crate and pulled the lid over her head.

Through the cracks in the wood she saw the room's lights come on.

"It's all here, as you can see," said Veronica. "Would you care to check the crates yourself, Mr. Trott? Or do you trust me now?"

"I have no time for that. They must be moved immediately."

"I hope Mr. Van Weldon appreciates the trouble we've gone to, keeping these safe. He did promise there'd be compensation."

"You've already taken yours."

"What do you mean?"

"Your profit from selling the Eye. That should suffice."

"That was *my* idea! *My* profit. Just because I borrowed the bloody thing for a few weeks…"

There was a momentary pause. Then Clea heard Veronica suck in a sharp breath. "Put the gun away, Mr. Trott."

"Move away from the crates."

"You can't—you wouldn't—" Suddenly Veronica laughed, a shrill, hysterical sound. "You *need* us!"

"Not any longer," said Trott.

Clea flinched at the sound of a gun firing. Three bullets in rapid succession. She pressed her hand to her mouth, clamped it there to stifle the cry that rose up in her throat. She felt as if all the air had been sucked out of the crate and she was suffocating in her fear, choking on silent tears.

Then she heard the sounds of terrified sobbing. Veronica's. She was still alive.

"Just a warning, Mrs. Cairncross," said Trott. "Next time, I'll hit my target."

Trott crossed to the doorway and called out, "In here! Get these crates in the truck!"

More footsteps approached—two men and a squeaky loading cart.

"The large one first," said Trott.

Clea heard the cart move closer, then the men grunted in unison. She braced herself as the crate tilted. She found herself wedged between the side of the crate and something cold and metallic: the bronze torso of a man.

"Christ, this one's heavy. What's in here, anyway?"

"That's not your concern. Just get it moved."

Every little bump seemed to squash Clea into a tighter and tighter space. Only when the crate at last thumped to a rest in the truck was she able to take in a deep breath. And take stock of her predicament.

She was trapped. With the men constantly shuttling back and forth, loading in the rest of the crates, she couldn't exactly stroll out unseen.

The scrape of a second crate being slid on top of hers settled the issue. For the moment she was boxed in.

By the glow of her watch she saw it was 8:10.

At 8:25, the truck pulled away from the warehouse. By now, Clea's calves were cramping, the wood shavings had worked their way into her clothes and she was battling an attack of claustrophobia. Reaching up, she strained to push off the lid, but the crate on top was too heavy.

She pressed her face to a small knothole and took in a few slow, deep breaths. The taste of fresh air took the edge off her panic. *Better,* she thought. *Yes, that's better.*

Something hard was biting into her thigh. She managed to worm her hand into her hip pocket and found what it was: Jordan's watch. The one she'd stolen.

By now he knew she'd taken it. By now he'd be hating her and glad she was out of his life. That's what she'd wanted him to think. What he should think. He was a gentleman and she was a thief. Nothing could close that gap between them.

Yet, as she huddled in that coffin of a space and clutched Jordan's pocket watch in her fist, her longing for him brought tears to her eyes.

I did it for you, she thought. *To make it easier for you. And me, as well. Because I know, as well as you do, that I'm not the woman for you.*

She pressed the watch to her lips and kissed it, the way she longed to kiss *him,* and never would again. She wanted to curse her larcenous past, her transgressions, her childhood. Even Uncle Walter. All the things that would forever keep Jordan out of her reach. But she was too weary and too frightened.

So she cried instead.

By the time the truck wheezed to a stop, Clea was numb in both spirit and body. Her legs felt dead and useless.

The other crates were unloaded first. Then her crate was tipped onto a cart and began a roller coaster ride, down a truck ramp, up another ramp. She knew there were men about—she heard their voices. An elevator ride brought her to the final destination. The crate hit the floor with a thump.

After a while she heard nothing. Only the faint rumbling of an engine.

Cautiously she pushed up on the lid. The weight of the other crate had redriven the nails into the wood. Luckily she still had the crowbar. It took some tight maneuvering, but she managed to work the tip under the lid and yanked on the bar.

The lid popped open.

She raised her head and inhaled a whiff of diesel-scented air. She was in a storage bay. Beside her were stacked the other crates from the warehouse annex. No one was around.

It took her a few moments to crawl out. By the time she dropped onto the floor, her calves were beginning to prickle with renewed circulation. She hobbled over to the steel door and opened it a crack.

Outside was a narrow corridor. Beyond the corner, two men were laughing, joking in that foul language sailors employ when they're away from the polite company of women. Something about the whores in Naples.

The floor lurched beneath Clea's feet and she swayed sideways. The engine sounds were grinding louder now.

Only then did she focus on the emergency fire kit mounted on the corridor wall. It was stamped with the name *Villafjord.*

I'm on his ship, she thought. *I'm trapped on Van Weldon's ship.*

The floor swayed again, a rolling motion that made her reach out to the walls for support. She heard the engine's accelerating whine, sensed the gentle rocking of the hull through the swells, and she understood.

The *Villafjord* was heading out to sea.

Chapter 14

Hugh Tavistock's limousine was waiting at the side of the road just outside Guildford. The instant Jordan and his two Scotland Yard escorts pulled up in a Mercedes, the limousine door swung open. Jordan stepped out of the Mercedes and slid into the limousine's rear seat.

He found himself confronting his uncle Hugh's critical gaze. "It seems," said Hugh, "that I retired from intelligence simply to devote my life to rescuing *you*."

"And a fond hello to you, too," answered Jordan. "Where's Richard?"

"Present and accounted for," answered a voice from the driver's seat. Dressed in a chauffeur's uniform, Richard turned and grinned at him. "I picked up this trick from a certain relative-to-be. Where's Clea Rice?"

"I don't know," said Jordan. "But I have a very good

idea. Did you confirm the shipping schedule for Portsmouth?"

"There is a vessel named *Villafjord* due to sail at midnight tonight. That gives us plenty of time to stop the departure."

"Why all this interest in the *Villafjord?*" asked Hugh. "What's she carrying?"

"Wild guess? A fortune in art." Jordan added, under his breath, "And a certain little cat burglar."

Richard pulled onto the highway for Portsmouth. "She'll jeopardize the whole operation. You should have stopped her."

"Ha! As if I could!" said Jordan. "As you may have surmised, she doesn't take to instruction well."

"Yes, I've heard about Miss Rice," said Hugh. "Uncooperative, is she?"

"She doesn't trust anyone. Not Richard, not the authorities."

"Surely she trusts *you* by now?"

Jordan gazed ahead at the dark road. Softly he said, "I thought she did…"

But she didn't. When it came down to the wire, she chose to work alone. Without me.

He didn't understand her. She was like some forest creature, always poised for flight, never trusting of a human hand. She wouldn't *let* herself believe in him.

That lifting of his pocket watch—oh, he understood the meaning of that gesture. It was part defiance and part desperation. She was trying to push him away, to test him. She was crazy enough to put him to this test. And vulnerable enough to be hurt if he failed her.

I should have known. I should have seen this coming.

Now he was angry at himself, at her, at all the circumstances that kept wrenching them apart. Her past. Her mistrust of him.

His mistrust of *her*.

Perhaps Clea had it right from the start. Perhaps there was nothing he could do, nothing she could do, that would get them beyond all this.

With renewed anxiety he glanced outside at a passing road sign. They were still thirty miles from Portsmouth.

MacLeod and the police were already waiting at the dock.

"We're too late," said MacLeod as Hugh and Jordan stepped out of the limousine.

"What do you mean, too late?" demanded Jordan.

"This, I take it, is young Tavistock?" asked MacLeod.

"My nephew Jordan," said Hugh. "What's happening here?"

"We arrived a few minutes ago. The *Villafjord* was scheduled to sail at midnight from this dock."

"Where is she, then?"

"That's the problem. It seems she sailed twenty minutes ago."

"But it's only nine-thirty."

MacLeod shook his head. "Obviously they changed plans."

Jordan stared out over the dark harbor. A chill wind blew in from the water, whipping his shirt and stinging his face with the tang of salt. *She's out there. I feel it. And she's alone.*

He turned to MacLeod. "You have to intercept them."

"At sea? You're talking a major operation! We have no firm evidence yet. Nothing solid to authorize that sort of thing."

"You'll find your evidence on the *Villafjord*."

"I can't take that chance. If I move on Van Weldon without cause, his lawyers will shut down my investigation for good. We have to wait until she docks in Naples. Convince the Italian police to board her."

"By then it may be too late! MacLeod, this could be your best chance. Your only chance. If you want Van Weldon, move *now*."

MacLeod looked at Hugh. "What do you think, Lord Lovat?"

"We'd need help from the Royal Navy. A chopper or two. Oh, we could do it, all right. But if the evidence isn't aboard, if it turns out we're chasing nothing but a cargo of biscuits, there's going to be enough red faces all around to fill a bloody circus ring."

"I'm telling you, the evidence *is* on board," said Jordan. "So is Clea."

"Is that what you're really chasing?" asked Hugh. "The woman?"

"What if it is?"

"We don't launch an operation this big just because some—some stray female has gotten herself into trouble," said MacLeod. "We move prematurely and we'll lose our chance at Van Weldon."

"He's right," said Hugh. "There are too many factors to weigh here. The woman can't be our first concern."

"Don't give me any bloody lecture about who's dispensable and who isn't!" retorted Jordan. "She's not one of your agents. She never took any oath to protect queen and country. She's a civilian, and you can't leave her out there. *I* won't leave her out there!"

Hugh stared at his nephew in surprise. "She means that much to you?"

Jordan met his uncle's gaze. The answer had never been clearer than at this very moment, with the wind whipping their faces and the night growing ever deeper, ever colder.

"Yes," said Jordan firmly. "She means that much to me."

His uncle glanced up at the sky. "Looks like some nasty weather coming up—it will complicate things."

"But…they'll be miles at sea by the time we reach them," said MacLeod. "Beyond English waters. There's no legal way to demand a search."

"No *legal* way," said Jordan.

"What, you think they'll just invite us aboard to comb the ship?"

"They're not going to know there *is* a search." Jordan turned to his uncle. "I'll need a navy helicopter. And a crew of volunteers for the boarding party."

Troubled, Hugh regarded his nephew for a moment. "You'll have no authority to back you up on this. You understand that?"

"Yes."

"If anything goes wrong—"

"The navy will deny my existence. I know that, too."

Hugh shook his head, agonizing over the decision. "Jordan, you're my only nephew…"

"And with a bloodline like ours, we can't possibly fail. Can we?" Smiling, Jordan gave his uncle's shoulder a squeeze of confidence.

Hugh sighed. "This woman must be quite extraordinary."

"I'll introduce you," said Jordan, and his gaze shifted back to the water. "As soon as I get her off that bloody ship."

* * *

The men's voices moved on and faded down the corridor.

Clea remained frozen by the door, debating whether to risk leaving the storage area. Before they docked again, she'd have to find a new hiding place. Eventually someone would check the cargo, and when that happened, the last place Clea wanted to be was trapped in a crate.

The coast looked clear.

She slipped out of the storeroom and headed in the opposite direction the men had taken. The below-decks area was a confusing maze of corridors and hatches. Which way next?

The question was settled by the sound of footsteps. In panic, she ducked through the nearest door.

To her dismay she discovered she was in the crew's quarters—and the footsteps were moving closer. She scrambled across to the row of lockers, opened a door and squeezed inside.

It was even a tighter fit than the crate had been. She was crammed against a bundle of foul-smelling shirts and an even fouler pair of tennis shoes. Through the ventilation slits she saw two men step into the room. One of them crossed toward the lockers. Clea almost let out a squeak of relief when he swung open the door right beside hers.

"Hear there's rough weather comin' up," the man said, pulling on a slicker.

"Hell, she's blowin' twenty-five knots already."

The men, now garbed in foul-weather gear, left the quarters.

Clea emerged from the locker. She couldn't keep ducking in and out of rooms; she'd have to find a more permanent hiding place. Some spot she'd be left undisturbed...

The lifeboats. She'd seen it used as a hiding place in the movies. Unless there was a ship's emergency, she'd be safe waiting it out there until they docked.

She scavenged among the lockers and pulled out a sailor's pea coat and a black cap. Then, her head covered, her petite frame almost swallowed up in the coat, she crept out of the crew's quarters and started up a stairway to the deck.

It was blowing outside, the night swirling with wind and spray. Through the darkness she could make out several men moving about on deck. Two were securing a cargo hatch, a third was peering through binoculars over the port rail. None of them glanced in her direction.

She spotted two lifeboats secured near the starboard gunwale. Both were covered with tarps. Not only would she be concealed in there, she'd be dry. Once the *Villafjord* reached Naples, she could sneak ashore.

She pulled the pea coat tighter around her shoulders. Calmly, deliberately, she began to stroll toward the lifeboats.

Simon Trott stood on the bridge and eyed the increasingly foul weather from behind the viewing windows. Though the captain had assured him the passage would present no difficulties for the Villafjord, Trott still couldn't shake off his growing sense of uneasiness.

Obviously, Victor Van Weldon didn't share Trott's sense of foreboding. The old man sat calmly beside him on the bridge, oxygen hissing softly through his nasal tube. Van Weldon would not be anxious about something so trivial as a storm at sea. At his age, with his failing health, what was there left for him to fear?

Trott asked the captain, "Will it get much rougher?"

"Not by much, I expect," said the captain. "She'll handle it fine. But if you're that concerned, we can turn back to Portsmouth."

"No," spoke up Van Weldon. "We cannot return." Suddenly he began to cough. Everyone on the bridge looked away in distaste as the old man spat into a handkerchief.

Trott, too, averted his gaze and focused on the main deck below, where three men were working hunched against the wind. That's when Trott noticed the fourth figure moving along the starboard gunwale. It passed, briefly, under the glow of a decklight, then slipped into the shadows.

At the first lifeboat the figure paused, glanced around and began to untie the covering tarp.

"Who is that?" Trott asked sharply. "That man by the lifeboat?"

The captain frowned. "I don't recognize that one."

At once Trott turned for the exit.

"Mr. Trott?" called the captain.

"I'll take care of this."

By the time Trott reached the deck, he had his automatic drawn and ready. The figure had vanished. Draped free over the lifeboat was an unfastened corner of tarp. Trott prowled closer. With a jerk he yanked off the tarp and pointed his gun at the shadow cowering inside.

"Out!" snapped Trott. "Come on, *out*."

Slowly the figure unfolded itself and raised its head. By the glow of a decklight Trott saw the terror in that startlingly familiar face.

"If it isn't the elusive Miss Clea Rice," said Trott.

And he smiled.

* * *

The cabin was large, plushly furnished and equipped with all the luxuries one would expect in a well-appointed living room. Only the swaying of the crystal chandelier overhead betrayed the fact it was a shipboard residence.

The chair Clea was tied to was upholstered in green velvet and the armrests were carved mahogany. *Surely they won't kill me here,* she thought. *They wouldn't want me to bleed all over this pricey antique.*

Trott emptied the contents of her pockets and her knapsack onto a table and eyed the collection of lock picks. "I see you came well prepared," he commented dryly. "How did you get on board?"

"Trade secret."

"Are you alone?"

"You think I'd tell you?"

With two swift steps he crossed to her and slapped her across the face, so hard her head snapped back. For a moment she was too stunned by the force of the blow to speak.

"Surely, Miss Rice," wheezed Victor Van Weldon, "you don't wish to anger Mr. Trott more than you already have. He can be most unpleasant when annoyed."

"So I've noticed," groaned Clea. She squinted, focusing her blurred gaze on Van Weldon. He was frailer than she'd expected. And old, so old. Oxygen tubing snaked from his nostrils to a green tank hooked behind his wheelchair. His hands were bruised, the skin thin as paper. This was a man barely clinging to life. What could he possibly lose by killing her?

"I'll ask you again," said Trott. "Are you alone?"

"I brought a team of navy SEALs with me."

Trott hit her again. A thousand shards of light seemed to explode in her head.

"Where is Jordan Tavistock?" asked Trott.

"I don't know."

"Is he with you?"

"No."

Trott picked up Jordan's gold pocket watch and flipped open the lid. He read aloud the inscription. "Bernard Tavistock." He looked at her. "You have no idea where he is?"

"I told you I don't."

He held up the watch. "Then what are you doing with this?"

"I stole it."

Though she steeled herself for the coming blow, the impact of his fist still took her breath away. Blood trickled down her chin. In dazed wonder she watched the red droplets soak into the lush carpet at her feet. *How ironic,* she thought. *I finally tell the truth and he doesn't believe me.*

"He is still working with you, isn't he?" said Trott.

"He wants nothing more to do with me. I left him."

Trott turned to Van Weldon. "I think Tavistock is still a threat. Keep the contract on him alive."

Clea's head shot up. "No. No, he's got nothing to do with this!"

"He's been with you this past week."

"His misfortune."

"Why were you together?"

She gave a shrug. "Lust?"

"You think I'd believe that?"

"Why not?" Rebelliously she cocked up her head.

"I've been known to tweak the hormones of more than a few men."

"This gets us nowhere!" said Van Weldon. "Throw her overboard."

"I want to know what she's learned. What Tavistock's learned. Otherwise we'll be operating blind. If Interpol—" He suddenly turned.

The intercom was buzzing.

Trott crossed the room and pressed the speaker button. "Yes, Captain?"

"We've a situation up here, Mr. Trott. There's a Royal Navy ship hard on our stern. They've requested permission to come aboard."

"Why?"

"They say they're checking all outbound vessels from Portsmouth for some IRA terrorist. They think he may have passed himself off as crew."

"Request denied," said Van Weldon calmly.

"They have helicopter backup," said the captain. "And another ship on the way."

"We are beyond the twelve-mile limit," said Van Weldon. "They have no right to board us."

"Sir, might I advise cooperation?" said the captain. "It sounds like a routine matter. You know how it is— the Brits are always hunting down IRA. They'll probably just want to eyeball our crew. If we refuse, it will only rouse their suspicions."

Trott and Van Weldon exchanged glances. At last Van Weldon nodded.

"Assemble all men on deck," said Trott into the intercom. "Let the Brits have a good look at them. But it stops there."

"Yes, sir."

Trott turned to Van Weldon. "We'd both better be on deck to meet them. As for Miss Rice..." He looked at Clea.

"She will have to wait," said Van Weldon, and wheeled his chair across the room to a private elevator. "See that she's well secured. I will meet you on the bridge." He maneuvered into the elevator and slid the gate shut. With a hydraulic whine, the lift carried him away.

Trott turned his attention to Clea's bonds. He yanked the ropes around her wrists so tightly she gave a cry of pain. Then quickly, efficiently he taped her mouth.

"That should keep you," he said with a grunt of satisfaction, and he left the room.

The instant the door shut behind him, Clea began straining at her bonds. It took only a few painful twists of her wrists to tell her that it was hopeless. She wasn't going to get loose.

Shedding tears of frustration, she slumped back against the chair. Up on deck, the Royal Navy would soon be landing. They would never know, would never guess, that just below their feet was a victim in need of rescue.

So close and yet so far.

She gritted her teeth and began to strain again at the ropes.

"You're certain you want to go in with us?"

Jordan peered through the chopper windows at the deck of the *Villafjord* below. It would be a bumpy landing into enemy territory, but with all this wind and darkness as cover, there was a reasonable chance no one down there would recognize him.

"I'm going in," Jordan said.

"You'll have twenty minutes at the most," said the naval officer seated across from him. "And then we're out of there. With or without you."

"I understand."

"We're on shaky legal ground already. If Van Weldon lodges a complaint to the high command, we'll be explaining ourselves till doomsday."

"Twenty minutes. Just give me that much." Jordan tugged the black watch cap lower on his brow. The borrowed Royal Navy uniform was a bit snug around his shoulders, and the automatic felt uncomfortably foreign holstered against his chest, but both were absolutely necessary if he was to participate in this masquerade. Unfortunately the other seven men in the boarding party—all naval officers—were plainly doubtful about having some amateur along for the ride. They kept watching him with expressions bordering on disdain.

Jordan ignored them and focused on the broad deck of the *Villafjord,* now directly beneath the skids. A little tricky maneuvering by the pilot brought them to a touchdown. At once the men began to pile out, Jordan among them.

The pilot, mindful of the hazards of a rolling deck, took off again, leaving the crew temporarily stranded aboard the *Villafjord.*

A man with blond hair was crossing to greet them.

Jordan slipped behind the other men in his party and averted his face. It would be bloody inconvenient to be recognized right off the bat.

The ranking officer of the naval team stepped forward and met the blond man. "Lieutenant Commander Tobias, Royal Navy."

"Simon Trott. VP operations, the Van Weldon company. How can we help you, Commander?"

"We'd like to inspect your crew."

"Certainly. They've already been assembled." Trott pointed to the knot of men huddled near the bridge stairway.

"Is everyone on deck?"

"All except the captain and Mr. Van Weldon. They're up on the bridge."

"There's no one below decks?"

"No, sir."

Commander Tobias nodded. "Then let's get started."

Trott turned to lead the way. As the rest of the boarding party followed Trott, Jordan hung behind, waiting for a chance to slip away.

No one noticed him duck down the midship stairway.

With all the crew up top, he'd have the below-decks area to himself. There wasn't much time to search. Slipping quickly down the first corridor, he poked his head into every doorway, calling Clea's name. He passed crew's quarters and officers' quarters, the mess hall, the galley.

No sign of Clea.

Heading farther astern, he came across what appeared to be a storage bay. Inside the room were a dozen crates of various sizes. The lid was ajar on one of them. He lifted it off and glanced inside.

Swathed in fluffy packing was the bronze head of a statue. And a black glove—a woman's, size five.

Jordan glanced sharply around the room. "Clea?" he called out.

Ten minutes had already passed.

With a surging sense of panic he continued down the

corridor, throwing open doors, scanning each compartment. So little time left, and he still had the engine room, the cargo bays and Lord knew what else might lie astern.

Overhead he heard the sound of rumbling, growing louder now. The helicopter was about to land again.

A mahogany door with a sign Private was just ahead. Captain's quarters? Jordan tried the knob and found it was locked. He pounded on it a few times and called out, "Clea?"

There was no answer.

She heard the pounding on the door, then Jordan's voice calling her name.

She tried to answer, tried to shout, but the tape over her mouth muffled all but the faintest whimper. Frantic to reach him, she thrashed like a madwoman against her bonds. The ropes held. Her hands and feet had gone numb, useless.

Don't leave me! she wanted to shriek. *Don't leave me!*

But she knew he had already turned from the door.

In despair, she jerked her body sideways. The chair tipped, carrying her down with it. Her head slammed against an end table. The pain was like a bolt of lightning through her skull; it left her stunned on the floor. Blackness swam before her eyes. She fought the slide toward unconsciousness, fought it savagely with every ounce of will she possessed. And still she could not clear the blackness from her vision.

Faintly she heard a thumping. Again and again, like a drumbeat in the darkness.

She struggled to see. The blackness was lifting. She could make out the outlines of furniture now. And she realized that the thumping was coming from the door.

In a shower of splinters the wood suddenly split

open, breached by the bright red blade of a fire ax. Another blow tore a gaping hole in the door. An arm thrust in, to fumble at the lock.

Jordan shoved into the room.

He took one look at Clea and murmured, "My God..."

At once he was kneeling at her side. Her hands were so numb she scarcely felt it when he cut the cords binding her wrists.

But she did feel his kiss. He pulled the tape from her mouth, lifted her from the floor and pressed his lips to hers. As she lay sobbing in his arms he kissed her hair, her face, murmuring her name again and again, as though he could not say it enough, could never say it enough.

A soft beeping made his head suddenly lift from hers. He silenced the pager hung on his belt. "That's our one-minute warning," he said. "We have to get out of here. Can you walk?"

"I—I don't think so. My legs..."

"Then I'll carry you." He swept her up into his arms. Stepping across the wood-littered carpet, he bore her out of the room and into the corridor.

"How do we get off the ship?" she asked.

"The same way I got on. Navy chopper." He rounded a corner.

And halted.

"I am afraid, Mr. Tavistock," said Simon Trott, standing in their path, "that you are going to miss your flight."

Chapter 15

Clea felt Jordan's arms tighten around her. In the momentary silence she could almost hear the thudding of his heart against his chest.

Trott raised the barrel of his automatic. "Put her down."

"She can't walk," said Jordan. "She hit her head."

"Very well, then. You'll have to carry her."

"Where?"

Trott waved the gun toward the far end of the corridor. "The cargo bay."

That gun left Jordan no choice. With Clea in his arms he headed up the corridor and stepped through a doorway, into a cargo bay crammed full with packing crates.

"The landing party knows I'm on board," said Jordan. "They won't leave without me."

"Won't they?" Trott glanced upward toward the rumble of the chopper rotors. "They're about to do just that."

They heard the roar of the helicopter as it suddenly lifted away.

"Too late," said Trott with a regretful shake of his head. "You've now entered the gray world of deniability, Mr. Tavistock. We'll claim you never came aboard. And the Royal Navy will have a sticky time admitting otherwise." Again he waved the gun, indicating one of the crates. "It's large enough for you both. A cozy end, I'd say."

He's going to shut us inside, thought Clea. And then what?

A ditching at sea, of course. She and Jordan would drown together, their bodies locked forever in an undersea casket. Suddenly she found it hard to breathe. Sheer terror had drained her of the ability to think, to act.

When Jordan spoke, his voice was astonishingly calm.

"They'll be waiting for you in Naples," said Jordan. "Interpol and the Italian police. You don't really think it's as simple as tossing one crate overboard?"

"We've bought our way into Naples for years."

"Then your luck is about to change. Do you like dark, enclosed places? Because that's where *you're* going to find yourself. For the rest of your life."

"I've had enough," Trott snapped. "Put her down. Pry the lid off the crate." He picked up a crowbar and slid it across the floor to Jordan. "Do it. And no sudden moves."

Jordan set Clea down on her feet. At once she slid to her knees, her legs still numb and useless. Dropping down beside her, Jordan looked her in the eye. Something in his gaze caught her attention. He was trying to tell her something. He bent close to her and the flap of his jacket sagged open. That's when she caught a glimpse of his shoulder holster.

He had a gun!

Trott's view was blocked by Jordan's back. Quickly she slipped her hand beneath Jordan's jacket, grabbed the pistol from the holster and hugged it against her chest.

"Leave her on the floor!" ordered Trott. "Just get the bloody crate open!"

Jordan leaned close, his mouth grazing her ear. "Use me as a shield," he whispered. "Aim for his chest."

She stared at him in horror. "No—"

He gripped her shoulder with painful insistence. *"Do it."*

Their gazes locked. It was something she'd remember for as long as she lived, that message she saw in his eyes. *You have to live, Clea. For both of us.*

He gave her shoulder another squeeze, this one gentler. And he smiled.

"Come on, get the lid off!" barked Trott.

Clea hooked her finger around the pistol trigger. She had never shot anyone before. If she missed, if she was even slightly off target, Trott would have time to squeeze off his entire clip into Jordan's body. She had to be accurate. She had to be lethal.

For his sake.

His lips brushed her forehead and she savored their warmth, knowing full well that the next time she touched them they might carry the chill of death.

"It seems you need a jump start," said Trott. He raised his pistol and fired.

Clea felt Jordan shudder in pain, heard him groan as he clutched his thigh. In horror Clea saw bright red droplets spatter the floor. The sight of Jordan's blood seemed to cloud her vision with rage. All her hesitation was swept away by a roaring wave of fury.

With both hands she aimed the pistol at Trott and fired.

The bullet's impact punched Trott squarely in the chest. He stumbled backward, his face frozen in surprise. He weaved on his feet like a drunken man. The gun slipped from his grasp and clanged to the floor. He dropped to his knees beside it, made a clumsy attempt to pick it up again, but his hands wouldn't function. As he sank to the floor, his fingers were still clawing uselessly for the gun. Then they fell still.

"Get out of here," gasped Jordan.

"I won't leave you."

"I can't leave, period. My leg—"

"Hush!" she cried. On unsteady legs she stumbled over to Trott's body and snatched up his gun. "There's no getting off this ship, anyway! They've heard the shots. They'll be down here any minute, the whole lot of them. We might as well stick together." She tottered back to his side.

He sat huddled in a pool of his own blood. Tenderly she took his face in her hands and pressed a kiss to his mouth.

His lips were already chilled.

Sobbing, despairing, she cradled his head in her lap. *It's over,* she thought as she heard footsteps pounding toward them along the corridor. *All we can do now is fight till the bitter end. And hope death comes quickly.* She bent down to him and whispered, "I love you."

The footsteps were almost at the cargo door.

With a strange sense of calmness she raised the gun and took aim at the doorway...

And held her fire. A man in a Royal Navy uniform stood blinking at her in surprise. Behind him stood three other men, also in uniform. One of them was Richard Wolf.

Richard shoved through into the room and saw Jordan and the growing pool of blood. Turning, he yelled, "Call back the chopper again! Have the Medevac team standing by!"

"Yes, sir!" One of the naval officers headed for the intercom.

Clea was still clutching the pistol. Slowly she let the barrel drop, but she did not release the grip. She was almost afraid to let go of the one solid thing she could count on. Afraid that if she did let go, she would drop away into some dimensionless space.

"Here. I'll take it."

Dazed, she looked up at Richard. He regarded her with an almost kindly smile and held out his hand. Wordlessly she gave him the pistol. He nodded and said softly, "That's a good girl."

Within fifteen minutes a team of medics had appeared, helicoptered in from the nearby Royal Navy ship. By then, Clea's legs had regained their circulation and she was able to stand, albeit unsteadily. Her head was aching worse than ever, and a medic tried to pull her aside to examine the bruises on her temple, but she shrugged him away.

All her attention was focused on Jordan. She watched as IV lines were threaded into Jordan's veins, as he was lifted and strapped onto a stretcher. In numb silence she squeezed onto the elevator that carried his stretcher up to the deck.

Only when one of the officers held her back as they lifted Jordan into the chopper did she understand they

were taking him from her. Suddenly she panicked, terrified that if she lost sight of him now, she would never
see him again.

She shoved forward, elbowing aside the naval officer, and would have run all the way to the chopper
were it not for a grip that firmly closed around her arm.

Richard Wolf's.

"Let me go!" she sobbed, trying to fight him off.

"He's being transported to a hospital. They'll take
care of him."

"I want to be with him! He needs me!"

Richard took her firmly by the shoulders. "You'll
see him soon, I promise! But now *we* need you, Clea.
You have to tell us things. About Van Weldon. About
this ship."

The roar of the rotor engine drowned out any other
words. With despairing eyes, Clea saw the chopper lift
away into the wind-buffeted darkness. *Please take care
of him,* she prayed. *That's all I ask. Please keep him
safe.*

She watched the taillights wink into the night. A
moment later the rumble had faded, leaving only the
sounds of the wind and the sea.

"Miss Rice?" Richard prodded gently.

Through tears Clea looked at him. "I'll tell you everything, Mr. Wolf," she said. And an anguished laugh
suddenly escaped her throat. "Even the truth."

It was two days before she saw Jordan again.

She was told that Jordan had lost a great deal of
blood, but that the surgery had gone well, without com-
plications. She could learn no more.

Richard Wolf installed her in an MI6 safe house outside London. It was a sweet little stone cottage with a white fence and a garden. She considered it a prison. The three men guarding the entrances did nothing to dispel that impression.

Richard had told her the men were a necessity. The contract on her life might still be active, he'd explained. It was dangerous to move her. Until Van Weldon's topple from power became general knowledge, Clea would have to be kept out of sight.

And away from Jordan.

She understood the real purpose of the separation. It did not surprise her that his aristocratic family would, in the end, prevail. Clea was not the sort of woman one allowed into one's family. Not if one had a reputation to uphold. No matter how much Jordan cared about her— and he *did* care, she knew that now—her past would come between them.

The Tavistocks had only Jordan's well-being in mind. For that she could not fault them.

But she did resent them for the way they had taken control of her freedom. For two days she tolerated her pleasant little prison. She paced in the garden, stared at the TV, leafed without interest through magazines.

By the second day in captivity, she'd bloody well had enough.

She picked up her knapsack, marched outside and announced to the guard posted in the front yard, "I want out."

"Afraid that's quite impossible," he said.

"What're you going to do about it, Buster, shoot me in the back?"

"My orders are to ensure your safety. You can't leave."

"Watch me." She slung the knapsack over her shoulder and was pushing through the gate when a black limousine rolled into the driveway. It came to a stop right in front of her. In amazement she watched as the chauffeur emerged, circled around and opened the rear door.

An elderly man stepped out. He was portly and balding, but he wore his finely tailored suit with comfortable elegance. For a moment he regarded Clea in silence.

"So you are the woman in question," he said at last.

Coolly she looked him up and down. "And the man in question?"

He held out his hand in greeting. "I'm Hugh Tavistock. Jordan's uncle."

Clea momentarily lost her voice. Wordlessly she accepted his handshake and found the man's grip firm, his gaze steady. *Like Jordan's.*

"We have much to talk about, Miss Rice," said Hugh. "Will you step into the car?"

"Actually, I was just leaving."

"You don't wish to see him?"

"You mean... Jordan?"

Hugh nodded. "It's a long drive to the hospital. I thought it would give us a chance to get acquainted."

She studied him, searching for some hint of what was to come. His expression was unreadable, his face a cipher.

She climbed into the limousine.

They sat side by side, not speaking for a while. Outside the window, the countryside glided past. The brilliant hues of fall were tingeing the trees. *What do we possibly have to say to each other?* she wondered. *I'm a stranger to his world, as he is to mine.*

"It seems my nephew has formed an attachment to you," said Hugh.

"Your nephew is a good man," she said. She stared out the window and added softly, "A very fine man."

"I've always thought so."

"He deserves…" She paused and swallowed back tears. "He deserves the very best there is."

"True."

"So…" She raised her chin and looked at him. "I'll not be difficult. You must understand, Lord Lovat, I have no demands. No expectations. I only want…" She looked away. "I only want him to be happy. I'll do whatever it takes. Even if it means vanishing."

"You love him." It was not a question but a statement.

This time she couldn't keep the tears at bay. They began to fall slowly, silently.

Sighing, he sat back in the seat. "Well, it's certainly not without precedent."

"What do you mean?"

"A number of women have fallen for my nephew."

"I can see why."

"But none of them were quite like you. You do realize, don't you, that you are almost single-handedly responsible for bringing down Victor Van Weldon? For smashing an arms shipment empire?"

She shrugged, as if none of it mattered. And at the moment, it didn't. It all seemed irrelevant. She scarcely listened as Hugh outlined the ripple of developments since the *Villafjord* was boarded. The arrests of Oliver and Veronica Cairncross. The new investigation into the *Max Havelaar*'s sinking. The cache of surface-to-air missiles found in the Cairncross Biscuits warehouse. Unfortunately, Victor Van Weldon would probably not live long enough to go to trial. But he had, in some measure, met justice. The final rendering would have to come from his Maker.

When Hugh had finished speaking, he looked at Clea and said, "You have performed a service for us all, Miss Rice. You're to be congratulated."

She said nothing.

To her surprise he chuckled. "I've met many heroes in my time. But none so uninterested in praise."

She shook her head. "I'm tired, Lord Lovat. I just want to go home."

"To America?"

Again she shrugged. "I suppose that *is* my home. I... I don't know anymore..."

"What about Jordan? I thought you loved him."

"You yourself said it's not without precedent. Women have always been falling in love with your nephew."

"But Jordan's never fallen in love with them. Until now."

There was a silence. She frowned at him.

"For the past two days," said Hugh, "my normally good-natured nephew has been insufferable. Belligerent. He has badgered the doctors and nurses, twice pulled out his intravenous lines and commandeered another patient's wheelchair. We explained to him it wasn't the right time to bring you for a visit. That contract on your life, you know—it made every transfer risky. But now the contract's off—"

"It is?"

"And it's finally time to fetch you. And see if you can't restore his good humor."

"You think I'm the one who can do that?"

"Richard Wolf thought so."

"And what does Jordan say?"

"Bloody little. But then, he's always been close-mouthed." Hugh regarded her with his mild blue eyes. "He's waiting to speak to you first."

Clea gave a bitter laugh. "How distressing it must be for you! A woman like me. And your nephew. You'd have to hide me in the family closet."

"If I did," he said dryly, "you'd find half my ancestors lurking in there with you."

She shook her head. "I don't understand."

"We Tavistocks have a grand tradition of choosing mates who are most…unsuitable. Over the centuries we've wed Gypsies, courtesans and even a stray Yank or two." He smiled. For the first time she recognized the warmth in his eyes. "You would scarcely raise an eyebrow."

"You'd…allow someone like me in your family?"

"It's not my decision, Miss Rice. The choice is Jordan's. Whatever will make him happy."

How can we predict what will make him happy? she thought. *For a month, or a year, he might find contentment in my arms. But then it will dawn on him who I was. Who I am…*

She clutched her knapsack in her lap and suddenly longed for escape, longed to be on the road to somewhere else, anywhere else. That was how she'd survived these past few weeks—the quick escape, the shadowy exit. That, too, was how she'd always resolved her romantic relationships. But now there was no avoiding the encounter that lay ahead.

She'd simply have to be straight about this. Lay her cards on the table and be brutally honest. She owed it to Jordan; it was the kindest thing she could do.

By the time they reached the hospital, she had talked herself into a benumbed sense of inevitability. She stood stiff and silent as they rode up the service elevator. When they got off on the seventh floor and walked toward Jordan's hospital room, she was composed and prepared for what she knew would be a goodbye. Calmly she stepped into the room.

And lost all sense of resolve.

Jordan was standing by the window, a pair of crutches propped under his arms. He was fully dressed in gray trousers and a white shirt, no tie—casual for a Tavistock. At the sound of the door's opening, he turned clumsily around to face her. The crutches were new to him, and he wobbled a bit, struggling to find his balance. But his gaze was steady on her face.

Her escorts left the room.

She stood just inside the door, longing to go to Jordan, yet afraid to approach. "I see you came through it" was all she said.

He searched her face, seeking, but not finding, what he wanted. "I've been trying to see you."

"Your uncle told me. They were afraid to move either one of us." She smiled. "But now Van Weldon's gone. And we can go back to our lives."

"And will you?"

"What else would I do?"

"Stay with me."

He stood very still, watching her. Waiting for a response.

She was the first to look away. "Stay? You mean… in England?"

"I mean with *me*. Wherever that may happen to be."

She laughed "That sounds like a rather vague proposition."

"I'm not being vague at all. You're just refusing to recognize the obvious."

"The obvious?"

"That we've been through bloody hell together. That we care about each other. At least, I care about *you*. And I'm not about to let you run."

She shook her head and laughed—not a real laugh. No, it felt as though her heart had gotten caught in her throat. "How can you possibly care about me? You're not even sure who I am."

"I know who you are."

"I've lied to you. Again and again."

"I know."

"Big lies. Whoppers!"

"You also told me the truth."

"Only when I had to! I'm an ex-con, Jordan! I come from a family of cons. I'll probably have kids who'll be cons."

"So…it will be a parenting challenge."

"And what about *this?*" She reached into her knapsack and took out the pocket watch. She dangled it in front of his face. "I *stole* this. I took something I knew you cared about. I did it to prove a point, Jordan. To show you what an idiot you are to trust me!"

"No, Clea," he said quietly. "That's not why you stole it."

"No? Then why did I take it?"

"Because you're afraid of me."

"I'm afraid? *I'm* afraid?"

"You're afraid I'll love you. Afraid you'll love *me*.

Afraid it'll all fall apart when I decide you're hopelessly flawed."

"Okay," she retorted. "Maybe you've got it figured
out. But it does make a certain amount of sense, doesn't
it? To get the disillusionment over with right at the start?
You can put a nice romantic spin on all of this, but
sooner or later you'll realize what I am."

"I know what you are. And I know just how lucky I
am to have found you."

"Lucky?" She shook her head and laughed bitterly.
"Lucky?" Holding up the pocket watch, she let it swing
in front of his face. "I'm a thief, remember? I steal
things. I stole this!"

He grabbed her wrist, trapping it in his grip. "The
only thing you stole," he said softly, "was my heart."

Wordlessly she stared at him. Though she wanted
to pull away, to turn from his face, she found that her
gaze was every bit as trapped as her hand.

"No, Clea," he said. "This time you don't run
away. You don't retreat. Maybe it's the way you've
always done things. When life gets rough, you want
to run away. But don't you see? This time I'm offering you something different. I'm giving you a home
to run *to*."

She stopped struggling to free herself and went very
still. Only then did he release her wrist. Slowly. They
stood looking at each other, not touching, not speaking.
His gaze was all that held her now.

That and her heart.

So many times I've tried to run away from you, she
thought. *And it was really myself I was running from.
Not you. Never you.*

Tenderly he stroked her face and caught the first

tear as it slid down her cheek. "I'm not going to force you to stay, Clea. I couldn't, even if I wanted to. But I've already made a decision. Now it's time you made one, too."

Through the veil of tears blurring her vision, she saw his look of uncertainty. Of hope.

"I...want to believe," she whispered.

"You will. Maybe not now, or next year, or even ten years from now. But one of these days, Clea, you will believe." He edged his crutches forward and pressed his lips to hers. "And that, Miss Rice," he whispered, "is when your running-away days will finally be over."

She looked at him in wonder through her tears. *Oh, Jordan, I think they already are.*

She threw her arms around his neck and pulled him close for another kiss. A sealing kiss. When she pulled away, she found he was smiling.

It was the smile of the thief who had stolen *her* heart. And would forever keep it.

* * * * *

USA TODAY bestselling author **Rita Herron** wrote her first book when she was twelve but didn't think real people grew up to be writers. Now she writes so she doesn't have to get a real job. A former kindergarten teacher and workshop leader, she traded storytelling to kids for writing romance, and now she writes romantic comedies and romantic suspense. Rita lives in Georgia with her family. She loves to hear from readers, so please visit her website, ritaherron.com.

Books by Rita Herron

Harlequin Intrigue

A Badge of Honor Mystery

Mysterious Abduction
Left to Die
Protective Order
Suspicious Circumstances

The Heroes of Horseshoe Creek

Lock, Stock and McCullen
McCullen's Secret Son
Roping Ray McCullen
Warrior Son
The Missing McCullen
The Last McCullen

Visit the Author Profile page at
Harlequin.com for more titles.

BENEATH
THE BADGE

Rita Herron

To Rickey and Delores for making me
fall in love with the Rangers...

Chapter 1

"Taylor Landis needs protection."

Sergeant Hayes Keller pushed his half-eaten bloodred steak away, his appetite vanishing. He knew Brody McQuade, his lieutenant, was still pissed at him for sleeping with his sister, Kimberly, and forcing him to *babysit* the richest, prissiest heiress in Texas must be his way of punishing him.

"But Montoya killed Kimberly," Hayes said, "and Carlson tried to kill Caroline, and you took care of him."

Brody cleared his throat. "We have to tie up loose ends. I'm at the crime lab in Austin, and we got the results of Carlson's autopsy. Egan said Carlson acted as if he'd been drugged, and the coroner found ketamine in his system."

"Ketamine—that's Special K on the streets. I'm not surprised," Hayes said. "Carlson had money. He ran with the party crowd."

Brody sighed, sounding weary. "We need to search Carlson's place, see if we find evidence of the drug."

"Why? He's dead. Good riddance."

"Yeah. But during the shoot-out, when Egan confronted Carlson about being on drugs, he denied taking anything."

"So you think someone else drugged him?"

"That's what I want to know."

Hell. He wouldn't be at all surprised that someone else wanted Carlson dead.

"And we still aren't sure who planted that bomb that blew up Taylor's car. It looks as if it was intended for her, not for Caroline. Which means that if Carlson tried to kidnap Caroline because she had him fired and he didn't commit all these murders, someone else wanted to hurt Taylor."

"So she's still in danger." Hayes slapped his beer down on the bar. He so wanted this case to be over, so he could leave Cantara Hills. "Carlson probably set the bomb."

"Maybe, maybe not. Caroline is worried sick about Taylor. She said that Taylor admitted that Kimberly and Kenneth Sutton had argued before the hit-and-run. I want to know what that argument was about."

Damn. Kenneth Sutton—the powerful and ambitious chairman of the City Board who was now running for governor. Kimberly had been interning in the man's office before her murder.

And she *had* been upset about something that had happened with the board, that was the reason Hayes had been comforting her the night they'd ended up in bed. Although she'd refused to confide the reason.

Brody was right. They had to tie up every unanswered question. He owed Brody, and he owed Kimberly.

The waitress glanced at his beer to see if he wanted a refill. He did, but he shook his head and indicated he needed the check. Duty called.

"So who would want to hurt Taylor Landis?"

Brody grunted. "That's what you need to find out. Could be related to her family's foundation, or Sutton's hiding something." Brody hesitated. "Miles Landis is also suspect."

Miles, Taylor's half brother. The snotty brat had rubbed him wrong the moment he'd met him. "Yeah, I heard he's had money troubles."

"Right. And Taylor is supposed to inherit a boatload of money in four weeks, on her thirtieth birthday," Brody continued. "That's motive for Miles."

Hayes grabbed the check and tossed down some cash, then strode toward the door. Tonight he'd wanted to drown himself in cheap beer, listen to country music and hang with the real people.

Instead, he had to head back to the neighborhood of the rich and greedy and Taylor Landis.

Could this day get any worse?

First the confrontation with Kenneth regarding his possible tampering with the bid for the new city library, then that ordeal with Miles at the restaurant.

The only highlight was the excitement about her best friend Margaret Hathaway's upcoming wedding. Margaret had been alone a long time, had never gotten over giving her son up for adoption when she was fifteen. She'd even hinted at hiring a P.I. to look for him, but her father, Link, had insisted against it. Poor Margaret. Her friend's pain had prompted Taylor to hire the P.I. herself. Finding out that her son's adopted family loved him would make a perfect wedding gift to Margaret. Then she could finally have the happiness she deserved.

Her cell phone rang, and she checked the number as she turned into Cantara Hills. Miles.

Not again.

She let it ring until it went to voice mail, but a second later, it started all over again. Knowing he wouldn't give up, she hit the connect button.

"I knew you were there," Miles snarled.

"Listen, I already told you that I'm not giving you any money right now. Grow up and start being responsible."

"You'll be sorry for turning your back on me, Taylor."

A chill swept up Taylor's spine. "Is that a threat?"

His bitter laugh echoed over the line. "It's a promise."

The dial tone buzzed in her ear as he abruptly ended the call.

Taylor shivered. After her mother's death, her father had quickly remarried. But his marriage to Miles's mother hadn't lasted long, and both she and Miles had been bitter and had tried repeatedly to milk him for money. But she'd never heard Miles so out of control. As she pulled down the drive to her mansion, she saw the crime scene tape in her driveway, and her senses jumped to alert.

The tape and the smoky, charred debris that had stained the imported Italian brick reminded her that someone had tried to kill her. That her body parts, instead of her BMW's, could have been all over the lawn...

If she hadn't rescheduled her appointment, she would have been driving home at the time the bomb exploded. According to Sergeant Egan Caldwell, the device had been set on a timer. Which meant that someone had known her routine and had intentionally planned for the car to explode with her inside.

Could Miles have done it? Or was Carlson Woodward responsible?

But why would Carlson have wanted her dead?

Hugging her arms around herself, she scanned the front of her estate, feeling paranoid as she let herself in and checked her security system. Ever since the break-ins had started in Cantara Hills, she'd been nervous. Had expected to be hit. After all, her mansion held expensive furniture, paintings, vases, collectibles, and she had several exquisite customized one-of-a-kind pieces of jewelry her father had given her over the years.

All tucked away in her safe because she rarely wore them. She enjoyed the advantages money offered, but didn't flaunt her wealth. In fact, that money was sometimes a curse. While most girls had to worry about men wanting in their pants, she had the added hassle of wondering if they wanted to get into her bank account. Even her father used his wealth to replace his feelings for her with expensive gifts.

And the break-ins—did the police believe that Carlson Woodward was responsible for them? She frowned and walked through the kitchen to the foyer and the spiral staircase, then wound her way up to her suite.

But why would Carlson steal from the neighbors? He didn't need the money. Her little brother, Miles, was a different story. He was so desperate for cash and angry with some of her friends who'd begun refusing him loans, that he might resort to theft.

She slipped into a bathing suit, sighing as her bare feet sank into the plush Oriental rug. Padding barefoot down the steps, she exited through the sunroom, grabbed a towel from the pool house and dropped it, along with her cell phone, onto a patio chair. The last vestiges of sunlight had faded hours ago, but the pool lights illuminated the terrace, bathing the intricately patterned stonework in a pale glow. The smell of roses from the garden along with hydrangeas bordering the patio scented the air, disguising the hint of chlorine, and she stared into the shimmering aquamarine water.

Still, thoughts of Carlson's attack on Caroline haunted her. She and Caroline had been neighbors and friends for years now. Apparently, Carlson had spread rumors in the community about Caroline having an affair with Sergeant Egan Caldwell, and had even called her father to stir up trouble.

Then he had attacked Caroline. Thankfully Ranger Caldwell had rescued Caroline and shot Carlson. Unfortunately Egan had been injured in the confrontation. Now Caroline had accompanied him to Austin to take care of him while he recuperated. Taylor still couldn't believe that Caroline had fallen for the surly ranger.

She dove into the water and began a crawl stroke. She and Caroline had joked about the three cowboy cops who'd invaded their country club community with their big bodies, hard attitudes and...guns. They'd dubbed Lieutenant Brody McQuade, Kimberly's brother, the intense one. Sergeant Egan Caldwell, the surly one. And Sergeant Hayes Keller—he had a chip on his shoulder the size of Texas.

Still, an odd tingling rippled through her as she thought about him—he was all bad attitude. Big, brawny, muscular, with eyes as black as soot and a temper as hot as fire. He was just the kind of man she normally avoided because he looked as if he could snap a person into pieces with just one look. But still, he was dangerously sexy...

Her stomach clenched. Where had that thought come from?

She didn't even like the guy. When he'd questioned her, she'd felt his disdain carving a hole through her.

She'd be glad when he left the area.

She swam another lap, counting strokes, but suddenly the lights flickered off, both outside and inside, pitching the terrace into darkness. Her breath hitched. There wasn't a storm cloud in sight, no reason for a power failure.

Something was wrong.

Scanning the terrace and garden for signs of an intruder, she swam to the pool edge to get out and call security. Suddenly a movement at the edge of the gardens by the pool house caught her eye.

A man?

Panic shot through her. She had to call for help. But the chair where she'd put her phone was next to the gardens.

And the only unlocked door was the sunroom door. She'd have to pass the pool house to reach it.

Taking a deep breath, she took off running, but before she reached the door, someone clamped a gloved hand over her mouth and encircled her neck with the other. She clawed at his hands, but he dug his fingers into her larynx, cutting off her air. Remembering the self-defense moves she'd learned, she jabbed her elbow in his chest, brought her knee up then stomped down on his foot.

He growled in fury and tightened both hands around

her throat. Blind panic assaulted her. She couldn't breathe, couldn't see. Desperate, she reached for something to use as a weapon as they fell against a patio chair. Her hand closed around a garden shovel and she stabbed backward with it, but he knocked it from her hand and it skittered across the terrace.

Enraged, he punched her jaw so hard her ears rang and she saw stars.

She had to fight back. But he hit her again, her legs buckled and her knees hit the stone with a painful thud. He shoved her face down, and she tasted blood as her head slammed against the brick wall encircling the patio. Then he dragged her toward the pool.

Summoning her last bit of strength, she flailed and kicked, clawed at him, but they tumbled into the pool.

Gasping, she struggled to fight her way back to the surface, but he was too strong. She held her breath, but her lungs were on fire, and he squeezed her throat so tightly that she choked and inhaled water.

Then an empty darkness sucked her into its vortex.

Hayes pulled to a stop at the iron-gated entrance to Taylor Landis's estate, and pressed the intercom button. He tapped his fingers on the steering wheel as he waited, but she didn't respond. Dammit, even if she wasn't home, didn't she have servants at her beck and call day and night?

He pressed the call button again, his impatience growing. What the hell was she doing? Lounging in some hot bath with cucumbers over her eyes, sipping champagne? Entertaining one of her rich guy friends? Maybe they were wallowing in bed with all their money.

Hell, maybe she wasn't home. Probably out shopping.

Still, he had to make sure she was safe. Resigned, he scanned the key card through the security system. But the card didn't work. Dammit, had she changed the system without informing them?

Or could something be wrong?

His heartbeat slammed in his chest, and he climbed out, removed his weapon, vaulted over the fence and jogged through the oaks lining the mile-long driveway, scanning the property for an intruder.

As the house slid into view, he searched the front yard, the sign of the crime scene tape a reminder that Brody might be right—that Taylor Landis might be in danger. He sped up until he reached the house, a cold monstrosity made of stone and brick with arches and palladium windows.

The hair on the back of his neck prickled. Why were the lights off?

The lingering odor of smoke and charred grass assaulted him, and he paused, a noise breaking the quiet. Water? A sprinkler maybe? But it had rained last night so why would Taylor have the sprinkler on?

He hurried to the front door and rang the doorbell. The sound reverberated through the cavernous inside, an empty sound that came unanswered. He pressed it again, then glanced through a front window. Nothing looked out of place. But it was pitch-dark inside. Quiet. No movement. And there hadn't been a storm to knock out the power.

What if someone had disarmed Taylor's security or cut her lights?

Another noise jarred him, and he jerked his head toward the side of the house, then realized the noise had come from the back.

Sucking in a breath, he wielded his gun and slowly inched along the length of the house to the side, then around the corner where a terrace held a pool, sitting area, fireplace, cooking pit and a pool house. A clay flowerpot was overturned, dirt spilled across the stone.

Senses alert, his gaze swept the perimeter and the gardens. A water hose lay on the ground, spraying the stone. He shut off the water, wondering why someone would have directed it toward the pool instead of the lawn.

His breath caught as he neared the pool. A body was floating facedown inside.

God.

It was Taylor Landis.

Chapter 2

Heart pounding, Hayes laid his gun beside the pool, threw off his Stetson and boots, then dove into the water. He flipped Taylor over, cursing at the bruises on her face and neck as he carried her up the steps. Her long blond hair was a tangled mass around her slender face, and her arms dangled beside her, limp and lifeless.

He eased her onto one of the pool chairs, guilt nagging him for thinking that she'd been out shopping while she'd obviously been struggling for her life.

He quickly checked for a pulse. Hell, he couldn't find one.

He punched the number for security. "Taylor Landis was assaulted. I need an ambulance and CSI team ASAP, and have your people search the surrounding area!"

He disconnected the call, then started chest compressions, tilted her head back, gently moved aside her hair, pinched her nose and began mouth-to-mouth resuscitation. "Come on, Taylor, breathe."

Instead, she lay as limp as a rag doll, deathly pale.

Sweat exploded across his brow as he continued CPR.

Another breath. More chest compressions. Sirens wailed in the distance, coming closer. "Come on, Taylor, don't die on me. Fight, dammit."

He inhaled, closed his lips over hers again, and said a silent prayer that he hadn't lost her already. Suddenly her body jerked and she gasped, a strangled plea for air. She was alive...

He muttered a silent thanks as he watched her eyes flicker.

She coughed, choking and gulping in air, and he tilted her head sideways so she could release the excess water trapped in her lungs. Her body trembled, then she slowly opened her eyes and her terrorized gaze met his.

Did she remember what had happened? Could she identify her attacker?

Taylor shivered, clawing her way through the darkness. She was cold and shaking and ached all over. And she was so weak... What had happened?

Muddied, terrifying memories crashed back and panic bolted through her. The pool...the attack...she'd been fighting off the man, but he'd pushed her under water...

She had almost died.

A strangled cry escaped her, and she blinked to clear her vision, then stared in confusion at the man above her.

Sergeant Hayes Keller.

His black eyes pierced her like lasers, while his hands gripped her by the shoulders. For a brief mo ment, fear seized her, but he stroked her cheek so gently that a tidal wave of emotions welled inside her and tears flowed down her face.

"Shh, you're going to be all right now, Taylor. I've called an ambulance."

She gave a slight nod, then swallowed hard to stifle another cry, but the pitiful sound came out anyway. Embarrassed, she pressed her hand over her eyes to regain control and shield herself from his probing look.

She hated to appear weak in front of anyone. Especially this big tough guy with the bad attitude. He didn't like her, and she didn't like him.

"Are you hurt anywhere?" He lifted her fingers from her face, his voice husky and low.

"I'm…okay," she whispered, although her throat felt raw and her voice sounded strained and broken. The effort it took for her to talk triggered a coughing spell, and he lifted her at an angle, murmuring comforting words until the fit subsided, and she sagged back against him.

"Taylor, did you see your attacker? Do you know who did this?"

She shook her head. "Too dark…"

"Was he on foot? Did you hear a car?"

"I don't know." An involuntary shudder rocked her. "He jumped me from behind…"

He clenched his jaw, looking harsh, yet his hands were tender as he stroked her back. "Just relax," he said. "Let me get you a towel or something."

He eased her back down on the chair, and she clutched his arm, not wanting him to leave.

"I'll be right back." He rushed away but returned in seconds and wrapped a thick, plush bath towel around her.

"I need to open the gate for the ambulance," he

said. "The security system was off and I couldn't get through."

She frowned, then realized that her attacker must have disarmed the alarm. But when? And how?

"Inside," she said in a ragged voice. "By the mudroom entrance."

He nodded, raced to the side entrance then disappeared inside the house. Terrified that her attacker might still be lurking nearby, she glanced around the terrace. There hadn't been a car in the drive when she'd arrived home. And she hadn't heard one after she went in the house. He must have come in on foot.

The rose garden with its canopy of trees, bushes and elaborate labyrinth of flower beds normally looked inviting but now it seemed eerie, a place for an intruder to hide. Even her home with its fortress of rooms would provide cover. He could be in a closet or one of the extra suites or even in her bedroom, for that matter.

Another chill swept through her.

What if her attacker was inside? What if he killed the ranger, then returned to finish her off?

Hayes had to hurry. He didn't like leaving Taylor alone for a minute. She was too pale, scared to death, and her attacker might still be on the premises. With ten thousand square feet of house and three acres, no telling where the bastard might be.

He could even be in the house. Had he tried to kill Taylor so he could rob her? Or could her brother, Miles, have attacked her because of her inheritance?

He yanked his boots back on, and they squeaked on the Italian marble tile as he entered the mansion. He paused to listen, but it was quiet. Too quiet. If the security system had been breached because of the power outage, it should be beeping. The security team would also have been notified and would have shown up by now.

Someone had disarmed the alarm intentionally.

He located the security system panel and pushed the manual button to open the gates, grateful to hear the sirens approaching. Then he jogged back outside to Taylor. He'd do a thorough search of the property, house and system once she was taken care of.

She was crouched in the lounge chair, clutching the towel around her, trembling. He scanned the area, walked to the edge of the gardens and checked. But he saw no movement in the carefully tailored layout of trimmed bushes and rose vines. Something caught his eye on a low tree branch. A hair had gotten caught in the twig. A long blond hair but not as blond as Taylor's. A woman's hair.

But Taylor said she'd been attacked by a man.

He bagged the hair anyway for trace.

On edge, he strode back to Taylor, this time standing guard. His jaw clenched at the sight of the scrapes and abrasions on her knees and hands. A bruise darkened her cheek and her nails were jagged and bloody, indicating she'd fought her assailant. Good for her.

Damn bastard. He couldn't stand the thought of any man beating on a woman. Maybe they'd find some trace evidence or DNA.

"What happened?" he asked bluntly.

She winced, biting down on her lip as if the horror of the memory was haunting her. "I came down for a swim," she whispered, coughing in between the words.

He grimaced, knowing her throat was hurting, her vocal chords damaged from the attack.

"He attacked you inside or out here?"

"Out here." She shuddered visibly. "I was swimming laps, then the lights went out." She paused, and her hand went involuntarily to her throat. Whether from pain or trauma he didn't know. Maybe both.

"Then I saw a movement beside the garden and got scared, so I swam to the edge and climbed out. I tried to make it inside, but he grabbed me from behind."

The siren screeched, announcing the arrival of the paramedics, and Hayes leaned over Taylor. "I'll take you around front to them, then I'll search the premises."

She nodded although she tensed when he lifted her and raced to the ambulance. The EMTs met them, and two security officers screeched to a stop, also vaulting into motion. The CSI unit followed a second later.

A thin wiry security guard for Cantara Hills spoke first. "We have other teams dispatched, searching the surrounding houses, canvassing the neighborhood."

Hayes nodded while the EMTs examined Taylor. The CSI tech approached with a kit.

"Process her," he told them. Although the chlorinated water might have washed away or destroyed trace evidence.

"We'll need to take her in for X-rays, an EKG and lab work," one of the paramedics said.

Hayes angled his head toward Taylor. "I'll meet you at the hospital. I want to search the house first in case the perp is inside or left evidence."

Taylor's gaze sought his, and he offered a brusque smile. She looked incredibly small and fragile, as if she didn't want him to leave, but that was shock talking. She'd never given him the time of day before.

Shaking off the thought, he left her with the medics so he could focus on the crime scene.

One of the CSI agents began with Taylor while the second one followed him around to the terrace. "Consider the crime scene as the pool area and backyard," he told the criminologist. "Our victim first saw her attacker by the gardens, so check for footprints, trace, anything you can find."

He gestured around the terrace. "My guess is he knocked over that plant while trying to escape. He probably ran through the gardens, jumped the fence and disappeared on foot, so look for footprints. Maybe his car was parked on a neighboring street. Or maybe he lives nearby." Hell, by now he might have cleaned up, disposed of the clothes he'd worn during the attack and be safely in his house or bed.

Then again, Taylor hadn't been in the pool that long. Maybe he hadn't escaped.

Hopefully one of the security guys would turn up something. "I'm going to check the inside premises, see if our guy might be hiding in one of the rooms."

He hoped to hell he *was* inside Taylor's. Then he could arrest the SOB and make him pay for hurting her.

But first, he'd like to take a fist to him for the bruises on her face and neck.

And if he'd hired Montoya to kill Kimberly…

Well, if he had, Hayes had a good excuse to kill him.

Taylor couldn't shake the realization that she'd almost died as she allowed the EMTs to examine her. If it hadn't been for Sergeant Hayes Keller, she would still be floating in that pool. Dead. Her life over.

And who would care?

Her opulent mansion with its thirty-plus rooms

mocked her. She had Caroline, Margaret and Victoria, but no significant male…

The CSI technician, a young woman with sandy-blond hair, offered her a friendly smile. "We need to photograph your injuries, ma'am."

Taylor frowned, feeling violated all over again as she dropped the towel and the woman began to snap pictures.

While she tried to lift prints from Taylor's neck, then scraped beneath her fingernails, Taylor closed her eyes, focusing on anything besides the attack. But images of the Texas Ranger's eyes flickered in her head. She could still feel his breath on her face, his touch on her mouth. His dark eyes had held worry…

Impossible.

He didn't even like her. He was simply a cop doing a job.

But no man had ever treated her as gently as he had when he'd comforted her.

Good grief, she was pathetic. Was she so desperate for comfort that she'd conjure an attraction between them, and a heart in the cold man beneath that badge?

Her ping-ponging emotions must be due to her upcoming birthday. She was turning the big three-oh. Her biological clock was ticking like a time bomb. And although people assumed she'd host a big bash to celebrate, she wouldn't.

Besides, turning thirty had its own consequences. She'd inherit the millions from the trust fund her father had reserved for her.

Yet he wouldn't personally show to celebrate the big day.

And Miles, her half brother, would hate her even more.

The argument she'd had with him earlier taunted her. The resentment in his tone, the accusations in his eyes. For a moment, she'd been afraid of him. He'd gripped her arm and shouted at her, had sounded out of control, almost threatening. And then that phone call...

No. She didn't like the path her mind was taking.

Miles wouldn't try to kill her, would he?

Chapter 3

Hayes checked the circuit breakers and restored power before searching the mansion. Throwing some light in the house might drive out the perp, or at least strip the guy of his advantage.

He gripped his weapon in one hand and kept his eyes trained for the intruder as he moved through the lower level. Taylor's basement housed a fully equipped gym, rec room with pool table, bar and a movie theater, as well as a separate kitchen and two suites. Hell, her basement furnishings were nicer than anything he owned.

He slowly climbed the stairs, pausing to listen, but other than the hum of the air conditioner and the padding of his boots on the kitchen tiles as he eased through the breakfast room, the house was silent. He crossed the formal dining room, to the living room, to the office. Built-in bookshelves held a variety of titles, while the room held a state-of-the-art computer system, sitting area and conference table. Photographs of Taylor and her father, then Taylor at various charity functions, decorated the walls, along with award plaques and a framed diploma from a private school in Switzerland. She'd apparently earned a business degree and now ran the Landis Foundation.

So she was not only beautiful and rich but smart.

He stored that information while he checked the family room with fireplace and twelve-foot ceilings and a ballroom with Palladian windows which obviously was used to host her elaborate parties. He'd seen photographs of them in the society section of the newspaper.

A place where he wouldn't be caught dead.

Finally, he found his way through a hallway to a bedroom suite the size of an apartment.

He wondered if this was Taylor's suite, but saw no personal belongings in the room. Decorated in earth tones, it held a king-size brass bed, dresser, flat-screen TV and sitting room. A massive bath in gold and white with a Jacuzzi and dozens of plush towels overflowing a baker's rack opened to a large walk-in closet.

The suite was empty, so he headed back to the foyer, then climbed the curved staircase, again pausing to listen. But he heard nothing. He still couldn't relax, not until he'd searched every square inch of the house.

Taking a deep breath, he clenched his hand tighter around his gun and combed the suites to the left, then retraced his steps back to the bank of rooms on the right. In the first bedroom, a white four-poster bed draped in blue-and-white satin drew his eye.

Judging from the lived-in look and feminine furnishings, he guessed it was Taylor's room. A black satin robe lay draped across the bed and a pair of slippers peeked from beneath the footboard. The room looked like her—tasteful, classy, soft.

For a moment, he imagined her sprawled on the satin sheets wearing nothing but a skimpy teddy or…nothing at all, and his body hardened with desire.

He quickly shook off the image. What in the hell was wrong with him?

An iPod and speaker system sat opposite the bed on a cluster of shelves holding candles, and in the corner a dresser held a silver brush and comb set and a jewelry box. He wondered if Taylor kept all her jewelry so accessible, but assumed she had a built-in safe somewhere in the house for her more expensive pieces. When she was released from the hospital, he'd have her check the house to see if anything was missing.

A bay window with chaise and reading lamp occupied one corner with a window seat separating two oversized chairs. He bypassed them and entered an elegant bath in blue and white, and a set of closets. Inside, he clenched his jaw at the sight of glittery gowns, expensive wraps, designer shoes and business suits. The second closet held Taylor's casual clothes, he assumed, since it was filled with sundresses, slacks, designer sweaters, and one wall housed shelves holding bathing suits and summer wear.

He snarled. His yearly salary wouldn't equal her monthly clothing allowance.

It didn't matter. He had to focus on his mission.

The rooms were empty, and didn't look as if they'd been touched by an intruder, meaning the perpetrator probably hadn't attacked her with the intention of theft.

So not a break-in gone awry. The perp's intentions had been more sinister—murder.

Moving on, he searched the other rooms, sighing as he descended the steps. Just as he was bypassing the office, he noticed a broken fingernail caught on the edge of the rug by the desk. He stooped and picked it up, wondering who it belonged to. The phone jangled so he bagged the fingernail, then hurried to the desk and checked the caller ID. An international call. Her father?

He picked up the receiver. "Taylor Landis's residence."

A long moment of silence. "Who in the hell is this?"

"Sergeant Hayes Keller, Texas Ranger. Whom am I speaking with?"

"Lionel Landis. What's going on? Why are you at my daughter's house? And why are you answering her phone?"

Hayes grimaced at the man's condescending tone. But he had a right to know his daughter had been attacked. And Hayes had to explore every angle. If the assault on Taylor wasn't related to Kimberly's murder, it might have something to do with the wealthy Landis family. Then he'd need information on the family and their business dealings.

"Sir, I hate to have to tell you this, but your daughter was assaulted tonight."

"What? My God, is she all right?"

"Yes, sir. But the paramedics transported her to the hospital for X-rays and observation."

"I heard about those break-ins in the community. Was that what this was about?"

"I don't know yet, but I can assure you I'll find out."

A long pause. "Maybe I should hire a bodyguard to watch her around the clock."

Hayes clenched his jaw. Odd that her father didn't offer to fly back to see her himself. Instead, he wanted to send hired help.

A private bodyguard would mean Hayes wouldn't have to spend time with Taylor himself.

But damn. He was a ranger, and he had to finish this case, find the man who'd tried to kill Taylor. "That won't be necessary, Mr. Landis. I'll personally provide protection for your daughter 24-7."

He hung up the phone but noticed the desk drawer ajar and examined it. The bottom drawer had been jimmied, papers tossed around.

The killer had been in this room. He'd have CSI dust it for prints.

What had he been looking for?

Exhaustion weighed on Taylor as the nurse helped her settle into the hospital bed. She'd been treated, had blood drawn, undergone an EKG, then wheeled to X-ray, where they'd x-rayed her chest and lungs. Thankfully all the tests were clear.

Other than nearly dying tonight, she was healthy.

Still, they'd hooked her up to an IV, checked her vitals, then the nurse offered her a sedative. But Taylor expected Sergeant Keller to show up any minute to question her, and she wanted to be coherent.

Besides, she avoided taking pills or medications unless it was absolutely necessary. Too many people she'd met at parties relied on drugs or alcohol for recreation and survival, and she was determined not to fall into that dangerous lifestyle so often portrayed in the tabloids as the rich and careless.

Still, fatigue pulled at her, and she finally dozed off.

But nightmares of the attack haunted her, and she tossed and turned, battling the terrifying memories.

She was running, fighting, struggling for air, being pushed under the water, held down...drowning.

She woke, gasping for air, her heart racing. Gray had settled over the room like a fog, the sound of someone breathing echoing in the quiet. Panic shot through her.

Oh, God, her attacker had come here to finish killing her.

She threw off the covers to run, but suddenly two firm hands gripped her arms. "Shh, Taylor, it's me. Hayes."

She was just about to scream, but the sound of his husky voice registered, and she stifled a sob.

"I didn't mean to scare you, but you were sleeping."

She relaxed against him, but her heart was still pounding. "I was dreaming about the attack..."

He smoothed her hair from her cheek, then eased down onto the edge of the bed. "It's over now. You're safe."

She nodded and forced herself to block out the terrifying images from her nightmare. Despite her efforts, her hand went to her throat.

"You didn't find him at the house?" she asked.

He shook his head, and she noticed he was wearing the same jeans and shirt he had on when he'd pulled her from the pool. They were still damp, and he must be uncomfortable, but he didn't seem to notice.

"Your assailant caused the power outage by tampering with the circuit breakers, but I didn't find anyone inside. CSI is dusting for prints and searching both the inside and outside, as well, for footprints, fibers, anything that might help us identify him."

"He didn't steal anything?"

"Not that I could tell. But you'll need to inventory your valuables, jewelry, etcetera, to verify if anything is missing."

"I'll do that tomorrow when I get home."

He gave a clipped nod. "The desk in your office had been ransacked. Do you have any idea what the intruder might have been looking for?"

She shook her head. "Maybe financial information on the foundation?"

"It's possible. You should examine your files and follow up on any credit cards."

She bit her lip. "Yes, I will."

"I left a guard at the house overnight in case he returns or someone else shows up."

"Thank you, Sergeant."

"You can call me Hayes." He hesitated, then his gaze zeroed in on her nails. "Your nails are real?"

She nodded. "Why?"

"I found a broken red nail, looked like an acrylic, inside your house."

She frowned. "I often have guests over, females. It could have come from any one of them."

"You're sure your attacker was male?"

His question threw her off guard. "I think so."

"I also found a blond hair caught in a twig in the tree by the garden."

She rubbed her temple. "I have parties out there, too. It could belong to anyone."

"I'll see what forensics says." He paused. "Can you talk about the attack now?"

She propped herself up against the pillows. "I told you what happened already."

"Indulge me and go over it again. Sometimes the passage of time allows victims to remember more details."

She sighed, hating to rehash the night but knowing it was imperative. "Okay. I got home around ten, but I was restless, antsy after all that's happened in the neighborhood lately." In fact, she hadn't slept well since Kimberly McQuade had died. If she hadn't hosted the party that night, maybe the young woman would still be alive.

She glanced at Hayes, suddenly realizing that he probably felt the same way, probably blamed her.

"Go on," he said sharply.

She cleared her throat; it was still so dry it hurt to talk. "I couldn't sleep, so I checked the alarm and changed into my swimsuit. Then I went for a swim."

"Had you been drinking?"

Irritation gnawed at her. "I had a glass of wine with dinner, but I wasn't drunk if that's what you're implying."

"You usually swim alone at night?"

She tensed at the scrutiny in his tone. Did he think she was being stupid, that she'd brought the attack on herself? "Sometimes," she said truthfully. "I'm a good swimmer, and I had the security system set." She glared at him. "Besides, I thought you rangers had caught the killer and that I was safe."

A muscle ticked in his jaw, and she knew she'd scored a direct hit.

"Your attack may or may not be related to the other crimes," he said sharply. "You're wealthy, everyone knows that. You must have some enemies."

She tore her gaze away with a shiver. If he'd meant to scare her, he had.

"Were the lights on when you came out by the pool?"

"Yes, Sergeant. I would have called security if they hadn't been."

He simply arched a dark brow, his expression cold and hard, and she silently willed herself to stop reacting. What did she care what Hayes Keller thought of her?

When she continued, she tried to relay the events as if it had happened to a stranger, not to her. "I was swimming laps when the power flickered off. I got nervous, decided to see what caused the outage, then I saw a movement by the gardens. I got out and ran toward the door... Before I reached it, the man jumped me from behind." She paused, unable to breathe for a moment as she remembered his fingers around her throat.

Again, the ranger stared at her with an intensity that made her more nervous.

She could not break down in front of the man again. "We struggled and he tried to strangle me, then we fell into the pool."

"He fell into the pool with you?"

"Yes. I fought him, but he kept choking me, then pushed me underwater and held me down."

He made a low sound with his teeth. "That's probably the reason he turned on the water hose, to wash away his prints. But I'll have the pool dragged for trace." He paused. "You said you were a swimmer?"

"Yes, high-school swim team. I set the record for holding my breath the longest on my team."

"That's probably what saved you."

"No, Sergeant Keller, you saved me," she said with a tentative smile. "If you hadn't shown up when you had..."

He glanced away for the first time, his jaw clenched tight, then shrugged. "Just doing my job, ma'am."

She didn't like the way he said *ma'am,* as if it was an insult. "Well, thank you anyway."

His eyes darkened, narrowed to slits as if he was issuing some kind of silent warning. "You don't owe me thanks. Just answer the questions."

She tensed at his brusque tone. Just when she thought he was human, he turned back into a growling lion. "What else do you want to know?"

The bite to her voice echoed in the silence for a moment before he replied. "You didn't see the man's face?"

"No. He was wearing a mask."

"Like a ski mask?"

"Yes. And gloves. Latex gloves."

His brows pinched together with his frown. "Maybe those will turn up or we'll lift some trace off of your fingernails."

She nodded, glad she'd fought back.

"Anything else you remember about your attacker? A particular odor? His height, size?"

"No, it's all so foggy."

His dark gaze met hers. "Tell me about your day, what happened earlier, before the attack."

She scrunched her nose in thought. "I don't see how that's relevant."

"Just do it, Taylor. Retrace your steps."

"All right, but you don't have to be so ornery." She tried to think back. "I spent the morning handling routine business matters for the foundation. Had lunch there. Then a business meeting with the City Board at five that ran till about seven. After that, I met a friend for dinner in San Antonio."

"Did you notice anyone following you during the day? Or when you left the restaurant?"

She rubbed her temple where a headache pulsed. "No."

He folded his arms. "Who attended the board meeting?"

"All of the board members. Sarah DeMarco, Devon Goldenrod—"

"Kenneth Sutton?"

"Yes."

"I was told that he and Kimberly McQuade had an argument before she died. Do you know what their disagreement was about?"

She frowned. "No. Kimberly was looking over the campaign budget, and she'd also reviewed the other finances for the board. Maybe there was a problem."

"So they might have argued about money?"

"I really don't know. Why is that important?"

"I'm just tying up loose ends. Sometimes small details can offer clues."

She conceded his point. After all, he was the cop. The chip-on-the-shoulder one, but it looked as if she was stuck with him.

"So, did anything unusual happen at the meeting?"

She hesitated, hated to impugn Kenneth unnecessarily.

"Taylor, I can't help you if you don't tell me the truth."

"Kenneth seemed excited about planning ahead for the gubernatorial election, but we did have a tense moment."

He leaned forward. "About what?"

"The bid for the new city library and to extend the tourist area by the Riverwalk. There's talk that the bid was tampered with."

"And that Kenneth was involved?"

"That's what I've heard, but he denied it and I believe him."

Silence met her statement, making her wonder what he was thinking. "You don't like Kenneth Sutton, do you?"

"He's a politician. No, I don't trust him."

"And after the meeting? Who did you have dinner with?"

She hesitated.

"Taylor?"

She twisted her hands together. "Margaret Hathaway."

His jaw tightened again. "You two are friends?"

"Yes. We met at our favorite restaurant and sushi bar, Bluefish. Margaret's wedding to Devon Goldenrod is around the corner, and we were finalizing wedding plans."

"Did anything unusual happen while you were there?"

"Not unusual. But I ran into my half brother, Miles."

His mouth thinned. "How did that go?"

She sighed, knotting the bedsheet between her fingers. She hated to discuss family. But if the ranger asked at the restaurant, he'd find out on his own. Her problems with her brother weren't exactly a secret.

"Taylor, I know that Miles has been hitting up friends for loans. Caroline told us that already." He cleared his throat. "Is that what he wanted with you?"

So much for family privacy. Then again, she should be used to it. Just because she was wealthy, tabloids, reporters and neighbors thought her life was food for the gossipmongers. "Yes, but I turned him down again. He blew up, made a scene…"

She looked away, his phone call echoing in her head. Hayes narrowed his eyes. "He threatened you, didn't he?"

She sucked in a sharp breath. "Not exactly."

"What does that mean?"

She finally faced him. "He told me I'd be sorry for turning my back on him."

He stood, bracing his feet apart, and hooked his thumbs in his belt loops. "That sounds like a threat to me."

She shrugged, unable to voice the truth. That she was afraid of Miles.

"I've posted a guard outside your door."

"You think that's necessary?"

He nodded. "And your father called your house. I told him I'd protect you 24-7."

Taylor's stomach dipped.

"I'm going to talk to your little brother. Find out if he tried to make good on his threat." His snakeskin cowboy boots pounded the floor as he pivoted. "Meanwhile, think hard, Taylor. In the morning I want you to make a list of any enemies you might have, former boyfriends or current ones who might want to harm you. Is there one you can think of offhand?"

She lowered her head. "No. I haven't been involved with anyone recently."

"In the past?"

She hadn't broken any hearts if that's what he meant. She'd never let a man get that close. "Maybe this was a random break-in."

"Just make the list. If it wasn't a robbery then someone wanted you dead."

A chill went through her. "You don't have to remind me, Sergeant."

"No? Well, think about this. The person who tried to strangle you could be someone you know from the foundation, someone who has it in for your family, someone who wants your money."

His dark gaze pierced her. "And it very well may be someone you know and trust, someone you're even close to. Someone you think is a friend, or your very own brother."

Chapter 4

Taylor's heart raced. Surely the ranger was wrong. None of her friends would actually harm her. Although neither she nor Caroline had thought that Carlson Woodward was dangerous and they'd been mistaken.

And what about Miles? He'd always been jealous of her and had done some underhanded things when they were younger, but he'd never been violent.

Not until recently. But lately she'd seen a spark flare in his eyes that scared her.

His substance abuse and gambling problems had escalated, making him seem desperate at times, and... frightening.

A knock sounded at the door, and suddenly Margaret Hathaway rushed in, her face stricken with concern.

"Oh my God, Taylor, I heard what happened. Are you all right?"

Taylor clenched the sheets as Hayes gave Margaret a feral look, a look that nearly froze Margaret in her rush to hug Taylor.

"I'm fine, Margaret," Taylor said, although tears blurred her sight. She could hold herself together in the face of Hayes's brusqueness, but her best friend's tenderness unraveled her calm facade. Although Margaret was old enough to be her mother, they had bonded as soon as they had met. The one person in the world Taylor trusted, the one who loved her unconditionally, was Margaret. And Taylor felt the same way about her friend. Not only was Margaret smart but kindhearted, and she'd faced her own share of problems and pain, although she hid them well from the prying eyes of the public.

Margaret bypassed Hayes and swept Taylor into a hug. "God, this is awful, Tay. What happened?"

Taylor relayed the short version of the story, well aware of Hayes's scowl.

"Who in the world would want to hurt you, honey?"

"I don't know, Margaret." Taylor sighed. "But Sergeant Keller saved my life."

Surprise registered on Margaret's face, then she gave Hayes a curious look and smiled. "Sergeant, thank you so much for rescuing Taylor. I don't know what I'd do if anything happened to her."

Hayes's dark eyes turned icy. "Just doing my job, ma'am. Where were you this evening?"

"Sergeant Keller, you're out of line," Taylor said sharply.

"Like I told you earlier, Miss Landis, your attacker could be one of your friends."

"It certainly isn't Margaret," Taylor said between clenched teeth. "She would never hurt me."

"That's right," Margaret said, obviously insulted at the thought. "Taylor and I are best friends."

"Then you won't mind answering my question," Hayes said in a lethal voice.

Margaret tightened her jaw, and Taylor gripped her hand. "I told you she wouldn't hurt me."

"I had dinner with Taylor, then met my fiancé, Devon Goldenrod, at his house," Margaret said. "You can ask him."

Hayes arched a brow. "Right, the golden boy who's vying for votes in the next City Board election."

Taylor grimaced at the disdain in Hayes's voice. She'd heard he'd had a rough life but he didn't have to take his attitude out on her and Margaret.

Then again, for a moment, pain had flashed in his eyes when he'd seen Margaret hug her. Kimberly had mentioned that he'd been adopted, that there were some things he refused to talk about.

Margaret folded her arms. "Sergeant, what are you doing to find the person who attacked Taylor?"

His lips thinned into a deeper frown. "I've processed the crime scene and will be investigating everyone in Miss Landis's life for motive."

"What about keeping her safe?" Margaret asked.

An evil grin slid across the ranger's face. "Well, ma'am," he drawled mockingly, "I've got that covered."

"How?" Margaret asked.

"I've been assigned as her bodyguard day and night."

Taylor's stomach sizzled with nerves yet she pressed her fingers to her lips, remembering how gentle he'd been when he resuscitated her. How in the world was she going to endure being near this man when he obviously hated everything about her?

* * *

Hayes balled his hands into fists to control his temper. Dammit, Taylor Landis looked all soft and needy. And she'd touched those luscious lips and looked up at him as if she was remembering his mouth on hers when he'd brought her back to life.

Hell. He couldn't think about that. Couldn't touch her mouth or any other part of her body again.

So he lashed out at her by taking perverse joy in taunting her rich friend. Maybe it was payback for all the taunting he'd received as a kid.

Margaret narrowed her eyes. "For some reason that doesn't make me feel any better, Sergeant."

He threw his head back and chuckled. "Don't worry, Ms. Hathaway, I won't let anything bad happen to the little princess."

"You'd better not." Margaret's eyes flashed with emotions that Hayes refused to allow to get to him. "Because she's going to be my maid of honor at my wedding, and I don't want her showing up in a cast or on crutches."

Or not showing up because she was dead, Hayes thought, although he refrained from comment. "In light of the fact that someone tried to kill you tonight, Taylor, you shouldn't put yourself in the limelight right now."

Margaret's face blanched with fear, and Hayes's gut tightened.

"He's right," Margaret said. "I'll postpone everything until after the police find out who did this to you, Tay."

"No, you won't," Taylor said, shooting Hayes a harsh look.

"But I don't want to take a chance on you being hurt," Margaret argued.

"She's right, Taylor," Hayes said. "You need to go into hiding until we find the man who attacked you."

Anger sizzled in Taylor's sky-blue eyes. "I refuse to run and hide. I'm not going to let some creep scare me from living my life."

Hayes glared at her. "Then you're a fool and asking for trouble."

She turned a saccharine sweet smile on Hayes that was so fake it fueled his temper. "But, Sergeant, you'll be with me day and night to protect me."

He met her gaze with a sinister stare, but she smiled again, and focused on Margaret as if he was her minion.

Rage ripped through him. That was how she saw him, and he couldn't forget it.

As soon as Margaret left, Taylor fell into an exhausted sleep. Fitful images of the attack drove her awake several times, but when she opened her eyes, she saw Hayes Keller sitting in the chair in the corner watching her. She shouldn't have found comfort in having him close by, but his big masculine presence soothed her nerves, and she rolled to her side and drifted back to sleep.

The last time she woke, sunlight streamed through the hospital window, and she checked the chair. He was slightly slumped, his head having fallen sideways in sleep, and his massive chest moved up and down with his breath. Catching him off guard in sleep seemed somehow *intimate*.

She noticed the fine dark stubble along his rugged jaw, the way his thick lips formed a constant scowl, the little curl in his dark hair that made her want to run her hands through it. His jaw was broad, his nose blunt and slightly crooked as if it had been broken and his eyebrows were full and thick, arched to frame his eyes in a way that added to his intensity.

The sound of his breathing floated toward her, a coarse whisper just as masculine as his face and body.

Somehow in that moment, he looked almost...human. And approachable.

He suddenly opened his eyes, his gaze meeting hers, and a tingling started low and deep in her belly. Lord, he was potently sexy. Like a cowboy hero in a Western.

No, no, no. She couldn't allow herself to fantasize about him.

His eyebrows lifted slightly, and a heartbeat of silence stretched between them, fraught with tension.

She must be insane because at that moment she wanted him.

Then the door swung open and the doctor walked in. "Good morning, Miss Landis. Let's see if it's time to dismiss you."

Hayes pushed to his feet, his boots pounding as he walked to the door. "I'll be outside. Let me know when you're ready to leave."

She nodded, although her throat was too thick to speak. She could count on her hand the number of men she'd actually been this attracted to over the years.

Why did Hayes Keller have to be one of them?

Hayes paced outside Taylor's hospital room. What in the hell had just happened?

After endless hours of being tortured by watching Taylor toss and turn, of wanting to crawl in bed and comfort her when she'd cried out in terror from her nightmares, he'd finally dozed off, only to have his own demons haunt him.

He had been five years old, locked in that damn closet where his adopted parents stuffed him anytime they needed to go out. Or when they just needed some peace and quiet.

Or when they wanted to punish him for being bad. And according to them, he was bad all the time so he'd spent half his young life in that tiny dark closet.

He still had claustrophobia. Hated dark closets, basements and crawl spaces.

Hell, he was a grown man now. Had his own life. A nice little cabin he'd built himself on a small ranch with tons of light where no one could bother him, where he'd never be stuck in that dark place again.

And he wouldn't...not even in his mind.

He had escaped and had a job to do, and he'd damn well do it without allowing Taylor to get under his skin like she had earlier.

He'd survived that hellhole of a family. He could survive being assigned as her bodyguard.

All the more reason to find her attacker quickly, though, so he could leave Cantara Hills.

The door opened and the doctor appeared, Taylor's chart in hand. "She's dressing, then she can go home."

He nodded. Margaret had brought Taylor an overnight bag. A nurse appeared with a wheelchair, and he went and retrieved his SUV from the parking garage, then pulled up in front of the hospital. Taylor climbed in and fastened her seat belt, and he maneuvered into the early morning traffic and drove to Cantara Hills.

"If we're forced to spend time together, we should

get to know each other," Taylor said, filling the awkward silence.

He glared at her. "I intend to learn everything about you."

Her blond brows rose, eyes sparkling. "Really?"

He pressed his mouth into a frown. "Yes, and all your friends."

The light left her eyes. "Then tell me about yourself. About your family."

A muscle ticked in his jaw. "I'm here to do a job, Taylor. My personal life is off-limits."

For a brief second, hurt tugged at her expression.

He turned away from her, refused to feel guilty. "I need to go by my room at the country club and pick up my duffel bag."

"Excuse me?" she said quietly.

"I told you I'm your bodyguard. That means I'm moving in."

She shivered and hugged her arms around her waist. "I certainly hope you find whoever did this quickly."

He chuckled. She obviously didn't want him around any more than he wanted to be with her. "That's the plan. In fact, I'd like to clean up and then I want to talk to your brother and Kenneth Sutton."

She stared out the window, her expression pained. "I just can't believe one of them would try to kill me."

He clamped his mouth shut. She was too damn innocent. Just because these people were related to her or acted as if they were her friends didn't mean they didn't have secrets or a motive for murder.

Chapter 5

Taylor grimaced at the way Hayes had cut her off when she'd inquired about his family. She felt for him, but she couldn't continue offering friendship if he was going to be so rude.

Besides, as soon as he found out who'd tried to kill her, he'd ride out of Cantara Hills and never look back.

She'd had it with men either using her or disappearing when they'd finished their agenda.

He parked in the circular drive, and she jumped out, not bothering to wait for him to open the door for her. The inside of the car had been too crowded, too hot, too filled with his male scent.

So why did his eyes haunt her?

Frustration mingled with fear as she unlocked the door. But Hayes pushed her aside and ordered her to wait while he checked the house. She paced nervously.

She'd always felt safe here, but after the night before, would she ever feel safe again?

At least her estate was large so she and Hayes wouldn't be trapped in close quarters together. She noticed her office door ajar and veered inside to see if anything was missing. Thankfully, she kept her important papers, stocks and bonds, in a safe, and she examined it first, then breathed a sigh of relief. Next she searched the desk files, but didn't notice anything missing. Even the file she'd been reviewing regarding the discrepancy with the city council bids seemed intact.

What had the intruder been looking for? What had been important enough for him to have killed her to get it?

Hayes noticed the stricken look on Taylor's face. The reality of her home invasion had finally hit her. But he steeled himself against sympathy. "Did you notice anything missing?"

She shook her head, then tucked a strand of her long blond hair behind one ear. "The safe hasn't been open, and all my files are intact."

So what had the killer been looking for?

"Inventory your jewelry."

She nodded and he followed her to her suite. She looked wary as she entered her bedroom, and he remained at the threshold, shifting to lean against the frame while she sorted through her jewelry. The sight of diamonds and the glittering emeralds and sapphires served as a reminder of the yawning distance between them.

"Is everything there?"

She bit down on her bottom lip. "Yes...wait. Let me look at my other jewelry box."

She had two?

He tugged at his Stetson as she opened her closet and retrieved a smaller box from the top shelf. The box was intricately carved, black lacquered, an Asian design although small, almost as if it had belonged to a child. She traced a finger over it lovingly and he wondered if it held special meaning for her. Maybe a gift from Daddy or a former lover?

The thought sent a small pang of jealousy streaking through him, but he brushed it off. What did he care if she had a dozen lovers? He would never be one of them.

"Taylor?"

She inhaled sharply, then lifted the lid, and her chin quivered. "It's gone."

"What?"

"My charm bracelet," she said softly.

"What was it worth?"

She lifted her head, and emotions splintered her eyes. "Not much, but it was priceless to me. My mother gave it to me." Her voice broke. "She used to add a charm every year at Christmas."

And her mother had died when she was eight.

"Why would someone take that piece instead of all those jewels in your other chest?" he asked.

"I don't know," she said, although the odd catch in her voice told him she was lying. "It's not valuable, not monetarily, I mean. But it was special to me."

He cleared his throat. "It had to be someone who knew where you kept it." Meaning the thief had meant to hurt her because he knew she valued the piece. "You think your brother stole it?"

She hesitated so long he had his answer. "Let me clean up and I'll pay Miles a visit," she said.

"I'm going with you, but I'd like to shower first."

He wanted to question Miles without her, yet he couldn't leave her alone, not knowing she was in danger, so he agreed, then headed downstairs to the guest suite.

But as he stripped and climbed in beneath the warm water, he imagined her upstairs doing the same. They could have conserved water if they'd showered together.

A bitter laugh lodged in his throat. Hell, he had to be honest, at least to himself. He didn't care about conserving water.

He was a hot-blooded man. He just wanted to see the damn woman naked.

Taylor stewed over the bracelet while she showered. She didn't want to believe her brother would take the charm bracelet, because he understood its significance to her.

Yet he had been furious with her the last time they'd run in to each other.

She dressed in a pair of her favorite jeans and a sleeveless silk tank and hurried down the stairs. Hayes stood in the foyer in a crisp white shirt and jeans, his Stetson shadowing his face.

"Do you know where to find Miles?"

She glanced at the grandfather clock. "At this time of the morning, he'll still be sleeping off last night's party."

"Then let's go wake him up," Hayes said.

Her stomach quivered as they walked to his SUV, and she studied the landscape architecture of the community as he drove to Miles's house, an English Tudor her father had bought for him for his twenty-first birthday. Of course, Miles had pouted that it wasn't as large as the estate where Taylor lived, which had only increased the tension between the two of them.

But she actually earned a salary, and kept the mansion to host various charity functions for the foundation. She took pride in using her salary for her own personal causes—she and Margaret funded a special program for needy children and Margaret spearheaded one for pregnant teens.

"This is it?" Hayes asked as he parked in front of the Tudor.

"Yes."

"He lives alone?"

"Most of the time, but he entertains a lot. Mostly women."

"Your brother is the party guy, isn't he?"

"I'm afraid so." To the detriment of himself and anyone who cared about him.

They climbed out, and she led the way to her brother's front door. Hayes punched the doorbell, tapping his boot on the brick stoop as they waited. Impatience made Taylor stab the button again.

No answer, so she retrieved her keys from her purse and unlocked the door. "He has to be here. It's too early for him to be out for the day."

"Maybe he spent the night with his latest hook-up."

"That's possible," Taylor said as she pushed her way inside.

"Does Miles have a key to your house?" Hayes asked.

Her gaze swung to his, and she released a sigh. "Yes."

He shook his head in disgust, and she bolted up the stairs toward his room. "Miles, it's me, Taylor. Are you up there?"

No answer.

"Miles, I hope you're decent, because I'm coming in."

She pounded on his door, and Hayes stood behind her, his presence oddly comforting as she opened it. "Miles?"

A low growl erupted, and she spotted him in bed, the covers half over him, a bottle of Scotch on the nightstand.

She stormed through the room, grabbed the slacks he'd tossed on the floor and threw them at him. "Get dressed. We have to talk."

"What in the hell are you doing here?" He scrubbed a hand through his scraggly hair and glanced at the clock. "Good God, Taylor. It's only ten o'clock in the morning."

"At ten o'clock, most people have already been at work for two hours," she snapped.

"Get out of here!" he shouted, then rolled over and pulled the comforter over his head.

Hayes jerked the covers from his face. "Either dress and join us downstairs or I'll drag you there myself."

Taylor smiled. If anyone could coerce the truth from her brother, it would be Hayes Keller.

Hayes ignored Miles's litany of profanities as he stepped outside the man's room. He, Egan and Brody had already speculated about Miles's motive. The twenty-four-year-old could have taken advantage of Kimberly's death to kill Taylor by pretending to be a vigilante killer, murdering suspects and witnesses involved in Kimberly's death to cover up his real target—his sister. All so he could gain access to Taylor's inheritance.

Taylor walked ahead down the staircase, her irritation with her brother evident by the strain on her face.

He followed her to the kitchen, where she brewed coffee. By the time Miles stumbled into the room, she'd poured both herself and Hayes a cup, then handed a third mug to her brother. He reeked of booze and cigarettes and a sour attitude.

"All right, Taylor. What is such a big freaking deal you came over here? And why is this ranger with you? You shacking up with him or something?"

Hayes knotted his hands, barely resisting the urge to ram his fist in the idiot's mouth. He'd put up with spoiled rich kids like him all his life, treating him like a third-class citizen.

Taylor's blue eyes glimmered with emotions. "Did you take the charm bracelet Mother gave me?"

Anger stained Miles's already flushed cheeks. "You dragged me out of bed because of that stupid trinket?"

"It's not stupid, Miles," Taylor said. "That was the only personal thing I have from Mom, and you know how much it meant to me."

He narrowed his eyes. "Yeah, but it's not worth anything, so why would I take it?"

"I don't know." Taylor's voice warbled with emotions. "Maybe you wanted to hurt me for not loaning you money."

Miles pushed his face into Taylor's like some childhood bully. "If I wanted to get back at you, I wouldn't pussyfoot around with some dinky bracelet. I'd go for something worth my time."

And money, Hayes thought grimly. Miles's daddy had probably bailed him out of trouble all his life, but if Hayes discovered he'd attacked Taylor, Hayes would make certain the guy paid.

He jerked Miles by the collar of his polo shirt. "So what would you do?" Hayes asked. "Try to kill her?"

Miles wheeled around on him. "Kill her? What in the hell are you talking about?"

"Where were you last night?" Hayes asked in a barely controlled tone.

Miles's eyes widened in alarm as he realized the implication. "Why do you want to know?"

Taylor crossed her arms over her chest. "Answer him, Miles."

Miles glanced back and forth between the two of them, fear and hate emanating from him. "I went clubbing. Took a cab home this morning."

"Can anyone vouch for you?" Hayes asked.

Though the earring in his left ear glinted in the sunlight, his face paled slightly. "I don't know, the bars were crowded."

"So you don't have an alibi?"

Temper flared in Miles's bloodshot eyes. "Do I need one?"

"Yes. Someone tried to kill your sister," Hayes said. "And you have a motive."

Miles backed up as if he thought Hayes might physically attack him. "Listen, I got drunk, went dancing. There's no way you're going to pin anything on me." He reached for the phone. "I'll call my attorney."

The weasel had shown no concern for Taylor at all. "You mean, you'll call your daddy to come to the rescue?" Hayes said snidely.

Miles's nostrils flared. "Guys like you have a chip on their shoulder," Miles muttered. "Everyone in Cantara Hills has talked about it. You'd try to railroad me because you're jealous of my money."

Rage burned Hayes's throat. "I'm not jealous of anything *you* have."

Miles jerked an accusatory look toward Taylor. "He is, isn't he, Taylor? He knows he's not good enough for the women here, so he's trying to make you doubt your own family."

Hayes's temper snapped. This time he jammed his face into Miles's, intentionally proving he was bigger and stronger. "If I discover you tried to hurt your sister, I'll come after you so fast you won't know what hit you. And no amount of Daddy's money will save you."

Deciding he had to leave before he pelted the little weasel, he stalked toward the door. He heard Taylor's footfalls as she hurried along behind him, but he didn't look back. Didn't want her to know how deeply her pissant brother's comment had cut him.

Chapter 6

Taylor almost laughed at the sheer look of terror on Miles's face.

Was he afraid of Hayes because he really believed the ranger was out to nail him or because he had something to hide?

"What do you think?" Hayes asked her as they settled in his car.

"I don't know," she said, scrunching her face in worry. "Over the years Miles and I have had our differences, but he is still my half brother."

"One who's jealous as hell of you," Hayes said. "And he has a substance-abuse problem, owes heavy debts and may be desperate."

All true. Still, the thought of one of her own family members trying to take her life made bile rise in her throat. "Families are supposed to love and trust each other," she said quietly. "They should stick together, support each other in difficult times."

"It doesn't always work like that," Hayes commented dryly.

Still, sadness weighed on her. When her mother had died, her father had thrown himself into work and travel, then sifted through women and marriages as easily as she did shoes. She'd needed him around, yet he'd chosen work and other women over raising his daughter. Then there had been the long line of nannies. And Miles had come along…

At first she'd been excited about having a little brother, but as he'd grown up, things had changed.

Miles had resented any attention their father had given her. One memory surfaced, a time when he'd cut off all of her dolls' hair, then blamed her. And another when he'd smashed the music box their father had given her.

Suddenly she felt a hand cover hers. When she looked up, Hayes was watching her, compassion in his eyes. He understood what it was like to be hurt by family.

"Let's talk to Kenneth Sutton now. He was upset with Kimberly for questioning him on the bids. And you asked him about it, too, didn't you?"

She nodded. "But I've worked with Kenneth for some time now, Hayes. I respect his ethics and his view on politics. I can't imagine him doing anything underhanded."

"He's a politician," Hayes said. "Maybe he thought no one would find out. With his campaign run for governor, it's even more important that anything illicit he was involved in be kept a secret."

She grimaced, praying Hayes was wrong and that she hadn't been fooled by Kenneth.

* * *

Hayes hadn't meant to take Taylor's hand, but she'd seemed so fragile and sad that he hadn't been able to resist. She'd been through an ordeal the past twenty-four hours and had shown amazing strength.

Even rich little girls had problems, he admitted silently. Even rich families could be dysfunctional.

Still, he kept his opinion to himself. He was here to do a job, not coddle Taylor. Miles's comment only further reminded him that their worlds might coexist but didn't mix.

"Taylor, do you mind calling Sutton to make sure he's at his office before we drop by?"

"Sure." She retrieved her cell phone from her purse and punched in the number. He started the engine but waited while she asked Sutton's secretary if he was in.

"Thanks, Dora, tell Kenneth that Ranger Keller and I will be right there."

She hung up, then he maneuvered into traffic. A strained silence stretched between them, the heat in the car climbing to an uncomfortable level.

"What made you decide to become a Texas Ranger?" Taylor finally asked.

He frowned, squinting through the bright sun glinting off the front window, and flipped the air conditioner up a notch. "I guess Brody paved the path. When he joined, he talked about the training and chasing down the bad guys…" He shrugged. "Figured it was better than being one of them, and I was headed down that path."

He'd had a lot of anger built up from the Kellers and would never have survived if he hadn't made friends with Egan, Kimberly and Brody.

"Kimberly told me you guys were all friends as kids."

"Yeah, we grew up in the same neighborhood, although our backgrounds were different."

"You don't have to come from the same background to get along," Taylor murmured.

He jerked his head sideways. "They weren't the same but they weren't that different." Not like the two of them.

"Kimberly said your foster parents weren't very nice."

He scrubbed a hand over the back of his neck and felt it sweating. "Kim talked too much."

"She cared about you," Taylor said softly.

A pang squeezed his chest, reminding him of her death and the events that had brought them to Cantara Hills. He couldn't discuss Kimberly with Taylor. Kimberly had understood where he'd come from, what it was like to be thrown away by a parent. What it had been like to want something that you'd never had.

Taylor had lived a charmed life and understood none of that. She might be drawn to him now but only because of the danger and the close quarters. Or maybe she saw him as a new kind of adventure in her life. Maybe she'd wanted to see what it was like to slum.

So he clammed up, intentionally killing any more personal conversation between them.

Thankfully, they arrived at Sutton's office, and Hayes parked. As soon as they entered, Hayes smelled the scent of old money, politics and secrets.

Mountains of posters advertising Sutton as the candidate to vote for in the upcoming gubernatorial election were stacked in every conceivable space and a flurry of workers were stationed in a bullpen answering phones, accepting donations and fielding questions.

Sutton's secretary buzzed them in immediately.

Dressed in a designer suit with polished shoes that shone as brightly as his pearly whites, Sutton gestured for them to enter. "It's a madhouse around here, but please sit down. Would you like coffee?"

"No, thanks," Hayes said. "We're here on business."

Sutton's neatly trimmed hair looked spiked with gel, his eyebrows waxed, his nails manicured, his forehead furrowed. "If it's about those bids, I have my people looking into that. I'm sure it's some kind of clerical error. That or someone is trying to sabotage my campaign by slandering my name and reputation."

"The bids are the least of your worries right now," Hayes said. "Where were you last night?"

Tension rippled between them, and Hayes saw the wheels turning in Sutton's eyes. Should he phone his lawyer?

Sutton glanced at Taylor. "What's this about, Taylor?"

Hayes ground his teeth. Sutton was smooth, intentionally using his personal connection to Taylor to his advantage. Just how personal was it?

Egan mentioned that Sutton's wife, Tammy, might be sleeping around, but what about Kenneth?

"Kenneth, I'm sorry," Taylor began.

"Last night someone tried to kill Taylor," Hayes said bluntly.

"Good God almighty." Sutton lurched from his chair and circled around to study Taylor. "What happened? Are you okay?"

"Answer my question first." Hayes cut in. "Where were you last night?"

Anger flashed in Sutton's eyes for a brief second, but he recovered quickly and pasted on his politician's smile. The man had appeared to be genuinely concerned for Taylor. Either that or he was a damn good actor. "I finished with meetings around eight, then had dinner with my wife, Tammy. We were home all evening."

Hayes grimaced silently. The perfect cover. A wife couldn't testify against her husband.

And from what he'd heard, Tammy Sutton was salivating for her husband to sit in the governor's chair, and would do anything to ensure his success.

Would she lie to protect him if he was a murderer?

Taylor's nerves pinged back and forth as she and Hayes drove to her estate. She hated putting her friends on the spot and hoped she hadn't damaged their working relationship today. She'd even considered the possibility that someone had framed Kenneth in an effort to degrade his name and throw off the election.

"Exactly what is your relationship with Sutton?" Hayes asked as they entered her house.

Her eyes widened in annoyance. "We work together, Hayes. I respect his decisions and appreciate the fact that he's contributed to several charities."

"What about those illegal bids?"

She bit down on her lip. "I'm still digging through the paper trail to figure out what happened. But I honestly don't think Kenneth would participate in anything illegal. He wouldn't take that chance."

"Not in an election year?" Hayes asked sarcastically.

Taylor grimaced. "Not at any time."

"Sometimes power and greed go to a man's head," Hayes said. "Maybe he thought the end justified the means."

Taylor shrugged, still not buying the supposition.

"Just because someone has political aspirations or money doesn't automatically make them bad."

He grunted in disagreement, and she gritted her teeth. "You're too judgmental, Hayes. But you're wrong about Kenneth. He's one of the good guys."

"Sounds as if you're in love with the man," Hayes said darkly.

Taylor whipped her head around in surprise. "No, Hayes. I admire him and think he'll make a great governor, but our relationship is totally professional."

"Really?" he said in a mocking tone. "He doesn't have any indiscretions to hide?"

Anger churned in her stomach at his implications. "Are you asking me if he's having an affair? Or if we've been together?"

Hayes's razor sharp gaze cut through her like a knife.

"No, he's not having an affair, Hayes, and we've *never* slept together," Taylor said. "I do have morals, and I would never sleep with a married man."

His jaw slackened slightly. "So he's happy in his marriage?"

Taylor pressed her fingers to her temple where a headache was starting to pulse. "He and Tammy seem to be in sync. They both have the same goal, Kenneth as governor. And I've never seen them argue." But still, she wasn't sure the love was there, at least not in his eyes. Sure, Tammy was obsessed with being his wife, and with him, but Taylor didn't see the passion she thought should be between a man and woman. The passion she wanted.

The passion she was starting to imagine between her and Hayes.

But she refrained from confiding her opinion. It would only make Kenneth look guilty in Hayes's eyes.

Suddenly his interrogation felt too invasive. He wouldn't talk about himself, but wanted to dissect her life, her friends, her family. Last night and today had taken their toll. She had to escape Hayes's probing eyes and questions. "I have some work to do now."

He simply stared at her, unnerving her even more. "Fine. I need to check in with Brody and Egan."

She nodded, then slipped into her office and shut the door. After downing some aspirin, she spent the afternoon and evening working on the fund-raiser for the teen center, throwing herself into her work and forcing Hayes from her mind as she concentrated on organizing an art auction to raise money.

By seven her stomach growled, and her headache told her she needed food. She hadn't eaten lunch, so she walked to the kitchen and began gathering ingredients for a shrimp stir-fry.

Hayes was working on his laptop at the table, and she began chopping vegetables. When she glanced up, he was watching her, his eyebrows arched, his look hooded. "I figured you had a gourmet chef on staff."

She laughed, but her huge kitchen seemed smaller now with him in it, more intimate with his big body taking up so much space. His masculine scent wafted around her, stirring other hungers that she couldn't feed. "I do." She tapped her chest. "Me."

He studied her for so long that she wondered at his thoughts.

"You're not exactly what you seem," he finally said in a gruff voice.

His quietly spoken words sent a tiny thrill through her because she knew it had cost him. Because maybe he felt the sexual tension charging the air.

Desire flared between them as they gazed at one another, but he turned away as if the connection between them had caught him off guard. Still, as she finished preparing the meal, the air thickened with his male scent and that odd feeling of intimacy intensified.

When she served him a dish and he dug into it with gusto, a sense of satisfaction filled her that she'd impressed him with her culinary skills. Her mind also took a dangerous journey as she imagined them sipping wine as they listened to music, cuddling on the couch, then slipping up to her suite hand in hand. He'd kiss her and trace his hands over her body, slowly undress her and feed her hunger with his mouth and tongue. And she'd tease him and prime his body for a night of hot lovemaking that would last for hours.

Her cell phone rang from inside her purse, and she was startled, her fork in midair. She didn't want to talk to anyone, didn't want to intrude on the serene moment, but it jangled again, and Hayes sipped his tea, obviously oblivious to her fantasies.

Thank God. The tension of the investigation must be making her insane.

"Aren't you going to answer the phone?" he asked.

She sighed, afraid it might be Miles ranting about their earlier visit. If so, she'd have to stand her ground. Clenching her hands, she crossed to the desk in the corner, removed the phone from her purse, then checked the number on the caller ID. Tony Morris, the private investigator she'd hired to locate information on the baby Margaret had given up for adoption years ago.

She grabbed the handset and walked to the living room out of earshot.

"Miss Landis," a deep baritone voice said, "I have that information you requested."

She inhaled sharply, running her fingers along the mantel as she glanced at a photograph of her and Margaret taken at a Christmas charity function. Margaret had talked about her baby that night, of all the holidays and birthdays she'd missed.

Nerves pinged inside her.

What if finding Margaret's child somehow caused Margaret more pain?

Chapter 7

"Miss Landis, are you there?"

Taylor's breath gushed out. "Yes. Did you find out what happened to Miss Hathaway's baby?"

"Yes," Morris said. "The infant Miss Hathaway gave birth to was placed with a couple in San Antonio. Their name was Keller."

"Keller?" Taylor staggered slightly. She couldn't have heard him right.

"Yes, Keller. Apparently someone paid them to take the child, and they didn't officially adopt him. They'd lost a son of their own, and never really connected with this boy. He got into some trouble as a teen and left home at seventeen."

Taylor's heart thumped madly in her chest. "What was the child's name?"

"They named the little boy Hayes."

The room spun sickeningly. It couldn't be possible, could it?

Hayes was her best friend's son?

"Do you have definitive proof?" Taylor rasped.

"Yes, I can fax it over—"

"No, no, don't do that." She couldn't chance anyone seeing the confidential information.

"Then we'll meet in person."

"Yes, that's better."

Footfalls clattered on the floor and Hayes appeared in the doorway, his brow furrowed.

What should she do now? She couldn't tell Hayes—he despised her and Margaret's lifestyle. How would he react if he learned Margaret had given him away? That her fortunes could be his own? That he could have grown up in Cantara Hills with so much more than he'd had?

And what about Margaret? How would she feel when she discovered the baby she'd given up, the one she'd pined for for years, the one she wanted to meet, was the brooding ranger who'd been staying in Cantara Hills? The man who was playing Taylor's bodyguard and would be following her every day as Margaret planned her wedding to Devon Goldenrod?

Margaret's father had assured her the child had been placed in a loving home, that the baby was better off being raised by two loving parents instead of a teenage girl, that he'd checked on him over the years and assured Margaret he'd led a picture-perfect life, that all his needs had been met and he'd wanted for nothing.

But he'd either been mistaken or he'd lied.

Something was wrong. Taylor's face had turned bone-white.

And as she disconnected the call, her hand trembled and she jammed it through her hair.

He had the oddest urge to pull her in his arms, to soothe her and assure her everything would be all right. But he remained rooted at the doorway, knowing if he did, he'd be crossing that invisible line that divided the two of them so distinctly in his mind. The one built by money and culture. "What's wrong, Taylor?"

Her breath whispered out. "Nothing."

He strode to her, then gripped her by the arms. "Then why do you look as if you just saw a ghost?"

She shook her head in denial, but she refused to look him in the eye. "I'm fine…"

He tipped her chin up with his thumb. "Then why won't you look at me?"

Her throat worked as she swallowed, drawing his gaze to the slender column of her neck. Damn. Her skin looked so incredibly soft, and it would probably taste like sin.

He hadn't tasted sin in a long time.

"What's going on, Taylor? Who was that on the phone?"

"Nobody," she said a little too quickly, rousing his curiosity even more.

"Don't lie to me. You're upset. Was it your brother or Sutton?"

Again she shook her head. "No, no, neither of them."

His mouth thinned. "Someone who threatened you?"

She pulled away, rubbing her arms where he'd gripped them, and regret slammed into his stomach. Had he hurt her? Been holding her too roughly?

"No, nothing like that." She paced to the Palladian window and stared outside. Night was falling, shades of gray slanting in shadows across the manicured lawn. He felt himself falling into those shades of gray himself, wanting to be her friend, to take care of her, when he needed to keep her at a distance just to guard himself.

"Taylor, it's my job to protect you and find out who tried to kill you," he said as much to remind himself as to convince her to talk. "I can't do that if you're not honest with me. Tell me what's going on."

When she turned to him, her eyes glittered with wariness and other emotions he couldn't read. "The call was personal business, Hayes. I swear, it had nothing to do with the attack on me."

"Maybe you should tell me and let me decide."

She shook her head. "No…it's not important, just some news about an old friend that took me off guard."

He narrowed his eyes, searching her face for the truth. But all he saw were lies.

Dammit, just when he'd begun to halfway think she was different from the other rich girls, that she was someone he could trust and like, she proved him wrong.

Taylor hated to lie to Hayes, but she couldn't very well confide the truth. Not now.

Not yet.

She had to talk to Margaret first. This was Margaret's secret to share, not hers. And Margaret would have to decide how she wanted to handle the situation, if and when she wanted to tell Hayes about his birth.

Worry knotted her insides, and she knew she had to escape. Hayes's look of disappointment ripped at her conscience. Relinquishing her privacy for a bodyguard was difficult enough, but trusting him with her emotions and Margaret's secret was impossible.

Men just wanted money or sex, not love.

Although Hayes seemed to want none of them from her…

But occasionally she noticed a spark of sexual interest flare in his eyes. Desire that he quickly hid.

Disturbed by his presence even more now after learning he was Margaret's son, she rushed to the sink to clean up from their meal. She needed to do something, keep busy, to occupy her confused mind and prevent her from acting on her raging hormones.

As she began to gather the dinner plates, he took them from her. "You cooked. I clean up. That was the rule at my house."

Her heart squeezed. "You're not there anymore," she said, feeling the slow burn of tears sting her eyes. He should never have been in that home, never suffered, felt unwanted…

His jaw tightened. "Taylor, look at me." His voice was so gruff that a tingle rippled through her. She didn't want to see the pain of his past in his eyes.

"You look exhausted," he said. "Let me take care of the kitchen, and you lie down."

"I'm fine," she said, although her protests sounded feeble to her own ears. She wanted to make him see that Margaret loved him and regretted giving him up, so everything would be all right.

Then she'd hold him and kiss him, and feel his lips on hers all night.

"No, you're not fine," he said more gently. "You just came home from the hospital this morning, and it's been a stressful day. Go on to bed."

His dark brooding gaze raked over her, and for a second, they connected again, and heat flickered in his eyes. She didn't want to go to bed alone. Was afraid she'd dream about that man trying to strangle her in her swimming pool.

But she couldn't ask Hayes to comfort her. Not when the secret she carried lay lodged in her throat like a rock. So she nodded, then disappeared up the steps.

Inside her room, she paced like an animal, her nerves tightening her throat, making it impossible to breathe. She was so agitated she couldn't sleep.

She had to know for certain that the information the private investigator had was correct. Tomorrow she and Margaret planned to meet for lunch to discuss wedding plans. If she had the proof in hand, then she could decide whether or not to show Margaret at the time.

She grabbed her cell phone and punched in the detective's number. She'd sneak out tonight, meet him and get that proof. Then she'd decide what to do with it.

Hayes loaded the dishwasher, his mouth watering over the delicious meal Taylor had prepared, his mind chasing suspicions about why the phone call had disturbed her. Who had been on the phone? Was she lying about the news pertaining to an old friend?

Maybe an old boyfriend had called?

For some reason that thought disturbed him, but when he'd asked her earlier if she had a boyfriend who might want to harm her, she'd denied it vehemently.

Hell, if the caller had phoned in on the landline, he could check the number for himself.

He needed to win her trust so he could extract the truth.

He finished stowing the dishes, then phoned Egan.

Two rings later, Egan answered. "How's it going babysitting the princess?"

He'd used that expression before himself, but hearing Egan say it grated on his nerves. "Fine. Did you hear anything from trace on the crime scene last night?"

"That hair you found belonged to Tammy Sutton."

"Hell, that doesn't do us much good. Taylor said Tammy is over here all the time. In fact, all our major players have been in this house for charity functions and other reasons during the past few weeks."

"I know, it's frustrating," Egan said. "What about you? You come up with anything?"

"We had a chat with Miles Landis. The punk is so spoiled he thinks his daddy will bail him out no matter what he does."

"I'm sure his daddy would," Egan said.

"Yeah, but if Miles tried to kill Taylor, he's not getting away with it."

"Did he have an alibi?"

"No," Hayes replied. "Claimed he was at the clubs, got drunk and passed out."

"Sounds like his routine," Egan said. "What about Sutton?"

"Sutton insists he was at a meeting until eight. Then he went home to the loving wife. So far his story checks out, but his wife is his alibi, so who knows?"

Egan barked a laugh. "Yeah, she loves money and power and knows how to obtain both."

"Right. Either way, if Sutton is our man, I don't see us turning Tammy." Another dead end. Hayes explained about Margaret Hathaway's upcoming wedding and Taylor's involvement.

"So I guess you'll be shopping for bridesmaids' dresses and flowers with Taylor," Egan said on a roar of laughter.

Hayes grimaced. Spending any time with Taylor and these country club women was torture, but to look at bridal stuff sucked big-time.

And Margaret Hathaway…something about that woman had thrown him off balance. She'd stood up to him just like Taylor had—in fact, he could see why they were friends. Both were attractive glitzy women with wealth and…dedicated to charity work. So were Victoria Kirkland and Caroline Stallings, two more Cantara Hills residents, and the women Brody and Egan had fallen for.

Frustrated, he hung up and paced the living area, itching to know who Taylor had talked to earlier and why she had withheld information from him.

Muscles coiled with tension, he checked the security system, then stretched out on the sofa, hoping to catch some sleep. The night before he certainly hadn't, not in that hospital room where Taylor lay a few feet away.

He closed his eyes and was about to doze off when the sound of a car engine sputtering to life startled him. It was Taylor's car.

Dammit, she was sneaking out. Where in the hell was she going this late at night?

He raced to the door to stop her, but he heard the automatic garage door shutting, and realized it was too late.

Maybe she had a secret lover she hadn't told him about and she'd gone to meet him. Or maybe the killer had phoned her for a rendezvous.

Anger railed inside him as he hurried to his car to follow her.

Taylor felt like a thief sneaking out in the night as she revved up her ice-blue Mercedes convertible and sped toward the private detective's office in San Antonio. Traffic was mild for the night, but the temperature had skyrocketed, the heat making her clothes stick to her skin. Still, she loved the freedom riding with the top down offered. A slight breeze tossed her hair around her face, then she noticed headlights zooming closer on her tail.

Was someone following her?

Nerves fluttered in her stomach, and she considered turning around or calling Hayes. But what could she tell him? That she was going to meet a private investigator about him?

As she rounded a curve, she noticed the car had fallen back several hundred yards. Relief surged through her. But she continued to check until she reached the city and the private detective's office. The building was nondescript and dark, except for a low light burning through a darkly tinted window. Her breath tight in her chest, she hurried to the door. Morris had promised he'd wait on her, so she knocked, then eased inside.

The door screeched and the inside light flickered off. Then a shot rang out, glass shattered from the front window and spewed across the room.

Taylor dove to the floor and screamed, crawling on her hands and knees behind the desk just as another bullet hit the carpet beside her.

Chapter 8

Hayes heard the gunfire, removed his weapon from his shoulder holster and eased up to the door of the P.I.'s office. What in the hell was going on? Who was firing?

Was Taylor hit?

Darkness shrouded the interior and he inched inside, pausing to scan the shadows. The sound of choppy breathing echoed in the silence, mingling with his own raging heart, and he searched the darkness again but saw nothing.

Outside, a car engine screeched to life, tires squealing as the vehicle lurched from the curb. He ran to the door, but all he could discern were the taillights of a dark sedan spinning around the corner.

He wanted to chase after it, but had to find Taylor. Hurrying back to the door, once again he scanned the office interior.

"Oh, God…"

"Taylor?"

She peeked from behind the desk, her silhouette a trembling shadow against the faint streetlight slanting through the blinds. "Hayes?"

"Yeah, are you all right?"

A whimper tore from her throat. "Yes, is he gone?"

"Yeah." Anger and fear knotted his insides, and he crossed the room to her, his boots clacking on the floor.

"Hayes," Taylor whispered, "there's a b-body here."

He glanced down at her feet and spotted a man sprawled behind the desk. The scent of blood and death rose to greet him, but he felt for a pulse. "It's too late," he said with a curse.

She whimpered in shock, and he grabbed her, pulling her away from the corpse. "What happened, Taylor?"

"I came in, but someone started shooting." Her voice broke, the horror of finding the man evident as a sob escaped her.

Gritting his teeth, he dragged her into his arms, pressed her head against his shoulder and soothed her. "Shh, it's okay."

"No…" she whispered. "He's dead."

"I know, but you're all right," he said, his own breathing choppy as he moved her to a chair in the corner and eased into it. "I have to call it in, Taylor."

She nodded against him, clinging to his shirt, and he held her tighter, well aware of his heart pounding in his chest. If something had happened to her…

No, he couldn't think like that. Taylor hadn't been hit.

On the heels of fear, anger shot through him. Before he called it in, he had to know what had happened, why she was meeting a P.I. in the night.

"You know this man?" he asked gruffly.

Her body stiffened, and he searched her face. "Who is he, Taylor? Why did you sneak out to meet him?"

"His name is Morris," she said feebly.

"He's a private investigator?"

She nodded, averting her gaze to stare at the body, and he trapped her face between his hands. "What were you doing here?"

Her breath rushed out, but she didn't answer.

"Taylor," he said more harshly. "Answer me. What's going on?"

She clamped her teeth over her bottom lip, shaking her head as if to deny him, and pure rage knotted his insides.

"Listen to me," he rasped. "Someone tried to kill you last night, and you're in my custody. If you're in some kind of trouble, if you know why someone wants you dead, you have to tell me."

"I really don't know," she said in a low voice.

"Why were you meeting this P.I.?" he asked again, more demanding this time.

"I can't tell you that," she said.

He released her abruptly, furious. "Why not?"

"Because it's personal," she cried.

"Is it business? Related to your father's foundation?" He hesitated. "Or personal as in a lover you forgot to mention?"

Her head moved from side to side, her face pale in the dim light. "No, nothing like that. It's…not about me."

"Then tell me," he shouted.

A strained second passed between them. "I can't," she finally said, then turned away from him and folded her arms around herself as if to shut him out completely.

Frustrated and furious with her, he phoned Egan to explain the situation.

"I'll get a crime unit there," Egan said. "Find out why Taylor Landis needed that P.I."

"I will," he said. Although he didn't know how he'd do that. She'd clammed up and was refusing to talk.

But this was the second time in two days she'd nearly died. And judging from the timing of their little midnight rendezvous, this man's death had to be related to her visit.

Taylor trembled, the sight of the blood pooling beneath Morris's chest so vivid that nausea rippled through her.

Did his death have something to do with the information he'd revealed to her on the phone? If so, she had to confide in Hayes and the police. But her loyalty lay with her best friend.

Fear clogged her throat. Hayes's face was a mask of fury as he greeted the crime scene unit, medical examiner and a local unit.

CSI began to process the scene, dusting for fingerprints, looking for trace evidence, and Hayes and a local officer approached her.

"Miss Landis, I'm Lieutenant Riley. Ranger Keller said that you and he found the body."

Hayes's gaze met hers, and she realized that he'd implied they'd arrived together. Her mind raced with how to answer, but she simply nodded.

"What were you doing here this time of night?" Lieutenant Riley asked.

She glanced at Hayes again, his jaw tense as he waited on her reply. "Mr. Morris called me and said that he had some information he wanted to give me."

"What kind of information?" he asked.

She chewed the inside of her cheek. "He didn't get a chance to give it to me."

"Was he working for you?" the lieutenant asked.

Again she hedged. Technically the investigation was for Margaret. "No."

His brow furrowed, and Hayes's eyes flickered with questions.

"Was he blackmailing you?" Lieutenant Riley asked.

She shook her head. "No. Like I said, he phoned me and said he had information to give me. When I arrived, someone shot at me. I ducked behind the desk and that's when I found his b-body."

The lieutenant gestured toward Hayes. "Ranger Keller said that someone also tried to kill you last night."

She shivered, then murmured that he was correct.

"And you don't have any idea why?"

"No."

One of the crime scene investigators approached, saving her from a lengthier interrogation. "Please don't leave town, Miss Landis," Riley said. "We may need to talk to you again."

She nodded, her hands tightening together as the investigator showed Hayes and the lieutenant a bullet casing he'd found by the doorway. "Looks like a .38."

"We'll bag it and send it to forensics," the investigator said.

Hayes squatted down, then removed a handkerchief and used it to pick up a small brass button with black etching on it that had rolled beneath the desk chair. "This might have come from our guy. Maybe from some kind of uniform?"

Riley bent to study it, as well. "The killer and Morris could have struggled first, and the button fell off, then the killer shot Morris."

"We'll send it to trace." The investigator bagged it.

Hayes pressed his hand to her shoulder. "Taylor, they need to take your prints for elimination purposes."

A numbness crept over her as she agreed.

Had this man died because of another case or because he'd dug into the past for her? If Hayes and the police searched Morris's files, would they find papers proving that Hayes was Margaret's son?

Dear heavens, she had to talk to Margaret and convince her to tell Hayes that she'd given birth to him. It would be difficult enough for both of them to handle the realization, but it would be far worse if Hayes learned his mother's identity from Morris's files instead of from Margaret.

"When CSI is finished, I want Morris's files and computer sent to me at Miss Landis's house in Cantara Hills," Hayes told the lieutenant. "Maybe one of his cases got him murdered."

Taylor gave him a wary look, but Riley nodded. "Just keep me abreast of anything you discover."

Hayes assured the lieutenant he would keep in touch. The button might prove instrumental in solving their case, especially if they identified the type of uniform it had come from. Hopefully, they'd find prints or DNA that would lead to the killer.

Although he'd vouched for Taylor in front of the lieutenant, anger still fueled his demeanor as he followed her back to her estate. He had to push her, find out what that P.I. had wanted with her.

Because he strongly sensed that she was lying. That

the private investigator had revealed his discovery to her on the phone.

Had that information brought a murderer to his door?

If so, why? The foundation business? The bids for the city council? Dirt on her brother? On her?

She pulled the sleek little convertible into the garage, hitting the automatic button to lower the door. He parked in the drive, a reminder that he didn't fit into her world and never would.

Was that the reason she wouldn't trust him with the truth?

She let him inside the front door, and he itched to pounce on her with questions, but the sight of the dark circles beneath her eyes made his gut clench.

"You look wiped out, Taylor."

"I am. I'm going to bed now."

He caught her arm before she could disappear up the stairs. "And this time stay there. No more sneaking out."

Fear flickered in her eyes, and she shook her head, her chin quivering. "Don't worry, Hayes. I won't. I... I'm sorry."

He didn't know if she was apologizing for sneaking out or lying about the P.I., and he didn't ask. But if she tried to sneak out again, he'd handcuff her to the bed and park himself in the room with her.

That thought triggered unbidden images he couldn't pursue, but they fed his libido anyway, making him even more frustrated.

Dammit. He needed to find the person after Taylor so he could get the hell out of Cantara Hills. He didn't want this simmering attraction to her.

Knowing he couldn't do any more tonight, he booted up his computer and ran a search on the button. Image after image of various uniforms spilled onto the screen, and he scanned the pictures.

Police uniforms, paramedics, firemen, postal and UPS workers, military uniforms, power company employees...the pictures continued. Finally an hour into the search he discovered a similar-looking button.

He clicked on the icon to enlarge the image, frowning as he recognized the crisp navy color, the hat, the row of shiny round brass buttons with black etching along the lapel—a chauffeur uniform.

His mind spun with jumbled thoughts of where he'd seen one like it before. The company that made it was based in Austin.

His throat thickened as recognition dawned. Egan's father, Walt, was Link Hathaway's chauffeur and wore an identical uniform.

But why would Walt be at a private investigator's office?

He wouldn't...

Perhaps he was covering for Link Hathaway. He was loyal to the man to a fault.

No. It had to be someone else. Another chauffeur who wore the same type of uniform.

But what if it wasn't? Would forensics be able to lift a print? And if they found out it belonged to Walt, what motive would he have to kill Morris, or Taylor?

He reached for the phone to call Egan, but decided to wait until he had some answers first. He couldn't accuse Egan's father without more proof. If he did, Egan would never forgive him.

When the case was solved, he had to make amends with his friends. Taylor wouldn't be a part of his life, but Egan and Brody had to be.

They were his only family.

* * *

Taylor climbed in the shower, desperately wishing she could wash away the images of the dead man's face as she scrubbed the scent of death from her body. Barring an occasional funeral, she'd never seen a dead person before, not in the first few moments when life had been snatched from them. Especially a life lost to violence.

Morris's wide gray eyes had stared up at her, and as she crawled along the floor, she'd brushed his skin. It had felt warm yet oddly like ice. And the smell…

Nausea gripped her, and she swallowed hard, willing it to pass as she leaned against the shower door and heaved for a breath. Hayes must see death all the time in his job. How did he handle it?

The water grew cold, and she flipped it off, dried off and bundled in her bathrobe. The air conditioner whirred, sending a chill through her. She hurried to the closet, pulled out a satin gown and slid it on, then climbed into bed, dragging the covers over her.

Exhausted, she closed her eyes but didn't think she'd sleep. Yet she was so drained and spent physically and emotionally that she slowly drifted off. But her sleep was fitful, and she jerked awake sometime later with a scream.

She'd felt a man's hands sliding around her throat, his fingers tightening, strangling her. Then the image of Morris's bloody body had floated in front of her, only his face faded to a dull black.

Then hers replaced it.

Chapter 9

At the sound of Taylor's cry, fear bolted through Hayes, and he raced up the steps to her bedroom. His gun drawn, he pushed open the door and searched the darkness. Moonlight shimmered through the window, casting a golden glow on the room. Taylor bolted upright to a sitting position, gasping for a breath as she pressed her hands to her chest.

"Taylor?"

"I'm sorry," she whispered hoarsely. "Bad dream."

Her voice caught, and his gut clenched. As angry as he'd been with her earlier, he'd recognized the shock in her eyes at the sight of Morris's dead body.

She was terrified but trying desperately not to show it.

Forgetting all rational sense, he strode toward her, placed his gun on her nightstand, lowered himself onto the mattress and pulled her into his arms. She fell against him, a soft, satiny female puddle of sexuality and vulnerability, and his body hardened as he admitted to himself how much he'd been wanting to hold her.

And taste her and touch her.

"I saw that man in my dreams, and all that blood," she whispered, "and then it was me, my face, my blood…"

"It's not you," he murmured.

She touched her neck. "I could feel hands around my throat choking me."

"Shh, it's over," he murmured. Her hair tickled his cheek and he stroked her back, cradling her in his arms. "You're safe now, Taylor. I've got you."

"I can't believe this is happening," she said on a sob. "First Kimberly dying, then someone attacking Victoria and Caroline."

And now her.

Someone definitely had targeted the women in Cantara Hills. Victoria Kirkland had been targeted because she'd freed her client from charges of trying to kill Kimberly, and she'd helped Ranger McQuade investigate. Then Carlson Woodward had tried to kill Caroline. Did it all lead back to Kimberly's murder, or was he right to suspect Miles or Kenneth Sutton? Although why would one of them murder the private investigator?

Only Taylor could tell him.

Or the man's files. Tomorrow…

The sweet scent of her bodywash and shampoo, something utterly feminine and sexy as hell, wafted to him, as she burrowed herself in his arms. "I don't want to go back to sleep," she said softly. "I'm afraid I'll see that man's eyes staring up at me. And his body was so cold…"

She shivered against him, so fragile that every primal male bone in his body screamed to protect her, to erase her fears and pain and replace that terror with other sensations. Pleasurable ones. Like his hands stroking her. His mouth tasting hers.

Just a taste.

Not a relationship, but just one sweet taste of her delicious lips.

"Don't think about it," he said in a husky whisper.

"How do you do it, Hayes? How do you deal with death all the time?"

"It's a job," he said. "I don't get close or let it get personal."

Except it felt personal right now.

Her breasts rose and fell, her soft mounds teasing his hard chest, eliciting wicked fantasies. His sex hardened, straining against his fly as he felt her curves beneath the softness of her gown. A gown that was so paper-thin that her nipples budding to life stirred his desires and made his breath catch.

He had to leave. Remove himself from her presence before he did something foolish like kiss her.

He started to pull away, but she clutched his shirt, then lifted her hands to cup his face. The rasp of his beard stubble sounded like sandpaper as her delicate fingers touched him, but he didn't have the power to move.

"Don't go, Hayes. Stay with me."

He closed his eyes, hating himself and the fact that he wanted her. That he was too weak to deny her or himself a moment of passion.

Still, somewhere he dredged up enough stamina to lift his hands and press them over hers. He meant to pry them loose, but instead she flicked out her tongue and traced it along the seam of his lips.

"Taylor—"

She shushed him this time by pressing her mouth to his jaw, then she nibbled her way to his mouth, and he opened for her, taking everything she offered as he claimed her mouth with his.

Taylor knew she was playing with fire, but she wanted to forget the horrible reality that had become her life. That her brother and friends were suspects and might be trying to hurt her. That tonight she had been touched by death again, and had escaped it herself by mere seconds. That an inch closer and that bullet would have pierced her heart and her blood would have been spilled across the floor, her life over.

That tomorrow she had to tell Margaret she'd found her son, and that Hayes might find out and it would give him another reason to detest her and Margaret.

For now, all she wanted to do was taste the sinfully sexy curve of his lips and feel his hard, tough body against her.

His kiss consumed her, demanding and urgent with need, and her stomach fluttered with desire. He raked one hand through her hair, while the other one slid along her spine, pressing her more tightly against the manly planes of his sculpted body. He probed her lips apart with his tongue, slid it inside and teased her, showing no mercy as he thrust deeper inside her mouth.

Heat speared her, making her nipples hard buds, tight, heavy, achy. She wanted his hands and mouth on her.

Like a cat, she purred into his mouth and rubbed herself against him, stoking the fire burning between them. As if he sensed the depth of her need, his hand encased her, kneading her weight, and an intense hunger sizzled from her breasts to her womb, igniting hidden desires and enflaming her senses with heat.

Desperate to strip him and feel his naked body gliding against hers, she lifted her hand to his chest and slowly unbuttoned the top button of his shirt. He groaned, then trailed kisses along the column of her neck. She threw her head back in abandon, whispering that she wanted him, and he licked his way down her throat, then untied the ribbon at the top of her gown, parting the satin so he could close his mouth over her tight nipple. Searing fire raced along her bare flesh, his sucking spiking the flames of desire to an inferno.

She dug her hands into his hair, holding him closer as he teased the bud with his tongue, sweeping his lips across her skin with nibbling bites that made her grow wet and warm and needy all over.

She craved more.

"Hayes…" She clawed at him, anxious, achy, throbbing for his full length to thrust inside her, stretching her, filling her, sating her.

Greedily, she ripped at his shirt, sending buttons flying then ran her hands across his bare chest. He moved his hand to her thigh, and she groaned his name.

"Please, Hayes, I need you…"

Suddenly his cell phone trilled, the sound shrill and vibrating between them like a whistle signaling the end of an exciting train ride before the train had reached its destination.

She caught his hand when he started to pull away, anxious that he ignore it and let them finish the ride together. "No, don't stop, please, Hayes—"

The phone trilled again, though, and he tore his mouth from her breast with a guttural groan, and looked up at her, his ragged breathing slicing the air between them as he checked the number.

"Dammit, it's your father." He growled and stood, putting distance between them.

"Don't answer it," Taylor whispered. "Come back to bed with me, Hayes. We can be good together."

She knew she sounded pathetic, and had never begged a man to make love to her. But she'd never wanted a man like she did Hayes.

She ached all over, felt empty and hungry inside. Her gown lay open, her nipples tight and wet from his tongue, her breasts heavy mounds that needed more, her skin a burning flame that needed stoking, her mouth watering to taste his salty skin, to close her lips around his throbbing member and lave him with her tongue.

He couldn't leave her like this.

But he did. He grabbed his gun, strode from the room, his boots pounding on the staircase as he charged from her bedroom away from her.

Hayes cursed, his body throbbing like the devil as he rushed down the stairs. His phone jangled again, and he yanked it from his belt and answered. "Keller."

"Yes, this is Lionel Landis. I apologize for calling so late, but I tried to reach Taylor earlier and there was no answer. Is she all right?"

Hayes ground his teeth at the man's formal tone. Taylor's father would dismiss him if he knew what he'd been doing with his daughter. "Taylor is fine," he said instead. In fact, she was more than fine. She was erotic as hell, and he wanted to run back up to her room, crawl in bed with her and make love to her until neither of them had the energy to walk.

Landis cleared his throat. "And the investigation?"

"We're still working on it."

"Do you have any suspects, Keller?"

Yes, your son, and Kenneth Sutton, who the man was probably buddy-buddy with. "I can't discuss the details of the case, but I'll let you know when we make an arrest."

"All right," Landis said curtly. "But, Keller, you'd better take good care of my little girl. If anything happens to her, you'll answer to me."

And Landis would use his power and money to make trouble for him. "Yes, sir," he said through gritted teeth. As if he needed a reminder of the different stations between him and Landis's precious daughter. "Don't worry."

Landis hung up, and Hayes cursed and walked out back to the swimming pool for fresh air, but the image of Taylor floating facedown, near death, haunted him.

He was here as her bodyguard. Not as her lover.

He needed to have his ass kicked for forgetting for one moment that he was the hired hand, that sleeping with Taylor would be a big fat mistake.

He lifted his hand to his badge. His badge was all that mattered. It was his life. The only reason he was in Cantara Hills was because Kimberly had been murdered and someone was after Taylor.

He wished to hell he had that P.I.'s files tonight. He needed something to do to keep his mind off of what had happened between him and Taylor.

Because her scent still lingered on his skin, her taste on his tongue, and he wanted more of her.

* * *

Taylor woke the next morning, agitated and irritable. She'd felt cold and vulnerable when Hayes had stormed from her bed without looking back, and more than a little confused by his withdrawal. Normally when stressed, she'd take her frustrations out in the swimming pool, but the memory of the attack sent a shiver through her.

Only Hayes could assuage this ache.

And he had wanted her. His body had been hard and pumped, his frenzied hands and mouth as anxious for her as she had been for him.

So why had he stopped?

And why had she begged him not to?

Because she was a fool. Hayes was a Texas Ranger, a man who didn't get involved, who hated her lifestyle and friends. How many times and ways did he have to tell her that?

Sure, his body had been primed for her, but what man would have turned down an offer of free, unattached sex? For all she knew, he had a woman—or maybe a dozen women—waiting on him when he left Cantara Hills.

Humiliation stung her cheeks as she showered and dressed. She could not have a repeat episode. Her self-confidence couldn't endure another rejection.

Besides, it was better that he'd halted before they'd made love. When he learned Margaret was his mother, and that Taylor had lied to him about hiring the private investigator, he would probably hate them both.

She twisted her hair into a low knot, added her diamond earrings and watch, then checked the time. Today she was meeting Margaret. Her stomach fluttered. She had to tell her about Hayes.

How would Margaret react?

Worse, how would she have felt if Taylor had slept with her son?

Good heavens, why was she so attracted to him anyway? They had nothing in common.

Nothing except…maybe that was what she liked about him. He wasn't interested in her money. Didn't want anything to do with her society life.

He was strong, protective, courageous. Rugged.

A cowboy.

God, he looked good in that Stetson.

Her stomach tightened. She'd like to see him wearing nothing but that hat. Her nipples jutted with arousal at the thought, a warm wetness tickling her thighs. He'd tip it low over those eyes, eyes framed by thick black lashes and brows, eyes that would watch her with passion beneath the hat brim as she slowly undressed for him.

Downstairs, his boots clattered on the marble floor, jerking her from her fantasy, and she pursed her lips, wondering how he'd fared after their interlude, if he'd fantasized about her instead of sleeping.

Evil thoughts speared her. She hoped he'd been horny as hell and had ached all night after leaving her unsated.

Sucking in a sharp breath, she checked the clock and realized she needed to hurry. She and Margaret had a dress fitting at ten, then lunch at the country club.

The intercom for the alarm buzzed, and she rushed to answer it, first glancing at the security camera to identify her visitor. A courier with a package, so she pushed the button to open the gate.

Hayes met her at the front door with a dark look in his eyes. "You just buzzed someone in?"

"A courier," she said.

"What if it was someone pretending to be a courier?"

She chewed her lip, feeling chastised. She hadn't thought of that. "I recognized his uniform."

She opened the door and accepted the package, her heart stuttering as Hayes took the envelope and examined it.

"It's not a bomb," she said, taking it back. "Just papers."

He narrowed his eyes but she simply smiled, then retreated to her office to examine the contents. It was the information from the private investigator. He must have had his mail sent out before he was shot. Inside she found Hayes's birth certificate and papers Margaret and her father had signed relinquishing custody of him. Another document proved that Hayes was Margaret's child, and that he'd been sent to live with a family named Keller.

"Is something wrong?"

She jerked her head up and saw Hayes watching her from the doorway, then jammed the envelope into her shoulder bag. The intensity in his brooding eyes sent a tingle of anxiety and arousal through her.

She wanted to tell him the truth. Wanted to comfort him if the news about Margaret being his mother upset him. Wanted to assure him that Margaret had loved and missed him all through the years.

But she couldn't. "It's fine."

He studied her for another long moment, a flicker of passion in his eyes as if he was remembering the night before, and her body quivered with longing. She wanted him to touch her again.

"About last night—"

"Don't." She waved a hand, warding off an apology. She had the good sense to know that throwing herself at him had been a mistake.

Unfortunately it didn't make her want him any less or douse the heat lingering between them.

Then his gaze changed, an emotionless hard mask sliding back into place, the walls between them being erected. "I'm hoping to receive those files from the P.I. today. What's on your agenda?"

"I have to meet Margaret for a dress fitting and then lunch."

He gave a clipped nod. "All right, I'll drive."

"That's not necessary," she said, knowing the day would be awkward enough already.

His frown deepened, drawing fine lines around his sexy, brooding mouth. "I promised your father I'd take care of you, Taylor, and I'm going to do my job."

But nothing else. The unspoken words lay between them.

Distress laced his eyes, though, as he followed her to the car. She dreaded the talk with Margaret, but it would be even more uncomfortable knowing Hayes was watching.

Chapter 10

Hayes gritted his teeth as Taylor exited the fitting room wearing a strapless, satin, sky-blue dress that dipped halfway to her navel. He'd imagined that babysitting her while she and Margaret tried on dresses would be painful, but the sight of her breasts spilling out of the rows of glittering sequins literally made him physically ache.

"What do you think, Margaret?" She twirled around, revealing the back of the dress which also dipped downward to the curve of her hips, tiny crisscrossing strips of fabric showcasing the skin beneath.

"It fits perfectly and enhances your eyes," Margaret said. "And you can wear the green one to the party."

Hayes grimaced. The damn dress would bring out the tongue-wagging men, as well, and have them salivating at her sequined-covered feet.

Her gaze shot to his, where he stood to the side of

the dressing rooms, feeling and looking like an awkward outsider.

"What do you think, Hayes?"

Holy hell. She might as well be naked.

A devilish light flickered in her eyes. The conniving woman was well aware of what the sight of her in that near-nothing fabric was doing to him.

Memories of the night before assaulted him, when his mouth had suckled her, when his tongue had bathed her nipple, when he'd almost slid his fingers all the way up her thigh and taken them both to heaven.

He couldn't forget the sweet taste of her skin or her sultry voice inviting him into her bed, the way she parted her thighs, the way his fingers itched to be inside her.

How the hell was he going to do his job when all he wanted was to take her someplace, strip her and crawl inside her?

Taylor took a modicum of delight in watching Hayes squirm. She pranced in front of the wall of mirrors, swaying her hips and purposely adjusting the straps of the dress to reveal more cleavage. Her nipples felt sensitive as the fabric rubbed against them, stiff points visible through the sheer fabric.

His look darkened.

She smiled at him in wicked delight. It served him right for abandoning her in the bedroom the night before.

But Margaret emerged from the dressing room wearing her wedding gown, decimating any romantic thoughts about Hayes. Her friend looked stunning in the strapless designer dress with overlays of brocade and lace, and a bodice that curved Margaret's gorgeous figure.

Tears stung Taylor's eyes as Margaret paraded in front of the mirror. Margaret had been alone so long; she wanted her friend to be happy. Taylor only hoped that Devon Goldenrod was as sincere in his affections for her friend as he appeared.

Something niggled at the back of her mind, worrying her, but she couldn't quite put her finger on it.

Hayes leaned against the wall near the mirrors, looking bored and completely out of his element. Yet for a brief second, she imagined modeling a wedding gown for him, and a sharp pang of longing rippled through her. She had grown cynical about men after her few disastrous experiences and had given up on marriage.

Would she ever find a man to love her, not her money and the power afforded by marrying into the Landis family?

"You like the gown, Taylor?" Margaret asked.

Taylor put aside her own selfish thoughts in lieu of her friend. "You look amazing, Margaret. Devon is lucky to have you."

Margaret hugged her, and they chatted about wedding plans for the next few minutes. Hayes yawned, and any fantasies of a possible future with him died.

Dread cramped her stomach, the slow burn of trepidation tightening her lungs as she and Margaret changed, then Hayes drove her to lunch.

Neither spoke on the drive to the country club. She was too nervous about the luncheon, and he was obviously bored out of his mind.

She and Margaret chose to sit at their usual corner table by the window, both preferring the view of the rose gardens and fountain to the golf course. Margaret ordered Perrier and a glass of pinot noir while Taylor ordered a glass of dry white wine.

Margaret glanced at Hayes, who had stationed himself at another table to allow them privacy. "Okay, what's going on with that ranger, Taylor? Has he discovered your attacker's identity?"

Taylor's stomach fluttered. "No, not yet."

Margaret sipped her wine. "I know it has to be awkward having him in your house. He seems so…angry all the time."

Goodness, this wasn't going to be easy. "That's what I want to talk to you about."

"About Ranger Keller?"

Taylor shrugged. "Yes, well, sort of."

Margaret's eyes widened. "Oh, no, don't tell me you like him?"

She shrugged. "That's not exactly what I wanted to talk to you about." She took a long swallow of her own glass of wine for courage. "You know how you're always talking about finding out more about your child?"

Margaret's smile faltered, and she dabbed at her mouth with her napkin. "Yes."

"Please don't be upset with me, Margaret, but as a wedding present, I thought I'd surprise you so I hired a private investigator to search for your baby."

Margaret's eyes widened, although she hesitated a moment as if debating whether she wanted to know more. Finally a labored sigh escaped her. "Did you find out something?"

Taylor nodded, rubbing at her temple. "Last night the P.I. called me and said he had information. But when I went to see him, someone shot him."

"Oh my Lord." Margaret pressed her hand to her chest.

"Whoever murdered him was still there and shot at me." Taylor shuddered. "But Hayes rushed in and saved me."

Margaret glanced at Hayes again, relief softening the startled look in her eyes. "Well, I must thank him."

Taylor slid her hand over Margaret's. "There's more."

"The information?" Margaret asked. "You know where my child is, Taylor?"

Emotions thickened Taylor's throat as she nodded. Then she removed the envelope and pushed it in front of Margaret. "The information is in there, Margaret."

Margaret's hand shook as she clutched the envelope, her chin quivering. "Oh my gosh, Tay. I've wondered about my baby, thought about finding him so much, but now I don't know if I'm ready."

Taylor gave her a sympathetic look. "I understand, Margaret. And I'm sorry if I've overstepped and done something to hurt you."

Margaret shook her head. "I could never be angry with you," Margaret said. "You're the one person in the world I trust."

Taylor couldn't speak. She felt the same way and would never hurt her friend. But the truth might.

Margaret inhaled deeply, closed her eyes as if in prayer for a moment, then opened them and unfastened the clasp of the envelope. Her chin quivered as she removed the documents and examined them.

"Oh my goodness…" Tears blurred her eyes and she lifted her gaze to Taylor's in question, then glanced at Hayes, shock straining her features.

"I was stunned, too," Taylor said.

Margaret was so overcome with emotions that she leaned her head on her hands, trembling.

"I'm sorry, Margaret," Taylor whispered.

Margaret jumped up and hurried toward the powder room. Taylor folded her napkin and followed, her heart in her throat.

What in the hell was going on?

Hayes trailed the women to the ladies' room in confusion. One minute Taylor and Margaret were modeling fancy dresses and drinking wine in celebration, the next Margaret had flown into tears and run to the powder room.

Because of the contents of that envelope. The envelope the courier had delivered this morning.

As he waited outside the door, standing guard, questions darted through his mind. What was in that envelope?

In light of the night before, could it have had something to do with the private investigator's death? Taylor claimed the information was personal. Did it pertain to Margaret instead of Taylor?

Both women worked on several charities and hosted fund-raisers together. Perhaps they'd discovered financial discrepancies? Or something else?

But what?

Another thought struck him, stirring more worry. If the envelope had come from the P.I. and involved Margaret, could she be in danger, as well?

He punched in Brody's number, grateful when he answered on the second ring. "It's Hayes."

"Yeah, what's going on?"

"Will you run a check on Margaret Hathaway, see what you can find out about her and her family?"

"Why? You got a lead?"

Hayes twisted his mouth in thought and explained about the envelope. "I'm not sure. But it might have something to do with that P.I.'s death. Maybe he had some dirt on Margaret and was going to blackmail her, or maybe someone else is." He scratched his head. "Hell, I don't know. It might be about the charity work she does or maybe about Goldenrod, the pretty boy she's going to marry. I just know something's wrong."

"All right. I'll dig around."

Hayes considered mentioning the button he'd found at the crime scene. After all, Egan's father, Walt, worked for Margaret's father. Maybe Walt had something to do with the P.I.'s death. Either way, the rich people in Cantara Hills seemed to have secrets.

Which one of those secrets was worth killing over?

"I can't believe it," Margaret cried.

Taylor pulled Margaret into her arms and hugged her, trying to soothe her tears. "I'm so sorry. I didn't mean to hurt you."

Margaret gulped, pulled away and leaned against the vanity, struggling for a breath. Taylor reached for the box of tissues and shoved them into Margaret's hand.

"From the talk around the club, Hayes Keller grew up in a bad home," Margaret sobbed. "If he learns I'm his mother, he'll hate me even more than he seems to now."

Taylor didn't know how to alleviate Margaret's anxiety. Hayes had suffered and had a chip on his shoulder because of being abandoned. "I didn't know whether to tell you or not, Margaret. But then that private investigator was killed last night, and Hayes was there, and he asked to have the man's files sent to him."

Margaret swung her gaze up to Taylor's, panic darkening her eyes. "What?"

"I'm sorry," Taylor whispered. "Hayes wanted to know why I snuck out to meet a private investigator. He even suggested that the man I hired was killed because of the information he had to give me."

The color drained from Margaret's face, her hand trembling as she reached for another tissue. "Do you think that's possible?"

Taylor bit down on her bottom lip. "I don't know. Maybe someone found out I was looking into your child's whereabouts and didn't want us to find that information."

"Good heavens," Margaret said. "What am I going to do?" She leaned over and splashed cold water on her face, then patted it dry with a hand towel. "All this time I've wanted to see my son, wanted to know he was happy. And he's been here in Cantara Hills and I didn't even know him." She turned to Taylor, pain slashing her features. "Maybe it would be better if he never knew the truth…"

Taylor gripped her friend by the arms. "Margaret, he's going to find out. It's only a matter of time before he sees Morris's files. You have to tell him first, instead of letting him read it in a folder from a private investigator."

Another sob caught in Margaret's throat, but she pushed her fist over her mouth to stifle it, a war of tumultuous emotions flickering in her eyes. "You're right, Tay. But I need to talk to my father first and let him know that I intend to tell Hayes the truth." Her voice cracked. "Will you go with me to talk to Father?"

"I'm not sure that's a good idea, Margaret."

"Please," Margaret begged. "I can use the moral support. My father will try to convince me not to tell Hayes."

"But he will find out," Taylor said. "The police are sending Hayes those files."

Margaret's labored breathing rattled in the air. "Right. But I have to tell my father first." Her voice faded. "And then I have to figure out a way to tell Devon, too."

Taylor clenched her hands together. Link Hathaway would do anything to protect Margaret. And from what Margaret had confided over the years, he'd been adamant that she not search for her child.

Her heart pounded as questions pummeled her. Had Link known all along that Hayes was suffering and left him there anyway? How far would he go to make sure that Margaret didn't reconcile with her child?

Chapter 11

Hayes paced outside the ladies' room, feeling conspicuous in his jeans and Stetson amongst the rich and snotty. A birdlike woman with platinum-blond hair narrowed her eyes. "Can I help you, sir?"

He tipped his Stetson. He hated this bodyguard job. "No, ma'am, I'm waiting for Miss Landis and Miss Hathaway."

She shrugged, then strolled across the plush rug at the threshold of the doorway.

Others stared, as well, but his dark glare kept them from approaching. Finally Taylor and Margaret emerged. Margaret's eyes were slightly red although the women must have done a repair job with makeup. Margaret Hathaway had a timeless beauty and sophistication yet something about her also seemed soft and…kind.

A kindness that belied her money and station in life.

Although when she looked up at him, her expression crinkled with sadness.

Confused, he fell into step beside Taylor, something moving inside him at the troubled expression lining her face. "What's going on, Taylor?"

"We're leaving. Margaret wants to visit her father."

"Fine. I'll drive you home."

She caught him by the arm. "Actually, I'm going with her."

"Then so am I."

Her shoulders stiffened. "Hayes, I don't think that's a good idea."

He arched a brow, daring her to argue. "I told you that you go nowhere without me. Remember what happened the last time you did?"

Her face paled, and he felt like a jerk for reminding her, but he couldn't forget she was in danger. And she shouldn't, either.

"I'll sign the bill," Margaret said in a shaky voice.

Margaret gave him another odd look, spoke to the waiter, returned and offered Taylor a strained smile. "All right. I'm ready."

Taylor nodded and they followed Margaret to her silver Jaguar, then he and Taylor went to his SUV. Just the sight of his utility vehicle next to Margaret's and the other expensive toys in the parking lot reminded him of the differences between them.

When Taylor settled in and buckled her seat belt, he angled his head toward her. "What was in that envelope, Taylor?"

Her labored breathing reverberated through the small confines of the SUV. "Nothing."

"Don't lie, Taylor. Whatever it was upset Margaret. Was it some kind of threat to you or Margaret?"

Taylor's gaze shifted to look out the window, and she twisted her hands together. "No," she whispered hoarsely.

Tension rattled her voice, and he reached out and laid a hand over hers. "I can't help you or her if you don't confide in me."

Her eyes looked tortured. "Just drive to Margaret's, Hayes. She and I will explain later."

He studied her for a second, then reluctantly accepted her answer. Whatever was wrong involved Margaret, and she had to discuss it with her father.

Before the day was over, he would find out what was in that file.

Guilt nagged at Taylor as Hayes parked in front of Link Hathaway's Spanish mansion. What would Hayes think if he knew he was about to meet his grandfather?

The man who had insisted Margaret give him away. The man who'd lied to her and assured her that Hayes was happy and lived with a loving family.

The man who had enough money that he could have kept Hayes, even if it meant raising him by nannies. The man who probably wouldn't want anything to do with Hayes now.

Link was a formidable man. Driven by guilt over a teenaged pregnancy, Margaret had always had a difficult time standing up to him.

Margaret pulled into the six-car garage, and Hayes parked in front of the impressive mansion, a frown marring his face as they walked up the tiled path to the arched doorway. When they entered, his gaze swept the interior, a scowl deepening the grooves around his mouth as he assessed the imported chandeliers, two-story winding staircase and Spanish decor.

"Mr. Hathaway likes history," she said, earning a sideways look of disdain.

Margaret appeared through a set of double French doors and glanced at Hayes with such longing and pain that Taylor's heart clenched.

"Father's in the study, Taylor. Ranger... H-Hayes," Margaret stammered. "Would you like to sit on the veranda? Elda can bring you something cold to drink."

"I'll wait here," Hayes said, shoulders squared.

She shot a nervous glance toward Taylor, then nodded. "All right. Make yourself comfortable."

He gave them both a look that said that was impossible, and Taylor's stomach churned. As soon as they entered Link Hathaway's office, Taylor sensed he was angry. That perhaps he even knew the reason for this meeting.

But how was that possible? No one knew about the file but her...

Unless the man who'd killed the private investigator had found the files. Would he phone Link if he had? Maybe for blackmail money?

"Father, I just discovered the truth about my baby," Margaret said in a surprisingly strong voice. She dropped the folder from the private investigator onto her father's desk. He glanced at it then up at Margaret, and slanted a furious stare toward Taylor.

"Don't you think we should discuss this in private?" he said sharply.

Margaret shook her head. "Taylor knows everything, Father. She hired a private investigator to find my son. The file came from him."

His thick gray brows drew together as he scowled. "You should have minded your own business, Taylor. Are you trying to ruin my daughter's happiness?"

"I thought I was helping her," Taylor said.

"She knew I wanted to know more about my baby," Margaret folded her arms. "Why did you lie to me, Father? Why did you tell me he was in a happy home when that file proves otherwise?"

Link paced the room, agitated. "I did what I thought was best to protect you and your future."

"But my baby suffered," Margaret cried. "And he was, *is,* your grandson. How could you leave him in a bad situation when we could have taken care of him so much better?"

Link Hathaway's nostrils flared. "You were fifteen years old, Margaret. Just a child, and an immature, irresponsible one at that, or you wouldn't have found yourself pregnant."

Margaret's face crumpled at his harshness. "I was in love with my baby's father."

"Yes, but he was young, too, and in no better position to get married than you were. You could barely take care of yourself, much less an infant."

"But you could have done something to make sure my son was happy like you promised, not leave him in a home where the people didn't love him."

"He was a bastard child," Link snarled. "He got what he deserved."

Margaret's face blanched. "That's cruel and untrue. He didn't ask to be born."

Link growled. "I wish to hell you'd had the abortion like I suggested."

Margaret wiped at a tear. "I could never have done that, and you know it."

"I gave him a mother and father, and that was enough," Link said, his voice tight. "It was better for all of us not to look back. Not to keep in touch. And my biggest mistake was that I didn't send him overseas to live with strangers instead of with the Kellers."

"Why them?" she asked.

"They'd lost a son and wanted a replacement. At the time, I thought it was best."

Taylor sighed. But the family obviously hadn't connected with Hayes.

"No." Margaret ran a hand through her hair. "It wasn't better for my son. He should have had loving parents. And some of this." She gestured around the room. "All our money and he had nothing."

"He will never have our name or our money," Link said. "I've worked too hard to build my reputation and to keep yours untainted for you to ruin it now. Leave the past behind, marry Goldenrod and look toward your future."

A long silence ensued, anger and accusations stretching between them. "I can't do that, Father. I know where my son is. I know the name those people gave him." Her voice turned shrill, growing nearly hysteric. "His name is Ranger Hayes Keller. And he's in your house, Father. A house that should have been a home to him all these years."

Link circled his desk and gripped Margaret by the arms. "But he doesn't know that, and he doesn't have to. What purpose would it serve now, Margaret? You're marrying Devon. Don't spoil that by dragging some bastard kid into the picture."

"Stop calling him that," Margaret snapped. "He deserves the truth. And I'm going to tell him."

She spun around and headed to the door, then swung it open. Taylor rushed behind her, and Link followed, his heels pounding angrily on the floor. He grabbed Taylor by the shoulder and forced her to look at him.

"This is your fault, Taylor. Fix it, and keep Margaret quiet and away from that ranger, or you'll be sorry."

Chapter 12

"Take your hands off of Miss Landis," Hayes ordered in a menacing tone.

Link Hathaway cut his gaze toward Hayes, a mixture of cold bitterness and another emotion Hayes couldn't define in his gray eyes. Eyes that chewed Hayes up and spit him out as if he was a nasty rodent who had invaded his lavish, ostentatious house and his perfectly orchestrated life.

"I said, take your hands off of her." He took another deliberate step toward the pompous ass. "And don't threaten her again or you'll deal with me."

"This is between me and my daughter," Hathaway said sharply. "Stay out of it, Ranger Keller."

"You're wrong about that," Hayes said. "I'm working a murder investigation, Mr. Hathaway, so anything that involves Taylor is my business. And from where I'm standing, you just threatened her."

"Get out," Hathaway barked.

"Father, stop it," Margaret said. "Hayes has a right—"

"He has no right." Link shot a warning look toward Taylor. "Tell her, Taylor."

Margaret's words echoed in Hayes's ears. What did she mean, he had a right? He searched her face, and a dozen tumultuous feelings darkened the depths of her eyes.

Taylor folded her arms around her waist. His mind boomeranged between all the elements of the case, all the questions that needed answers, the pieces that didn't quite fit into the puzzle yet.

"Does this have to do with that P.I.'s report?"

A thick unwavering silence stretched across the room, then Hayes addressed Link. "Mr. Hathaway, you're aware that a P.I. named Morris was murdered last night and that someone shot at Taylor."

A muscle ticked in Hathaway's jaw. "Maybe Miss Landis was simply in the wrong place at the wrong time."

"This is the third attempt on her life." He whirled around toward Taylor. "You're obviously keeping something from me. If the P.I. discovered something on Sutton and the city council, or if someone's blackmailing you or Margaret, then I need to know the reason."

Margaret moved closer to Taylor, a low sigh escaping her. "Taylor, it's all right."

Hayes glared at Taylor, tired of all the secrets and lies. "Maybe you had something to do with the illegal bids, Taylor."

Hurt registered on Taylor's face. "I would never do that."

"Then stop lying and tell me what the hell is going on."

"Taylor has done nothing wrong," Margaret said, drawing his gaze back to her. "In fact, she's been covering for me, trying to protect me."

He narrowed his eyes. "Protect you from what?"

Link cleared his throat and reached for Margaret's arm but she jerked away, fury flaring in her eyes. "No, Father. I'm going to tell him the truth. He deserves to know." Her voice cracked. "Besides, this man Morris might have been killed because of what he uncovered."

Hayes made a low sound in his throat. "Go on."

Margaret wet her lips with her tongue, and Taylor inched closer to her, placing a supportive hand on her back.

"When I was fifteen years old, I gave birth to a baby out of wedlock," Margaret said in a strained voice. "I gave that baby up for adoption, but I've always regretted it and wanted to know where my son was, if he was safe and happy." She hesitated, clenching her hands together, then brought them to her neck, twisting at a silver chain around her neck. "Taylor hired Mr. Morris to locate my child."

Hayes scowled. "And he did?"

She nodded, her face etched in pain.

"You think this is why Morris was killed?" Hayes asked.

She shrugged. "I don't know. I'm sure my case wasn't the only one he was working on."

"But it's possible," Hayes said. Rich people covering up their secrets.

"Stop this now." Hathaway reached for Margaret again, but she spun on him, planting her fisted hands on her hips. "No, Father, you lied to me, told me my son was happy, that he had a good life, but that wasn't true."

Hayes's chest began to throb, some germ of a thought sprouting as he began to connect the dots. Hathaway said he didn't belong here... Margaret had argued that he did...

He jerked his head toward Taylor, saw emotions darken

her eyes, then Margaret's where tears began to trickle down her cheek.

"I'm so sorry, Hayes. I…"

"What are you saying?" Hayes asked through gritted teeth.

Margaret cleared her throat. "You're my son, the baby I gave up for adoption."

Shock rooted him to the spot, anger and humiliation and old feelings of abandonment clawing at him. "I don't believe you."

"It's true," Margaret said softly. "The papers were in that file Taylor gave me at lunch." She pushed them toward him, and Hayes took the papers and studied them, his jaw clenched.

He looked at Taylor for confirmation, and she nodded, sympathy in her eyes. He didn't want her damn pity.

Margaret reached for him. "I'm so sorry, Hayes—"

He cut her off. "You're sorry I'm that child?"

"No…" She shook her head and moved toward him again, extending her hand, her fingers sparkling with rubies.

Hayes held his callused one up to ward off her attempt to touch him. "Sorry I didn't turn out like you thought."

"Hayes, listen," Taylor whispered. "Margaret wanted to find you. She cares about you."

He shot Taylor a glacier look. Through the years, he'd imagined a million different reasons his mother might have given him up.

Because she was ill. Dying. Had no means to raise a child on her own. No family to support her. That she was killed by a vicious murderer. Or that he'd been stolen and that he had a family somewhere wondering where he was, waiting to reconcile with their kidnapped baby and bring him home.

But never had he dreamt that a spoiled heiress and her rich father had gotten rid of him because he would have interfered with their social schedule and prestigious lifestyle. "Yeah, she cared so much she abandoned me." He narrowed his eyes, accusing. "And you knew about this, Taylor. That's why you lied to me." His voice thickened and he worked to swallow the rage and pain clogging his throat. "You knew I was *her* son? The baby she threw away like trash."

"I didn't know until last night, when that private investigator called," Taylor whispered. "But I had to talk to Margaret first."

"Please understand, Hayes," Margaret cried. "I was only fifteen…a kid myself. Father thought it would be better, that you'd have two parents, a loving home—"

"A loving home?" A sarcastic chuckle escaped Hayes, echoing shrilly through the grand two-story foyer and bouncing off the elegant walls. Slowly the realization was sinking in. Link Hathaway was his grandfather. Had said he didn't belong.

And he was right. "My home was anything but loving." He gestured toward the ornate crystal chandelier, the original oil paintings, the vases that had probably cost more than a year's paycheck. "And nothing like this."

"I know that now," Margaret whispered. "But I didn't know back then. If I had, I would have done something sooner." She twisted the necklace, pulling a locket from beneath the shimmery fabric of her silk blouse and flipping it open. "See, this is a picture of you when you were born. I always wear it."

Another bitter laugh rolled from deep in his chest.

"Right. Because you thought of me every day when you were hobnobbing with your rich friends."

"I did," Margaret cried. "I missed seeing you grow up and wondered what you were doing. And every year on your birthday I mourned for you, imagined what you looked like, how you'd changed, if you had a birthday party."

"I told you this was a mistake," Link Hathaway interjected.

It all came together in Hayes's mind, why Hathaway hadn't wanted her to tell him. He wanted to protect what was his. His money, his wealth, his power and image.

"Well, there weren't any parties," Hayes said dryly. "But I understand how you wouldn't want a kid messing up your rich snotty lifestyle or your social calendar." He directed a condescending look toward Hathaway, hating the man. "You people don't care about anything but your wealth and how you look. But don't worry. I don't want your damn money."

"Hayes, please, listen…" Margaret pleaded.

Hayes's fists tightened. "Just answer me one question. Who is my father?"

Margaret gulped. "I'm sorry, but I can't tell you that."

"Can't or won't?" Hayes barked.

"I can't," Margaret said in a choked whisper. "He doesn't know about you. He was young, too… I never told him I was pregnant."

Hayes felt sucker punched. His heart pounding, he spun around and rushed outside. He had to escape these people, wished he'd never come to Cantara Hills.

Wished he didn't know the truth and had never met the woman who'd given birth to him and hadn't wanted him.

* * *

Taylor's heart ached for Margaret and for Hayes. She turned to fold Margaret in her arms, but Margaret shook her head. "Go after him, Taylor. Please…make sure he's all right. He needs someone right now."

The pain and desolation in her friend's eyes tore at her, but Margaret was right. The best thing she could do for her was to comfort Hayes. To convince him that Margaret loved him. That they could have a relationship now.

If only he'd give her the chance.

"You'll be all right?"

Margaret nodded and gently coaxed her toward the door. "Please, he shouldn't be alone."

Not that he'd want her with him, but Taylor nodded and rushed outside anyway. Hayes was sitting in his SUV, the engine sputtering to life, anger emanating from his icy glare as she settled in the passenger side.

"Why don't you stay here with your rich friends?"

"Don't be a snob, Hayes," Taylor said.

His eyes darkened, a muscle ticking in his jaw. "You took me along today to watch the two of you try on those damn dresses, and you knew all along and didn't tell me."

His accusation stung. "I wanted to, Hayes, but it wasn't my secret to share."

Walt Caldwell, Link Hathaway's chauffeur, drove up then and climbed out. Taylor glanced up and noticed his uniform. Her breath caught as the shiny brass button on Walt's uniform flickered in the sunlight. Hayes was studying it, too.

No… It was a perfect match.

"Who else was aware you'd hired that private investigator?" Hayes asked.

"No one that I know of," Taylor said.

His shoulders stiffened, but pain edged his voice. "Who else knew about me?"

She glanced at the Hathaway mansion. "Just Margaret's father... I think." She reached for his hand, covered it with her own. "He told Margaret that he'd checked on you over the years, that you were healthy and happy and in a good home, Hayes. Margaret...loved you. You have to believe that, to try and understand the circumstances—"

"I understand perfectly." Hayes jerked his hand from hers, then spun from the driveway and onto the main road. "But your case just took on a new list of suspects, Taylor. Hathaway obviously didn't want Margaret to find me, and if he discovered you'd hired a private investigator, he would have tried to bury the search. I'm going to have to question him about that but I'll get a warrant first."

Taylor winced and buckled her seat belt as Hayes pushed the gas and accelerated. But his words haunted her.

Link certainly would do anything to protect his daughter. He'd lied to Margaret to prevent her from looking for her child.

Had he discovered the P.I. was searching for Hayes, and killed Morris to keep the truth about Hayes quiet? She gripped the seat edge as Hayes took a turn too fast. Had Link tried to kill her to keep her from finding Margaret's son?

Hayes cursed as he checked the rearview mirror, then increased his speed. "Hold on, we've got a tail."

She glanced over her shoulder and saw a dark sedan with tinted windows speeding up their rear. Tires screeched as they careened around a curve, then a shot pinged off the back glass, shattering the window.

Chapter 13

"Hellfire and damnation!" Hayes swerved, tires screeching as another bullet bounced through the car and grazed the seat. The SUV skidded toward a stop sign, sliding through and barely managing to miss an Expedition flying the other way. The driver honked madly, and Hayes checked the rearview mirror to get a look at the shooter, but the windows were so dark that he couldn't distinguish a face. Then the sedan spun off on a side street and headed the other way.

"Taylor, are you okay?"

She'd ducked in the seat and covered her head with her hands. "Yes. Are you?"

"Yeah, but I'd like to choke that son of a bitch in the sedan."

"Is he gone?"

"It looks that way."

He turned into Cantara Hills, then on to the street to Taylor's estate. She uncovered her head and sat up, eyes wide with fear. Adrenaline had flooded his system, and he had to force himself to ease up on the gas and slow down.

"Did you see him?" Taylor asked.

"No, the windows were tinted too dark." He pulled up to the gate and slid the key card into the slot, then drove up the winding drive to her garage. Sweat had beaded on his neck and forehead, and he wiped it away, grateful at the moment to be at Taylor's mansion with closed gates.

At least she'd be temporarily safe.

They both climbed out, the silence a deafening roar charged with questions and the tension from the past hour.

He verified that the security system was on, then allowed Taylor to unlock the door and punch in the code.

"I need to bag these bullet casings and send them to forensics."

She nodded. "Is there anything I can do, Hayes?"

Her question was loaded with innuendo, with a reference to the fact that he'd just learned Margaret Hathaway was his mother. But Hayes couldn't deal with that now, not with her. He felt too raw, too...exposed.

"No. I'm going to call Brody and Egan so we can discuss the investigation."

"I'm sorry, Hayes. For everything."

The sincerity in her voice tugged at his heart, one he'd guarded for too long. One he couldn't open to her now, especially with her close friendship to the woman who'd given birth to him then tossed him away.

"You realize that the man who rummaged through

your office the night he tried to strangle you in the pool might have been looking for the information from Morris."

Her eyes flickered with distress. "I suppose it's possible."

"When did you hire him? Before the car bomb?"

Her face paled and she nodded. "But I didn't tell anyone."

Hayes frowned. "If Morris was poking around, Hathaway could have heard about it. And judging from his reaction, he might have hired someone to find that report."

Pain darkened her eyes. "Hayes, I know he was tough tonight, but I don't really think he'd hire someone to kill me."

Hayes arched a brow. "Why not, Taylor? He'd do anything to protect his wealth, his daughter and his social standing. And your search threatened all of that."

"He only wanted to protect Margaret, Hayes. She was so young when she had you—"

He jerked his hand up, cutting off any further discussion. "Please, spare me, Taylor. I know how you rich people think."

Anger reddened Taylor's face. "You are such a snob, Hayes. I understand you're hurting now and that you received a bum rap, but if you'd knock that chip off your shoulder for a second, you'd see that not everyone who has money is evil." Her ragged breath pierced the air. "Margaret is kind and loving and has felt guilty about giving you up for years. Why do you think she never married? She didn't think she deserved happiness because she regretted giving up her child."

"I've seen her picture in the society pages," Hayes snapped. "She didn't look so miserable to me."

"She tried to make a life," Taylor argued. "But she thought about you every day, she told me that. She even funds a teen center for pregnant girls to offer them counseling because she never received any when she needed it most. Only pressure from her father to give you up for adoption and his assurance that you'd be better off."

"Right." His voice dripped sarcasm. "The truth was that Link Hathaway was better off without a bastard child ruining his life. But don't worry, Taylor, I don't intend to ask him or Margaret for anything." His chest ached from the pressure of not shouting at her.

Memories of their heated interlude the night before rose to taunt him. She'd known the truth then. "Is that why you kissed me, why you came on to me, Taylor? Because you felt sorry for me and wanted to soften the blow for your friend, hoping I'd understand and not make trouble?"

Hurt and anger reared in her eyes, and she reached back and slapped him. "I can't believe you'd suggest such a thing. You can be a bastard, Hayes."

His jaw stung. "Yes, well, that I am."

Taylor sighed. "Oh, God… I'm sorry. I didn't mean it like that, Hayes."

He spoke through clenched teeth. "I don't want pity sex because you feel sorry for me."

Her lip quivered, a dozen emotions flaring in her eyes. Hurt. Anger. Sympathy. Compassion. Desire.

She wet her lips, then reached up and cupped his face with her hands. "I didn't kiss you out of pity," she whispered. "And you know that, Hayes."

She dragged him toward her, fusing her mouth with his.

Pure hunger and raw primal need raced through his blood, obliterating his fury and erasing common sense. He wanted to forget the case. Forget that she'd kept secrets from him and made him feel inadequate and vulnerable. That she was best friends with his birth mother, the woman he'd tried so hard to forget all his life.

That she'd seen him endure one of the most painful moments of his life.

A maelstrom of emotions clogged his throat, but she ran her hands along his jaw, scraping rough beard stubble, and moaning as she plunged her tongue inside his mouth.

He sucked it in, drawing in the essence of her sensuality as he tasted the passion seeping through her pores and flaming his body with a need so strong that he clutched her to him and deepened the kiss. She stroked his shoulders, then lowered her hands to claw at his back.

His body hardened, his sex throbbing and aching for fulfillment, for her. But reality gnawed at him, chopping away at his hunger and rekindling the pain raging below the surface of that unbidden lust.

He ordered himself to pull away, but she tore her mouth from his, her eyes hooded and molten hot with hunger and the unbridled passion that steeped below the surface. Her ragged breathing echoed in the tense silence between them.

"Did that feel like pity to you, Hayes?"

She squared her shoulders, a dare glinting in her eyes.

No, it didn't. But the passion between them was strictly physical. Stemmed from the danger confronting her and the adrenaline from their earlier attack.

When things returned to normal, she would write him off and go back to her rich men.

But he'd remember that for a moment he'd had a beautiful heiress in his arms. And he'd be haunted by the fact that he'd just met his mother.

Hell, he was a Texas Ranger. He couldn't forget that he was here to protect her.

And that the reason someone had tried to kill her might be because of him. Because she'd hired a P.I. to find Margaret's son. That his own grandfather wished he would go away and blamed Taylor for screwing things up.

"Did it, Hayes?"

He steeled himself against the blatant hunger threatening to rob him of his sanity.

"It doesn't matter what it is," he said coldly. "I'm here to do a job. To find out who's trying to kill you." He took another step back, knowing if he didn't, he'd cave and drag her back into his arms. He possessed only so much resistance, and she was hacking at it with a sharp knife.

"You almost died three times, Taylor. And now I know it might be because of me."

Her soft gasp filled the air. "Hayes…no, it's not your fault."

He clenched his jaw. "I'm going to find who's targeted you, Taylor. Then I'll leave Cantara Hills, and you and Margaret and Link Hathaway will never have to worry about me bothering you again." His voice held a razor-sharp, firm edge, yet feelings for her simmered beneath the edge of his calm. Feelings he didn't welcome but was helpless to stop.

As much as he didn't want to admit it, he admired her loyalty to her friends, the fact that she'd faced his wrath because she'd respected Margaret's right to tell him the truth. That she even fought to convince him that Margaret really cared.

And when that SOB had shot at them earlier, all he had thought about was protecting Taylor, not letting any harm come to her because he couldn't stand to see her in pain.

Or dead.

"Hayes—"

"Shh." He raked his gaze over her, knowing that if he didn't leave her this second, he'd do something stupid, like make love to her.

Or fall for her and lose his heart.

So he simply stroked her hair behind her ear. "I promised to keep you safe, and I will. And if Hathaway tried to kill you or hired someone to do his dirty work, I will put the SOB behind bars, even if he is my grandfather."

Barely holding on to his ironclad control, he retreated to the guest room to sort out the clues to the case. First he had to call Egan and inform him of what he'd learned. That now they had additional suspects.

That a button from his father's uniform had been found at the scene of a murder investigation. An investigation that now led back to Egan's father's boss.

That Walt was now at the top of their list of suspects because he would do anything for Link Hathaway, was loyal to him to a fault.

God...how had things gotten so screwed up?

Egan and his father had never been close. In fact, Walt had been cold to Egan. But how would Egan feel when he found out that his father might be the killer they were working their asses off to find?

Taylor's body tingled with need as she retreated to her office. Never had a man gotten her so tied up in knots. One minute she wanted to slap Hayes out of his ever-loving mind, and the next she wanted to take him to her bedroom and make love for hours. Maybe days.

He was so darn stubborn.

So sure that her money was a barrier between them when it didn't have to be that way. Love was all that mattered...

Love? Good grief, she couldn't be falling in love with Hayes Keller.

Not Margaret's son, a man who had too much pride for his own good. Would that pride prevent him from forgiving Margaret?

And what about Margaret's father?

Had Link Hathaway tried to have her killed because she'd nosed into his business? God...if so, Margaret would be devastated.

Why was all this happening, especially right before Margaret's wedding, when she was finally going to be happy?

She pinched the bridge of her nose, her head throbbing from tension. Knowing she'd go crazy if she didn't keep busy, she accessed her computer files to finalize the plans for the party she was giving to honor Margaret's engagement.

She flipped on the small television in the corner and listened to the news while she worked, a news clip catching her eye. Kenneth Sutton onstage, giving a speech about his political views and plans for the state when he was elected governor. Tammy, dressed immaculately in a linen designer summer dress, smiled behind him, the perfect politician's wife. The camera panned sideways and landed on Devon Goldenrod, Margaret's fiancé. Devon's sandy-blond hair and Armani suit showcased his handsome face and athletic build, but something about his smile seemed forced.

He had always been second to Kenneth Sutton, second in the city council election four years earlier. Second in the class where the two men had graduated together.

Hmm…had Devon minded?

She shook off the thought. Now that Kenneth was running for governor, Devon was a shoe-in for the city council.

So who would want to make Kenneth look bad or frame him for the illegal bids? She dug through the files again searching for answers.

Anything to distract herself from Hayes in the other room and to keep from going to him.

Hayes had set up the sitting room that adjoined the guest bedroom suite as an office with a whiteboard for notes and a corkboard where he tacked photos of each of the suspects in the case and the crimes and arrests leading up to Taylor's attack. Montoya, who had killed Kimberly McQuade. Carlson Woodward, who had tried to kill Caroline Stallings.

And his main suspects. Miles Landis. Kenneth Sutton. Tammy Sutton. Now he needed to add Link Hathaway and Walt Caldwell. But he had to talk to Egan first. He owed his friend a heads-up.

He phoned Egan and asked him to get Brody and meet him at the estate. While he waited he reviewed the case from the beginning, trying to piece it all together.

Wet shoe prints had been found on Caroline's floor during the break-in and attempt on Caroline's life, but forensics hadn't determined the source. The print belonged to a size eleven but anyone could have worn them to conceal his real foot size. The Rangers believed those shoes belonged to Miles because they'd seen them on the surveillance video footage and seen a pair in Miles's gym bag. Of course, someone could have stolen them.

The explosive devices in Caroline's garage and Taylor's car were set on timers and were low-tech, meaning they didn't require a skilled person to make them. With the Internet, any of their suspects could have found directions and followed them.

The house key that Caroline had given Tammy and Kenneth was still missing. And the toxicology report on Carlson Woodward proved that he'd been drugged. The drugs could have triggered his violent behavior and spurred him to try to kill Caroline.

The question was—had he voluntarily taken the drugs or had someone else drugged him?

Someone who was now trying to kill Taylor?

Although Taylor claimed no one else knew about the private investigator's search for Margaret's son—him— so that wouldn't have been their motive.

On to the more recent facts. The hair he'd found the night of the pool attack on Taylor belonged to Tammy Sutton and proved she'd been at Taylor's, but it could have been left at any time.

The button from Morris's office belonged to Walt Caldwell who they had to question.

The bullet casings from the private investigator's office, and the bullet casings from his SUV had both come from a .38. But where was the gun?

Several prints had been found at the private investigator's office, including Taylor's but not Link's or Walt's. And two others that weren't in the system but might be useful later if they needed to match them with an arrest.

The buzzer for security chirped, and he answered it, then let Egan and Brody in. A frown marred Brody's face as he strode into the room.

The tension was only going to get thicker, Hayes thought. Especially between him and Egan.

Egan jammed his hands in his jeans pockets and leaned against the wall. "You got a lead on Taylor's attacker?"

He shrugged. "Maybe. There's definitely been a new development."

Brody crossed his arms. "Spill it, Keller."

Hayes took a deep breath. "I found out the reason Taylor went to meet that private investigator and maybe the motive for his murder."

"Good work," Egan said. "Fill us in."

Hayes cleared the cobwebs from his throat. "Margaret Hathaway had a baby when she was fifteen, but gave the baby up for adoption. Taylor hired Morris to find out where the child was." He hesitated. "And he did."

"You think that's what got him killed?" Brody asked.

"It's looking that way." He dragged in a breath. "It also turns out that that kid was me."

Brody's eyes shot up and Egan's mouth opened and closed. "Margaret Hathaway is your mother?" Brody croaked.

Hayes swallowed hard and nodded.

"You saw proof?" Egan asked.

Hayes nodded again. "Yep. Saw the birth certificate and adoption papers where my mama signed me away."

"Holy hell, Hayes," Egan said. "That means your family is rich."

"Yeah, rich." He grunted in disgust. "But I don't want

their damn money. And Link Hathaway made it plain and clear that I'd have no part in their happy little family."

"What about Margaret?" Brody asked quietly.

A sharp pain twisted his insides. "I don't want to talk about it." He cleared his throat, forcing a calm veneer to his voice. "Anyway, the point is that Link calculated to keep my existence a secret. He didn't want Margaret locating her child."

"Which would give him a motive for murdering the private investigator," Egan said, jumping on his train of thought.

"And Taylor," Hayes added. "I overheard him tell her that it was her fault, and that she would be sorry for nosing into his business."

Brody whistled, and Hayes tacked Hathaway's picture onto the corkboard, then pointed to the picture of the button. "I found this button at the private investigator's office beside his body."

He waited, watched, saw the moment Egan recognized the button. His gaze swung to Hayes's, questions exploding in his eyes.

"You know who that belongs to?" Tension strained Egan's voice.

Hayes nodded.

Disbelief, then pain and worry flashed in Egan's eyes. "And you think my father killed Morris for Link Hathaway."

Chapter 14

Hayes lifted his shoulders in a shrug. "I don't know," he said honestly. "But we have to question him and Hathaway."

"What about your father?" Egan asked in a low voice. "Maybe he didn't want Taylor snooping around. And maybe he didn't want you found, either."

Egan's comment cut to the bone. "That's possible." He ground out the words. "But Margaret claims he doesn't know I exist. She never told him she was pregnant."

"He could have found out," Egan pointed out.

Hayes couldn't argue that point. Meaning Hayes's father would be a suspect, as well.

Egan phoned Walt and requested they meet at his old house but offered no explanation.

"I'll call for a warrant for Link Hathaway's house and Walt's," Brody said.

"Remember we're looking for a .38, probably unregistered." Hayes gestured toward the photos on the corkboard and the whiteboard information. "In our preliminary research, I discovered that Hathaway has a .45 and a .38, Tammy Sutton a .22 and Kenneth owns a .38." He turned to Egan. "Does your father own a gun?"

Egan shook his head. "Not that I know of."

But he could have bought one without Egan knowing.

Egan clapped his hands together. "I say we pick up that warrant, then get this over with."

"I'll work on obtaining Hathaway's phone records while you're gone," Brody said.

Hayes grimaced. Recently Walt had called Egan and apologized for giving him such a crappy childhood. Egan hadn't totally forgiven him but they'd started to mend their relationship.

This would throw a kink in that reconciliation.

Hayes caught Egan's arm. "Listen, man, I'm sorry."

Egan stared him in the eyes, his jaw tight. "Yeah, so am I."

Hayes nodded. Neither of them had expected this investigation to be turned on its tail and implicate their own family members.

But now they had, they had to follow through. After all, they were Texas Rangers and the badge required it.

The pain in Hayes's eyes roused emotions and protective instincts that Taylor had never felt for a man.

Yet she also felt protective over Margaret, and knew her friend was in turmoil, too. Besides, Hayes was wrong. Margaret had missed him, had seen his face in every child she'd tried to help since.

She didn't simply donate money to charities. She

spent time at the teen center, had even earned a counseling degree and counseled girls on teen pregnancy.

A knock sounded on the door. "Come in."

She expected to see Hayes's face, but Ranger McQuade
appeared instead. "Miss Landis, I just wanted to let you
know that I'll be downstairs filling in for Hayes for a
while. He and Egan went to question Link Hathaway
and Walt Caldwell."

She nodded and picked up the phone as he closed
the door. So that was the way Hayes wanted to play it.
He'd leave his friend to babysit her so he could interrogate Margaret's father.

She had to warn Margaret.

She punched in the number for Margaret's cell phone,
hoping to avoid Link and speak directly to her friend.
Margaret answered on the third ring, her voice hoarse.

"Margaret, are you all right?"

Margaret sniffled. "I don't know, Taylor. Part of me
wants to jump for joy that I finally found my son. But
he hates me, and I don't know how to make it up to him
for all that he lost."

Taylor winced. "He doesn't hate you," she said gently. "He's just bitter right now, and in shock."

"I never meant to hurt him," Margaret said in ear-
nest. "I did think Daddy was right at the time."

"And if the people who took Hayes in had loved him,
he probably would have been. You were only a kid yourself and needed to finish school, Margaret."

"But he'll never forgive me," Margaret said. "And I
want to have a relationship with him."

"Give him time," Taylor advised. "You both need
that, Margaret." Maybe Hayes would come around at
the party Saturday night.

"I suppose you're right." A long pause ensued. "But I have to tell Devon. Maybe postpone the wedding."

"Margaret, do you think that's necessary?" Taylor clawed her hand through her hair. It had taken Margaret months to agree to marry Devon. She hated for her to postpone it any longer.

Devon would understand. Wouldn't he?

Or would it affect his run for the city council if Margaret's illegitimate child were revealed?

"How are things between you and your father?" Taylor asked.

"Tense," Margaret said. "He encouraged me to let Hayes go without even trying to get to know him, but I can't do that. I won't."

Relief surged through Taylor at the conviction in her friend's voice. Link had manipulated Margaret far too long. He needed to see that forging a relationship with her son would finally fill the void in Margaret's life.

"Speaking of your father and Hayes," Taylor said. "I think he's on his way over there to talk to him now."

Margaret's soft gasp echoed over the line. "About me?"

A ripple of panic darted through Taylor. "About that private investigator's murder."

"Oh my Lord," Margaret rasped. "Hayes thinks that my father killed Mr. Morris because he didn't want me to find out about him."

Unable to verbally answer that question, she let the silence serve as her reply.

"He's wrong," Margaret insisted. "My father would never hurt anyone, Taylor."

Again, Taylor couldn't respond. She hoped Margaret was right, but Link had never intended for his secrets about Hayes to be revealed. He probably feared that if Margaret discovered his lies, he'd lose his daughter.

Egan insisted on driving, and Hayes agreed. The silence between them was deafening as they parked at Egan's father's house, a modest home in the same neighborhood where he, Egan and Brody had grown up and connected as kids. Three boys who'd liked rough-housing, sports and fighting, who'd been like brothers.

Now this case might tear them apart.

He followed Egan up the overgrown sidewalk, wondering why Walt didn't take more pride in his own place and why he was so ridiculously dedicated to Link Hathaway. Obviously not because he earned an exorbitant salary or had been given a fancy car.

Not like the limousine Walt drove for Link.

As kids, the boys had begged Egan's father to take them for a ride in the swanky black vehicle, but Link had refused Walt the privilege, saying the car was too nice for hooligans like them.

They had all despised Link Hathaway.

And now that Hayes knew the man was his grandfather, he hated him even more.

Although this house had once been Egan's home, Egan balled his hand into a fist and pounded on the door, alerting his father to the fact that he had stopped by.

"Dad, it's Egan. We have to talk."

Walt approached from the back bedroom, looking disheveled. "What in God's name is going on?" Walt bellowed. "I need to be at work, Egan."

Egan shoved the search warrant into his father's hands. "Dad, this is official. We have a warrant to search your house and car."

Walt's shocked gaze swung to Egan, then Hayes. "You've got to be kidding."

Egan chewed the inside of his cheek. "I'm afraid not. One of the buttons off your uniform was found at the scene of a murder investigation, Dad."

Walt sucked air between his teeth. "How do you know it's mine?"

"It's identical to the one on your uniform," Hayes said, cutting in. "And we matched your prints, as well."

Walt sighed shakily and sank into his big plaid recliner. "I can explain."

"Yeah?" Egan snapped. "I bet you can."

"Don't disrespect me, son," Walt snarled.

Hayes cleared his throat. "We have to follow every lead. Can you explain your relationship to a P.I. named Mr. Morris?"

"Morris?"

"Yes."

Walt cut his steely blue-gray eyes sideways, shifting restlessly. "I don't have a relationship with the man."

"Look, Dad, there's no need to lie or deny that you knew him," Egan said in a clipped tone. "We have prints proving that you were in his office. And Morris is dead."

"I did go there," Walt admitted. "But he was already dead when I arrived."

"What was the nature of your visit?" Hayes asked.

"I'm not at liberty to say," Walt said.

"You work for Link Hathaway," Hayes accused. "You went there for him, didn't you? You knew that his daughter had a baby when she was a teenager and gave it up for adoption?"

Walt's eyes widened. "How did you find that out? No one was supposed to know."

Hayes's jaw tightened. "You obviously did. Did you help Link get rid of the kid when he was born?"

Walt's face turned a pasty greenish white, and Hayes's stomach clenched. "You did, didn't you?"

Walt gripped the chair edge. "I was his driver. I did what he told me to do."

The picture of the events of that night rolled through Hayes's mind in a sickening drunken rush. Margaret giving birth. Link sending Walt off to dispose of the child.

To dispose of him.

"Link discovered that Taylor Landis had hired Morris to find Margaret's child," Egan said, his tone hard, yet pain darkened his eyes. "And he sent you to take care of his business, didn't he, Dad?"

Walt lurched to his feet. "I went there, yes, but I didn't kill Morris. He was already dead when I arrived."

Hayes arched a brow. "Really?"

"I swear it." Walt turned a panicked look toward Egan. "Honest, son, I smelled blood the minute I walked in, and stooped down to see if the man was alive." His hand combed over his uniform finding the missing button. "That's when I must have lost the button. He didn't have a pulse, and I heard a sound and thought the killer might still be there, so I ran as fast as I could."

"You didn't call 9-1-1?" Hayes accused.

Walt swiped a hand over his sweating face. "I...was going to, but then sirens wailed and I figured someone else heard the shots and had called it in."

"And you didn't want to stick around and answer questions?" Egan asked.

"I...didn't want to expose my reason for being there. Link Hathaway's interests had to be protected."

"What about yours?" Egan asked.

Walt reached for Egan, but Egan snapped a hand back. "Stop it, Dad. I don't know why you're so dedicated to that man."

Walt glanced back and forth between the two of them. "He's not a bad man. He only wanted to protect his daughter."

"Do you have a gun in the house?" Egan asked.

Walt shook his head. "No, you know I don't like guns, Egan."

"I have to look anyway, Dad." He paused. "You know that if you're covering for Link Hathaway or lying, you can be charged as an accomplice to murder."

"I didn't kill anyone, son," Walt said firmly.

But he still might be covering for Hathaway. Egan stared at his father for a long moment, then strode toward the hall desk and started to search.

Hayes gritted his teeth. "Answer me one more question, Walt. Did you know that I was Margaret's son, the one Hathaway threw away?"

Walt staggered backward, then slumped into the chair again. "No, I had no idea. All Link said was that he told Margaret the kid was happy."

So that part of Margaret's story was true. But it didn't mean that his grandfather wasn't a killer.

"What about my father?" Hayes's throat felt dry as if he had sawdust clogging it. "Do you know his name?"

Walt gave him a steady look. "Mr. Hathaway never told me his name, and I never asked. Didn't think it was any of my business."

But it was *his* business, and his father might be the killer.

Chapter 15

By the time they reached Cantara Hills, Hayes had adopted his poker face. He refused to allow Hathaway to know how much he was hurting. On some level, he realized Margaret had only been a kid herself and under the direction of an overbearing powerful father when she'd given him up.

Keeping him would have ruined her life.

But the ache of being unwanted ate at him, especially knowing Hathaway had had the money to give him a decent home.

His gut tightened as Egan parked in front of the mansion. Margaret's pricey car still sat in the enormous garage.

Egan whistled. "I still can't get used to walking up to these damn estates." He eyed Hayes. "Unbelievable, man, that your mother grew up here."

Hayes growled. "I can't think of Margaret Hathaway like that."

"They owe you," Egan said in a low voice.

"I don't want anything from them but the truth." And to know if Hathaway had tried to kill Taylor.

He focused on that thought as he and Egan crossed the path to the front door and knocked. A minute later, a butler answered the door.

Egan cut straight to the point. "We need to speak to Mr. Hathaway. And we have a search warrant for the premises."

The butler's expression was stony, but he led them to Hathaway's office. "I'll call Mr. Hathaway."

Egan and Hayes both nodded, Hayes's gaze traveling around the glitzy interior again and landing on a portrait of Margaret hanging over the fireplace. She wore a graduation cap and gown, so it must have been in high school, probably a finishing school. If she had been fifteen when he was born, this picture was taken afterward. He stepped closer, studying her youthful face, yet something about her eyes disturbed him. They held a haunting sadness that made his throat thicken.

Had she regretted giving up custody of him? Had she missed him and thought of him over the years?

Was it possible that she really cared about him?

The sound of Hathaway clearing his throat jerked him back to the present. "What are you doing back here?"

Hayes gritted his teeth. "We have a search warrant."

"You can't think that I killed that private investigator?" Hathaway barked. "Unlike you, I'm a prominent well-respected citizen of this community."

Unlike him. The words echoed through his head, rousing his temper.

"Father, don't speak to him like that." Margaret moved into the arched doorway, her frame elegant and graceful, although wariness filled her eyes.

Hathaway pivoted, his jaw set. "He practically accused me of murder. Now he knows who he is, he wants to get revenge on us. Hell, he's probably going to plant a gun to frame me so he can go after my money."

Margaret's eyes flared with anger. "Stop it, Father. He's not here to do any such thing." She gave Hayes an odd look, a mixture of hurt that he'd accuse her father of a crime and acceptance that he had to ask questions. "Hayes, is this really necessary?"

Egan cleared his throat. "Yes, ma'am. We have to check out every lead. And right now, your father is a prime suspect in Mr. Morris's murder." His voice turned low. "We also questioned my own father and searched his house."

He didn't have to add that explanation, but Hayes realized that Egan was smoothing things for him.

Hayes wasn't ready to latch on to the olive branch.

Hathaway reached for the phone. "I'm going to call my attorney. Don't say anything else, Margaret."

"I need you to tell me my father's name," Hayes said.

Margaret winced. "I told you he has nothing to do with this, Hayes. He really doesn't know about you."

"But he could have found out, so you have to tell me."

She hesitated, tears blurring her eyes. "All right. But please let me talk to him first. He has a right to hear that he has a son from me."

He hesitated, considered what she was asking. If his father really didn't know, then he deserved the truth from Margaret. But allowing her to tell him might put her in danger.

Her eyes were so pleading, though, that he relented. "All right. But do it soon."

She nodded, the anguish in her eyes tearing at him.

Still, if she was wrong, his father could have offed Morris to keep Hayes from finding the truth.

Link Hathaway could have done the same thing.

"Mr. Hathaway, you keep a gun here?" he asked.

A vein bulged in Hathaway's forehead but he nodded.

"Would you get it, please?" Egan said.

Hathaway reached inside the cherry credenza, retrieved a key and unlocked the top desk drawer. "Holy hell," he muttered.

"What is it?" Margaret asked.

He jerked his head up, his gaze wide-eyed. "My .38 is missing."

Margaret gasped, and Hayes and Egan exchanged looks. Was Hathaway feigning surprise or had he known the gun was gone?

"You always keep it in that drawer, not a safe?" Egan asked.

"Yes."

Hayes narrowed his eyes. "When was the last time you saw it?"

Hathaway scratched his head. "A few days ago."

"Dad?" Margaret's voice sounded shaky.

"I haven't had any reason to get it," Hathaway said defensively.

Egan crossed his arms. "Who has had access to your office?"

Hathaway furrowed his brow in thought. "The

staff…" He glanced at Egan. "Walt. But none of them would steal it."

"Are you sure? Any of them or another visitor might have seen where you keep the key," Egan pointed out.

"Who else has been here?" Hayes asked, unconvinced that Hathaway hadn't used it to kill Morris, then ditched it.

Hathaway glanced at Margaret and hesitated.

Margaret twisted the silver chain again, drawing Hayes's eyes toward the locket, the one holding his baby picture. "Dad, who?" Margaret whispered.

A long-suffering sigh escaped him. "Devon stopped by yesterday morning. And Kenneth and Tammy Sutton were here for lunch."

Hayes grimaced. Sutton once again. But another thought niggled at him. "Devon knows you had a child, Margaret?"

Panic blazed in her eyes. "Yes."

"He knew you were looking for him?"

Her expression turned wary. "I mentioned it to him."

"What was his reaction?" Egan asked.

She hesitated. "He thought I should leave the past in the past."

Hayes grunted. "If he knew Taylor had hired the P.I., he could have tried to stop him from giving her the information."

"But he didn't know that Taylor had hired Mr. Morris," Margaret argued.

"How did you know about Morris, Mr. Hathaway?" Hayes asked.

Hathaway shifted and jammed his hands in the pockets of his pleated designer suit. "The damn fool came to me and showed me the documents he'd found."

Hayes's suspicions rose. "And what did you do?"

Hathaway glanced at Margaret, his shoulders tensing. "I offered to pay him to keep quiet."

Bribery, Hayes thought sourly. "Did he accept your offer?"

Hathaway shook his head. "Said he had already been compensated. And he refused to tell me who hired him."

But Hathaway had somehow found out. Hayes would bet money on it.

And he might have told Goldenrod. Then Margaret's father and fiancé could have conspired to keep Taylor and Margaret from learning about him.

"I have to talk to Devon Goldenrod," Hayes said.

Margaret thumbed her hand through her hair. "He's out of town and won't be back until tomorrow right before the party at Taylor's."

"Party?"

Margaret winced. "Yes, Taylor insisted on throwing it in honor of the wedding."

A wedding he would have to attend as Taylor's bodyguard. A wedding where he'd watch his mother marry a man who had just been added to his list of murder suspects.

Chapter 16

Taylor's stomach was so tied in knots, she found herself in the kitchen again. She made homemade pasta
with fresh salmon, a spinach salad, appetizers of pro-
sciutto and melon, garlic bread, and a decadent chocolate turtle pie.

She wondered if Hayes liked chocolate turtle pie.
Or salmon.

And what was happening with him and Margaret
and Link Hathaway.

Ranger McQuade was poring over Link's phone records in the living room when Hayes returned. Her
stomach vaulted to her throat as he entered.

The other ranger was missing in action—had he
gone back to Caroline?

At first, she'd thought Caroline crazy for falling for
Egan Caldwell, but now she understood the earthy sen-

sual magnetism of these rangers. They were real men. Down to earth, strong, gutsy, protective…masculine and sexy as hell.

Heaven help her, but he looked so damn tempting in that dark Stetson with his dark eyes so brooding. His permanent five-o'clock shadow only added to his mysterious soulful look, and her hands itched to touch him.

Instead she placed the appetizers on the bar along with a bottle of red wine, Scotch and a beer mug, just in case she could convince Hayes to have a drink with her.

Or more…

She'd never actually tried to seduce a man, but her imagination had had a field day the past hour, and she'd fantasized about the two of them working their frustrations out in bed.

What would Margaret say if Taylor slept with her son?

If she knew that Taylor was starting to have feelings for him?

He glanced at the bar as he entered, an eyebrow arched at the display of food. "Expecting company?"

"Just you," she said, her cheeks heating.

An odd look simmered in his eyes…desire? Heat? Surprise?

Then he quickly masked it and grunted at Ranger McQuade when he loped in. "What's the scoop?" Brody asked.

Hayes frowned. "Walt Caldwell claims Morris was dead when he arrived. He didn't stick around because he heard a noise and thought the killer might still be there. We didn't find a gun at his place."

Brody harrumphed. "So he knew about you?"

"He claimed he didn't know my name," Hayes said.

"Just that Hathaway was asking questions. He intended to bribe the P.I. to keep quiet, but was too late."

"How'd Egan take it?" Brody asked.

Hayes shook his head. "He didn't say much. But I think he believes his father."

"And Hathaway?" Brody asked.

Hayes glanced at Taylor, his expression hooded. "Hathaway has a .38 but it was conveniently missing. The staff, Margaret's fiancé, Devon Goldenrod, Egan's father and the Suttons all had access to his office."

Brody leaned one palm against the granite bar. "The suspects keep piling up."

"Yeah," Hayes agreed. "We stopped by Sutton's after we left Hathaway's, and he offered his weapon. I checked it and it hasn't been fired recently. No GSR on his hands, either."

"So Sutton didn't shoot Morris?"

"Could have hired someone," Hayes suggested.

"True. What else did Hathaway say?"

Hayes blew out a breath. "Link Hathaway admits he knew Morris was looking for Margaret's child, but Morris refused the bribe."

"A P.I. with morals," Brody muttered. "That's original."

Hayes's mouth almost twitched with a smile, and something tickled inside Taylor's belly. She wanted to see him smile, see him happy.

Good grief. What was wrong with her? She poured herself a glass of wine then gestured in offering, but Brody shook his head and Hayes declined, as well, mumbling that he was on duty.

Yeah, being her bodyguard.

She wanted his body instead.

"Another twist, though," Hayes said. "Apparently Devon Goldenrod knows that Margaret had a baby and didn't want her looking for the kid."

Taylor's lungs tightened. Hayes uttered the comment as if he was a distant observer and this was just a case, not his mother, his life, they were discussing. Tears burned the back of her eyelids, and she looked up at him, her heart in her throat. His gaze caught hers, questioning, lingering, then he visibly flinched and jerked his head back toward the other ranger.

"You talked to Goldenrod?" Ranger McQuade asked.

Hayes shook his head. "No, he's out of town. Margaret said he'll be back Saturday for the big party." He gave Taylor a scathing look. "Which I think you should cancel."

Taylor opened her mouth to reply, but Ranger McQuade spoke first. "No, let her have it. All the major players will be present. Something may happen."

"That's what I'm worried about," Hayes said. "There will be too many people in one room. It'll be harder to protect Taylor."

"We'll all be there for extra security," Brody said.

Hayes nodded, his expression stony. He obviously wanted to end the investigation so he could leave Cantara Hills. Leave Margaret and her behind.

Taylor sipped her wine. She didn't know why that thought bothered her so badly.

Because she wanted him to forgive Margaret, to have a relationship with her best friend?

Or because she wanted time to make him fall in love with her?

The next day, tension tightened Hayes's shoulders as he entered the ballroom inside Taylor's estate with Taylor on his arm. She looked stunning in the emerald-green satin ball gown that showcased her curves and cleavage.

Hellacious desires bombarded him. The woman was torturing him. The night before she'd been almost solicitous. Sweet, smiling at him, offering him a cold beer— a beer, for God's sake, when he figured the woman wouldn't allow it in her house. And that dinner she'd prepared had been mouthwatering.

Gorgeous and she could cook…

Was she as good in bed as she was in the kitchen?

Today, watching her calmly organize the details of the event tonight, he'd realized that she was…amazing. Organized and businesslike, but kind and respectful to the vendors and staff, treating them almost like friends or respected coworkers, not as if they were her underlings. And she cared about Margaret.

Still, she was way out of his league.

He tugged at the tie to the suit she'd had sent over for him, feeling completely out of place. He wanted his jeans and Stetson.

But Taylor had argued that if he wore the suit, he'd blend in.

He didn't want to blend in.

Except that out of uniform he'd put the guests more at ease, and maybe catch them off guard.

Taylor smiled at him from across the room, and his heart tripped. Hell, he was a red-blooded man and he wanted Taylor Landis. At least his body did. His mind protested, but his hunger seemed destined to ignore logic.

For the next hour, he followed her around like a damn puppy, making sure she was safe, yet salivating as she greeted strangers with a hug. These people were her friends, her kind of people.

He wasn't.

And of course, every man in the room appeared smitten with her, which only stoked his irritation as the night wore on.

Violin and piano music played from the orchestra on the stage and an ice statue of two doves created a centerpiece. Flowing chocolate fountains were interspersed throughout the room, along with dozens of fresh flower arrangements.

Food he'd never heard of or considered eating was artfully arranged on white linen tablecloths, and waiters dressed in monkey suits carried silver trays laden with appetizers, crystal flutes of champagne, wine and martinis. The attendees wore glitzy evening gowns and tuxes, and diamonds and other gemstones glittered beneath the chandeliers.

His stomach growled for a burger and brewsky.

But he wasn't here as a guest, he reminded himself, just to guard Taylor and investigate her friends. Link Hathaway, dressed in a gray tux that matched his silver-gray hair, stood by a staging area, watching his daughter as if he was afraid Hayes might get too close to her. Margaret smiled at him across the room, although sadness flickered in her eyes when he didn't return the gesture, and his gut clenched. Pretty boy Goldenrod had arrived with her, his manicured hand lying possessively across her back as they wove through the crowd.

Against the women's wishes, Brody and Egan had kept Victoria and Caroline away, but they insisted they would attend the wedding. Hopefully, the Rangers would have solved this case and Hayes and the Rangers could skip the ceremony. He didn't want to be anywhere near that shindig—instead he'd be riding his horse across his land while his birth mother married into politics.

Kenneth and Tammy Sutton rolled in to applause, although Hayes noticed Goldenrod's smile seemed forced.

Was there tension between the two men? And if so, why?

Politics? Maybe something to do with those illegal bids? Or was it personal?

A cloud of perfume swirled around Tammy Sutton as she glided past him, but she ignored him as if he was invisible and swept Taylor into a hug. "This is marvelous, darling. You always throw the best parties, Taylor. I don't know what we'd do without you around here."

"Thanks, Tammy," Taylor said. "I'm so glad you and Kenneth could make it. I understand how busy your schedule has been with the campaign."

"Yes," Tammy said, brushing a bejeweled hand up to pat her husband's cheek. "It has been hectic, but well worth it. Soon Kenneth will be sitting in the governor's chair where he belongs."

Or in jail, Hayes thought sourly.

"I know," Taylor agreed. "It's an exciting time for both of you."

Kenneth took Taylor's hands in his. "I couldn't have accomplished all I did for the city council without a great team. I'll be forever grateful to you, Taylor."

Taylor smiled. "Of course. You know you've earned my loyalty."

Link Hathaway moved up beside Devon Goldenrod while Margaret approached Taylor. "This is lovely, Taylor." She glanced at him, a softness in her eyes that twisted at him. "I'm glad you're here, Hayes."

"I'm here to protect Taylor, nothing more," Hayes said curtly.

Taylor glared at him, and Margaret's smile faltered. "I know, and I'm thankful for that. She doesn't deserve to be in danger, especially because she was trying to do something nice for me."

He couldn't argue with her over that, or stand to see her looking at him as if she wanted his forgiveness, so he excused himself. He needed to focus, to talk to Goldenrod.

Eyes trained on the man, he cut him off before Hathaway reached him, although he had no doubt that Margaret's father had already warned Goldenrod that Hayes would be asking questions.

He wanted to observe the man's reaction personally. Feel him out and see if he had a hidden agenda.

Did he love Margaret?

Hayes adjusted his tie, a smile cracking his lips when he noticed Goldenrod's thumb raking up and down the stem of his champagne flute as if he was nervous.

"Mr. Goldenrod," Hayes said. "I'm Ranger Keller."

"I know who you are," Goldenrod said with an edge to his voice that indicated he was also aware that he was Margaret's son.

"Then you realize why I'm here."

"Because you want access to Margaret's wealth."

Anger surged through Hayes. "No, because of the attempt on Taylor Landis's life and Morris's murder. I intend to find the person responsible and lock him behind bars."

The two of them indulged in a stare-off for several tense seconds.

"I don't know how I can help you."

"Do you own a gun?" Hayes asked.

Goldenrod shook his head. "No. Haven't felt the need."

"Where were you night before last?"

"Why are you asking?"

"Don't play dumb," Hayes said. "Even if Margaret didn't tell you about my visit to her and her father, Hathaway did. You know the private investigator who was working for Taylor was murdered."

"I was in Houston," Goldenrod said. "On business."

"I suppose you have witnesses?"

He nodded, not a blade of his sandy-blond hair moving. "A roomful."

Hayes twisted his mouth in thought. For some reason he didn't like this man. Didn't trust him.

"Now, I suggest you leave me and Margaret alone," Goldenrod said, dropping his voice a decibel. "She and I are to be wed, and I don't intend to let anything stop the ceremony." His eyes glinted like ice. "I won't allow you to cause trouble for her or hurt her."

Hayes raised a brow. That was rich, Goldenrod threatening him.

"Do you understand what I'm saying?" Goldenrod asked.

Hayes gritted his teeth at the bastard. "Oh, yeah, I hear you." He pushed his face into Goldenrod's. "But you don't scare me, pretty boy. And if you had anything to do with the attacks on Taylor, then I'll lock your ass up and throw away the key."

He stormed away, leaving Goldenrod with that message. When he looked up, Margaret was watching, her face lined with concern.

The tinkle of spoons clinking against glass rippled through the air, and voices began to hush. Taylor walked up the steps to the stage, her delicious curves mesmerizing him as she took the microphone. "I want to welcome you all to the party tonight. We're here to honor my best friend Margaret Hathaway and her fiancé, Devon Goldenrod. Let's raise our glasses to toast their upcoming nuptials."

Taylor lifted her glass and a chorus of shouts rang out as guests whispered and cheered. Link Hathaway climbed the steps, a smile stretching across his face.

But suddenly a shot rang out, shattering the ice statue on stage, and chaos erupted. Guests screamed and ducked, running from the room.

Hayes jerked his gun from his holster, and yelled for Taylor to get down as another bullet zoomed toward her.

Chapter 17

Taylor screamed and ducked behind the statue, and Link Hathaway dashed down the steps toward Margaret. Guests yelled and ran, glasses shattered on the floor as people scurried for safety and another shot flew by her head.

"Stay down, Taylor!" Hayes braced his gun to fire as he scanned the room, then he must have zeroed in on the shooter's location because he ran toward the side entry to the stage behind a curtained off area, vaulted through the opening and fired a shot.

She couldn't see what was happening, only hear the panicked sounds of the guests and Margaret calling her name. But when she looked up, Link and Devon Gold enrod had sequestered Margaret between them. And the other Rangers were searching the room.

It seemed like hours but only seconds passed when

another shot rang out, and Taylor cried out again, terrified Hayes had been hit.

Her chest ached from the pressure of holding her breath, then he finally appeared, shoving her brother in front of him.

Taylor gasped. Miles was handcuffed and spitting out curse words. "Miles?"

"I'm sorry, Taylor," Hayes said in a gruff voice. "But he was the shooter."

"This is your fault, you bitch!" Miles lifted his hand, his shaggy brown hair falling over one eye.

"Why?" Taylor gasped. "Why would you try to kill me?"

He jerked his head around, gesturing at the room. "You spend all this money for a party and you won't help me. It's not fair."

Taylor's chest clenched, but anger assaulted her. "You had your own money, Miles, and you threw it away, wasted it on drugs and gambling when you could have done something with your life. Could have helped others."

Margaret hurried to her side for support, and Hayes sent her a look of regret, but she didn't blame him. Her own brother had tried to kill her, and he could have hurt others. She refused to allow Miles to make her feel guilty for his problems.

"Come on, Landis," Hayes growled. "You have an appointment with a cell tonight."

He shoved Miles through the crowd of guests who were finally settling down with hushed whispers after the chaos.

"Taylor, maybe everyone should leave," Margaret said.

Taylor shook her head. "I don't want this to spoil your night."

Margaret gripped her hands. "Honey, you are so

much more important than a party. And I know you're upset about Miles."

Taylor glanced around, saw that the guests were uncomfortable. Plus the room was a mess—broken glass splattered on the floor, flutes overturned and food trays wrecked.

Tears stung her eyes and embarrassment flooded her cheeks, but she blinked back the tears, held her head up high and walked back to the microphone. "Please forgive me for what just happened," she said, her voice steadier than her legs. "I apologize for my brother's actions and sincerely hope that everyone is all right. Under the circumstances, though, I suggest we call it a night."

Hayes pushed Miles from the room, and locked gazes with Taylor.

Once he took Miles into custody, he could close the investigation and life could return to normal.

Relief tickled her, yet a deep ache throbbed in her chest. Then Hayes would leave Cantara Hills and she would never see him again.

Hayes hated the pain in Taylor's eyes and wanted to throttle her brother for hurting her. The stupid arrogant little twit. He had money and family and he'd screwed all of it.

Brody and Egan hurried to calm the guests and make sure they departed safely.

"Stop shoving me," Miles growled.

"You should be grateful I didn't blow your damn head off, you idiot."

Miles glared at him with hate-filled eyes, and Hayes tightened his grip on the man's hands.

Voices echoed from the foyer, guests leaving, Taylor saying goodbye and thanking people for attending, car engines revving up and rolling away.

Brody met him at the exit. Hayes opened the side door and led Miles toward him. Miles actually jerked his arm, seeming to have the stupid idea that he might run.

Hayes dug his fingers deeper into the guy's arm. "I'll take him in," Brody said. "You should stay."

Hayes removed Miles's gun from where he'd tucked it in the waistband of his jeans. "I'm sure you'll find GSR on his hands, too."

"It's a .38," Brody said. "I'll see if it matches the other bullet casings we found."

"I'll go search for the bullet casings and send them over."

Brody nodded, then took custody of Miles, who gave Hayes another bitter look before Brody shut the car door.

"I'll keep you posted," Brody said.

Hayes nodded. He wanted to question the jerk himself, but Taylor was upset, and his gut warned him that she didn't need to be left alone. Not tonight.

Besides, what if Miles had only reacted this evening, and wasn't the man they were looking for? They had to tie up loose ends and make certain the threat to Taylor was over.

Then he could leave.

He strode back to the ballroom and spent the next half hour searching for the bullet casings. He dug one out of the stage floor, another from the wall only inches from where Taylor had stood, then another from behind the staging area. If Miles had hit her, Taylor might be dead.

A frisson of fear ripped through him and sweat beaded on his forehead. He didn't want to see her hurt. Not physically, by a bullet.

And not by her brother because families should stick together.

Not that he knew anything about families...

The waitstaff for the party had begun cleaning up and taking down the bar. He bagged the bullets to send to forensics, then headed back toward the entrance when Margaret appeared.

"Hayes?"

He froze, heart pounding. "Yes?"

"Thank you for saving Taylor tonight." Emotions glittered in her eyes. "I was terrified for her."

He gave a clipped nod. "I'm glad she's all right, ma'am."

Ma'am? This was his mother. Yet he barely knew her. Would never be able to call her that.

"I'm not sure she is," Margaret said gently. "Taylor appears tough and strong, but having her own brother shoot at her...that cut deep."

He supposed it would. "He's in custody now. He can't hurt her again."

"Well..." She hesitated as if she wanted to say more, then Goldenrod appeared behind her, and placed a protective hand at her waist.

Hayes gritted his teeth. Goldenrod had made it clear he didn't want Hayes near Margaret.

"Please take care of her tonight," Margaret said. "She seems all right now but it'll hit her later."

"Don't worry," Hayes said. "I'll stay with her."

Margaret's eyes softened with relief, and she turned to leave with Goldenrod. He watched her go, feeling an odd sensation in his chest.

And that strange sense of panic that maybe Taylor was still in danger.

* * *

Taylor hugged Margaret good-night, then forced herself to face the staff she'd hired for the party and oversee the cleanup. Emotions ping-ponged inside her as she remembered the frenetic scene that had erupted when that shot had rung out.

She still couldn't believe that Miles had tried to shoot her. He would face charges now, perhaps spend time in jail...

Her father would be crushed. Angry. And even more remote than he had been the past few years.

She only hoped that he would make sure Miles received the therapy he needed to get his act together.

And poor Margaret...she already felt the strain of finding out that Hayes was her son, and Taylor had sensed tension between her and Devon and Hayes all evening.

Tonight's episode certainly hadn't helped.

"I think we have things covered," the caterer said. "We'll bill you as usual."

Taylor thanked the woman, then sighed and left the ballroom. Hayes was talking to Ranger Caldwell, and handed him the bullet casings to take to the lab.

"I'll check in with you tomorrow," Hayes said.

Ranger Caldwell nodded and left, and Taylor bypassed him and headed up the staircase. She wanted a shower, to wash the scent of fear off her body, to warm herself so she could finally stop trembling.

She ripped the hairpins from the bun at the base of her neck, tossed them on her dresser, then removed her diamonds and placed them in her jewelry box.

Then she stripped her gown and walked into the bathroom, flipped on the shower and climbed inside.

The tears fell as she drowned herself in the warm spray, her body shaking from the aftermath of the night.

She allowed herself to spend her emotions and scrubbed with her favorite bodywash, willing away the image of her brother in handcuffs, but memories of the night she'd almost been strangled haunted her. Had Miles done that, too?

She donned a robe and walked into her bedroom, wondering how she would sleep in her house tonight.

When she entered the bedroom, Hayes was standing by her bed, looking concerned. "I knocked, but you didn't answer so I got worried." His voice was low, husky. "Are you all right, Taylor?"

She clutched the thin robe to her, her body tingling as his gaze raked over her. She was still cold, still trembling, still felt so damn vulnerable. "Yes."

His eyes narrowed. "You're lying."

"I will be fine," she whispered. "I just need some time."

Hayes lifted his hand and tucked a strand of hair behind her ear. The movement was so gentle that she shivered, but not from being cold, from arousal.

"I understand that Miles is family." He rubbed his thumb down her cheek. "I'm sorry I had to arrest him."

"It's not your fault," Taylor said. "He was out of control. He could have hurt someone…me, Margaret… you…"

"Shh, he didn't, though," Hayes said. "Margaret is safe and so are you."

They stared at one another, emotions pummeling her as she felt his arms encircle her.

She slid her arms beneath his, clutched his back and breathed in his scent. He smelled like a man, masculine, rugged, strong. And he held her with such tenderness that her heart swelled. Beneath that tough facade and badge, his heart beat strong and solid. He was a good man. The kind heroes were made of.

Heaven help her, she was falling in love with this cowboy.

But he would leave soon. Ride out of town and never come back. She couldn't let him go without tasting him again. Without a night in his arms where she could show him that they could fit together.

She licked her lips, cradled his face between her hands and dragged his head toward her. He stiffened, but she fused her mouth with his and traced her tongue over his lips. He moaned deep in his throat, then his hands slid lower to yank her against him. She felt his hard length press into her, and knew he wanted her.

Adrenaline was still churning through Hayes, that and the fear that had robbed his breath when the shot had broken out. He hadn't been able to reach Taylor fast enough.

And now…now all he'd meant to do was comfort her. But those damn lips teased him, and so had the sight of her in that skimpy robe. Her nipples were tight, turgid peaks, the sheer fabric giving him a glimpse of her pale-pink areolas beneath. He wanted his mouth on them.

And his hands on the rest of her naked flesh.

She licked at his jaw and rubbed her foot up his calf, and his arousal stabbed the fly of his damn suit pants.

He had to stop this insanity.

He forced himself to pull away but she gripped his arms and kept him from leaving.

Still, his chest was pounding. "Taylor, you're scared. Tonight was traumatic." His voice cracked. He was a ranger first, had to take charge, stay in control. "I can't take advantage of you."

"You're not," she murmured raggedly. "I want you, Hayes. Please make love to me."

"Taylor…"

Her breath brushed his cheek as she kissed him again, robbing him of words, of anything but the raw primal lust burning inside him.

Then she teased his lips with her tongue again. He opened, so starved for her that he murmured her name and trailed his hands over her breasts, deepening the kiss as he stroked her nipples through the satiny robe. The buds hardened to peaks, her chest rising and falling erratically, arousing sensations that rippled through every muscle in his body.

"I want your hands and mouth on me," she said into his throat. "And you inside me."

No woman had ever talked to him like that. Had ever sounded so starved for him. So passionate…

He parted the fabric, rubbed his thumbs over the turgid peaks, then lowered his head and licked the tip. She gasped and thrust herself at him, clinging to him as if she'd fall apart if he released her.

He sucked one nipple into his mouth, stroked his hand over her hips, then to her inner thigh where he feathered his fingers along the delicate skin of her legs, parting them slightly to allow him better access to her precious secrets. Heat shot through him, firing his sex to a raging need that destroyed any common sense.

"Yes," she rasped. "Take me, Hayes. I need you."

His breath caught and he dragged his mouth from her breast to watch as she dropped the flimsy robe to the floor and stood beautifully naked before him.

Chapter 18

Hayes paused to drink in Taylor's beauty, his chest heaving with the need to make love to her. She reached for his tie and yanked it off, then tossed it to the floor. Her hands tore at his dress shirt, buttons flying as she hastily pushed it off his shoulders and slung it behind her. As soon as her fingers began to fumble with his belt and zipper, he thought he would explode.

But he reined in the need raging through him, kicked off his shoes, then shoved off his pants and socks.

"Hayes…"

Taylor's whispered sigh spiked his hunger, and when she kissed him again, he backed her against the wall, taking all that she offered as her tongue danced with his.

She tasted so delicious that he groaned, and raked his hands over her shoulders, her back, her breasts again, his sex throbbing with the need to stroke her, to fill her, to make her his.

He tore his mouth away, and her breath bathed his neck as he lowered his head and teased her nipples again with his tongue, sipping greedily as her hair brushed his neck. Her scent made his heart race, and he trailed kisses down her abdomen to her thighs and teased the sensitive skin guarding her secrets.

She moaned and clawed her hands through his hair, and he used his tongue as he would his length to slide between her legs and tease her until she parted her legs. Then he plunged his tongue inside her to taste her sweet essence.

"Hayes…"

He held her still, his movements bolder, his own excitement growing hotter as she whispered her pleasure and offered herself to him. Seconds later, her body quivered beneath his onslaught, and her wet juices filled his mouth, a taste so erotic he would never forget the headiness.

Or how much he wanted her.

Dizzy with the blinding sensations spiraling through her, Taylor closed her eyes and relented to the intense climax riding through her, a climax made more satisfying and erotic by her growing feelings for Hayes.

Tears threatened, but she blinked them away, quivering as Hayes's mouth played havoc with her senses. He held her, loved her, pleasured her as if she was a fine treasure he'd found, one that was meant to be treated with loving care. A fire erupted deep inside her belly, flaming hotter with each sensation exploding through her and burning out of control.

She clawed at his arms, dragged him back up to stand, then lowered her hand and stroked his hard length. He was huge, bulging beneath the boxers, and she was frantic to feel his naked flesh inside her, frantic to pleasure him as he had her.

She breathed, her passion spiraling out of control, and pulled at the boxers, freeing him so she felt the damp fullness of his erection pulsing with need. She moved to go down on him, but he caught her arms, kicked off his boxers and lifted her. She looped her arms around him and rubbed her wet, aching heat against his hard length, begging him to take her.

"Taylor... I want you now."

"Yes," she pleaded. "I need you, Hayes."

He moaned, deep and throaty, hunger lacing the sound, then tore away from her.

"Can't," he muttered gruffly. "No condom."

"The nightstand," she whispered, and he grinned and reached inside the drawer and ripped one out, her legs still wrapped around him.

They laughed together as she tried to help him roll it on, his huge size making it difficult. The flare of raw passion in his eyes heated her skin and ignited her desires to a frenzied fever.

She threw her head back in wild abandon, then tightened her legs around his waist, crying out his name as she impaled herself on him.

He growled, pushing deeper, gripping her legs as he thrust farther into her warm chamber. She lifted her hips, angling herself to feel him pulse against her sensitive nub, her breath erratic as he pulled himself out, then thrust again, more forcefully this time, delving deeper into her body until she panted his name again. Perspiration dotted her skin as she rode him up and down.

Any semblance of control evaporated like rain on hot pavement. The sounds of their bodies slapping together, their husky whispers and choppy breathing filled the room. Raw, primal, sensual noises that intensified the trembling in her body and sent another mind-shattering climax to overtake her.

Her insides clenched, and he thrust into her again, their bodies climbing to the heavens together as his own orgasm ripped through him.

The erotic outpouring rippled in wave after wave of mind-numbing pleasure until Taylor dropped her head forward against his neck, heaving for a breath. He leaned into her, his face buried between her breasts, as his body shook from the pleasure.

They stood like that for what seemed like hours, each drawing in breaths, holding each other, their bodies entwined, her heart soaring with love. Finally he carried her to bed and they fell onto it, exhausted. But she curled into his arms and he wrapped them around her and held her.

Emotions overwhelmed her, feelings that ripped away the fear she'd had earlier, yet another fear fought its way through the clouded recesses of her pleasure.

Hayes would leave soon, and she couldn't stand to lose him.

No man had ever made her feel this heartfelt knot of love and happiness bursting inside her.

She had to find a way to convince him that they belonged together.

Sunlight streaked the sky as Hayes stirred from a deep sleep. He smiled, sensations rocketing through him. He was dreaming. Dreaming of having sex with Taylor. Featherlight strokes massaged his hard length, a damp tongue laving him. He opened his eyes and groaned as erotic tension pummeled him. He wasn't dreaming.

Taylor had crawled beneath the covers and was going down on him. Had his throbbing length inside her mouth, wetting it with her tongue, sucking it, applying pressure...

He threw the covers back with a guttural groan, the sight of her long blond hair spilled across his bare belly sending a shot of pure lust through him. She trailed her tongue along his length, teasing the tip, her other hand massaging the insides of his thighs, stoking him to degrees of pain-pleasure that made her name rip from deep in his throat.

If she continued, he was going to lose it.

"Taylor, honey, you have to stop..."

She lifted her head, her eyes hooded and dark with desire, and his excitement skyrocketed. "No," she said softly.

He shook his head as she closed her mouth around him again. Her warm wet mouth enflamed him, and he clenched the sheets, struggling for control. But she was determined to torture him. She sucked him long and hard, riding up and down until he forced her to stop.

"I want inside you," he said gruffly.

She laughed, reached for a condom and ripped it open. They barely got it on before she crawled on top of him and straddled him. With one hand she guided his throbbing member inside her. Her beautiful breasts fell heavy in front of him and he leaned on his elbows, biting at her nipples, licking and drawing one into his mouth as she moved up and down on him. She tossed her hair over her shoulder, crying his name as spasms made her insides clench tighter around him.

Unable to stand the tension any longer, he threw his

head back, gripped her hips and they found a frenzied passionate rhythm that sent them both over the edge together.

Her breathing erratic, she collapsed on top of him, their sweat mingling, their bodies still joined, and he closed his arms around her. Holy hell, he could get used to waking up like this.

No, he couldn't fantasize about other mornings with Taylor on top of him.

"That was so wonderful." Taylor pressed a kiss to his chest, stroking him.

"I thought I was dreaming when I woke up," he mumbled gruffly.

She laughed against his chest. "See how good we are together, Hayes?"

Something about her tone flamed his desire again, but fear also darted through him. He couldn't let her think this was anything but sex. That he would stick around after the investigation.

He'd go back to his world and she would return to hers. He wouldn't allow himself to think otherwise or to offer her hope of more.

Margaret's wedding was Saturday. With Miles in jail, and loose ends still unclear, he'd take her away to his place until the wedding. Maybe by then they'd know for sure if the danger to her was over.

When she saw how he lived, his lifestyle, she'd realize that the two of them weren't suited at all.

Except in bed...and there he'd found a slice of heaven.

While Hayes showered, Taylor slid from bed and prepared breakfast, then placed it on a bed tray and carried it back to her bedroom. When Hayes emerged from the shower, his hair damp, a towel knotted around his waist, her mouth watered.

"That looks delicious," he said.

"So do you."

His gaze locked with hers, heat and memories of their lovemaking lighting the flames of desire again. But his stomach growled, and she put her needs on hold and patted the bed.

"Sit and eat, Hayes. You're going to need your energy again later."

A chuckle rumbled from his chest. "Is that so?"

She nodded, plucked a fresh strawberry from the tray and offered it to him. He sucked it into his mouth, licking the tip of her fingers when he was finished, then he joined her on the bed and they devoured the omelet and muffins.

She raked her hands over his chest. "Now, I want you again."

He gripped her hands. "Taylor, Egan and Brody are going to interrogate Miles today and hope to tie up loose ends. Why don't we ride out to my place, get out of Cantara Hills till the dust settles?"

"We'll be back for Margaret's rehearsal dinner?"

"Yeah. But the press will probably be all over Miles's arrest and will hound you. I thought it might do you good to get away."

Her heart stuttered. "Oh, goodness. I'm not ready for the media circus. Not yet…"

He nodded. "Then pack a bag."

She grabbed his hand and kissed it. "Thank you, Hayes. I'm looking forward to seeing your home."

Affection flickered in his eyes, and he twisted his mouth, uncomfortable. "I'll call Brody and tell him where we'll be while you get dressed. Oh, and pack casual, jeans if you have them. My place is country, not country club."

She winced at his comment, but blew it off. Did he think she didn't like the country? That she had to have a mansion?

She kissed him, then hurried to the shower, determined to prove him wrong. Hayes must be starting to have feelings for her, otherwise he wouldn't invite her to his home.

She couldn't think of anything nicer than leaving town with him, getting away from the ugliness of the investigation. A place where no one could bother them, and she and Hayes could make love day and night.

Where she could prove to him they had a future.

Hayes braced himself for Taylor's reaction as they drove to his cabin. Rustic would best describe the home he'd built for himself. He liked the open space, pasture for his horses, the huge ancient trees with their gnarled branches, the stream where he could fish and the peace and quiet of the land.

There was no sauna, outdoor swimming pool, marble in the bathroom nor gourmet kitchen. A woodstove served as the main heat source in the winter although he had installed central air for the unbearably hot summers.

He'd added the front porch at the last minute so he could enjoy coffee and morning sunrises.

As soon as he pulled down the three-mile drive to his secluded property, Taylor perked up, a smile spreading across her face that shocked him and caught him off guard.

"Oh my God, this is breathtaking, Hayes. I can't believe you own it."

He swallowed, gripping the steering wheel tighter. "It's not fancy, Taylor."

He maneuvered the gravel road, still expecting her to look down on his cabin, but she "oohed" and "aahed" as he parked, her exuberance making his heart pick up a notch.

"This is wonderful, Hayes. So secluded and quiet and, oh, look at that stream in back and your horses." She clapped her hands, unfastened her seat belt, jumped out and jogged over to the gate.

Apache trotted straight to her like a pathetic love-struck male, whinnied and nuzzled up to her as she petted him.

Hayes grimaced. He was in deep trouble, had vastly underestimated Taylor Landis.

Tucking his hands in the pockets of his jeans, he loped over to the fence, glaring at Apache.

"He's gorgeous," Taylor said, her face glowing with excitement. "Can we ride while we're here?"

"You ride?" he croaked, then figured she rode dressage, show horses if anything, not trail riding.

"I love to ride," she said with such a softness to her voice that her sincerity rang through loud and clear. "Each year, I host a summer camp for handicapped and underprivileged children at a ranch." She turned to him, eyes sparkling with emotion. "Maybe this next year, you can come and visit with the children."

His gut clenched, emotions that he didn't want hitting him. He'd thought Taylor a rich snotty heiress, yet she offered more than money to her charities. She gave her time and her heart.

A heart that he was beginning to fall for.

He sucked in a sharp breath. Remembered how he'd awakened this morning with her loving him. Remembered the delicious way she tasted and how sweetly she'd offered herself to him.

Remembered that someone wanted to kill her.

That would not happen. If it did, it would be over his dead body.

Chapter 19

Taylor spent the next few days in total bliss. Two days of relaxation, picnics outside, wading in the stream, riding across his property on horseback, feeding each other in bed and making love.

He was surprised when she'd saddled her own horse, and even more so at the way she settled into his home. It was cozy and comfortable, with wood floors, braided rugs, a fireplace and handmade quilts on his massive oak bed. He'd built most of the furniture himself including the rocking chair by the fireplace and the porch swing where they sipped their coffee.

All the place needed was a cat curled in the corner and a couple of children running in the yard. *A little boy with dark hair and big dark eyes....*

Their last night together, their lovemaking felt even more frantic as they both felt the clock counting down the minutes until they had to return to Cantara Hills, to reality and the investigation.

He took her against the wall, on the floor, outside on his back porch with the stars twinkling above the Texas sky, his horses prancing across the open pasture and coyotes howling in the distance.

During the ride back to her estate, Taylor broached the subject of Margaret again. "Please give her a chance," she said. "She cares about you, Hayes."

"But she still hasn't told me my father's name," he said bitterly.

"She will, Hayes, just give her time."

He grunted, and Taylor bit her lip, the rest of the ride strained and silent.

Finally, as they pulled into her drive, Hayes cleared his throat. "I talked to Brody this morning while you showered. Your father showed up with a lawyer. Miles admits to the shooting at the party, but not to Morris's murder or the pool attack. We did find your charm bracelet at his house, though."

She sighed. "He knew that would hurt me."

He nodded. "But this means that you could still be in danger, Taylor."

Fear slithered through her. "Then you won't leave yet?"

He studied her, his expression indicating that he heard the double meaning underlying her words.

"No, not yet."

She nodded, a sharp pain clawing at her heart. She'd intended to tell him that she loved him at the ranch, but had decided to hold back, to show him instead of saying the words. And she thought she had.

She only hoped it was enough.

"What time is the rehearsal dinner?" Hayes asked.

"Seven." She climbed from the car. She had a million things to do before then.

The rest of the day flew by. She had lunch with Margaret and an appointment to pick up her dress. Hayes tagged along, looking awkward and quiet but so damn handsome that she could barely keep her eyes off of him.

Margaret traced a finger along her water glass. "Last night I told Devon that I'm meeting with Hayes's father to tell him about Hayes."

"How did Devon react?" Taylor asked.

"Not well. He begged me to reconsider." Anguish laced Margaret's voice. "But I think he should know, and Hayes has a right to know his birth father's identity."

"Devon probably just feels threatened," Taylor said softly.

Margaret's face looked pinched. "I know. But it's not like Hayes's father wants me. He's married."

Taylor sighed. "I'm sorry. Are you going to see his father before the wedding?"

Worry filled Margaret's eyes as she glanced at Hayes where he stood by the wall of the restaurant. "Right after I leave here. I'm not looking forward to it."

"Good luck, Margaret." Taylor squeezed her hand. "And call me if you need me."

"I will."

Taylor murmured a silent prayer for her friend as Margaret left. She still hoped Hayes would come around. Maybe if she and he stayed together...

If they married...

With visions of the two of them celebrating their own

ceremony on his ranch in her head, she rushed to her spa appointment. Her father phoned during her massage and she called him back on the way to the hair salon. "Are you all right, Taylor?"

She bit her lip at his concerned tone. "Yes, Dad."

"I can't believe Miles tried to hurt you."

Tears blurred her eyes. "It was awful. He needs help."

"And he'll get it. But he may have to spend some time in jail to learn his lesson."

At least he wasn't going to let Miles off this time.

"Do you want me to come to the house tonight, Taylor?"

"No. Ranger Keller is there."

"He'd better take care of you," her father said.

She smiled, although she wondered how her father would react if he knew about them.

After she hung up, she met with the hairstylist. Hayes waited in the lobby, his dark look imposing, reminding her that someone still wanted her dead.

He also looked bored and disgusted, triggering anxiety to sprout again in her belly. Was she being foolish to hope that he loved her?

As she dressed for the rehearsal dinner that evening, anxiety riddled her. Hayes met her at the bottom of the steps wearing his Stetson and jeans as if to remind her again that they belonged to different worlds, that he wasn't here as a guest but as her bodyguard. She had fit into his world fine.

Would he even try to fit into hers?

She struggled to stifle her doubts as he drove her to the church for the rehearsal. The stained-glass cathedral with its ornate windows and candelabras looked stunning with candles burning, but Margaret acted nervous and fidgety, and she and Devon both looked strained as they went through the motions of the rehearsal.

Twice she caught Hayes watching Margaret with an odd look in his eyes, and she wondered if he might be softening.

She stumbled, the strap of her heel slipping free. He caught her, and she gazed into his eyes, heat rippling between them as she recalled their erotic lovemaking. His hands stroking and touching her, his mouth loving her body from her head to her toes, the two of them riding each other day and night.

"Are you all right?" he asked gruffly.

She licked her lips. "Yes. Just hot."

A smile twitched at his mouth. "It is hot in here," he agreed in a low voice.

She smiled and he knelt and fastened her shoe for her, his finger tracing a path along her bare toes that sent a chill of longing through her. "Later," she whispered.

He stared at her, but he didn't answer.

When they arrived at the country club, a host of cars filed down the drive, and two reporters with cameras stood on the entrance steps. Margaret Hathaway's marriage was society news, especially with Devon running for city council and Kenneth in attendance. Camera lights flashed as Devon and Margaret exited their limo, and they paused to pose for photos and to address the reporters.

Taylor hung back in the car, allowing them their moment, and curious about how Margaret's talk with Hayes's father went.

Finally satisfied they'd given the press what they'd come for, one of the reporters moved to interview other guests.

Hayes accepted the parking stub from the valet and she climbed out. He circled around the car to accompany her, but just as they reached the top of the steps and neared the entrance, the other reporter zoomed toward her. Cameras flashed, capturing her on Hayes's arm and she smiled, but felt Hayes stiffen.

"Miss Landis, Connie Winstead. We heard your brother was arrested for attempted murder."

Hayes cleared his throat, but Taylor spoke up, aware she had to deal with the fallout. "Yes, that's true. Unfortunately, my brother has some emotional difficulties. The family is going to do all we can to support his recovery."

"Is it true that Texas Rangers have been assigned to protect you?" The reporter pivoted toward Hayes with a raised brow.

Taylor swallowed but kept her smile intact. "Yes, temporarily."

Connie leaned closer with a wink. "We also heard that the two of you went away together. Give us the scoop, Miss Landis. We heard two of Cantara Hills' finest residents have become engaged to rangers. Is there a romantic relationship between you and Ranger Keller?"

Taylor barely restrained a gasp. Hayes stiffened, looking intimidating and furious, while she glanced up and saw Margaret watching her with interest. She couldn't very well divulge such personal information in front of the press.

"Ranger Keller simply escorted me to a safe place to allow me to get away for a few days."

A devious look sparkled in Connie's eyes. "So you're not having an affair with Ranger Keller?"

"Certainly not," Taylor said matter-of-factly. "Now,

please excuse me. This is Miss Hathaway's rehearsal dinner."

At that moment, Kenneth and Tammy Sutton rolled up, someone shrieked about their arrival and the reporters darted toward them.

She swept forward, and Hayes followed, his expression stoic. Taylor pulled Hayes into the entryway and headed to the ladies' room to recover.

Hayes fisted his hands by his sides to control his raging temper. He'd never been rough with a woman before but he'd wanted to grab that damn woman reporter and shake her senseless. And Taylor...he'd been poleaxed by the reporter's questions, but she had remained cool, aloof, had replied without even thinking about her answer.

Because she'd never admit to her friends and social circle that she'd stooped low enough to bed a cowboy.

All that lovemaking this weekend, those sweet smiles, intimate moments, how she'd pretended to like his cabin and ranch...she'd just been slumming.

"Hayes, I'm sorry about that," she said. "I wasn't expecting the press to be interested in me tonight."

"Why not?" he growled. "You're high-society news, Taylor. You always will be in the spotlight."

She frowned at his cutting tone. "That may be true, but I don't like my personal life plastered across the papers for everyone in the world to read."

"No, I don't imagine you'd want people knowing you slummed with me."

Her eyes widened, anger sparking. "Slummed?"

He shrugged. "That's what you did, didn't you? Wanted to see how the other half lived?"

"That's ridiculous." She grabbed his arm. "I enjoyed every minute we spent together, Hayes. And making love to you had nothing to do with wanting to see how the other half lived. I'm in love with you."

"Right." He made a throaty sound of disbelief. "Don't confuse love with sex, Taylor. That's all we had together. Great sex."

"It was great," she said, her voice breaking. "Great because I love you, Hayes. Because we're good together."

"It was great sex," he said through clenched teeth, "because someone taught you how to pleasure a man, Taylor."

Hurt flickered across her face, and tears pooled in her eyes. He felt like a jerk, but he couldn't retract the words. It had been painfully obvious that she didn't want her friends to know she'd been intimate with him. He hadn't expected different, but these past few days, for a few moments, he'd almost allowed himself to forget who she was. Where she'd come from. Where he'd come from.

That they had no future together.

She spun around, swiping at the tears, then bolted inside the ladies' room.

His stomach churned, but he watched her go. They had to part when the case ended, anyway. No use living a fantasy that wouldn't come true.

She'd realize he was right in no time, and then she'd move on to a man of her caliber.

And he'd be alone again, just as he always had been. Just as he liked it.

Taylor felt like the biggest fool in the world. Hayes didn't love her, didn't see her as anything more than a good lay that he'd enjoyed on the job.

She wiped at the tears, sucked in a deep breath and reminded herself that her heart would heal. Tonight was about Margaret, and she wouldn't spoil her happiness for anything in the world. She doctored her makeup, powdered her nose and jutted her chin as she left the lounge.

Hayes stood like a sentinel outside the doorway, his Stetson pulled low, shading his eyes. "Taylor—"

"Don't," she said sharply. "I'm going to hire a private bodyguard so you can be dismissed immediately."

A sardonic sound echoed from his throat. "You can hire some pretty boy if you want, but I have a job to do here and I'm not leaving until it's done."

She glared at him. "Fine. Just keep your distance."

"Don't worry," he muttered in a low voice.

She brushed past him and rushed into the ballroom, weaving between the guests who were greeting Margaret and Devon and seating themselves for dinner. Hayes followed her, and stood away from the table by a stage area draped in red velvet.

Margaret rose and went toward him, then gestured for him to join them, but he shook his head. Taylor sipped her water, sensing he felt out of place amongst their group, but he really belonged at the table with Margaret. Still, hurt prevented her from insisting he sit and eat with them.

The dinner seemed strained, Devon and Margaret exchanging uncomfortable looks as Kenneth and Tammy joined them. Link claimed his place beside Margaret, his expression stoic. Tammy plastered herself to Kenneth all evening and Devon refused to leave Margaret's side. But Margaret and Kenneth exchanged odd looks occasionally, making Taylor wonder what was going on.

Kenneth even went over and spoke to Hayes—she assumed he was asking about the investigation, but Kenneth seemed more ruffled than usual and tugged at his collar as he returned. Her gaze caught Margaret's and pained emotions flickered across Margaret's face.

Link offered a long-winded toast to Margaret and Devon, and Margaret smiled, although she glanced again at Kenneth. Taylor tensed, something passing between her friend and Kenneth, triggering a distant memory of another time when she'd seen Margaret and Kenneth together, laughing and looking at each other as if they shared something intimate.

She gasped and nearly choked on her water as the truth dawned on her. Was Kenneth the reason Margaret had never married? Had she been in love with him all these years?

Could Kenneth be Hayes's father?

Margaret excused herself to go to the powder room and Taylor followed, well aware that Hayes dogged their movements. But as she'd requested, he maintained his distance.

Just as Taylor pushed at the door to the lounge, a loud noise ripped through the air. God, a bomb!

Taylor screamed as the door shattered, wood and glass splintered and smoke burst from the inside.

Chapter 20

Hayes's heart raced as he pushed Margaret and Taylor to the floor. Dammit, someone had just tried to blow them up!

When was this madness going to end?

Smoke poured from the lounge, pieces of wood, tile, glass pelting the outer area. Screams reverberated across the grand entryway, guests running and shouting in horror.

"Taylor, Margaret, are you okay?"

Taylor turned toward him, her face streaked with soot and a line of blood. "I'm all right. Margaret?"

Margaret made a soft moan, and Hayes's breath tightened in his chest as he gently helped her sit up. "I'm fine," she said, although terror streaked her voice and a bruise marred her arm where she'd fallen.

"Was anyone else inside?" he asked.

Taylor shook her head. "I don't know."

He called 9-1-1. "We need an ambulance." He gave the address, then punched in Brody's number and explained what had happened. "Get a crime scene unit here ASAP and I need help questioning the guests."

Link Hathaway, Devon Goldenrod and Kenneth Sutton all stormed toward Taylor and Margaret, concern on their faces as they hovered over the women.

Hayes crossed to the doorway where guests were trying to escape, then held up his hand and shouted. "I'm sorry, folks, but no one is leaving yet. This is a crime scene now. Everyone has to be questioned, so just settle down and relax."

The next two hours were total chaos. Brody and Egan arrived along with two local officers, and they herded the guests back inside the ballroom and divided up to question them.

He, Brody and Egan took the major suspects while the paramedics tended to Margaret and Taylor and CSI searched the lounge. Security for the country club managed to confine the area outside to prevent others from entering or leaving.

Link, Devon and Kenneth stood guard around Margaret and Taylor, while Tammy Sutton hovered nearby, acting concerned, although she looked irritated with the attention her husband was bestowing on the other two women. Goldenrod kept one hand on Margaret's shoulder as if to remind himself that she had survived.

Or that she was his?

Egan joined him as he walked toward the group. He desperately wanted to talk to Taylor and his mother...

His *mother?*

A sharp pang of fear clutched at him. He'd just found

her and had almost lost her. And he hadn't even made an attempt to get to know her.

Where did they go from here?

Did he want to try?

Then Taylor's terrified gaze met his, and his heart clenched. He closed the distance between them, needing to verify she was safe.

Remembering the night before when they'd made love, he itched to hold her, but she frowned when he approached as if to remind him of their earlier conversation, that she'd proclaimed her love and he'd thrown it in her face.

Kenneth Sutton edged up beside him, authority in his tone. "What's going on? Do you know who did this?"

"Not yet, but I will," Hayes growled. "I need to speak to each of you alone."

Kenneth frowned, and Link and Devon exchanged annoyed looks. "Margaret, you and Taylor first."

Egan ushered Link aside to question him, and Kenneth and Tammy moved to a sofa nearby, while Brody appeared to interrogate Devon.

"Margaret, Taylor," Hayes said, "did you see anyone leaving the lounge when you got there?"

"No," they both murmured at once.

"Either this attempt was made on Taylor alone and you got caught up in it, Margaret, or someone wanted you out of the way, too. It obviously has something to do with that P.I.'s death."

Margaret clutched Taylor's hands, trembling.

"Who else knows about me?" he asked.

She wet her lips. "Devon, and…this afternoon I told your father."

Hayes's stomach churned. "How did he react?"

"He would never do this, Hayes, I can assure you that." Margaret's voice cracked.

"How did he react, Margaret?"

"He was upset, angry, hurt." Her eyes implored him to believe her. "He insisted that if he'd known, he would have been part of your life, that he would have stood by me. But he was so young and so was I."

"Who is he?" Hayes skimmed the room. "Is he here?"

She hesitated, then nodded and lowered her voice. "Hayes… Kenneth Sutton is your father."

Her declaration echoed in his ears. Kenneth Sutton, the city councilman? The man running for governor?

A man who wouldn't have wanted a kid to stand in his way years ago…or now.

No wonder Margaret hadn't told Kenneth. No wonder she'd shipped him away.

Shock and hurt clouded his thoughts, the pain so intense he thought his chest would explode.

He had to control himself, couldn't let emotions interfere. Had to think like a Texas Ranger.

Which meant Kenneth Sutton had just jumped to the top of his suspect list for this bombing.

Would Sutton kill Taylor and Margaret to keep the truth from being revealed?

Goldenrod also had a lot to lose. He'd been all over Margaret tonight. Had been second in line to Kenneth Sutton for years. Maybe he feared that when the truth finally came out, that Margaret and Kenneth might get together and he'd lose to Sutton again.

Taylor hugged Margaret as Hayes strode toward Kenneth.

"He wouldn't do this," Margaret insisted in a pained

voice. "Kenneth wouldn't hurt you or me, Taylor. He wants to make amends to Hayes. Said he'd make their relationship public, but he wanted to talk to Hayes first."

"Does Tammy know?" Taylor asked, remembering how she'd clung to Kenneth's side all evening.

"I don't know." Margaret sighed then looked up at Taylor. "What's going on with you and Hayes, Taylor? I thought you two were…maybe involved."

Taylor winced. She'd never been good at hiding her feelings.

"You're in love with him, aren't you?" Margaret asked. "If you are, it's okay, Taylor. I'd like nothing better than to see you with my son."

Taylor sighed. "It doesn't matter, Margaret. He made it clear that he doesn't have feelings for me."

"It's all my fault," Margaret whispered. "I can't blame him for the way he feels about us. He must be so hurt."

Taylor winced. He was hurting, but she was hurt, too. She couldn't go to him tonight or ever again, not after the things he'd said.

A minute later, Hayes returned with Kenneth in tow and escorted the four of them into a private room. Margaret gave Kenneth an apologetic look, but he shrugged it off, watching Hayes as if searching for some semblance of himself.

"Let's lay all the cards on the table," Hayes said dryly. "Mr. Sutton, Margaret just informed me that she told you that you have a son."

Kenneth scrubbed a hand over his chin. "Yes. I swear I didn't know, Hayes."

"Not a clue?" Hayes asked bitterly.

Sutton hesitated. "No. Although…maybe I should have figured it out."

"What do you mean by that?" Hayes asked.

Kenneth paced the room. "A while back, when Kimberly was working for me, she came to me with speculations."

"Kimberly did?" Hayes asked.

"Yes. She claimed that you had a rare blood type, AB negative. That's also my blood type."

"How did she know your blood type?" Hayes asked.

"She answered the phone for me. I get constant requests to donate blood. Then she saw a picture of me as a kid and thought there was a resemblance between us. Apparently she did some digging on her own and heard gossip that Margaret had given up a child." He whirled around. "But I didn't believe her. I assured her that she was wrong, that if Margaret had given birth, she would have told me. That she would never have kept a secret like that."

Tears trickled down Margaret's cheeks, disbelief and hurt on Kenneth's.

Kenneth dragged his hand down his face. "I thought Kimberly was going to blackmail me so we argued and she left."

"So you hired Montoya to kill her?" Hayes asked.

"No," Kenneth said sharply. "Absolutely not. I would never hurt a person." He stepped closer to Hayes, a muscle ticking in his jaw. "If I'd known about you, I would have married Margaret and been a father to you."

"I couldn't trap you like that," Margaret cried.

"Our son deserved to know us," Kenneth said emphatically. "And we could have made it work, Margaret."

"Yeah, right," Hayes said sarcastically. "Having a kid would have ruined your political aspirations, Sut-

ton. And now with your bid for the governor's chair…"
He paused, and anger flared in Sutton's eyes.

But Hayes continued, "As a last resort, you hired
someone to plant a bomb to kill Taylor and Margaret
tonight to protect your career."

Kenneth reared back as if Hayes had punched him
in the face. "You're wrong. I would never hurt Margaret." He turned a pained look her way. "Never in a
million years."

Taylor saw the truth in his eyes then and wondered if
Hayes could see it. Kenneth was still in love with Margaret. She wondered if Margaret saw it, too.

Or if Tammy or Devon knew.

If so, one of them might want to get rid of her and
Margaret. One of them could have set the bomb.

But Hayes said he had confirmed that Tammy was
with Kenneth the night of the pool attack.

Had she lied?

Or could Devon have tried to kill her to stop her from
finding the truth?

Chapter 21

Emotions ran high as Hayes drove Taylor home. Thankfully the medics had released both her and Margaret, but he had to wait until the next day to get the results on the forensics evidence from the bombing. Of course, nearly every female guest at the country club that night had been inside the lounge, so they needed fingerprints on some part of the actual bomb to pinpoint its maker.

She unlocked the door and he followed her in, willing his hands to stay put when what he really wanted to do was drag her into his arms and feel her breath on his cheek, to know that she was safe forever.

"Can I get you something, Taylor?" he asked.

She looked exhausted, her hair was disheveled, her dress stained. But he'd never thought her more beautiful. "I just want to go to bed."

He started to follow her up the staircase, but she waved him off. "Don't, Hayes. Just find out who set off the bomb so we can both get on with our lives."

Her dismissal cut, but she was right.

Still, he didn't sleep at all that night. Kept replaying the scene where he heard the explosion, where he saw his mother and Taylor both nearly die.

Dammit, he was all tied in knots.

The next morning, he called for the forensics results first thing, but they didn't have them yet. Taylor spent most of the day in her suite, obviously avoiding him. When she finally emerged, she was dressed for the ceremony, although her eyes looked slightly puffy as if she hadn't slept much, either.

They drove in silence to the church for pictures, and he stood to the side, again feeling like an outsider. But today as he watched Margaret, he saw the softness about her, the tender way she treated Taylor, the fear in her eyes that he would never accept her.

He had to forgive her.

But Kenneth…he didn't quite trust that the politician would have sacrificed his life years ago to include him in his family.

"I don't know if I can go through with the wedding." Margaret paced the bride's room. "Last night Devon and I had a terrible argument. He accused me of sneaking behind his back and seeing Kenneth, but that's not true. I've always respected Kenneth's marriage to Tammy. And I wouldn't do anything to jeopardize Kenneth's future."

Taylor thrust a tissue into Margaret's hand, then adjusted her veil. "Because you're in love with him," Taylor said quietly. "You've never stopped loving him, have you, Margaret? That's the reason you stayed single all these years."

Margaret's face fell. "Is it so obvious?"

Taylor shook her head. "No, but you forget you're talking to your best friend here. I saw the way the two of you were looking at each other last night."

"It's such a mess," Margaret cried.

"It's going to be all right," Taylor said.

"How?" Margaret's voice choked. "When I told Kenneth and saw how hurt he was, and then saw him talking to Hayes…"

She gulped back tears. "I'm going to call off the wedding. It's not fair to Devon."

The door squeaked open, and Tammy Sutton appeared in the doorway. Taylor frowned, wondering if Tammy had overheard them.

Then Tammy slid a gun from her purse and pointed it at them, and Taylor had her answer.

"You had to tell Kenneth and ruin everything," Tammy snarled. "But you won't stop this wedding."

Margaret gasped. "You knew?"

Tammy nodded, bitterness lacing her voice when she spoke. "Your father told me years ago. And then Devon phoned to warn me that you were going to tell Kenneth."

Margaret pressed a hand to her chest. "Devon did what?"

Tammy's sinister laugh echoed through the room. "Yes, he wants you, Margaret. Now this is what you're going to do," Tammy said. "You're going to march yourself out there and marry Devon. He loves you, and Kenneth is mine. You and that bastard kid of yours aren't going to ruin our lives and keep him from the governor's chair. Not after all I've done."

She swung the .22 toward Taylor. "This is all your fault. You had to go nosing into things. You should have stayed out of our business."

"You…you're the one who tried to kill me?" Taylor choked out.

A crazed rage flashed in Tammy's eyes as she nodded. "And if you don't keep quiet, I will shoot you now, Taylor."

Margaret clutched Taylor's hand. "Please don't hurt Taylor."

Tammy nudged her with the gun. "Then let's go. Your fiancé is waiting."

Hayes positioned himself at the back of the church directly beside the center aisle. The guests had filled in, the church overflowing, the scent of lilies and roses hanging heavily in the air.

The music for the wedding party piped up, and Taylor appeared, then Margaret on her father's arm. He was momentarily mesmerized when he looked at Taylor.

All night he'd craved her, had thought of nothing but crawling into her bed and making love to her again. His body reacted now, hardening, yet fear slipped into the mix. Not a fear of loving her, but a fear of never telling her.

Of losing her forever.

He froze, reality hitting him. He was in love with Taylor.

But what in the hell did he have to offer her?

She started down the aisle, but she was trembling. He frowned, but Hathaway stepped up, and Margaret gave Hayes a strange look, emotions darkening her eyes. Then the wedding march began, the guests stood and Margaret and Link began their walk down the aisle.

Egan approached him and leaned over, speaking in a

low voice. "I just talked to forensics. They found a print on the remainder of that explosive device last night."

His breath stalled in his chest. "Sutton?"

Egan shook his head. "Close, though. His wife, Tammy."

Hayes stiffened, then his gaze swept the room, searching for the couple. Kenneth and Tammy were seated in the third row, the seats on the end by the center aisle. As Taylor walked past her, sweat beaded on Hayes's forehead. He gestured for Egan to move up one side while he took the other. There were too many people here to arrest her now. It was too dangerous.

But just as Taylor took her place at the front of the church, he noticed a pistol in Tammy's hands. She held it hidden beneath her handbag, but pointed toward Margaret.

He had to do something. Stop the wedding and clear everyone out.

Moving silently, he inched toward the front, but Tammy caught his gaze, and pure rage and fury flared on her face. She must have realized his intent, and she shot up from the seat, her expression crazed. "Don't think about it. This wedding will go on."

Gasps and screams echoed through the packed church, and shock reddened Kenneth's face. "Tammy, what in the world is going on?"

She threw a spiteful look his way. "You're mine, Kenneth, and no one is going to take you away or ruin our future."

Kenneth vaulted up and reached for her, but she swung the gun wildly. "No, Kenneth, the wedding has to go on." She rushed into the aisle, waving her hands like a wild woman. "I'll kill everyone here if you try to stop it."

People ducked in their seats, crying and screaming, and she aimed the gun at Margaret.

"Mrs. Sutton," Hayes said calmly, "give me the gun. You don't want to hurt anyone."

She pointed the gun at him, her voice shrill. "You should have stayed out of Cantara Hills."

"It's not his fault," Margaret said. "Please, Tammy, don't hurt him."

Her hand trembled, her eyes twitching, her jerky movements indicating she was out of control. "You whore, you ruined everything!" Then she spun toward Taylor. "And so did you. This is all your fault."

"I didn't hurt anyone," Taylor said.

"You should have minded your own business!" Tammy shouted.

Hayes shielded Margaret and Taylor with his body. "Stop it, Tammy," Hayes said. "You don't want to do this."

"I have to," she cried. "Don't you see, Kenneth, they're ruining everything we've worked for our entire lives."

"You did that when you conspired to kill Taylor and Morris," Hayes said. "How many more people did you kill, Tammy?"

Kenneth's face paled. "My God, Tammy, what have you done?"

"Everything I did I did for us," she screamed.

"Tammy, wait." Kenneth lowered his voice, trying to reach for the gun. "Give the gun to me and let's talk. I'll help you…"

"No," Tammy shouted. "You know about that bastard kid now. After everything I did to keep it from you. And Devon. For God's sake, Margaret, he wanted you so badly he killed that man Morris to protect your dirty little secret."

Everyone turned toward Devon whose face brightened with anger. "That was an accident," Devon argued. "I only went to pay him off, to keep him from divulging that information, but he fought with me."

Kenneth's eyes widened. "You both knew I had a son and didn't tell me?"

"Of course, I didn't tell you," Tammy screeched, waving the gun toward one of the press as the reporter captured a photograph. The reporter dropped his camera and gestured for her not to shoot, and she wheeled back around on Kenneth.

"Then you would have married her instead of me. And we wouldn't have had our wonderful life."

"Our wonderful life has been a lie," Kenneth barked.

"No…" Tammy said on a ragged cry. "When they're all gone, we can go back to normal."

She was delusional, Hayes thought. Had completely lost her mind.

Tammy's hand trembled as her finger tightened around the gun.

Kenneth vaulted in front of Tammy, shielding Hayes just as the bullet was fired.

Margaret and Taylor screamed as Hayes pushed them out of the line of fire. Kenneth's body bounced backward, then he collapsed to the floor, unconscious, blood pooling on the floor.

The next few hours were chaotic. Taylor clung to Margaret as the Rangers arrested Devon and Tammy, and the ambulance arrived. "I have to go to the hospital with Kenneth," Margaret said.

Link insisted on driving Margaret, and Hayes and Taylor rushed to his SUV. He flipped on his siren, racing to meet the ambulance as it arrived. The press met them at the hospital, but Hayes ordered security to keep them outside.

The next two hours dragged by in slow motion as Kenneth was rushed to surgery. Victoria and Caroline huddled with Taylor and Margaret, offering comfort.

When Hayes joined them in the waiting room, he stood aside, looking morose and torn over what to do. The doctor appeared and announced that Kenneth needed a transfusion, and Hayes immediately volunteered his blood.

Tears burned Taylor's eyes. Kenneth had saved his son, and now Hayes was going to save his father's life. Maybe somehow, out of all this, the men could be friends.

When he returned, Margaret rushed to him. "Thank you, Hayes. I know this is difficult for you, and I can't tell you what it means to me to have you here."

He nodded and started to speak, but Link approached. "Thank you for saving my daughter's life." He extended his hand.

Hayes stared at it as if unclear what the gesture meant, but shook it. "That's my job."

Her heart ached for him. Hayes looked so out of place, like a lost boy who wanted to belong. But protecting Margaret had been more than a job. She could see Hayes softening toward her, the concern in his eyes when Tammy had aimed that gun at her. Maybe in time, he and Margaret and Kenneth could develop some kind of a relationship.

She turned away and wrapped her arms around her waist. Only she'd have no place in his life.

Hayes's chest hurt from the emotions bombarding him. Fear for Kenneth hit him, though he didn't know why. The man had never done anything for him…except to save his life.

Brody and Egan strode in, and he met them at the door. "That was fast."

"They spilled their guts," Brody said.

Taylor, Margaret and her father hurried over, as well. "Tell us everything," Hathaway said.

"Tammy admitted that she was afraid she'd lost Kenneth and that she had to make sure everyone who knew of Margaret's baby died. She panicked when she found out it was you, Hayes, and that you were in Cantara Hills. She figured it was only a matter of time before the truth came out, so she conspired with Montoya to kill Kimberly. Then she tried to kill Taylor because she'd hired the P.I." He paused. "And Link sent Walt to bribe the P.I., but Devon beat him to it."

"What about Carlson Woodward?" Hayes asked.

"Tammy drugged him, hoping we'd blame everything on him and Montoya," Brody said. "She also knew how much Devon wanted you, Margaret, so she conspired with Devon to keep you from finding out the truth. Only Taylor got in the way. Devon was jealous of Kenneth and stole the sealed bid so Link's company would win the bid on the new city library project, and he'd earn favors with you, Mr. Hathaway." Brody paused again. "Then Tammy made it appear as if Kenneth had stolen the bids so she could trap him into staying with her if he tried to leave her for Margaret. She was going to squeal on Goldenrod."

Margaret looked at Link. "But why did you tell Tammy about my baby?"

Link clenched his jaw. "We had an affair back then. I let it slip."

"So helping you with the bids was payback."

He shrugged.

"It's finally over then?" Taylor asked.

Brody nodded. "Yes. You should be safe now."

The doctor stepped into the doorway and cleared his throat. "Mr. Sutton is in recovery now. It was touch and go and he needs rest, but he should make a full recovery in time."

Margaret twisted her hands together. "Can we see him?"

The doctor peered over bifocals. "Only for a minute. And just one at a time."

Clearly relieved, Margaret hurried behind the doctor. Hayes was Kenneth's son. He should be with him, too. But he remained rooted to the spot.

Brody elbowed Hayes. "Victoria and Caroline are going home together. Egan and I are going for a beer to celebrate putting this one to rest."

Egan seconded it, and Hayes glanced at Taylor, then walked away with the Rangers. Taylor was safe now. He could leave her with her friends.

And he could get the hell out of Cantara Hills and back to the badge.

He'd thought he'd feel excited but all he felt was a deep gaping hole in his chest, along with anguish.

He'd found his real family, but he didn't belong with them any more than he did with Taylor. It was time to let them go.

Chapter 22

As soon as they reached the end of the hallway, Brody turned to him. "What in the hell are you doing, Hayes?"

He frowned. "What do you mean?"

"You just found your family. Your mother and father. You need to be with them."

"I don't belong there," Hayes said.

"Why not?" Egan asked. "Because they have money?"

"That's part of it."

"It looked to me like they wanted to mend things. You should give them a chance," Brody said.

"Yeah," Egan said. "Don't cut off your nose to spite your face."

"I don't want anything from them, especially their money," Hayes snapped.

"Maybe. Maybe not. But you want Taylor Landis, so don't let your damn stubborn pride get in the way," Egan said.

Hayes glared at them both. Just because they'd found love they were suddenly experts.

Hayes glanced at Brody, still worried about the tension between them. "About Kimberly..."

"Don't," Brody said. "I've had time to cool down. I know you cared for Kimberly and she did you."

"I did," Hayes said. "She was one of my three best friends."

A silent moment of understanding passed among them where they all acknowledged their love for Kimberly and the fact that they mourned her death. She would always be a part of their disjointed family, a part they'd never forget.

Finally Brody spoke. "I miss Kimberly like crazy, but she would want you to be happy, Hayes. To be with your family." He hesitated, his voice thick. "And with Taylor, if you love her."

"*Is* that what you want?" Egan asked.

Hayes scrubbed his hand over his head, barely able to breathe. "Yes."

"Then get your sorry ass back to her," Brody growled.

Egan clapped him on the back. "Yeah, we'll have that celebratory beer at your wedding."

"I don't know if she'll have me," Hayes admitted. "Not after the things I said."

Brody laughed. "Hell, then get on your knees like a real man and grovel your heart out."

A chuckle rumbled from him. "You're right. Pride is overrated." And Taylor was worth chucking his.

His heart stuttering, he turned on his heels. Taylor had been dead-on in reading him, in understanding him. He'd been the snob, not her. He'd been the coward.

But he'd prove he could change.

And he wouldn't take no for an answer. He was stubborn, and when he wanted something like he'd wanted to be a ranger, he hadn't let anything stand in his way.

Right now he wanted Taylor Landis.

Taylor wiped at the tears she'd tried not to let fall after Hayes left. Then he suddenly appeared in the doorway, and her breath caught. Before she could ask him why he'd returned, Margaret came back to the waiting room, her eyes red rimmed, her father standing by quietly. "How is he?" Taylor asked.

"He's groggy and in some pain, but coherent." She squeezed Taylor's hand. "He said he loved me, Taylor, that he had all these years. That he didn't blame me for not telling him about the baby, that he had been cocky and full of ambition back then, and knew I'd done what I thought was right." She sniffed. "When this dies down, he wants us to be together."

"What do you want, Margaret?"

"I want to be with him. I've always loved him," Margaret said softly. She turned to Hayes. "And we both want to make it up to you, Hayes, to have a relationship if you'll let us be part of your life."

Emotions strained Hayes's face, and Taylor held her breath until he nodded. She forced a smile and decided it was time for her to leave. She suddenly felt like the stranger, out of place.

"I guess I'll go home now," she said, then hugged her friend. "I'll talk to you later, Margaret."

Margaret nodded, and Hayes took her arm. "Come on, I'll drive you."

"I can call for a car," she said, still hurt.

"No, I'm driving you."

They rode in silence to her estate, and she wondered if perhaps he had more bad news, that the case wasn't really closed.

When they arrived, he asked her to step aside to the pool, making her nerves stretch even thinner.

Taylor paced along the pool edge. "Hayes, what's going on? Is something wrong?"

He nodded. "Yes."

She paused and stared at him. "What?"

"I'm in love with you," he blurted.

She shook her head, uncertain she'd heard him right. "What?"

"I'm in love with you." His voice was stronger now, but heat, desire, other emotions flickered in his eyes.

Hope tickled her, but she remembered what he'd said at the country club and tamped it down. "And that's a problem?"

"Hell, yeah, because I've been an idiot." His voice turned gruff. "I didn't mean to hurt you earlier at the club, but I don't know what I have to offer you." He gestured around the estate. "You already have everything."

"You can give me your love." A soft mellow warmth spread through her, excitement spiking her blood at the same time. "Don't you get it, Hayes? That's all I want, all I need."

His eyes darkened. "Is it enough?"

She nodded, then looped her arms around his neck. "Yes, you big sexy idiot. You're all I've ever wanted in a man."

He tilted his head. "I want to marry you," Hayes said gruffly, "but I don't think I could live at your estate. I won't be a kept man."

She smiled and traced a finger over his badge. She'd

known that beneath that badge lay the heart of a loving man. One who'd make a great husband and father. "Me neither. I'd much rather live on your ranch."

His eyes flared with emotions. "You really liked it?"

"I loved it," she declared, then kissed his neck. "Just like I love you. But we might have to make a few changes."

His expression turned wary. "What kind of changes?" He paused. "You want a pool? To get rid of the country furniture? The handmade quilts?"

"No." She threaded her fingers in his hair. "I was thinking we could get a cat to curl up on the rug."

He shrugged. "I'm more of a dog person, but I guess I could live with a cat."

She brushed a kiss along his jaw. "There's something else."

"What?"

"Maybe we could finish one of those upstairs rooms for a nursery."

A smile twitched at his mouth. "You want babies?"

She kissed him again, teasing his mouth with her tongue. "Let's start with just one."

"A little girl," he said in a husky tone.

She unbuttoned the top button of his shirt. "A boy."

He laughed and so did she. They would always have differences but they'd work them out together.

"At least we agree on one thing," he whispered against her ear.

His hard length throbbed against her belly. "That we're made for each other in bed?"

He nibbled at her ear. "Right. I guess we'll just have to spend a lot of time there."

She took his hand and led him inside, then up the stairs to her bedroom. The stars were twinkling through the window, the moon beaming bright, and her heart was overflowing with love.

It was going to be a long and wicked but wonderful life.

* * * * *

Five years of memories didn't compare an ounce to the man
they'd been made about. Not when he seemingly materialized
out of midair, wrapped in a uniform that fit nicely, topped
with a cowboy hat his daddy had given him and carrying
some emotions behind clear blue eyes.

Eyes that, once they found Mel during her attempt to flee
the hospital, never strayed.

Not that she'd expected anything but full attention when
Sterling Costner found out she was back in town.

Though, silly ol' Mel had been hoping that she'd have more
time before she had this face-to-face.

Because, as much as she was hoping no one else would
catch wind of her arrival, she knew the gossip mill around
town was probably already aflame.

"I'm glad this wasn't destroyed," Mel said lamely once
she slid into the passenger seat, picking up her suitcase in the
process. She placed it on her lap.

She remembered leaving her apartment with it, but not
what she'd packed inside. At least now she could change out
of her hospital gown.

Sterling slid into his truck like a knife through butter.

The man could make anything look good.

"I didn't see your car, but Deputy Rossi said it looked like someone hit your back end," he said once the door was shut. "Whoever hit you probably got spooked and took off. We're looking for them, though, so don't worry."

Mel's stomach moved a little at that last part.

"Don't worry" in Sterling's voice used to be the soundtrack to her life. A comforting repetition that felt like it could fix everything.

She played with the zipper on her suitcase.

"I guess I'll deal with the technical stuff tomorrow. Not sure what my insurance is going to say about the whole situation. I suppose it depends on how many cases of amnesia they get."

Sterling shrugged. He was such a big man that even the most subtle movements drew attention.

"I'm sure you'll do fine with them," he said.

She decided talking about her past was as bad as talking about theirs, so she looked out the window and tried to pretend for a moment that nothing had changed.

That she hadn't married Rider Partridge.

That she hadn't waited so long to divorce him.

That she hadn't fallen in love with Sterling.

That she hadn't—

Mel sat up straighter.

She glanced at Sterling and found him already looking at her.

She smiled.

It wasn't returned.

Don't miss
Accidental Amnesia *by Tyler Anne Snell,*
available May 2022 wherever
Harlequin Intrigue books and ebooks are sold.

Harlequin.com

Love Harlequin romance?

DISCOVER.

Be the first to find out about promotions, news and exclusive content!

Facebook.com/HarlequinBooks

Twitter.com/HarlequinBooks

Instagram.com/HarlequinBooks

Pinterest.com/HarlequinBooks

YouTube.com/HarlequinBooks

ReaderService.com

EXPLORE.

Sign up for the Harlequin e-newsletter and download a free book from any series at **TryHarlequin.com**

CONNECT.

Join our Harlequin community to share your thoughts and connect with other romance readers!
Facebook.com/groups/HarlequinConnection

HSOCIAL2021